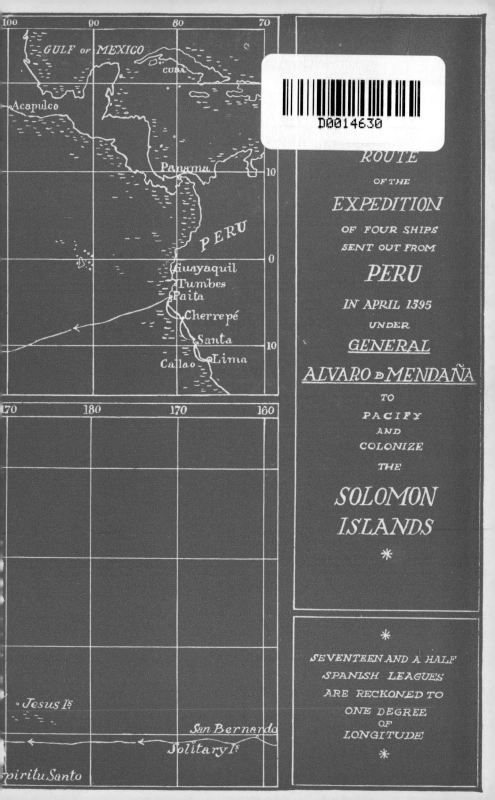

The Islands of Unwisdom

Historical Novels by Robert Graves

The Islands of Unwisdom

BY ROBERT GRAVES

DOUBLEDAY & COMPANY, INC.

Garden City, New York, 1949

. . . la tragedia *de* las *islas* donde faltó *Salamon:* esto es, la prudencia. [The tragedy of the islands where no Solomon was found: *that is* to say, no *wisdom* . . .]

'Varios *diarios* de *los viajes* à *la* mar del Sur y descubrimientos de las Islas de Salamon, las Marquesas, *las* de San-ta Cruz, etc. . . . *1606.'*

Contents

MEMBERS OF THE EXPEDITION
MENTIONED BY NAME

Sergeant Luis Andrada, Sergeant-major of settlers
Juan de la Roca, orderly to Captain Barreto
Raimundo, orderly to Ensign de Buitrago
Gil Mozo, orderly to Ensign de Ampuero
Salvador Aleman   } soldiers
Sebastian Lejia
Federico Salas
Miguel Geronimo, with wife and seven children
Melchior Garcia   } soldier-settlers
Miguel Cierva
Juarez Mendés   } veterans of the previous expedition
Matia Pineto

NAVAL

Captain Don Pedro Fernandez of Quiros, Chief Pilot and master of
  the *San Geronimo*
Don Marcos Marin, Boatswain of the *San Geronimo*
Damian of Valencia, Boatswain's mate
Don Gaspar Iturbe, Purser
Jaume Bonet, Water-steward
Don Martin Groc, Pilot of the *San Felipe*
Don Francisco Frau, Pilot of the *Santa Catalina*

RELIGIOUS

Father Juan de la Espinosa, Vicar
Father Antonio de Serpa, his Chaplain
Father Joaquin, priest in the *Santa Ysabel*
Juan Leal, lay-brother and sick-attendant

OTHERS

Don Luis Barreto, Doña Ysabel's youngest brother
Don Miguel Llano, the General's secretary
Don Andrés Serrano, his assistant
Don Juan de la Isla, merchant-venturer, with his wife
Doña Maruja de la Isla, his daughter
Don Andrés Castillo   } merchant-venturers
Don Mariano Castillo

Elvira Delcano ⎱
Ysabelita of Jerez ⎰ Doña Ysabel's Spanish maids
Pancha, her Indian under-maid
Pacito, the Colonel's page
Leona Benitel, his washerwoman
Myn, the General's negro, veteran of the previous expedition

Introduction

Most of my readers will be as surprised as I was to find Spaniards trying to discover Australia and settle the South Sea Islands a generation before the Pilgrim Fathers landed at Plymouth Rock. This expedition, though it failed in its main objects, deserves to be better known because the Marquesas Islands and the South Solomons were discovered in the course of it, and because on the death of the leader, General Alvaro de Mendaña, his young widow Doña Ysabel Barreto* assumed command of the flotilla and exercized the absolute power he bequeathed to her—a unique episode in modern naval history. But what has interested me most in the story is its bearing on the history of Spanish colonization. When the missionary spirit predominated, as in the Philippines, the natives benefited in the long run, despite governmental corruption; when precious metals excited the greed of conquest, as in the New World, they suffered cruelly; but when there was an irreconcilable conflict of motive, as on this occasion, they were abandoned (in the Spanish phrase) 'to the claws of him who held them first.'

The story also explains why England, with a far smaller fleet, managed to wrest the command of the sea from Spain: her forces were not so rigidly organized. An English galleon was not readily distinguishable from a Spaniard, and had much the same armament; but the Spanish seamen, though they knew their trade well, only worked a ship and did not fight her, while the soldiers, who were the best-disciplined

---

*It was still unusual for a woman to adopt her husband's surname. Cervantes mentions as a novelty in Don Quixote (1605) that Sancho Panza's wife Teresa had done so, the custom having recently spread to La Mancha from France. Ysabel Barreto did not tack on a descriptive 'de Mendaña' to her signature even in official documents.

in the world, fought, but disdained to work her. Their naval and military officers were almost always at loggerheads, and the larger the vessel, the worse the mistrust and confusion. In the English navy the arts of navigation and war were closely co-ordinated, to the especial improvement of gunnery; the same men would handle sail or repel boarders, and the only rivalry was between commanders of sister ships.

I have not had to rely on English translations of the relevant documents. The first account of the voyage appeared in 1616, when Suarez de Figeroa included a carefully excised version in his biography of the Marques de Cañete, who had sponsored the expedition; and it was not until 1876 that the original anonymous report, from which he borrowed, was published in Madrid by Don Justo Zaragoza. What seems to be the only English translation of Zaragoza's text appeared in 1903, under the title *Voyages of Pedro Fernandez de Quiros, 1595–1606*. The translator and editor was the then president of the Hakluyt Society, Sir Clements Markham, who possessed a wide store of geographical and nautical knowledge, but so little Spanish that he guessed at the meaning of almost every other sentence, and usually mistook it. A typical instance occurs in the starvation passage at the close of the voyage: *Todo el bien vino junto*, 'All the good wine appeared too,' which is almost in a class with *Le peuple ému répondit à Marat*, 'The purple emu laid Marat another egg.' No wine was, in fact, served to the men dying of thirst and the sense of the passage, which literally means: 'All that was well came together,' is that the general situation suddenly improved when the *San Geronimo* approached Corregidor Island at the entrance to Manila Bay.

Yet even in accurate translation this original report, which was largely inspired by Pedro Fernandez of Quiros, the Chief Pilot, makes difficult reading. It demands for its understanding a fairly comprehensive knowledge of the contemporary Spanish and Spanish-American scene, of late sixteenth-century navigation, and of native Polynesian, Melanesian and Micronesian customs. Moreover, the author, not caring to enlarge on some of the more discreditable episodes, often falls back on this sort of reporting:

Nine men were sent ashore to buy food. The business reached a point when Don Diego ordered an arquebus to be fired at a sailor who went up the mizzen-mast. The Chief Pilot advised Doña Ysabel that it was greatly to her advantage to finish the voyage in peace. That was a foolish affair, and so I will say no more about it.

or:

This was not the only false testimony borne by the malcontents; for another lie was told of another person. A friend said to one of them . . .

What lie was told, and by whom, or who the friend was, we are left to guess from hints dropped elsewhere.

I have done my best to reconstruct the real story, inventing only as much as it needed for continuity; and though I am on dangerous ground in accounting for the tense relations between Doña Ysabel and the Chief Pilot, something very much like my version of events must have taken place. The Vicar's religious anecdotes are genuine, though condensed; and I have not had to invent names even for Doña Ysabel's maids or the settler Miguel Geronimo's children, Dr. Otto Kübler having recently found the real ones in the archives at Seville.

I must here express my thanks to Dr. Kübler, who first called my attention to the story and has kindly checked the opening chapters; to Don Julio Caro for lending me a copy of Zaragoza's now very rare book *Historia del descubrimiento de las regiones Austriales*, which escaped the destruction of his library during the Spanish Civil War; to Robert Pring-Mill for research at Oxford; to my neighbour Don Gaspar Sabater for placing his Spanish encyclopaedia at my disposal; to Gregory Robinson, a leading authority on Elizabethan seamanship, for correcting my nautical errors; to Kenneth Gay for constant help with the novel at every stage.

R.G.

Deyá,

Majorca, Spain.

1949.

The Islands of Unwisdom

Chapter 1

THE BLIND GIRL OF PANAMA

In the visible firmament which (according to my learned Sevillian friends) is but the eighth of a grand series—the other seven being designed only for the reception of saints, martyrs and their attendant angels—God has placed many thousands of stars. Some are great, some of middle size, some so small that only the keenest eye can distinguish them on the clearest of nights. Yet, as Fray Junipero of Cadiz who taught me Catholic doctrine in my childhood once assured me, every one of them is numbered and registered and twinkles with a certain divine destiny. 'If even the least of them were to be quenched, my son,' he said, 'an equivalent loss on earth would soon be observed.'

From where I knelt on the cold sacristy floor, before the image of Saint Francis, I asked dutifully: 'Father, what moral are we to deduce from this?'

'Little Andrés, my son,' he answered, 'the moral is as plain as the nose on your face. Even the most minute event that may to all appearances be wholly finished and done with, whether proceeding from a good intention or from a bad one, must necessarily, in God's good time, have its effect upon the people concerned in it: an effect consonant with the quality of the intention—as grapes are fruit of the useful vine, and thistle-down flies from the thistle, food of asses.'

Fray Junipero's philosophic doctrine was as memorable as his discipline was severe, and with this particular conclusion I have always been in perfect accord. All the troubles, for example, that occurred during the famous and terrible voyage across the South Seas which is the subject of this history may be said to have sprung, and spread like thistle-down scattered by the wind, from the tale of the Blind Girl of Panama. This tale therefore, though raw and indelicate, I will quote in full as I heard it, not indeed for your amusement (the Saints forbid!) but—by one of those paradoxes beloved and exploited by the schoolmen—for your moral edification.

On the morning of the fourth day of April, in the year of our Lord 1595, at Callao, the port of Lima where the viceroys of Peru reside, I stood with two companions in the waist of our flagship, the *San Geronimo*, a fine galleon of one hundred and fifty tons; and from the mastheads above us two royal banners of Spain and the pendant of General Don Alvaro de Mendaña y Castro fluttered bravely in the land breeze. This celebrated explorer, a nobleman of Galicia and nephew of a former Lord President of Peru, had been appointed to command our expedition, by royal letters patent signed by King Philip II himself. Our destination was the Isles of Solomon, which Don Alvaro had himself discovered twenty-seven years before, but which no one had visited since; our purpose, to colonize them. My companions were the valiant Ensign Juan de Buitrago, a scarred and grizzled veteran of many wars, and tall, hook-nosed, mild-mannered old Marcos Marin, the Aragonese boatswain.

'That is very true, Don Marcos,' the Ensign was saying. 'Some women will never be put off, try how you may. I remember when I was a young soldier at Panama, billeted in the house of an ebony-merchant from Santander, a very respectable man whose name I have now forgotten . . . Shortly after my arrival, as we sat drinking in doublet and shirt, he said to me earnestly: "Don Juan, may I ask you to do me a kindness?"

' "I am entirely at your disposal, host," I said.

' "It is this. In a garret of this house lives a beautiful girl, an orphan, who spends her days carding and spinning wool. Very industrious she is, and proficient at her work; but can do no other, because, poor creature, she is blind. This girl greatly desires to handle your arms and speak to you, for her grandfather who brought her up once served under the great Pizarro, and though a model of piety, she is always curious to hear tales of soldiers and camp life."

' "To refuse a blind orphan a few minutes of my long day would be uncharitable indeed," I said. "I am ready to humour her this very moment, if you please." With that I rose, made an armful of my ac-coutrements and told him: "Lead on."

'We went upstairs to a garret room where the girl sat spinning at the open window; and beautiful she was, by the eleven thousand virgins of Saint Ursula, with her pale skin and broad brow like the Madonna's, her glossy hair, slim waist and rounded bosom. My host made us acquainted, and a few compliments and nothings were exchanged, when presently he was called away on a matter of business and she and I were left alone.

'Well, first she asked permission to examine my armour; and I handed her my headpiece, my corslet and my tassets, which she tapped with her nails and stroked with her fingers, greatly admiring their lightness and toughness. Next, she reached for my Venetian scabbard and fingered it thoughtfully from end to end; she cried out with delight at the silver chasing which, indeed, was curiously intricate and graceful—as you can see for yourselves, for here is the very scabbard. Next, she drew my sword out a hand's breadth or two and tried its edge with her little thumb—"as keen as a razor!" she exclaimed—and her finger-tips traced the fine Toledo inlay on the flat of it. Next, my Mexican dagger and its copper scabbard with the turquoise studs. Next, my trusty arquebus, with its match; my powder-horn, my bag of bullets. Everything pleased this poor blind girl beyond expression. But then, then——'

Don Juan paused and his face, that had been serious, took on a droll expression between triumph and shame. 'But then——?' the Boatswain prompted him.

'—But then: "Is that all, soldier?" she asked in tones of dissatisfaction.

' "It is indeed all, daughter," I replied. "Though I am heartily sorry to disappoint you, I have nothing else." But some women will never be put off, try how you may. She came close up to me and her eager hands went all about me, deft as a Neapolitan pick-pocket's, remorseless as a Venetian sea-captain's when he searches his captive Turk for concealed jewels; and pretty soon she caught firm hold of a something. "Aha," she cried, "my brave comrade, what concealed weapon is this?"

' "Take your little hands out of the larder!" said I. "That is no weapon of offence: it is no more than a prime Bolognian sausage hanging from a hook against time of need."

' "Hanging?" she exclaimed with surprise. "But it hangs upside-down!" And then in a voice of deepest reproach: "Oh, noble Don Juan, would you tell lies to a poor blind girl, and an orphan too?" '

The intention of the tale cannot by any means be described as a good one, and its effect was altogether lamentable. At the very moment that the Ensign reached this climax, lowering his voice be-

cause Father Antonio de Serpa, the Vicar's keen-eyed Chaplain
was edging near, a boat drew alongside and the Colonel, Don Pedro
Merino de Manrique climbed ponderously aboard. The Boatswain and
I were so beguiled by the tale that we did not turn round, and
what with the sailors' singing and shouting, and a duet of carpenters'
hammers, it was excusable that the Colonel's arrival should have
escaped our attention; we supposed that a bum-boat had come with
fruit, or perhaps the skiff that had been sent to fetch the laundry.

The Colonel staggered aboard, three parts drunk with *chicha*, the
maize liquor of Peru—for this was the feast of Our Lady of Joy—
slipped on a pool of oil, caught his scabbard between his legs and went
flying, head first, into the scuppers; not a second before the Boatswain,
though a most respectable old man, burst into a hoarse cackle of
laughter at the Ensign's tale. I laughed too, till the tears flowed,
being young and gay and no longer so devout as when I was Fray
Junipero's acolyte.

'God's blood!' cried the Colonel, hauling himself to his feet with
the help of the bulwarks and a loaded stick he still grasped in his
hand. 'God's blood and nails!'

The Boatswain gasped: 'Upside-down, by the miraculous Virgin of
Pilar, upside-down! That's wonderful! Ho! ho! ho!'

I tried to move off quietly. To tell the truth, I had no right to
be gossiping on deck on so busy a morning and only three days
before we were to sail. My place was below, checking the stores as
they were piled in the hold: this forenoon, five hundred tubs of salt
beef and four tons of biscuit, together with a ton of chick-peas,
fifty jars of vinegar and a ton and a half of dried beans were being
fetched aboard. But the Colonel roared at me to come back. 'You,
sir, with the fat cheeks! You too laughed at me when I slipped and
fell!' he cried. 'To sneak off and leave your companions to bear the
brunt of my wrath is certainly the act of a coward. Are you a rat,
sir, or are you a man?'

I swept off my plumed hat and made him a deep obeisance. 'My
lord,' I said, 'I am no rat: I am the General's assistant secretary
and your very humble servant. But I fear that you have caught the
wrong bull by the horns. I was laughing at a droll tale told me by
the Ensign, and since I did not observe your lordship's fall, I had
no occasion, as I should not have had the presumption, to laugh at
your lordship.'

The Ensign supported me boldly: 'What Andrés Serrano has told your lordship is the plain truth, and if it had been otherwise I should have at once defended your lordship's honour.'

The Colonel glared at the two of us and fired a thunderous broadside at the Boatswain, whose face was still wreathed in smiles. 'As for you, you Aragonese snail-guzzler, you tall, tottering, rotten ladder, will you also deny that it was at me you laughed? "Upside-down, by the Virgin of Pilar, upside-down!"—were not those your very words, you tarry-tailed dog, you Jew's bastard?'

The Boatswain was not used to be treated with such contumely. His captains had always trusted him, his crews spoke well of him, and he had grown old in the King's service. For the Colonel to revile him in the hearing of the sailors, indeed in the hearing of the whole port of Callao, because Don Pedro Merino had the most powerful parade-ground voice I ever heard in my life, was hard to bear in silence. He kept his temper but strode close up to the Colonel, who was a little turkey-cock of a man, and looked down on him with his head gravely bent. Then he said in his atrocious Castilian, his mother-tongue being a sort of Languedoc French: 'With the greatest respect to your lordship, I was referring not to your unfortunate posture, but to that of a fine Bolognian sausage which figured in the Ensign's tale; and I should be glad to think that I misheard your lordship a moment ago and that the evil names you pronounced were meant for the same sausage, not for the Boatswain of the *San Geronimo*.'

The Colonel, though he understood that he had made a fool of himself, was too far gone in drink to take the opportunity of honourable retreat which the Boatswain offered him. Standing on his yard and a half of dignity, he roared back: 'The Devil fly off with your fine Bolognian sausage! Do you expect me to believe this trumpery lie? You laughed at me, you sweepings of an ass-stall, you scurfy-headed camelopard—instead of drumming me aboard with the respect due to my rank and honours, you laughed at me—at me, Don Pedro Merino de Manrique y Castellon, the Colonel appointed by the Viceroy himself to command the troops of this expedition! What is more, my fall, which might have broken both my legs, was caused by your unseamanlike slovenliness. My foot slid on oil slopped over the deck by your ruffianly sailors!'

'Believe what you are in the humour to believe, but permit me to remind your lordship that it is not customary in any royal ship for a military officer, be he ever so exalted, to abuse a boatswain except with the permission, and in the presence, of the ship's master; and even then not before the crew. I humbly beg pardon for not having drummed your lordship aboard, but arriving at an awkward moment as you did, unannounced by tuck of drum, you were on deck in an instant. Moreover, deeply though I regret your lordship's fall, I cannot offer apologies as the person responsible, since my men have handled no oil-jars. If you seek satisfaction, your complaint had best be directed to Doña Ysabel, the General's lady, whose servants have been carrying oil aft to her private larder.'

'O sweet Saint Barbara and all the loud artillery of Heaven!' burst out the Colonel. 'If this is not insolence beyond any remedy but death!' He clapped his hand to the pommel of his sword and would certainly have spitted the Boatswain like a sucking-pig had I not darted forward, with Miguel Llano the General's secretary, and caught at his wrist, while Father Antonio and the Ensign between them hustled the Boatswain away.

We could not long restrain this raving officer, he struggled and swore so hard, spitting in our faces like a llama, but the Boatswain had escaped below deck before the Colonel could free his sword and go charging after him, hallooing as loudly as a Morisco on a feast day.

Doña Ysabel stood on the half-deck watching the scene below her with impassive face, but her blue eyes danced like stars under her crown of wheat-coloured hair. As I went off to the forecastle, giving her the respectful salute to which both beauty and rank entitled her, the Chief Pilot, Don Pedro Fernandez of Quiros, who stood by her side, gestured to me to wait; I suppose he wished to question me about the origin of the affray. I obeyed, and could not but overhear what Doña Ysabel said to him: 'Our Colonel is a man of more than usual severity. If this is the way he means to assert his position throughout the voyage, he may, of course, come to a good end, but I think that most improbable.'

Pedro Fernandez shook his head glumly. 'I am forced to agree with your ladyship,' he said. 'I only wish that he might be given a warning before it is too late.'

'And why not?' she answered lightly. 'The sooner the better.'

The Colonel, finding that his quarry had gone to earth, sheathed his sword and marched towards the forecastle, still puffing fire and smoke. Doña Ysabel called down to him: 'Why, Colonel, what has come over you this fine morning? What savage insect of the tropics has found its way into your peascod-bellied doublet? By the violent way you behave I can only conclude that something has bitten you where you are ashamed to scratch. But listen to me, my lord: if my husband comes to hear of this morning's doings, I undertake that he will be little pleased to know that his ship's officers are treated with contumely, and served with language that would better suit the mouth of a brothel-keeper than a Colonel with the King's commission; especially when so slight an occasion for your outburst has been offered.'

The Colonel turned half about when Doña Ysabel began to address him. Now he grimaced like a schoolboy and, jerking his thumb over his shoulder, cried with great insolence to the sergeant who attended him: 'Why, upon my word, what have we there on the poop?'

This lubberly retort brought the Chief Pilot into the quarrel. He grew indignant, and with good reason. 'My lord,' he said, 'in the absence of the General it devolves on me to resent the gross insult that you have offered the virtuous and high-born Doña Ysabel. It were better for you to ask her pardon publicly; for every one of us respects her, not only as the General's Lady, but as the flower and glory of the womanhood of His Most Christian Majesty's possessions overseas.'

'Hold your tongue, insolent Portuguee!' the Colonel roared back. 'I offered Doña Ysabel no insult. My remark was meant for that fabulous Bolognian sausage, hanging upside-down—though upon my honour, it would puzzle me to distinguish one end of a sausage from the other—not for any woman whatsoever, least of all the General's distinguished Lady. But I do not hesitate to insult you, as suits your inferior rank and calling. Understand, numbskull, that I am the Colonel, and that if we sail together in this ship I command her in battle, and if it pleases me to order you to run her upon a rock, what then? Answer me, dog, what then? Will you obey my order?'

The Chief Pilot made a politic reply: 'When that time comes, your lordship, I shall do whatever seems best, but the case is a hypothetic and dubious one. As things stand, I recognize no superior in naval affairs except his Excellency the General, to whose high-born Lady, though you protest that you intended no insult, you have at least failed to render the civilities due from every nobleman to every noblewoman. The General has appointed me to navigate this vessel, and to act as her master while he controls the movements of the flotilla as a whole; when he comes aboard, as I trust he soon will before this scandal grows worse, he must define my powers in so far as a conflict of authority may arise between your lordship and myself. But you may believe me when I tell you, without oaths and objurgations, that if it is your aim to become lord and master of all lands which we hope to discover, I will resign my appointment at once rather than come under the orders of an officer who takes so much upon himself and shows so little discretion.'

The Colonel gestured to the sergeant. 'Up into the pulpit, fellow,' he said, 'and bring me down that gabbling Portuguese preacher. I mean to beat the Devil's tattoo on his hide with this stick of mine!'

The sergeant saluted, shouldered his weapon and started reluctantly for the quarter-deck; but before he could execute his orders, two of Doña Ysabel's brothers, Captain Don Lorenzo de Barreto and Ensign Don Diego de Barreto came rushing up with drawn swords, having been warned of what was afoot. Don Diego hauled the sergeant off the ladder by a leg, and Don Lorenzo kicked him across the deck, where he stumbled into the Colonel and sent him flying once more. Then they went up to their sister and each kissed one of her hands deferentially, before turning to the Chief Pilot and clapping him on the back. 'Sir,' Don Diego said, 'you may be only a Portuguese, but for the bold and honourable way in which you championed our sister against the rudeness of that soused Bombastes yonder, you deserve to be a Spaniard. Our swords will always be at your disposal, should you ever have need of them in the course of this voyage.'

Pedro Fernandez thanked them gravely and declared that he valued their goodwill beyond measure. 'Nevertheless, my lords, I could never consent to join a faction within an enterprise that will succeed only if perfect unanimity exists between all who serve in it.'

Doña Ysabel smiled pleasantly at the Chief Pilot, who was a fine-looking man, above the usual height, slim but muscular, with clear grey eyes and a short, curly beard; he was then in the thirty-sixth year of his life. When he excused himself, pleading great press of business, and kissed her hand with ceremony, she said in a voice that had a keen edge to it: 'As for what I told you a few minutes ago, my friend: I am now convinced that it is against God's will and wholly impossible for the Colonel's end to be in the least degree fortunate.' Doña Ysabel was a Galician through and through, and having already had close dealings with that bold, tenacious, clannish, close-fisted, secretive people, who are three parts Suevian and one part aboriginal devil, I crossed myself involuntarily and thought: 'That drunkard's life is not worth a maravedi* if he sails in Doña Ysabel's company.'

The Chief Pilot came down from the quarter-deck and taking me affectionately by the arm, said in urgent tones: 'Little Andrés, for the love of the Saints, help me to repair this mischief. Take the Colonel below to his quarters and sober him up by any means you please, but be careful to humour him as though he were a Duchess with the jaundice; and make sure that he is recovered before the General comes aboard.'

The Colonel had been struck insensible by his fall against the port bulwarks. The sergeant had now lifted him on to a coil of rope abaft the mainmast and was supporting his bruised and lolling head with both hands. Among the gaping crowd I saw our barber and called him to me; together we carried the Colonel below, where he vomited a good quart of drink. Then the barber bled him and gave him restoratives; so that he was soon sitting up in his bunk, sober enough, but weak and confused. Being well-intentioned at heart, he repeatedly exclaimed in our hearing: 'Ai, ai! If only this had not happened!' And once he groaned: 'But in the name of God, what was I to do? Those swine would not allow me an honourable retreat from the position into which they had forced me. They should have seen that I had a skinful of fiery chicha and was not to be crossed; they should have treated me with greater regard. For the officers I do not care a fig, but that I should have failed in respect to a lady of high rank, who is also young and beautiful, and the wife of the leader of this expedition—man, that is a catastrophe!' He felt the disgrace keenly in his chivalrous soul, and after repairing his bruises with a plaster and further sobering himself with cups of a hot Turkish drink, he dressed in his best clothes—those that he wore being stained with oil and tar from his tumbles—and went to the Great Cabin to offer his apologies to Doña Ysabel, but found her gone ashore.

Fate, like Love, the poets say, is blind; yet her fingers are all the defter for that, like those of the Blind Girl of Panama.

*32 copper maravedis = 1 silver real
  8 reals (or 'pieces of eight') = 1 gold peso (worth about 4 shillings in English money of the period)

Chapter 2

AN AUDIENCE WITH THE VICEROY

The General had been detained in Lima by the Viceroy, Don Garcia Hurtado de Mendoza, Marquis of Cañete, to whom he had gone to kiss hands at a final leave-taking. The Marquis was never an early riser and today the General was kept cooling his heels in an ante-room until long past noon; but he remained patient, despite the thousand and one affairs that still remained to be settled, and improved the hours by telling his beads many times over. He was confident that he would never again need to wait upon the pleasure of a Viceroy. 'Of patience,' he had told me a week or two before, 'I have a cellarful.' Then he turned with a smile and took me by the ear: 'I hear you are a rising poet, little Andrés: how does your inspired fancy picture a cellarful of patience?'

'Your Excellency,' I answered, 'I see patience as a virtue compounded of faith, hope and resilience. Its emblem is cork, which when struck a heavy blow springs back undented into shape, though all but flattened, and is light enough to buoy up the heavy heart struggling in dark waters of despair. A cellarful of patience, you say? I see a huge mound of corks, cut to every size, enough to seal all the vials of wrath and indignation that the Devil ever blew in his infernal glass-house.'

'And the cellar itself?' he asked. 'How do you picture the cellar?'

'My fancy flags when it comes to that, your Excellency.'

'Then permit me to tell you, my poet,' he said with much feeling, 'that the cellar of patience smells of mice and musty cloth and has no other way out than the way in. It is furnished like a viceregal ante-room with handsome but uncomfortable chairs, overrun with gorgeous but surly lackeys, and papered from floor to ceiling with innumerable unread despatches, applications and memorials, all

signed with the name and embossed with the seal of General Don
Alvaro de Mendaña y Castro, of Neira.'

When the Marquis, who was a veteran of the Dutch and Milanese
wars, but still in vigorous health and a great dandy, at last summoned
the General to the audience chamber, he embraced him and offered
many excuses for the delay. An important letter to the Indies
Council at Madrid, he said, had called for immediate despatch by
way of Panama; the Bishop had paid a visit to notify him that a
relapsed heretic would be handed over to the secular authorities on
the coming Sunday; and a horde of other matters had unexpectedly
forced themselves upon him.

The General listened politely, though aware that the Bishop was
down with fever, that arrangements for accepting the heretic from
the hands of the Holy Office had been made on the previous afternoon; and that the Panama packet was not due to sail for another
three days. He also knew from Doña Ysabel, who had once been a
maid of honour at the Viceregal Court, that the Marquis's Lady
grudged him every minute devoted to business of state rather than
to herself and had made him promise to take her off, that very afternoon, for a month's holiday at Cuzco, high in the hills. This noblewoman was as prudent as she was beautiful and never interfered
directly with her husband's affairs; but when the royal order which
forbade the use of carriages in the New World was relaxed in her
favour, it became clear who wore the breeches. I happen to know
that Doña Ysabel acted as her confidante in many delicate affairs,
and that but for these services, which are of no concern to my story,
our expedition would never have left Peru.

The Viceroy clapped his hands for wine and sweet biscuits, which
a negro servant brought on a heavy Potosi salver, and proceeded
briskly: 'So you are leaving us at last, Don Alvaro, and upon my word,
much as I esteem you and your charming Lady, I shall draw a sigh
of relief when I see your pendant disappear over the western horizon.'

'No deeper a sigh, your Excellency, than I shall heave to see the
snowy peaks of the Andes bob like distant icebergs in our wake. Only
consider my case: no less than twenty-one years have elapsed since
His Majesty King Philip II signed these letters patent and wished me
God-speed at a brilliant audience. Pray look at the parchment, how
yellow it has grown, how faded the ink! And my black beard: streaked
with veins of silver. I cannot sufficiently express the emotion with
which I now kiss the generous hand that has annulled the animosity

of Don Francisco de Toledo—for vipers sting, though dead—and has set my table upon four legs again.'

'It is nothing, my friend,' said the Viceroy, running a finger around his neck, which was adorned with the largest and laciest ruff in the entire Western hemisphere, and stroking his scented, yellow-dyed beard. 'It is nothing, or no more than your due, though I agree that my predecessor's report upon you, of which I have a copy in my archives, can hardly have influenced the Indies Council in your favour. It is based for the most part on the testimony of one Hernan Gallego, your chief pilot, who evidently bore you much ill-will and deposed that you had proved yourself in no way fit to lead another enterprise in those same Southern waters.'

'So it was Gallego's hand that guided Don Francisco's pen! In my simplicity I had put it all down to the inveterate malice of Captain Pedro Sarmiento de Gamboa, who caused me so much trouble and anxiety during the voyage and whom I finally degraded for his cruelties and insubordination. It was Gallego after all! By the Holy Mother of God, what foul ingratitude! My fellow-countryman, whose fortune and reputation I secured by making him my chief pilot when I might have chosen a score of more capable and deserving men!'

'Of Gallego's capacities I cannot judge. But he alleged that so far from conferring reputation on him, you robbed him of it: that he conceived and planned the expedition himself and made the preparations for it. And that it was only at the personal plea of your uncle, the illustrious Licentiate de Castro, that His Majesty conferred the command upon yourself—yourself who (if I may be permitted to quote his words) "neither before you sailed, nor after, knew stem from stern, tar from turpentine, or the Pole star from the planet Venus." According to this same memorial you so grossly neglected your duties that—to mention only one instance of the many there adduced—on your precipitate return to California, your task only half accomplished, it was left to him to pay for the refitting of your two ships with fourteen hundred gold pesos out of his own pocket, and for their re-victualling with another four hundred—a sum for which he had not, at that date, received a maravedi of compensation, though his account had been a dozen times presented.'

The Viceroy paused to watch the effect of this revelation, but Don Alvaro never moved an eyelash. (I heard the tale from my godfather, the Marquis's secretary, who was present.) 'I knew well, your Excellency,' he answered with a sad shake of his head, 'that Gallego was an unlucky choice for chief pilot: that he was jealous, treacherous, tale-bearing and devoid of even a spark of Christian charity. I must admit, alas, that our Galicia breeds the worst of men as well as the best. Gallego was raised among the mists of Cebrero, whose rude inhabitants have a thousand times more respect for a witch than for a priest, and are so avaricious that when a stranger stops to water his mare at one of their streams they will detain him by force and seize his boots or cloak, if he refuses to pay in coin. But I had no notion that even Gallego would tell such shameless lies and, disregarding all obligations of loyalty, embody them in a secret report to Don Francisco. But enough of Gallego: he had his just deserts five years ago, when the Devil claimed him in a shipwreck at the mouth of the River Saña.'

'And how did you happen to fall foul of Don Francisco? He was a stiff-backed man, but neither unreasonable nor quarrelsome. I see that he accuses you of returning from the Isles of Solomon with forty thousand pesos of gold, and failing to declare them in your report to His Majesty. On this point, by the way, neither Gallego nor Sarmiento was his informant.'

Here Don Alvaro was on safer ground: 'No, indeed! Sarmiento's complaint was that I had not remained long enough in the islands to conduct mining operations, but hurried home empty-handed. As for Gallego (who hated Sarmiento as one snake hates another): if I had found even one-tenth of the amount you mention, would he have dared to claim that I was so ungenerous that the refitting of my storm-tossed vessels was left for him to pay? But what care I who told lies to Don Francisco? Your Excellency must have heard of the deep grudge which this thief—for I can call him thief since the King's justices consigned him to the prison of Seville, there to repent his huge misappropriations of government funds—the deep grudge, I say, which this thief bore my sainted uncle, his predecessor. His spite was directed against me only as my uncle's nephew. When six years later I returned to this country from Spain, with the letters patent in my pocket, he pretended the most loyal obedience to His Majesty's wishes, but declared that the country had been so sadly impoverished under my uncle's misrule that for the time being it was out of the question to equip and man a flotilla of the authorized strength. Yet all these were lies.'

'Don Alvaro,' said the Viceroy, 'try to be just to the man, however bitter your feelings may be. There is a saying: "Of the dead, speak nothing but good"; and though much of the gold and silver that passed through my predecessor's hands stuck to his palms, yet never a day passes but I feel grateful to him for the vigour with which he consolidated the conquests and gains of the heroic Pizarro, of my sainted father, and of your sainted uncle. It was Don Francisco who established the magnificent constitution under which Peru is still governed. And it was he who, with the help of your enemy Sarmiento, took care that the loyalty of its people should be secured for all time to the crown of Castile, by extinguishing the ancient, absurd dynasty of the Incas. If he could not furnish you with ships, why, neither can I, for all the good will I bear you; the silver mines of Potosi and Huancavelica are no longer what they were and the increased demands for treasure made by the King force me to be thrifty in the extreme. The ships and stores you have, I suppose, purchased yourself. All that I have done is to lend you arms from the royal arsenal, detail capable soldiers to serve under your pendant, and permit you to recruit sailors and settlers on your own initiative. And apropos of that: I have at last found you the very man you need for Colonel, and this morning, if one of his famous celebrations has not prevented him, he has already gone aboard your flagship. He is a brave and pious soul who has fought on a hundred fields of battle; you must know him at least by reputation—I refer to Don Pedro Merino de Manrique.'

'Merino!' echoed the General faintly, gripping the back of a chair. 'Alas, your Excellency, if only you had told me sooner. I would rather the Devil himself commanded my troops. He was once a close friend of this same Sarmiento, and a week ago in a wine-shop at Callao he fell out with one of my officers, Don Felipe Corzo, who captains our galeot. It was only the quick-wittedness of a pretty girl who was the subject of the dispute, that prevented this fire-eater from running my Captain through. She tossed a cupful of wine in Merino's face, pushed Don Felipe into the street, bolted the door and herself took refuge in a certain slight out-building at the back, where the Colonel's delicacy forbade him to pursue her. When the two men meet again, as in the end they must meet, though they sail in different ships, they will recognize each other at once, the quarrel will flare up again and murder be done.'

'Here in Peru,' said the Viceroy authoritatively, drawing himself up in his chair. 'Here in Peru, Don Alvaro, you are a private person and have no right to quell even a wine-shop dispute without reference to myself or my officers. But it behoves you to remember that, once your flotilla is under way, you are the trusty and beloved deputy of His Most Christian Majesty and exercise absolute power under him. If any of your subordinates dare to fall out and commit a breach of the peace, it is your duty to investigate the matter at once, fall upon the culprits like a sledge-hammer and flatten them on the anvil of discipline. "Let him who rules, rule!" This lesson I was taught by my sainted father who restored order in this country by knocking head against head, without respect for rank or fear of retaliation; and during my governorship in Chile I proved myself—if I may make the boast—a true son of his begetting . . . But tell me, my friend, what truth is there in the rumour that you found much gold and many large pearls in the Isles of Solomon?'

'As for gold,' the General replied with a disarming smile, 'we found it and we did not find it. The natives who came aboard my flagship from the great islands of Santa Ysabel and Guadalcanal all venerated the golden cross and chain around my neck, and when I showed them some nuggets that I had with me, they nodded and pointed towards the mountains, saying "Yaro bocru!", *bocru* signifying "much" in their language. And when I asked their word for gold, they told me *areque* and made signs that it was found near running water. However, being unable, because of the fewness of our soldiers and the scarcity of ammunition, to carry war into the hills, we did not, in the event, handle any gold at all; the yellow ore we found on Guadalcanal was what our miners called "fool's gold." I sent one Andrés Nuñez with thirty soldiers to see what the land produced, and to search for true ore in cracks or broken ground, because a couple of miners who understood the business said that it seemed a land for precious metals. But while they were washing for gold in a river of the interior, so many natives crowded around them with threatening gestures that they had to abandon the project; besides, the stream was running too swiftly for their pans. Yet the sand, they reported, glinted bright. Moreover, the women of Aytoro are said to wear necklaces, which they call *aburu* . . .'

'And the pearls?' asked the Viceroy, drumming impatiently on the table.

'As for the pearls—now there I can speak with perfect certainty. On the island of Veru I both saw and handled many small pearls of a good colour. The natives thought nothing of them, not understanding the use of the drill. Again at Estrella Bay I found very large pearls with which the children were playing at marbles; but these were

scorched and discoloured because their parents, who value only the
meat of the oyster, had placed the shells on red-hot stones to roast.
In the other islands, too, we found abundance of pearl shells of
enormous size, and if the pearls were of the same proportion they
would be jewels fit for a crown. But, unlike gold, pearls are a luxury—
and if there is no gold in the islands that God has granted me to
discover, then you may write me down as a dunce. Here, at least, I
am at one with Sarmiento: it is my opinion that they teem with
precious metals.'

'In that case, Don Alvaro,' said the Viceroy, 'you were far from wise
to proclaim their riches to the world by naming them the Isles of
Solomon, as though you had re-discovered the Land of Ophir from
which King Solomon brought prodigious quantities of gold for the
beautifying of his Temple.'

'Your Excellency will pardon me. The name was not my invention,
but issued from Sarmiento's rash brain and gained such currency
among the crew that I could not persuade them to call the group
by any other. Yet I own that I was much surprised by the Jewish cast
of features in a great number of the islanders—descendants, as Sarmiento would have it, of Solomon's mariners—and by the practice of
circumcision which is widespread. The name, at all events, proved
my undoing. Don Francisco, jealous of my success, placed frivolous
obstacles in my path and delayed me here for six years, though I sent
memorial after memorial to the Indies Council and others directly
to the King—he even threw me into prison when once, by great mis-
chance, one of these letters fell into his hands——'

'I seem to remember that in it you not only reflected sharply upon
the Viceroy's treatment of yourself, but accused him of having sent
unauthorized expeditions to the South Seas for his own profit, and of
planning to send yet another to your islands—if I may call them so—
in search of contraband treasure.'

'I stand by all I wrote, your Excellency. And since I was not the
only witness against him, was he not recalled? However, I had no
better fortune with his successor, Don Martin Enriquez. . . .'

The Viceroy leaned back in his great carved ebony chair, and
cooled himself with a light fan of lace and tortoise-shell. His eyes
roamed idly among the gold traceries of the ceiling. 'Oh, by all the
sores of Lazarus!' my godfather sighed to himself, 'is Don Alvaro
going to recapitulate the history of his grievances chapter by chapter?'
My godfather had been secretary to each of these Viceroys in turn

and had heard it fifty times, if he had heard it once, always with new additions and embroideries. 'I wonder that the Marquis has not cut him short already.'

'. . . Don Martin, as I was saying, must have read the adverse report upon me, bequeathed him by Don Francisco. Taking no pity on the poor wretches whom I had brought from Spain to colonize my islands and who were now reduced to the utmost misery—one half of the women had been forced to walk the streets, which caused me infinite shame. . . . Taking no pity on them, he told me that enough lands had already been discovered, and that what mattered now was to settle and people these rather than squander the King's resources in search of new countries, especially in regions so distant that even when they were pacified they would still be a great and useless burden to maintain. He even dared to question the authenticity of my letters patent, saying that when next he had occasion to write to his friends of the Indies Council he would ask for more information about me. Don Martin died in the following year, and the old Count of Villardompardo, your Excellency's immediate predecessor could hardly, I admit, have helped me, even if he had wished, because of the earthquakes, followed by pestilence and famine, which made his term so ill-fated. Also, by that time the news of our discovery had spread far and wide—a Genoese sailor is to be blamed for that—and the report reached England that the Isles of Solomon were the eighth wonder of the world. That lure drew Francis Drake into the South Seas, where he began to prey on our shipping. Drake's name cast a black shadow over my life, because his piracies were everywhere pleaded as an argument against my project. "It would be folly to colonize these islands and set the natives to work in the mines," I was told, "when Drake and his captains are bound to reap where you have sown!" Such talk I hold to be both cowardly and unpatriotic. Only last year your Excellency proved that resolute Spanish hearts and well-aimed Spanish guns can subdue Englishmen even more daring than Drake——'

The Marquis smiled complacently. 'It is indeed cause for great satisfaction to have the gallant Richard Hawkins safely confined in our City jail. You should see him tramp up and down in his cell, Don Alvaro, even in this pestilential heat, up and down, up and down, like a lion in a cage! Blessed be the Virgin, we heard of his arrival sooner than he expected! When our men-of-war surprised his *Dainty* in the Bay of San Mateo, and denied her sea-room for manoeuvre, he fought his guns to the last, and would not yield even when he was dismasted and sinking, having lost half his crew. Our targeteers poured aboard from both sides and the scrimmage washed clean over him. My brother, Don Beltran Hurtado, who commanded that day, declares that he fought superbly.'

'That is high praise indeed, your Excellency. But, if I may be permitted to continue my dismal tale: the Indies Council then advised His Majesty that the Isles of Solomon should not be colonized for the time being, in order, they said, to prevent English freebooters who might sail through the Straits of Magellan, in back-door raids on the spice islands of Molucca, from refitting or revictualling at our expense on the way. And this policy was followed for many years until now, at last, when my hopes were nearly extinguished, your Excellency's generous intervention—in gratitude for which I propose to honour the first new land of importance that I may discover by giving it your Excellency's own name——'

'Of course, of course, it stands to reason. If this piracy continues, what greater advantage could His Majesty possess than a well-found base in the South Seas, midway between Peru and the long-established colony of the Philippines, from which our ships could actively deny the privateers that assistance in water and victuals which the Indians might otherwise give them? Last year your charming Lady presented this argument to me with such eloquence that I had no word left in contradiction; and that very day, as you know, I wrote to the King on my own responsibility. She also made a certain proposal about gold and pearls, doubtless with your approval. . . . Your Galician women of every rank and station show remarkable independence and fortitude: while passing through the province on a journey to Corunna I was astonished to see them guiding the plough, sowing, harrowing, felling trees, in short, doing all the work of men, yet keeping their modesty and piety in a way that would shame many women of the South.'

'Ah, piety!' exclaimed the General, catching gratefully at the word, his eyes aglow with religious fervour. 'By Heaven, that is a subject which should have been earlier on my lips. Though discovery is glorious, trade necessary, gold desirable and courage the justification of manhood, yet is not piety a jewel worth a thousand times more than all the rest? The first object of our enterprise is not to discover in order to conquer, to conquer in order to find gold, to find gold in order to enrich ourselves, to enrich ourselves in order to lead lives

of sloth and luxury! It is a nobler and more glorious object by far:
to perform the solemn duty which Our Saviour has laid upon us;
to bring those benighted, cannibalistic heathen the inexpressible joy
of the Faith; to baptize them with the holy ritual of our Mother the
Church, to teach them that they have immortal souls, to warn them of
the horrid nature of sin, to guide them along the narrow path that
leads to redemption . . .'

But the Marquis was no longer listening. 'Tell me, Don Alvaro,'
he said, stroking his beard thoughtfully. 'If you should find gold in
plenty, whether in the rivers or the rocks, or large and well-shaped
pearls, would it be possible, as your Lady so generously suggested . . . ? Do you think . . . ?'

He hesitated, searching for the word, but at this delicate moment a
door behind the General slowly opened, a plump white hand glittering
with rings slid into view, a dainty finger beckoned.

The Viceroy stopped, sighed deeply, and did not complete his
question. 'In a minute, in a minute, my Lady,' he pleaded to the
owner of the hand. 'I have not yet done.' Then he snatched a scroll
from the table, opened it, cleared his throat and, in a firm, if hurried
voice, began at once to read out a speech which my godfather had
composed at his direction:

'Don Garcia Hurtado de Mendoza, Marquis of Cañete, Viceroy of
Peru, to the intrepid General Alvaro de Mendaña y Castro of Neira,
in the presence of the chief officers of the Church and State here
assembled in our Viceregal audience-chamber at Lima, the City of
Kings, in the year of our redemption, 1595—greeting:

'My Lord the General, I may well wish you God-speed as you embark upon this enterprise with as vigorous a company of men as can
be found anywhere in the world. Prodigious indeed have been the
deeds of Spaniards at various times and in different places, especially
when led by valorous Generals who know how to face and overcome
adversity; who have met danger with prudence; who have kept a
cheerful countenance despite the frowns of Fortune, and maintained
the spirits of their followers with high promises and encouraging
words; who have rewarded them, cherished them, succoured them;
and who, ruling by kindness, have taken wise advantage of every
opportunity that offered. There are so many glorious leaders of our
nation who have acted thus in times past, that I should undoubtedly
weary brain and tongue if I attempted to bring them all to mind.
Yet I must not omit to praise their valiant followers, who always,

on every occasion, showed themselves loyal and obedient, overflowing in courtesy and virtue, in word as well as in deed. If in respect of the present age my praises must be qualified in part, that is no fault of the men. Some years yield better harvests than others. Latterly, our bold husbandmen have garnered scanty sheaves and their overseers have earned little praise—especially those going in search of adventure on the high seas, where dangers and difficulties abound but remedies are few.

'Old sailors may decry the men of today as being inferior to our ancestors who drove their deep furrows through the eastern seas. Those were bold fellows, I grant you, but how little they achieved in the Western hemisphere, an almost limitless field of conquest and exploration, and what a galaxy of brilliant navigators we can here display! In the front rank of these stands Christopher Columbus who, despised and rejected by many crowned heads, set sail at last under the patronage of the Catholic Sovereigns Isabella and Ferdinand, and revealed this continent of America, the firm foundation upon which so many important edifices, alike spiritual as temporal, have since been raised. He was succeeded by Hernan Cortez, the conqueror of Mexico, famed for his huge extensions of Empire and his prodigious deeds. Here, to Peru, came Francisco Pizarro and his glorious little band that was to conquer such rich and populous provinces. Next, Ferdinand Magellan, a loyal servant of Spain, though a Portuguese, who would have sailed completely around the world, had he not met an untimely and less fortunate end than his brave spirit deserved. Next, Vasco da Gama sought remote regions and opened up to his nation, and so to ours, the commerce of the East. Audacious, it need not be denied, have been the feats of the Englishmen Drake, Candish and our prisoner Hawkins who, envious of Magellan's fame, traversed the straits called after him and disturbed the seas which for many years had been secure and peaceful under our sway and trident.

'All this notwithstanding, I behold in you a discoverer neither less distinguished nor less famous than any I have named. In every country, throughout history, the leadership of great expeditions is entrusted to men who, by reason either of their genius, the dignity of their bearing, the purity of their lives, or their authority and tact, have acquired universal fame as just arbiters of peace and war; the prosperous conclusion of the tasks in which they were engaged depending upon their exercise of consummate wisdom. All these qualities, I am assured, are combined in your person. Your actions confirm the choice made by His Majesty for so great a service to God and to him: namely, the pacification and conversion of the infidels who inhabit the distant Isles of Solomon, hidden in the great gulf that divides the coasts of New Spain and Peru from those of the Philippines and Japan. In my own mind there is not the least doubt that the government which you are about to establish will be glorious and triumphant, and that the people under your sway will remain faithful; so that great praise may already be awarded you in anticipation of your signal industry, prudence and valour.'

His speech concluded, the Viceroy tossed the scroll aside, offered his hand to be kissed and then said in brisk tones: 'My friend, I have two more things to add. First, let me repeat that your flotilla will clear the port of Callao by Friday, three days hence. The second: that I shall hold you to the undertaking made by your Lady. Now goodbye and God-speed! The Admiral-General of the South Seas will deputize for me at the port, and the day of your departure will be proclaimed a public holiday.'

He rose and disappeared quickly through the small door. Don Alvaro, on the point of delivering a prepared speech of gratitude, was taken aback. He blinked, stared, then slowly replaced his plumed hat and was about to retire, when my godfather politely detained him with the warning that he must expect to stay a little while yet.

'Why, man, the audience is at an end!'

'That is so, Don Alvaro, but the Viceroy's court-painter has been ordered to depict you standing there against the open window with these letters patent under your arm, modestly listening to the Viceroy's speech. Your flotilla, by a pictorial licence, will be shown riding at anchor behind you. The canvas is somewhat spacious.'

'But the work will take months to complete,' the General gasped, 'with the Marquis so overwhelmed by business.'

'No, no,' said my godfather soothingly. 'You misunderstand me. The audience-chamber is already fixed on the canvas, and so are the figures of most of the lords spiritual and temporal who, as you learned from his Excellency's gracious speech, were present in spirit on this auspicious occasion, though unfortunately not in person. The picture will be completed, as a witness to posterity of the great honour conferred on you, when his Grace the Bishop and his

Excellency himself can spare the time to pose; and I promise you it
will be a very fine and life-like work.'

'Alas, I have a thousand matters of the greatest urgency to settle
before nightfall. Why could not the painter have begun during my
long wait in the ante-room?'

'Come, Don Alvaro,' said my godfather politely, 'if you go to him at
once, it will soon be done. His Excellency's orders are precise and not
to be flouted. But perhaps you would prefer first to eat something a
little more substantial than these thin, sweet biscuits?'

'O blessed Saint Lorenzo on your red-hot griddle!' groaned the
General, 'teach me to suffer in silence for just a few hours longer!'

Chapter 3

THE VICAR'S BAGGAGE

Father Antonio, our Chaplain, went below to examine the quarters which the Vicar, Father Juan de la Espinosa, was to share with him. Though one who cared little for bodily comforts, he found the cabin so cramped, dark and stifling, that he recoiled in dismay. It seemed to him a studied affront to the Church that this kennel should have been allotted to a frail old man, who had given his life to good works and dangerous missions among the Indians of the interior. Indeed, it bordered upon sacrilege: was this place fit to house the sacred accessories of religion, blessed by the Bishop of Lima, that were to be conveyed to the Isles of Solomon—the chalice, the pyx, the vestments, the Holy Scriptures, and the elements of the Blessed Sacrament?

In a royal ship, as he remembered from his voyage to Peru many years before, there were two secular services: the naval and the military. Here in the *San Geronimo* the Chief Pilot, as master, commanded the crew, the Colonel commanded the troops. The General controlled both services and, once the flotilla was on the high seas, his powers equalled those of the Viceroy of Peru, to whom he then ceased to owe allegiance; being answerable only to the Indies Council at Madrid, presided over by the King. Yet in matters spiritual not only the Chief Pilot and all his sailors, the Colonel and all his troops, but even the General must defer to the Vicar, or suffer the consequences. King Philip himself, the mightiest and most absolute monarch that the world had ever known, owed spiritual vassalage to the Pope, who held the keys of Heaven and Hell in direct succession from Saint Peter, who received them from Our Saviour. The honour of the Church demanded that the Vicar should be as well lodged as any man on board.

The good Father told the slaves who followed him with the ecclesiastical baggage to carry it back to the upper deck while he went to lodge a complaint with the Purser, in the hope of securing an exchange for his superior with some naval or military officer who had been better served.

Coming to the master's cabin (which Don Alvaro, in expectation of huge discoveries, grandiloquently styled 'the Chart-room'), he asked a page: 'Whose fine quarters are these, my child?'

'That's where the Chief Pilot lives, if it please your Reverence.'

'It pleases me very well,' said Father Antonio, and muttered to himself: 'Perhaps he will agree to an exchange; he has a name for piety unusual in a man of his calling.'

Pedro Fernandez had unpacked his sea-chest, and was now stowing his nautical instruments in racks built for them by the carpenter. He made his obeisance to the Chaplain and kissed the silver cross he wore.

'My son,' said Father Antonio, 'I bring you a message from my superior, the Vicar. It is this. Two rich merchants of Lima have lately been tried by the Supreme Court of the Holy Inquisition, and found guilty of a relapse into the damnable Lutheran heresy—dogs returned to their vomit . . .'

'Alas, reverend Father,' cried the Chief Pilot, drawing him into the Chart-room, closing the door and falling on his knees. 'Have you come to reproach me? How did you learn that I was implicated in their wickedness?'

'Your conscience accuses you, not I; but let me hear your confession, my son.'

'Bless me, Father, I have sinned. I confess that I have had an understanding with a customs clerk in this port, and have smuggled in small quantities of goods at the request of friends, and for a fee this clerk passes them. That is common practice here, and since he is paid very little and cannot support his family without taking bribes, it has never troubled my conscience to do what others do. But the fault of which I accuse myself was that I agreed to bring in a weighty parcel for these Lutherans, whom I knew to have been already once convicted of heresy; it was said to contain ledgers and bills of account and, though I knew that these are not contraband, I smothered my suspicions and did what they asked of me. Afterwards, when I learned that I had been instrumental in smuggling copies of the Holy Scriptures printed at Amsterdam in the vulgar tongue, I

felt as though a shot had furrowed my scalp and carried away my
bonnet. What if the Inspector of Customs had caught me with the
books? God was very merciful; indeed, I might well have burned
in these heretics' place. Absolve me, Father.'

'My son, what have you done with the gains of this abominable
traffic?'

'I have made restitution to God, reverend Father. I dropped every
maravedi of it into the alms-box of the Clarissas.'

'You are absolved,' said Father Antonio. 'For a penance you shall
repeat five Paternosters with five Ave Marias, and pray for my intention. Now make a good act of contrition. . . . As I was about to
tell you: of these two heretics, one has confessed and repented under
torture; he is to be granted his life, though forfeiting his whole
fortune. The other remains obstinate in error, averring that since die
he must, he will die in the Lutheran faith; and since his body must
burn he will not be strangled first, but will wear the beard of furze.'

'How did you say, reverend Father?'

'The customs of your country are what they may be, but in Peru,
as in Spain, before we light the fire at an Act of Faith, the cry
goes up: "Let the dog's beard be made!", which is then done by
thrusting flaming furze against the heretic's chin, until it is charred to
a coal. That is indeed a cruel sight, and a fearful reminder of what
lies in store for those who live scandalously and die unconfessed. The
flames of Purgatory are a thousand times hotter than any that can be
lighted on this earth, and they burn without respite until Judgement
Day. As an act of mortification, the Vicar has vowed to stand beside
the pyre this coming Sunday, and greatly desires the ship's company to
march to Lima behind him. Such a spectacle would strangle at birth
many an infant sin born of wantonness, which otherwise might grow
to manhood and deliver a soul to torment. Therefore, my son, he asks
you to do all you can to postpone our sailing until the Monday, and
God will reward you.'

'Ah, but reverend Father,' said the Chief Pilot, 'I am under orders
from the General to make ready for our departure on Friday with all
possible speed. Last night he was fuming at the negligence of the
contractors who have so far delivered only one-half of the provisions
needed; and censured me because the spare sails and cordage—paid
for out of my own purse—which were to have been brought ten
days ago, are not here either. For my sick wife's sake I would willingly
give a hundred pesos to delay another week, until the crisis of her

fever has been passed. However, he is right to make haste; the south-easterly winds may fail us if we wait even a little longer. Submit your superior's plea to the General, if you will, but pray do not add my name to it, lest he suspect me of hidden motives; I dare not forfeit his trust.'

Father Antonio frowned, and said: 'There is another small matter in which you can show your gratitude to God.' He spoke sorrowfully of the little dark glory-hole that was to serve the Vicar both as oratory and living quarters.

'But, reverend Father, what can I do? The distribution of quarters is the Purser's business. He has nearly lost his wits trying to find decent accommodation for every person of importance in this ship, so crammed with soldiers, seamen, passengers, goods and livestock. Until it pleases God to bring us safely to the Isles, everyone must expect more than usual discomfort. The enlarging of the General's own store-room has eaten into the living quarters; that's where the trouble lies.'

'I do not notice, my son, that you are likely to suffer discomfort yourself. Would it not be a pious and charitable act to exchange this airy cabin of yours with the Vicar—an old man, who coughs all night like a cat with a fish-bone in his throat, and is so saintly that he never asks for anything better than is given him?'

'I would willingly yield my quarters,' said the Chief Pilot, 'and live with the common sailors in the forecastle, though they lie as close as salted sardines in a tub. I have not forgotten that I served six years before the mast until I rose to supercargo and assistant pilot. But now that I am both Master and Chief Pilot, my post is in the Master's cabin where these nautical instruments belong, and where I have a table to spread my charts; and my room must communicate with the Great Cabin so that the General can summon me on the instant, and must also be within a hop and a jump of the quarter-deck. Yet because all the cabins are crowded, and indeed over-crowded, I have agreed to share my quarters with the General's secretaries. More lodgers I cannot entertain. If your cabin will not hold the two of you, may I suggest in all humility that you ask permission to sail in the galeot, where they have no priest at all?'

'The Vicar cannot do without me, my son, and upon my word, your excuses show little devotion. Are the instruments of navigation to be accorded more honour than the instruments of religion?'

'I make no excuses, reverend Father; I only explain circumstances.

Go to the General, by all means, and ask for the exchange to be made; if he consents, I shall obey.'

The good Father went away, very discontented, and meeting with the Purser's negro, asked to be taken the round of the cabins and other living quarters. But it was as Pedro Fernandez had said: the ship was overcrowded, and even the berth which the Colonel was to share with his nephew and four other military officers seemed as dark and airless as a dungeon. However, when the negro told him that the best cabin of all, after the Barretos', had been allotted to a mere merchant-venturer, Don Juan de la Isla, he at once took his protest to Doña Ysabel.

Doña Ysabel showed him every respect, but little sympathy. She explained that Don Juan, an old friend of the General's and a veteran of the Philippine wars, had a larger investment in the enterprise than anyone else in the flotilla, with the exception of her husband; and that he was to share that cabin with his wife and daughter who, being women of rank, could not be accommodated elsewhere. As for the other two merchants who were installed in a smaller cabin alongside, they had been persuaded only with the greatest difficulty to embark on the expedition. 'Should the least mark of discourtesy be shown them now,' she said, 'they might change their minds and go ashore again.'

'If they have come unwillingly, that would do little harm, my daughter; and if this cabin were freed it would serve for the Vicar, who is old and has a bad cough.'

Smiling a little grimly, Doña Ysabel said: 'The merchants' room would be bought at a heavy price, reverend Father. All the pork and biscuit on board is their venture, and half the wine too. Why do you complain of your quarters? Not on your own account, I warrant; your Bishop tells me that you are used to poverty and hardship. Is it on your superior's account? That would do him little honour, since he is said to be a pious man, and a Franciscan in all but his habit. Is it on account of the sacramental plate, the vestments and such like? Yet did not Our Saviour Himself in His infinite mercy consent to hold court in a stable, lodged in an ass's manger, and our Blessed Lady with Him?'

This, though unanswerable, did not satisfy Father Antonio, as coming from a woman, and he determined to carry the matter to the General. Nor was he the only one who had complaints to make about his accommodation, and the Purser, run after by a swarm of angry people, went into hiding below, where the bilge-water stank so foully that he was safe from pursuit. When I saw him again he looked pretty sick, but told me philosophically: 'A stinking bilge, a sound hull.'

At last the General was drummed aboard, suspecting no trouble, like a man who looks cheerfully up at the sky and steps into a wasp's nest. The Chief Pilot was the first to salute him and, as they mounted to the quarter-deck where Doña Ysabel was waiting, contrived to explain what had passed between the Colonel and himself, adding that he had no wish to sail with a madman, but would far rather remain in Peru, even if this meant forfeiting the thousand pesos which he had invested in the enterprise. Doña Ysabel's brothers took his part against the Colonel, and protested that Pedro Fernandez could not be spared: of capable military officers we had no lack, they said, but here was the best navigator in Peru, or out of it. Let the Colonel hang or drown, it was all one to them; but it was not consonant with their honour to sail with the soldier who had insulted their sister, while parting with the sailor who had championed her at the risk of his life.

The General groaned and wrung his hands. 'Brothers,' he said, 'you do not know what you are asking. The Colonel has been appointed by the Viceroy, and I can no more dismiss him than I could tear up my letters patent. If we take any action against him, his cousin the Warden of Callao will hear of it at once and order the dock-masters to delay our taking in of stores; and even if we were foolish enough to leave without these, we might find on our arrival at Paita that the news had outrun us and that we were denied the eighty arquebuses which the Lieutenant of the port is to supply. Calm yourselves, I implore you! Pedro Fernandez, my friend, you are a reasonable man and must be aware that it is I, not the Colonel, who commands this expedition. I pledge you my word of honour that if you consent to stay, suitable remedies will be applied.'

But Father Antonio was still waiting with his complaint about the cabin, joined with a request for a postponement of the sailing. The General commiserated with him and said that, though he could neither enlarge the ship nor redistribute the quarters, yet when the Isles were reached, he would give the Vicar every facility for the erection of a splendid church and vicarage, which should take precedence of all other building whatsoever. He even agreed to send a messenger to the Viceroy asking leave to postpone the departure, though he held out no hope of a favourable reply.

That night Juarez Mendés and Matia Pineto, two gaunt old soldiers, were on guard outside the Great Cabin, and keeping them company was Jaume Bonet, the water-steward. These three formed a close junta, since they were the only men in the ship—except for the General and his negro Myn—who had been on the previous voyage when the Isles of Solomon were discovered. They sat cross-legged in the alley-way, playing a desultory game of cards, and drinking chicha; but most of the time they were recalling events in which they had taken part and commenting on their new ship-mates. The General and Doña Ysabel slept ashore, and the Chief Pilot was also away, attending to his sick wife; whether the junta were unaware that I lay close by in the Chart-room, hearing every word they said, or whether they knew and did not care, I cannot tell. I strained my ears to listen, because they were men who knew much but were not free with their opinions except when in drink.

I heard Juarez ask: 'What is your venture, Matia?'

'Chisels, knives, razors, needles and suchlike; fifteen pesos' worth: a pedlar's stock that I bought up-country a month ago.'

'Bought!' exclaimed Juarez, in tones of disbelief.

'With a soldier's prayer and blessing, not to mention the bull's pizzle with which I dusted his clothes for him. The savages will pay me a whole pig for a single needle. One of these days you'll see me surrounded by pigs, like the Prodigal Son, but with a plumper paunch. As for every chisel, a sackful of gold nuggets: that's my price. What's your venture, mutton-vender?'

'Thirty yards of arquebus match, borrowed from the Royal Arsenal by a friend to whom I have bequeathed my sweetheart.'

'What use will the savages have for wick, unless you also sell them your piece and powder-horn, which you'd never do?'

'Blockhead, the match isn't for them! Our first expedition, though far better supplied than this one, failed for want of match. In those islands a man's life depends on keeping his match alight; and mark my words, Matia, the time will come when you'll be ready to barter all your black pigs, and your sacks of nuggets too, against a span of wick.'

'I'd strangle you with it first, you Jew. But Juarez, do you recall that day on Malaita when the Indians attacked us, and I dropped that old man with the grey corded hair? God's passion, how the bastard fought, though all the rest had fled when we opened fire! Jaume, you should have seen him! There he stood, with a great gash

in his thigh, facing us all alone with his spear and shield. Four
of our targeteers went for him, but he defended himself like a devil,
dealing terrific thrusts at their targes with the miserable spear which,
had it been steel-tipped, would have pierced them through and
through, and warding off their sword-strokes with his wooden shield,
until they hacked it into fifty pieces. And even when we'd given him
a couple of good cuts on the shoulders, and a stab in the side, the
black devil fought on until I settled him with a blow that nearly split
his skull and felled him to the ground, and what was left of his spear
dropped from his hand.'

'Will I ever forget it?' said Juarez. 'Don Hernando Enriquez
ordered us to do him no more harm, and though he was dying, yet he
tried to rise, with the blood pouring in streams from his face, and
groped for the remnant of his spear, but could not find it and sank
down again. Nor will I forget your face, Matia, when presently you
ventured close and he shot you such a venomous look that you
jumped back three paces; and tried once more to lift himself up against
you, but could not, and plucked a handful of grass and flung that. . . .
It's only with fire-arms that these heathen can be controlled. I still
say that my wick is the best venture.'

'Jaume,' said Juarez presently, 'you look glum tonight. Another
cup, man, and tell us what you think of this ship and her company.'

A pause, while Jaume drank, then he pronounced slowly: 'In my
opinion, old cocks, the *San Geronimo* is pretty well; as good as any
Peruvian-built ship in which I've sailed, though they're all clumsy
in rough weather, and don't take it kindly when you work them to
windward. She came off the stocks at Guayaquil no more than two
years ago, and I've seen the Chief Pilot go over her from bowsprit to
lantern and from keel to masthead, warranting her to be sound.
You can trust that man; a Lisbon wharf-rat and a seaman to his
finger-tips, yet with more breeding than many a marquis. The crew's
pretty well too, on the whole; and as for Don Marcos Marin—I never
served under a better boatswain. What more remains to be said?'

'A great deal more, Jaume. On our last voyage we hadn't a single
skirt in the fleet, except when we kidnapped those five savages just
before our return; and then the General locked them up below, giving
the key of their quarters to Fray Francisco. But what have we now?
This ship might be a floating brothel, and I'm told and well believe
it, that fully half the girls have earned their living that way. Where
there are skirts, there's trouble, I say. For who can control them?
Not even the priests. Nor even God Himself.'

'As to that, I've no fears. The General's Lady has a cold blue eye, to exact obedience, and her maid Elvira tells me that if the least breath of scandal comes to her ears, she's capable of having the slut whipped well-nigh to death and the poor fornicator keelhauled. It takes a skirt to manage skirts, and the General's Lady is a tiger, if ever I saw one. Let any man who crosses her path beware; for my part, I've learned to doff my cap from half a league away when I see her approach, and remain frozen in a respectful posture for half an hour after she's passed.'

'How in the world did the General come to marry her?'

'She came out from Spain as companion to the Viceroy's Lady in the same ship as himself—she's a daughter of Don Francisco de Barreto, a Governor of Angola who died, they say, searching for gold in the mountains of Africa. The gold-fly seems to have bitten Doña Ysabel too, and her greed matches her courage; Elvira says that she often dreams of bathing in rivers of gold like the King of Bogotá. When she heard of Don Alvaro's letters patent, she very soon had her hook in his gills. It's my opinion that but for her the General would have been satisfied with his early laurels and spent the rest of his life on his estate at Guanaco. And this I know: she's used her interest with the Viceroy's Lady to get the expedition under way at last, forcing the old man to sell or mortgage all his worldly goods to equip it, and herself recruiting the merchant-venturers to make up what was lacking. Your deal, Matia, but remember old friendship. Your hands move a little too fast for my liking.'

'Come, Jaume, you know I'd never skin you! Indeed, I swear I love you so well, you whoremaster of Majorca, that if you'll pay me only half a peso, I'll teach you the whole art of dealing. After three days I warrant to make you an adept, and you'll never want again for the remainder of your life.'

Jaume grunted doubtfully, but Juarez said: 'Why grunt like a pig, man? It's a generous offer. Matia's the world's best artist in rigging a deck. *Primero's* his specialty, and I'm his faithful acolyte. Half a peso, sailor, it's nothing; and for that he'll teach you how to take a quick peep at the lowest card, how to shuffle it where it's of the greatest use, and then deal yourself a certainty. The trick is to give your partner fifty-two points, and then palm an ace to make fifty-five yourself or, if you like, deal yourself a neat fifty-four, so that you win either on the hand or on points. And another half-peso for myself, Jaume, and I'll teach you how to draw three cards and throw only two

without fear of discovery. Whenever Matia and I play together—
except, of course, with an old ship-mate like you—we play into each
other's hands like a couple of friars, and share the profits. How we
rig the deck is this: one of us either takes up good cards already
thrown and slips them on top of the pack for his partner to draw, or
changes it for a doctored pack while his partner raises a distraction.
It's easy pickings, sailor. Come in with us; we need a third.'

'I wonder that, with your mastery of the art, you can bring yourselves to play a straight game with me.'

'Why, Jaume, you might as well wonder that, being soldiers by
profession, we don't ransack the homes of our nearest relatives.'

'Yes, you're right there, Juarez. I might as well wonder, knowing
the reputation you built up in the late bloody rebellion.'

The soldiers laughed uproariously and, as the chicha went round
again, returned to their discussion of the General. Matia asked: 'And
what do you think of him, Jaume? According to Juarez he isn't
by any means the man he was when we knew him; but why say that?
He's half a century older, I grant, but so are you, and so am I. I don't
know how it is with you fellows, but though I'm a trifle slower on my
legs and more easily winded, I'm quicker on the mark with my
arquebus; and though less indefatigable in my pursuit of skirts, yet I
can deal with them when I catch them as well as ever I did, or better;
and if I haven't learned wisdom, I've learned at least to avoid the
appearance of folly. Am I to believe that the General has lost more
and gained less in these years than I have?'

'As to that,' said Jaume, 'Elvira tells me that he's taken a vow
of chastity for the length of the voyage, and that he's tried to persuade Don Juan de la Isla, and the Captain of Artillery, and the
other married men to do the same. Piety is his pretext, but from
what Elvira says, who's as deep in her mistress's confidence as I'm
in hers, the General who once had a splendid reputation as a gallant
has failed for years to give his Lady the tender attentions which are
her due; and this may well be the reason for her restlessness and
violent ill-temper—any fool can see by her gait and figure that she's
a full-blooded woman and, if I may believe Elvira, she's never yet
taken a lover, though many a nobleman has strained his guts in an
attempt to seduce her. In my opinion, the General is already senile;
the sap has ceased to mount and the leaves are falling. I only hope
that the courage and resolution which he displayed when we first
knew him haven't yet altogether deserted him.'

'I say amen to that,' said Juarez. 'But I've known him off and on during the intervening years, and it's my belief that he's never been the same since that affair at Panama. I don't think you know the story. Well, when he made his first attempt to set this expedition on foot, some twenty years ago now, he passed through Panama on his way here, with the volunteers he'd enlisted in Spain, myself among them. At the quay, when we'd disembarked, a bilious customs-clerk confiscated my sea-chest, pretending to find contraband in it. You know me; I called him a rogue and a robber and offered to break his teeth with the butt of my arquebus. At once the Inspector had me arrested, and all my comrades ran to the city to complain to the President—who proved to be an abominable cockroach by name Dr. Loarte.'

'Loarte? That would be the gentleman who seduced his step-daughter to prevent her from marrying and taking her fortune away with her.'

'I can well believe it; the gallows were marked all over his face. He not only supported the Inspector, who supported the clerk, but sent troops to arrest the General as leader of the riot; and then in compliment to the General's uncle, whom he hated for what he'd written against him as a member of the Indies Council, had him marched off to the common jail (where I was already confined) to lie among stinking negroes and poxy Indians. The people of the port sided with us, so far as they dared, and showed their detestation of that insect in a ruff, the President; but stood in fear of the Supreme Court which he controlled. Only one man came forward to plead his case, this same Juan de la Isla, who persuaded Dr. Loarte that to jail a high-born Spaniard with a Royal Commission in his pocket was to affront King Philip himself; so presently he was removed to the Town Hall, where Don Juan placed his purse at the General's disposal —everything he owned having been confiscated—and a week later we were both set free to continue our journey. Well, I hold that something in the General's soul, some airy creature of great merit, was mortally wounded in that jail; and that after lingering a few years in the unkind airs of Peru, it perished. I believe, in fact, and Jaume here has confirmed my belief, that though the General may play his part as leader of this expedition with dignity and courage, he walks already like one who treads his destined road to the grave or to the gallows. What drives him is not his own will, but the will of Doña Ysabel; who, when they step ashore on the Isles and take possession, will become a great land-owner and strut about in golden slippers. I'm heartily sorry for her serfs and her tenants. The chicha, Jaume! These things don't bear reflexion.'

His comrades did not seem to be paying much attention. 'No, no, Jaume, not that way,' scolded Matia. 'You're all thumbs, sailor. Let me show you again how to juggle the top-cards.'

'My fingers are too old and too well set in honesty to learn a thieves' trade now,' Jaume grumbled.

'And that's no way to palm an ace, man! You knocked on every door in turn, like the Vicar's Chaplain.'

Chapter 4

DEPARTURE FROM CALLAO

I shall never forget our labours and vexations of the Thursday, the last full day left us for taking in stores. We were now short-handed: fifteen of the seamen signed on for the voyage had deserted during the night, no doubt because the violent altercation between the Colonel and the Chief Pilot decided them—and I began to be of their opinion myself—that this was no ship in which to sail to the unknown ends of the world. Moreover, Don Gaspar Iturbe the Purser found to his disgust that though our list of stores was an imposing one, ample for six months or more, and included a multiplicity of items, such as saws, hatchets, spades, mattocks and a portable forge, needed for the building of a settlement; not to speak of bells, looking-glasses, beads, coloured kerchiefs, silken caps, German knives and other toys prized by savages; yet only two-thirds of the victuals and less than one-third of the tools and trade goods had so far been delivered. When he went to remonstrate with the contractors, he found that the General had not been able to lay down sufficient money to secure the remainder, and that they had no confidence in his notes of hand despite their Royal backing. Four out of every five expeditions to the South Seas miscarried, and though they could present their claims to the Treasury, it might be years before these were met; they had therefore promised, but not performed.

In effect, though the General had paid for the San Geronimo and contributed towards the purchase of two other vessels by mortgaging the income of his estate; and also contrived to buy some toys for the Indians, a few cattle to stock the Isles, and equipment for the smelting of precious metals, there he had stopped. He required all the pilots to provide their own nautical instruments and even to lend him money for the purchase of spare sails, spars and cordage; as for the pay of the sailors and soldiers, that would be found by the Treasury, except in the case of some fifty volunteers who served on the understanding that they would be granted estates in the Isles.

The Purser warned me not to tell a soul of the General's failure to lay down his share of the venture; to do so would not only lessen his authority with the ship's company but greatly displease our merchant-venturers, who did not yet know either that they had been left to bear the whole cost of victualling the flagship, or that important stores were still lacking. 'Let us be just,' said Don Gaspar, 'and admit that the fault does not lie wholly with him. Twenty years ago at his own expense he brought out a galleon from Corunna laden with merchandise and volunteers; but the President of Panama and the Viceroy of Peru combined against him, so that he had to sell the goods at great loss, besides paying off his volunteers, and has been in debt ever since. I cannot find it in my heart to blame Don Alvaro.'

I promised to keep silence, but when I saw how lavishly the General's own larder was being stocked with oil, dried meats, bladders of lard, barrels of Malmsey and Madeira wine, jars of honey, boxes of quince conserve, sacks of white flour and the like, I began to wonder. And when Doña Ysabel came on board that evening, in a stiffly brocaded silk dress with diamond buttons, flaunting a golden bracelet closely set with fine emeralds each the size of your thumb-nail, a necklace of the same design and a ruby ring on her little finger worth ten thousand pesos at the least, besides costly ear-rings and other jewels, I grew indignant. 'Don Gaspar,' I said to the Purser, 'the General's Lady should be ashamed to display riches that might have been pledged to buy much needed stores.'

'Hush, man!' he answered. 'She inherited those jewels from her mother and, as anyone with experience of the world will tell you, once a noblewoman begins to pledge her jewels, or allows her husband to do so for her, she loses pride and pleasure in life and sees herself already in rags, begging on the Cathedral steps. The General would never even hint that they should be sacrificed; besides, they have served us well. Doña Ysabel has succeeded in stocking her husband's wants at no cost either to herself or to him; because many of the rich Andalusians of Lima, though you might not think it, are men of chivalrous sentiments, which is to say, fools. When a lady of birth and beauty walks into a counting-house and confidently hands the merchant a long list of goods for the Great Cabin of the ship in which she and her husband are sailing to the South Seas in search of gold and pearls, and does not haggle, but merely stipulates immediate delivery, what then, man? Why, he agrees as if in a trance, dazzled by her smile and condescension, accepts her note of hand without a qualm, and never pauses to notice that the date of payment is not specified. He fulfils the order because it would go against his honour to retreat from his word—did she not address him as "my lord"?—and afterwards quiets his mercantile conscience with: "I can be sure of seeing my money again. She was wearing jewellery worth forty thousand pesos, and the goods are for herself, which makes her debt one of honour." All the same, he is hardly fool enough to show the note of hand to his wife, who would surely skin him alive if she knew what he'd done.

'So you see, little Andrés, her jewels have earned their keep, and give us cause to admire them without rancour. And you may be sure that if we are longer at sea than is expected, because of contrary winds, and provisions run short, Don Alvaro will relieve our hunger and thirst from the plenty of his private store. He is a man of compassion and on his first voyage, I am told, made it his rule to eat and drink no better than a common seaman; ay, and in time of danger he placed himself under the boatswain's orders and took his turn at the pumps, and even lent a hand with the sails.'

Three smaller vessels completed our flotilla. The *Santa Ysabel* galleon was of about one hundred and twenty tons burden, a decrepit old vessel which her commander, Captain Lope de Vega, had bought for a song on behalf of himself and the General. The *San Felipe* galeot was of seventy tons, wholly the venture of Captain Felipe Corzo, her commander; a fine little craft. The *Santa Catalina* frigate, of fifty tons, commanded by Captain Alonzo de Leyva, was the venture of a Lima merchant, but the General had a third-interest in her hull and also held the merchant's power of attorney; she was worn and crank, with a hogged keel and dry rot in her upper works, and should have been broken up years before—we nicknamed her 'The Holy Coffin.'

By midnight all the settlers were assembled aboard and we had the *San Geronimo* more or less ship-shape, the frigate and galeot reporting that they too were ready for sea. Only the *Santa Ysabel* was not yet in port; her captain had been sent to recruit respectable married settlers in the valleys of Saña, Santa and Truxillo, high up the coast, and to buy salt beef, flour and cheeses for the troops' rations, which were cheaper there than at Callao. The absence of the galleon was much remarked upon by the sailors. Some said that the General feared to produce so unseaworthy a vessel for inspection by the Admiral-General; others, that she had already foundered with all hands.

The business and excitement of departure repaired in some measure the discord between the high officers. Since the Colonel was now stark sober and very much at the General's orders, the Chief Pilot and Doña Ysabel's brothers agreed to treat him as though the scandalous events of the Tuesday had never occurred. Doña Ysabel herself showed him a graciousness that melted him like sugar stirred into hot wine, and because of his bad conscience towards them he was anxious to make amends, though careful of his dignity. When not in his cups, he was a correct and likeable old man, though he would always say the first thing that entered his head, without reflexion, and usually it was something unwise. He was much given to the reading of romances: *Amadis of Gaul*, *The Seven Champions of Christendom*, *The History of Palmyrin of England* and the like, and had brought a cloak-bag full of these books to kill the tedium of the voyage. The Cid was his hero; the manners of the world nowadays displeased him; and he would often complain that all had gone to wrack since the invention of gun-powder had made the knave the equal of the knight.

Friday dawned at last. To my chagrin I was detailed to stay on board, while all the soldiers and sailors who could be spared went ashore and were marched up to Lima, where they heard High Mass in the Cathedral and partook of the Sacrament. The General also made an intercession on their behalf to Saint Domingo, at the back of whose church stands the fine Basilica of Vera Cruz built by Pizarro more than fifty years before. Here a splinter of the True Cross is kept in a jewelled reliquary, a gift from Pope Paul III, which was now held up for the veneration of our people. The officers were ill content that Saint Domingo had been made our patron, as though we were friars, rather than Saint James of Compostella who favours and rewards daring enterprises when piety goes hand in hand with in-flexible courage. The three Royal Standards were then blessed; each bore the double-headed eagle of the Holy Roman Empire, embracing the royal arms of Spain, with a tall crucifix above and, below, the motto: 'Thou art my protection and defence.' The royal banners of purple watered silk with gold fringes were also blessed; and the pendant of each commander.

This being a public holiday, thousands of Lima citizens travelled the two leagues to Callao for a sight of the ships, although it was close and torrid weather, better suited for staying indoors, fan in hand, behind closed shutters. The procession wound down from the Cathedral with great pomp, the General and his Lady at the head of the ships' companies, preceded by friars of three different Orders who waved censers and chanted penitential psalms. Our people were surprised to see that the General had adopted the habit of a Franciscan lay-brother and that Doña Ysabel, to keep him decent company, was wearing a russet gown bare of adornments, except for a small gold crucifix. The garrulous Elvira had evidently been right about Don Alvaro's vow; but, to judge by their rich clothes, neither Juan de la Isla nor our other two merchant-venturers, Andrés and Mariano de Castillo, had been moved by the General's plea for sacrifices. The Chief Pilot carried a wooden image of Our Lady of Solitude in his arms, a parting-gift from the House of Clarissas to whom his brother-in-law was appointed father confessor. It can have been no easy burden.

The chanting ended at the quay-side, where our musicians struck up bravely with fife and drum while the General and his following were rowed back across the harbour in a fleet of decorated boats. The troops of the flagship formed up on deck under arms, and the Admiral-General of the South Seas, with his suite, was drummed aboard to inspect us. As had been foreseen, he found everything to his liking, being taken to see only what was fit to be shown, and did not trouble to have the military stores checked against the lists handed to him; nor did he inspect the frigate, or the galeot either. The Dean of the Cathedral-canons blessed the *San Geronimo*, sprinkled holy water over her anchor-cables, masts and helm, and gave his benediction to those of us who had been unable to attend mass that morning. Every craft in the harbour was dressed with bunting in our honour, great animation was shown, and rival bands of musicians began playing in the ships and on the quay-side.

The Admiral-General left us about the hour of vespers, and no sooner had his state-barge touched the shore than a galley put out and ran under our counter, with a gift of fifteen seamen in exchange for those who had run off. It was easy to see why they had not been sent until the inspection was completed: these were not seamen, but the sweepings of the water-front, and a more villainous consignment of gallows' meat I never saw in my life—branded, leg-and-neck-galled, lousy, thin as rakes, their backs well-patterned by the lash, one of them without a hand, another with a prop for a leg, all of them ragged in the extreme and lacking the barest necessities. The Boatswain made no complaint to the Harbour-master from whom he received the men, but pretended satisfaction and waited until the galley had put off, when he at once ordered every one of them to be confined below under guard. He told the General: 'Tonight, if it please your Excellency, I shall row these heroes ashore and let them find their way back to the City jail, where they belong.'

'Do so, by all means, Boatswain,' said Don Alvaro. 'They have been sent us in error. The Harbour-master must have misread the Warden's order to impress fifteen able seamen for our galleon, and given us galley-slaves instead.'

The Royal Standard was broken from the stern, the anchor was weighed with much stamping and singing, and the long-boat took us in tow, upon which the Captain of Artillery gave the order to fire a grand salute from our falcons and falconets. That was a fine simultaneous volley, at once taken up by the galeot and frigate; to which the other royal vessels and the fort at the harbour entrance replied thunderously, and then the soldiers discharged their arquebuses. The crowds cheered wildly, and so did the crews of the ships that lay near us. Rockets rose from the square in front of the customs house, and other fireworks were touched off. It was a memorable leave-taking. The long-boat's oars dipped raggedly, the foresail was set, and we drew slowly away from the quay; but the breeze was so light that we could not clear the harbour. I believe that it might have been managed, had the crew not considered Friday an unlucky day either for turning a mattress or for quitting port; and had not the Chief Pilot, recognizing their unwillingness to put their backs into the work, advised the General to contain his impatience until the morning.

All that night we rode at anchor, only a cable's length from the customs house, and when the middle watch was roused, the Boatswain sent the long-boat ashore, with muffled oars, to a remote part of the beach. In her bottom lay the fifteen ruffians, bound and gagged, and we were happy to see them go; however, half an hour later she returned, as deep in the water as before, the Boatswain's mate passing word that the whole length of the shore was patrolled by armed guards, who had forcibly resisted his landing. 'That's of no great consequence,' the Boatswain said placidly, 'we can always turn them out at Santa or Cherrepé.'

The Chief Pilot was sunk in grief for his wife, Doña Ana Chacon, whose fever was so high that she had not known him when he went to say goodbye, but took him for a priest come to give her extreme unction. Miguel Llano and I had great difficulty in calming him when, towards the end of his watch, a messenger in a skiff brought letters for the General: he was convinced that one of them was addressed to him and contained the report of her death. He trembled like a poplar and his brow was beaded with sweat. However, there was no news for him, either bad or good, and presently he composed himself by prayer and meditation, but did not sleep.

The wind freshened in the morning, that of the eighth of April. We weighed anchor again and rounded the massive Isle of San Lorenzo; then at last the flotilla stood out to sea under full sail, a sight to gladden the heart. The galeot was leading by half a league, which soon increased to two. She disregarded all our signals to keep within view, but crammed on more sail, until by noon we had lost sight of her. When we picked her up an hour or two later off the town of Ancon, she was drawing away from a small coaster headed for Callao and gave us the slip again. We learned afterwards that Captain Corzo had boarded and plundered this coaster of her cargo of salt beef and chick-peas, and that he then stopped two more vessels and forced them to hand over their stores, impressing three fishermen from one, and two seamen and a boy from the other, to make up his complement.

The wind blew fair from the south all day and all night. The sea was choppy, and most of the thirty women aboard, and many of the men, including myself, suffered from sea-sickness. But despite the long draught the coast, I owned, was noble, with its many islands and rocky promontories peopled by myriads of gulls and droves of sea-lions, and a grand backing of hills and mountains as far as the eye could reach.

We did not catch up with the galeot until the Monday evening. She lay in the port of Santa, sixty leagues higher up the coast, where her Captain had been bold enough to capture the *Santa Trinidad*, a merchant ship of about ninety tons, also bound for Callao. She was too large a vessel for him to handle alone, and as we entered the harbour he hailed us with: 'Captain Corzo's compliments to the General. We have shown our standard to the master of the *Santa Trini-*

dad—from Panama with a general cargo and fifty negro slaves—as a
warrant for her requisition in His Majesty's name. Will the General
be good enough to confirm the seizure?'

When I went to the Great Cabin and gave Don Alvaro the message, he turned pale. 'But, man!' he exclaimed, 'this is rank piracy!'

Doña Ysabel, seated at the window with her widowed sister Doña
Mariana Barreto de Castro, looked up sharply from the tambour on
which she was embroidering a design of doves and flowers. 'Piracy?'
she echoed. 'My lord, that is an ugly word; be sparing in its use, I
beg. The costs of enterprises approved by the Crown but left without
aid from the Treasury are bound to fall on private shoulders. Do not
your letters patent entitle you to commandeer what you please, whenever you please?'

'My lady,' the General cried, 'this is not to be borne! Would you
have me become a receiver of stolen goods? How will our voyage end
if we begin in this dishonourable and godless way?'

'Don Alvaro,' she replied, the colour rising in her cheeks, 'if you
considered our safety and the well-being of our people rather than the
impassioned dictates of your honour, it would be better for us all.
Confirm the seizure by all means, and if the ship is sound in hull and
rigging, add her to the flotilla.'

'Why, yes, brother-in-law,' Doña Mariana chimed in, 'to salve your
conscience you can always promise to repay the owners the full value
of ship and cargo—one day, in God's good time.'

He threw out his hands, rose, and summoning the Vicar, asked him
in the hearing of all whether he should countenance Captain Corzo's
wanton acts. Father Juan gave it as his opinion that to do so would
be a sin. Yet even with this guidance Don Alvaro dared not visit the
galeot and reprimand her captain, for fear that he might take offence
and sail away on an enterprise of his own. Besides, Doña Ysabel made
it clear enough by the way she pursed her mouth and stabbed her
needle into the breast of an embroidered dove that, if he attempted
to check the Captain, she would grant him little peace. We all saw it,
and it saddened us.

The Chief Pilot, who had somewhat recovered his spirits now that
we were fairly under way, grew gloomy again. He told me in low
tones as we returned to the Chart-room: 'Though Don Alvaro is a
man of honest intentions and excellent feelings, I fear he lacks the
strength to swim against this current.' Then he ran after the Vicar
and said: 'Father, to avoid trouble in the Great Cabin, would it not

be well to go aboard the galeot yourself and persuade the Captain to see reason? You could make it plain that the General has not sent you, but that you come in the name of the Church.'

Father Juan thanked him for his good advice, and while Doña Ysabel and her sister were trying to convert Don Alvaro to their way of thinking, had himself rowed to the *San Felipe*, where he paid a visit to Captain Corzo. It seems the Captain replied to his severe remonstrances that this was a matter for the General to decide, not a priest; which brought the good Father to a heat of righteous indignation. 'My son,' he said, 'do you know what you are saying? If you persist in your wicked obstinacy, I must excommunicate you, here and now, and we shall see whether your subordinates will sail under your pendant.'

Captain Corzo fell on his knees and promised to pay the master of the *Santa Trinidad* for all the merchandise already transferred to the *San Felipe*, and not to retain the stores which he had taken from the smaller vessels; then the Vicar absolved him, bound him to a good act of contrition, and went away well satisfied. But the Captain, having little money, compensated the master of the *Santa Trinidad* with his other plunder, and thereby kept at least to the letter of his promise.

Doña Ysabel, on the master-carpenter's report that it would cost him three weeks' labour and many barrels of pitch to make the *Santa Trinidad* seaworthy, resigned all claims upon her, but persuaded Don Alvaro to impress fifteen of her able seamen and replace them with the vagabonds from Callao; a decision that caused the Boatswain no little pleasure.

Her attention was soon diverted by a domestic interlude: besides her Spanish maids, Elvira Delcano and Belita of Jerez, she had a pock-marked Peruvian under-maid called Pancha. This Pancha, to tell the truth, though loyal to her mistress, was a perfect strumpet and sensual to a degree: despite her ravaged face, the men fought one another for her favours and it was her boast that she could draw any husband from his wife on their very wedding-night. Being in charge of Doña Ysabel's cow and goats, she was on her way to the Great Cabin that evening, carrying the full milk pail, when her eye fell on Raimundo Pons, Juan de Buitrago's orderly; she put down the pail and stopped to talk to him. He drew her into the cabin which his master shared with two other ensigns but which was unoccupied at the time, and began to bargain with her, swearing that she valued her kindnesses excessively high. They could not agree on a price, and losing all patience he called her a draggle-tailed bitch, seized her by the shoulders and tried to force her. That was all one to Pancha, who did not baulk at violence and would have made him pay twice over by stealing some part of his accoutrement and holding it to ransom, as I heard that she afterwards did with another of her victims. But Raimundo was clumsy and struck her head against the corner of a chest, which made her cry aloud in pain. At that moment she heard approaching footsteps and, fearing discovery, screamed 'Rape, rape! Murder!', and in rushed Juan de Buitrago, upsetting the milk in his haste, gripped his orderly by the collar, pulled him off her, and gave him in charge to a sergeant.

Later, the Ensign told his comrades that he should rather have paid the slut a real or two as the price of holding her tongue, and kicked his orderly soundly for turning their berth into a bawdy-house. Then there would have been no need for the affair to come to the General's notice, because Raimundo was a good soldier; but when the cry of rape went up he had acted without forethought. So Raimundo was taken before the Colonel, while Pancha hurried off with the empty pail to Doña Ysabel pretending great agitation. Since the matter had now been made public, she kept to her story that the soldier had tried to force her, as indeed was the case; and Doña Ysabel accepted her plea of injured innocence and undertook to have her assailant punished handsomely.

Now, the General believed that the success of our enterprise depended far less on the skill of his crew or the courage and resource of his troops, than on the purity of their conduct. He tried to lead them to a devout way of living by every possible means and, not content with the customary Ave Maria and Paternoster sung at matins and vespers, had enjoined the Vicar to lengthen these into a service whenever the weather would permit, with a sermon every Saturday evening and great doings on Sundays and the vigils of feasts. Thus, when Doña Ysabel came to complain indignantly that a soldier had tried to force one of her maids, he was scandalized and agreed that the man must be punished with the utmost severity.

The Colonel, at first, tried to make light of the matter, since in effect the rape had been forestalled, and when he learned that it was Doña Ysabel's pock-marked under-maid, proposed to dismiss the culprit with a caution. In his thoughtless manner he protested to the Ensign: 'But Don Juan, her lock is common to every key! As for the soldier, he's a marksman with a fine record, as you yourself testify.

Don Alvaro would surely not have him publicly flogged for so venial an offence? Settle the case in private, Ensign, with your rattan and the toe of your shoe. I have no time to waste on trivialities.'

The General sent for the Ensign, and took it very ill indeed that the Colonel should not only have accused his Lady of employing a maid known to be of bad character, but should regard rape as an everyday occurrence, to be sufficiently punished with a few strokes of the rattan and a kick in the buttocks. The Colonel, seeing how the land lay, recanted at once and, to placate Doña Ysabel, ordered an immediate strappado.

The ship's company were paraded on deck and Raimundo, his hands tied behind him, was marched to the mainmast by two halberdiers. He pleaded for mercy, which was refused him. Father Antonio had been asked to preach a sermon on concupiscence and evil-living, but did so in such general terms that it seemed he knew the true facts and, having once been a soldier himself, regarded the punishment as excessive. When he had done, the drummer beat a long roll, while a rope was tied round the prisoner's wrists behind his back and then cast over a yard-arm high aloft. He was hoisted slowly by a dozen sailors and then, at a sudden loud double-tap of the drum, released; but the sailors' end of the rope had been hitched to a belaying-pin, so that instead of crashing to the deck he was pulled up with a dreadful jerk, a foot or so above our heads, and the drop dislocated both his shoulders.

The heavy silence of the soldiers and crew, who laugh and joke on occasions of this sort if they agree that the prisoner has got his just deserts, was not lost on the Colonel. He let it be known that in arranging the hoist he had been obeying the General's orders, and that he regarded the prisoner as unlucky rather than criminal. Raimundo, groaning horribly, was made to swallow cup after cup of aqua vitae, and when he was thoroughly drunk, the Ensign himself with the aid of a block and tackle wrenched his shoulder-blades back into place— no easy task even for a surgeon; he was then put ashore as no longer fit for service, Juan de Buitrago raising a fund for his keep, to which the Colonel contributed two pesos and almost every soldier in the ship a real. This solicitude for Raimundo, which seemed a deliberate affront to Doña Ysabel, incensed her brothers against the Ensign to such a degree that they ignored his presence, except when on parade, in the rudest manner. He was forced, in self-defence, to cultivate the good will of the Colonel and become a member of his faction.

While we lay at anchor off Santa the General ordered the Chief Pilot to make five charts: one for the Great Cabin, one for the master's cabin, and one for each of the other vessels; but for fear of meeting with English privateers, who might make ill use of the knowledge, instructed him to include none of the islands in the South Seas, and to trace the coastline of Peru only from Arica upwards to Paita. Two vertical lines, one drawn in seven degrees south, the other in twelve degrees, would serve to indicate the position of the Isles of Solomon, which extended, he said, through five degrees of latitude. They were to be placed fifteen hundred leagues to the west of Lima, because this was the extreme distance to be covered on our voyage; the longitudinal distance of the more northerly Isles being only fourteen hundred and fifty leagues.* 'But come, friend Pedro,' said he, 'let us make it fifteen hundred, and if we arrive sooner than we expect, so much the better.'

The Chief Pilot promised to have the charts ready by the time we left Cherrepé, a port half-way between Santa and Paita, where we were to take in water; and the General then handed him the log of the previous voyage, which had been kept by Hernan Gallego. This he studied attentively; he had known Gallego and could trust his latitudinal reckoning though, as he told me, 'he may well have mistaken the longitude, which is always a matter of guess-work. Not even in Germany, where the best nautical instruments are made, has any mathematician yet hit upon an exact means of determining longitude by the observation of stars and planets. Latitude is easily enough determined by shooting the sun with back-staff or cross-staff, whichever is most convenient; but we pilots must be content to rely for our longitude upon dead-reckoning, which is difficult to compute, especially at night. However, Hernan Gallego is unlikely to have made any error that we may not ourselves make in the same waters; so perhaps it is all one.'

Since our voyage was now fairly begun, the General summoned a grand council of high officers, masters and pilots and read them a prepared speech. He discoursed piously and at length about chastity, forbearance and brotherly love, but kept the pith of the matter for the close, when he said that on the previous expedition certain malicious persons complained of his refusal to disclose his sailing orders and also accused him of actions conflicting with the royal will and mandate; but that the orders were secret, which prevented him from justifying himself. Fortunately, he continued, this was not the case

*Seventeen-and-a-half Spanish leagues were reckoned to one degree.

now, and he had therefore decided to read them the text of the capitulations signed by King Philip II on the 27th day of April, 1574, and witnessed by Don Antonio de Eraso, the then Secretary of State. The gentlemen present would henceforth know where they stood, and if he committed any breach of trust, or assumed any powers not specified in these royal letters patent—errors from which he trusted God would protect him—he begged them to call the matter to his attention, so that he might humbly correct the fault.

THE CAPITULATIONS

GENERAL DON ALVARO DE MENDAÑA, OF THE TOWNSHIP OF NEIRA, IN GALICIA, IS COMMISSIONED BY HIS MAJESTY, KING PHILIP II—

(1) To return at his own charge and expense to the Islands of the South Sea discovered by him, as described in the report which he presented on January 31st, 1569, to his uncle, the illustrious Licentiate Castro, Governor and Lord President of the Kingdom of Peru, and which is now filed in the archives of the Indies Council.

(2) To take with him five hundred armed men, fifty of them married, with their lawful wives and children.

(3) To take with him twenty cows in calf, ten mares in foal, ten chargers, twenty goats in kid with the necessary he-goats, twenty ewes in lamb with the necessary rams, also ten sows and two boars; to be used as breeding stock for the said Islands.

(4) To take with him the ships necessary to transport the aforementioned persons and livestock.

(5) To take with him all stores and victuals necessary for the voyage and for the colonization of the said Islands.

(6) To found three cities, one of them to become the capital, each with its own laws and municipality; this task to be concluded within the six years which the settlement of the Islands may be expected to require for its completion.

(7) To pay into His Majesty's Treasury ten thousand ducats of caution money, in guarantee that he will fulfil the terms of this commission.

In return the King made the following concessions, authorizing the General:

(1) To take title and prerogatives as Prefect of the said Islands for as long as he may live to enjoy them; this title to pass to his son,

heir or assign for a single lifetime, but then to become the gift of
the King of Spain.

(2) To take title and prerogatives as Governor and Captain-
General of the said Islands so long as he may live; this title to pass
similarly to his son, heir or assign for a single lifetime; together with
the salary fixed by himself according to the richness of the lands he
shall have pacified and settled.

(3) To take title and prerogatives as Lord Chief Justice of the
said Islands, so long as he may live; this title to pass, etc., etc.

(4) To export free of duty from His Majesty's settled possessions
overseas, twenty negro slaves, and to carry them to the said Islands,
but to no other place.

(5) To export free of duty from Spain, Portugal, the Cape Verde
Islands or the Guinea Coast, as many as eighty slaves in addition
to the twenty already mentioned.

(6) To convey from Spain one ship, not exceeding three hundred tons burden, fully laden with Spanish merchandise.

(7) Once a year to send back from the said Islands to the settled
parts of His Majesty's possessions overseas one ship, fully armed
and provisioned.

(8) To commandeer stores and provisions from merchants unwilling to deliver them, but at current prices, and this only on the
occasion of the first voyage to the said Islands.
This eighth concession he read twice, very slowly, to justify himself
against possible charges of piracy; but this was ill-considered because,
as it turned out, his captains misunderstood his intention and thought
that he was covertly prompting them to commit fresh acts of violence.

(9) To pay into His Majesty's Treasury no more than a tenth
part of the gold, silver and pearls that he may find in the said
Islands, or in others that he may discover.

(10) To be exempt from sales-tax for a period of twenty years
from his arrival in the said Islands.

(11) To be exempt from export duty on all goods brought to
the said Islands by himself or his companions for the first ten
years; this exemption to be extended to twenty years in the case of
himself or his successor in the Prefectship.

(12) To retain for himself and his heirs in perpetuity the fishing
rights of the said Islands, including the right to fish for pearls.

(13) To grant estates in the said Islands, and allot native serfs
to each of these.

(14) To grant land and building sites to pioneers of good repute who may apply for them; but if they need native serfs they must pay tax according to the number employed.

(15) To construct three fortresses, and fix the payment of the garrisons.

(16) To take and enjoy without payment during his own lifetime, and to bequeath to the heirs of his body for the period of two lifetimes, or to his widow if he should die childless, for her lifetime, one only of the estates mentioned in the thirteenth of these present concessions; the remaining estates there specified being allotted to settlers of good repute at the Prefect's discretion, and the tax fixed according to the number of serfs employed upon these.

(17) To continue to enjoy the rights and privileges of any estate he may hold elsewhere in His Majesty's possessions, notwithstanding that he remain domiciled in the said Islands.

(18) To assay and stamp with a distinctive mark all gold and silver found in the said Islands, or in others that he may discover.

(19) To nominate the officers of a Customs Service, for whose actions he will be answerable to His Majesty.

(20) To suppress armed rebellion, or any attempt to alter the form of government which these present articles shall have entitled him to set up.

(21) To issue regulations for the opening and working of mines.

(22) To be free to grant or refuse any appeal made against decisions of a Court of Law appointed by himself, whether the case be a civil or criminal one, and whether it has been judged by a mayor, a justice of the peace, a lord-mayor, or by the Prefect's own lieutenant.

(23) To be answerable for his acts, laws and decisions only to His Majesty's Indies Council.

(24) To share his supreme judicial rights in the said Islands with no other person whatsoever.

(25) To convey five hundred men to Spain or Peru from the said Islands, without hindrance from the justices at the ports where they are disembarked.

The document concluded with the Royal wish that when the said General Alvaro de Mendaña, in fulfilment of his commission, reached the Isles of Solomon, he should be granted the hereditary title of Marquis. Three later codicils were appended; one clarified the concession about the three fortresses, where it had not been stated whether the payment of the garrisons should be met by the Treasury or by local taxation; another amplified the General's dignity as Prefect, which was made equal to that of other South Sea Prefectships; the third further defined his authority as Lord Chief Justice.

His audience listened in deep silence to this recital, astonished and not a little dismayed at the wide powers which he had been granted. Later, the Colonel went to Miguel Llano and demanded a copy of the capitulations, which was given to him. He studied it intently, until he knew it by rote, and seems to have pointed out many weaknesses to his room-mates.

Chapter 5

WHAT HAPPENED AT CHERREPÉ

Whenever I read a chronicle of ancient Greece, Rome or my own country, which is often, I first ask myself how the author looked, and until his likeness takes clear form in my mind I cannot know how much credence to give him. For this reason, rather than from a desire to thrust Andrés Serrano forward as a person of consideration, I shall describe myself without ambiguity for the benefit of curious readers.

I write from Manila, in the year of Our Lord 1615, and my age is now forty-three, but I am little changed in appearance or habits since the day we sailed from Callao; so that the present account will serve equally well for 1595 as for today. I am short, plump, pale of face and inclined to indolence, with a small nose, scanty beard and wide mouth; my voice is flat and precise; my habits, orderly. I have never been a prey to the more violent passions, but I love food and drink, and am happier to watch and record events than to take part in them. I write verses, rather because rhyming comes easy to me than because I fancy myself touched by Apollo's fire; I wear a sword not to provoke quarrels but to remind the world that I am of good family. So far I have refrained from marriage, fearing to place a halter round my neck, though more women than one or two have been kind to me in my day. If I have enemies, they have never yet revealed themselves, and I am greatly blessed in friends. The worst I have ever heard said of me, and I own it rankled, was when later in the voyage the veteran Juarez was estimating how many men of the afterguard were capable of bearing arms, and included my name. His comrade Matia burst into a guffaw: 'What, our little Cupid? You count him a man? You might as well include Doña Ysabel's brindled calf!' Being a person of this sort—'more like a singing eunuch than a human being,' as my colleague Miguel Llano used to say of me, rather testily—and because, when I drink, I grow silent rather than talkative, men who feared to confess to a priest, or found none at hand, have often confided their troubles to me.

At dawn, on the 17th of April, after another good run, we put in at Cherrepé, the port of Santiago de Miraflores, where we found the *Santa Ysabel* at anchor. Captain Lope de Vega came aboard the flagship to report that he had got together a fine body of settlers, all respectable married couples, with their children, and that they had paid for their passages by contributing salt pork, biscuit, wine and other stores to the victualling of his ship, and had brought with them the tools of their various trades. The General showed great pleasure and relief at the news, and at once fulfilled his part of the bargain that had been struck between them: he conferred on Don Lope the title of Admiral, that is to say Second-in-Command of the flotilla, and married him then and there to his sister-in-law, Doña Mariana. Yet he made it a condition that the wedding should not be celebrated with feasting and dancing, and that, for chastity's sake, the bride should not be bedded until the Isles were reached but remain with her sister in the flagship.

The Colonel, when he heard that Don Lope had accepted this condition, raised his hands to Heaven. 'God's passion!' he said to the Ensign-Royal. 'What have we come to? Is a man to be forbidden to company with his lawful wife on his bridal night? It sticks in my mind that Saint Augustine, or some other saint of repute, laid it down that "whom God hath joined, let no man put asunder." Mark my word, before this voyage is over the Purser will be issuing a hair-shirt to every common seaman, and the Master-gunner ramming incense down the barrels of our falcons!'

Doña Mariana, who was a lively woman, had no intention of being widowed a second time if anything could be done to prevent it. She remarked to her sister that afternoon as they sat under the poop-awning: "Ysabel, my dear, that looks to me a very fine ship—the galleon lying over there, beyond the *San Felipe*. Pray ask the Chief Pilot what he knows about her.'

Pedro Fernandez was summoned. He knew the vessel by repute, he said, having sailed in convoy with her several times: she was the *Tres Reyes Magos*, of Panama, homeward bound with a cargo of flour and timber. He described her as sound and commodious.

'Then do you not agree,' asked Doña Mariana, 'that it is the greatest of pities to see such a large, fine ship wasted in coastal trade, when my poor husband must cross thousands of leagues of uncharted seas in a patched and leaking tub that the very rats have long ago deserted?'

'Why not ask Don Alvaro to make the exchange?' broke in Doña Ysabel, before the Chief Pilot had time to reply. 'I agree that this would be very much to the King's advantage.'

'I think,' her sister answered modestly, 'such a request would come better from my husband; the General would hardly listen to a woman.'

'Oh, that can easily be arranged, my child,' said Doña Ysabel.

Pedro Fernandez kept silent. He was in two minds: to commandeer the vessel would be high-handed in the extreme and might well ruin the owners; but he himself would have hesitated to sail so crank and rotten a ship as the *Santa Ysabel* even from Callao to Cherrepé; and he thought it little short of murder to embark in her more than one hundred and twenty trusting settlers, to say nothing of the crew and the slaves, for a voyage of two months and upwards in tropical waters.

Towards evening, sure enough, Admiral Don Lope de Vega presented a formal petition to the General that the *Tres Reyes Magos* should be commandeered for the King's service, and her owners offered the *Santa Ysabel* in exchange. Don Alvaro was shocked by this proposal, and replied that the Admiral's ship, though admittedly not handsome, was well found and fit enough in every way for the arduous service required of her. When he rejected the petition with virtuous firmness, Don Lope returned to his ship and ordered the boatswain to go below with an auger and secretly bore a number of holes in her bottom. It is said that Doña Ysabel had suggested this stratagem to the Admiral, promising to shield him from the General's displeasure should he ever come to hear of it; and I can vouch for this much, that she and Doña Mariana sat together on the poop, with their eyes fixed on the *Santa Ysabel*, whispering and giggling behind their hands like naughty little girls.

Presently we heard discordant shouts from the Admiral's ship: the cry was raised that she was settling, and that part of her cargo was already awash. 'Man the pumps, brave hearts!' her master sang out, and gave urgent orders to find the leaks at once and stop them. At this the Admiral's officers came to him with a plain refusal to sail another league in so rotten a vessel, and pressed him to make the exchange before it should be too late. The master and pilot ardently supported them, and together they drew up a memorial, which all signed: to the effect that since the *Santa Ysabel* leaked at every seam, she was unfit for the long and dangerous voyage contemplated, and that they begged his Excellency 'to apply the remedy that lay so close at hand.'

Don Alvaro saw that their concerted resistance was not to be overcome; but rather than admit defeat, or go against his conscience, he pleaded a sudden attack of the quinsy and referred the matter to the Colonel, giving him full authority to do whatever seemed right and just in the circumstances. The Colonel, who had few scruples on such occasions, then told Don Lope in everybody's hearing: 'My lord Admiral, you did well to force matters. Pray bore a few more holes in her bottom for good measure, so I may truthfully report to the General that she leaks like a sieve. And now we must seize the *Tres Reyes Magos* before she can slip away; already her crew show signs of suspicion and alarm.'

He hastened back to the flagship with his report and, at the General's request, set it down in writing. Don Alvaro read the document carefully, comparing it with the other, and then authorized him to commandeer the *Tres Reyes Magos*, but not before carpenters had been sent aboard both ships to estimate the difference in their values.

'Mark you, my lord,' said he, 'I will have nothing done in an irregular way, nor anything against the laws of God.'

The carpenters informed the Colonel that the merchantman, though of the same tonnage as the *Santa Ysabel*, was worth some nine thousand six hundred pesos more; but from this estimate he knocked off three thousand pesos out of kindness to the General and the Admiral, her joint-owners.

Now, as ill-luck would have it, the *Tres Reyes Magos* was also jointly owned, by a merchant and a Canon from Panama. The Canon had been ashore during these proceedings and when, strolling down to the quay, he saw negroes and sailors discharging the cargo that he had been at such pains to stow aboard, and soldiers stalking about with fire-arms, he raised an anguished yell, and charged into the midst of them. He called them bandits and infidels and worse names still, and forbade them to touch another sack or barrel, if they hoped for salvation, because all was the property of the Church and they were committing a heinous sacrilege. The boatswain of the *Santa Ysabel*, an impatient man and no great lover of priests, told him curtly to be off and take his complaint to the Admiral; he himself, he said, was acting under orders and doing nothing for his own gain. The men continued at their task with set faces, fearing the boatswain's rope-end far more than a priest's threats and objurgations; until finally the Canon, who was young and of noble family, was driven to an ecstasy of anger. He rushed at his adversary as if to tear him in pieces, but the boatswain stepped aside, and he would have fallen into the harbour if a soldier, posted at the edge of the quay, had not given him a timely push. 'Do you want a ducking, Father,' he shouted gruffly, 'in three fathoms of salt water?'

The Canon's fury was now turned against this soldier, whom he promised a vile death and eternal damnation; but the man hid his face to avoid being recognized again, and ran off. The Canon then went from one seaman to another, threatening them with all the torments of Hell, until the boatswain said in exasperation: 'As you wish, Father. If you don't want us to take out the rest of the cargo, let it stay in the hold. We can make good use of it and I assure your reverence that, in heat like this, my men don't lug barrels and baulks of timber merely for pleasure.' And he ordered the sailors to take a spell.

The Canon and his partner, a merchant of Cherrepé, jumped into their skiff and rowed awkwardly out to the flagship, where they demanded an immediate interview with the General. The Colonel was waiting for them on deck and greeted the Canon courteously enough, but gave him little satisfaction. He said that Don Alvaro was indisposed and had delegated plenary powers to himself and that, for his part, he greatly regretted the necessity that had forced him to make this exchange of ships.

The young priest burst into another torrent of invective, declaring that he had not only been robbed of his entire fortune, but buffeted by a common soldier and threatened with drowning in three fathoms of water; that he would carry his complaint to Rome itself, if need be, and ensure for those guilty of this outrage nothing but pain and sorrow in this world, and perpetual torment in the next.

'Calm yourself, calm yourself, reverend Father!' said the Colonel and, beckoning to Juan de Buitrago, gave him whispered orders to prevent the Vicar and the Chaplain from coming on deck; he could stand up to one priest, he said, but three was too great odds.

'You dare ask me to calm myself, you godless wretch?' shouted the Canon. 'You, who are in the direct line and descent of those Roman soldiers who played at dice for Our Lord's stolen vestment while He hung upon the Cross!'

'No one has stolen anything from your Reverence! With the authority of King Philip we are making a legal exchange of ships, and you stand to lose nothing by this transaction, but rather to gain. The General is an open-hearted and considerate nobleman, a true son of the Church, who would sooner think of robbing his mother than a priest.' He added, thoughtlessly: '—even a priest of Panama. He will pay you for your own interest in the vessel, deducting only the value of the ship we shall give you instead of it, which will serve your purpose well enough; and no one will lay a finger on your cargo.'

But the Canon, clenching his fists and setting his teeth, hissed at him: 'Those sons of Satan have not even troubled to remove the whole cargo, but threaten to keep for their own use what is left. I warn you, my lord, that every matins and vespers, when I offer my prayers to Our Saviour Jesus Christ, I shall not fail to carry this crime to His judgment seat, and implore Him to prevent my stolen ship from ever reaching port in safety. Our Lord's ears are always open to the prayers of His injured priests—even those of Panama!'

Upon my soul, I felt sorry for the Canon, but even more so for his partner, who could expect neither favour nor redress. This poor merchant pleaded his case with tears running down his cheeks, and protested that the loss would beggar him; but the Colonel told him coldly that he should thank God that he had not been robbed by English freebooters, but was permitted to show his loyalty to King Philip by a small, though useful, loan to one of his most distinguished commanders; and that in God's good time he, too, would be repaid in full.

Meanwhile, Juan de Buitrago had no difficulty with the task assigned to him, because the Vicar was prostrated by seasickness—there was a strong swell even in the harbour—and in no state to intervene in the dispute, and the Chaplain was busy attending to his needs. As for Father Joaquin, who sailed in the *Santa Ysabel*, he was timid and unworldly and kept well out of the way of trouble. At last the Canon persuaded the Colonel to order the unloading to be completed, which was done with the help of Indian serfs whom, at Don Alvaro's request, the District Officer had sent down from Santiago de Miraflores to water our ships. The whole cargo was laid out on the quay, and the Canon, having carefully separated his half-share from the merchant's, sat down in the middle on a pile of sacks and kept a watch all night, until he had seen us safely under way again. None of our people was hardy enough to remove the least thing from his heap.

When Don Alvaro learned what had been arranged, he sent the Canon a signed and sealed letter in which he engaged himself to pay the partners the sum of six thousand six hundred pesos—within two years, or as soon as he returned to Peru—and meanwhile mortgaged them the flagship in bottomry, generously throwing in his third-interest in the frigate. This document would not have satisfied the Canon, even if he had thought the valuation a just one; for short of sailing with the expedition he saw no means of securing payment within the period specified, or indeed afterwards.

The General complained bitterly to Doña Ysabel of the false position into which the Colonel had placed him, saying that the affair had been mishandled. 'Yes, husband,' she agreed, 'it is a pity that you did not face the Canon yourself, instead of delegating your authority to the Colonel, who has a quick tongue and a heavy hand. However, God be praised for this much at least, that my sister's husband now commands a ship not altogether unworthy of his new rank.'

'Whatever will the Vicar say,' he mourned, 'when he learns what has been done?'

'Tell him at once yourself,' she replied lightly, 'before he has had time to recover from his retching and vomiting, and he will say no more than "Ugh!", and "Ai, ai, Mother of God!", and "It is God's will that man should suffer for his sins."'

The provisions bought by the Admiral were distributed among the ships; but they proved neither of good quality nor of sufficient quantity and the Colonel, who had somehow learned that Don Alvaro had not yet supplied his quota of the venture, grew restive. He swore that, as a conscientious officer, he would see that his troops did not go short because of any man's negligence or avarice; and that night, when the General had retired, he commandeered the provisions unloaded from the *Tres Reyes Magos*, except the Canon's share, and had them taken aboard the flagship. He then broke into a warehouse containing foodstuffs brought down from the neighbouring valleys for sale to coastal traders, and had these shipped as well. The warehouseman, who slept on the premises with his wife and two young sons, was utterly dismayed; not all the goods were his, and the Colonel, who had been drinking heavily again, held out no hope of repayment.

At last, in desperation, he agreed to a suggestion made by the Purser: namely, that he and his family should join the expedition and that what had been seized from him should be regarded as his venture; and to this the Colonel offered no objection.

The difficulty now was to find accommodation for the warehouse-man, but the Purser, always resourceful, overcame it. He went to the Great Cabin at midnight, when the General was in the habit of rising for his devotions, and complained of scandalous behaviour among a small group of settlers recruited at Callao—an old cooper with two sons and three daughters. The men, he said, were very jackdaws, stealing everything that was not under lock and key, and the women were openly accosting the sailors.

'Turn them out, Don Gaspar, turn them out at once!' cried the General zealously. 'But search their baggage first!' So they were put ashore, protesting vociferously, and their quarters given to the ware-houseman's family. I might add that had Don Alvaro turned out the whole body of Callao settlers this would have been little loss, though as it proved, the Purser should certainly have thought twice before parting with a family of skilled coopers.

As dawn was breaking, the Colonel, who had taken frequent pulls at his bottle while supervising the removal of stores, ran into the Admiral and, being more than usually drunk, gave him an extravagant salute. 'Good morning, your Excellency!' he said. 'May I convey my sincerest condolences?'

'You are very kind,' said the Admiral, 'but I do not know that I stand in need of any.'

'Is it nothing to spend your bridal night working like a negro slave on the quay-side of such a piddling port as this, instead of proving your mettle between scented sheets, while the fiddles play and bride-men cheer outside your chamber door? They tell me that Doña Mariana is withheld from you by the sanctimonious orders of I need not say whom. But, by God's thunders, if I were you, I should resent that at the point of my sword.'

Don Lope was the more vexed because this was said in the hearing of the soldiers who escorted him; but answered mildly enough that he had lived unmarried so many years that two more months of bachelordom were no great penalty, and that he respected Don Alvaro's pious motives.

However, it is seldom easy to shake off a drunkard before he has had his say. The Colonel followed him and bawled: 'Stay a little,

Don Lope, my fine cock, I have thought of something to please you. There's a pretty little Callao whore named Dolores, a cooper's daughter, whom the General has turned out for plying her trade too openly. She's neat and clean and a splendid little worker—I'll vouch for that with my life—and just now she came to me in tears, begging me to find accommodation for herself and her father in one of the smaller ships. Now, Admiral mine, why not take her with you as a consolation for your ill treatment? I warrant she'll show you gratitude in any position you desire. Let You-know-whom go hang with his ventose sermons on marital chastity. What's a wife for, but to sleep with her husband?'

The Admiral, greatly provoked, though the Colonel's offer had been prompted by true pity for all concerned, put his hand to his sword; but thought better of it and passed on, not deigning to reply. At the time, it seemed an incident of little importance, but if ever the Devil finds a small ember of resentment, he blows it patiently into a conflagration; and when Don Lope went aboard his new ship, rechristened with the same name as the old, and hoisted the royal banners and his own pendant, he told his officers that he held the General greatly to blame 'for not keeping that old Momus under better control.'

Yet though the Colonel had been ill-advised to offer the Admiral a whore in public he had not over-rated his virtue, as the sequel will show. About breakfast time Don Lope called upon the General and asked permission to make an example of a sergeant who had defrauded a countryman of the price of a sucking pig; and the General granted this with alacrity, pleased that at least one high officer shared his zeal for fair dealing. At once, without ceremony, the sergeant was hoisted, maimed and put ashore; but his young and lively wife remained in the *Santa Ysabel*, protesting that, for all she knew, the friar who married them had been but a soldier in masquerade, and that her sergeant was reported to have another wife in Quito. Thereafter she spent part of her days and all her nights in the Admiral's cabin, caring for his clothes and smoothing his pillow; and nothing that Father Joaquin said could keep her out of it. The soldiers in the Admiral's ship, who had valued their sergeant, were not slow to say that his one fault had been to marry a woman with a slim waist and fine round breasts, and that Don Alvaro must be held responsible for this affair because he had kept Doña Mariana out of her legitimate bed. It would have been better for all, they declared, if Don Lope had taken the Colonel's advice and shown charity to the cooper's daughter. Others blamed Doña Ysabel, swearing that it was she who had made this chastity a condition, for fear that her sister might be got with child before the voyage was over, and so out-do her in womanly repute.

Our departure from Cherrepé was postponed until the evening because we had not yet taken on water; and when the District Officer, Don Bartolomé de Villavicencio, rode down to the port and found that the Indian serfs whom he had sent for that purpose were used instead to transfer the cargo of the old *Santa Ysabel* to the new, and to carry the contents of the warehouse aboard the flagship, he displayed anger and vowed that we were killing his men by overwork. He called them off at once, with their ponies and carts, and sent them back to Santiago de Miraflores.

Their departure was the occasion of a fresh dispute, this time between Don Alvaro and the Chief Pilot. The General ordered him to set sail for the Isles without further delay, but he objected that it would be madness to cross the widest and most perilous gulf in the world, with no more water than was in the kegs and jars which he himself had taken aboard at Callao for the use of his crew. 'What of the soldiers?' he asked. 'What of the settlers and their families?'

Don Alvaro grew restless and stammered that his officers were urging him not to visit another port, but to stand out to sea, because their men were already getting out of hand; and that, if need be, everyone could be put on half-allowance. 'Do as I say, friend,' he cried.

'But tell me, your Excellency,' demanded the Chief Pilot, 'even if we could do without water, are we not to call at Paita to collect arquebuses with powder, match and ball? Surely, your officers are not so negligent as to have forgotten these arms, which you yourself were at pains to secure?'

The General bent his head, not caring to meet the Chief Pilot's eye. 'Our soldiers have their fire-arms,' he said, 'also swords, halberds and targes, enough for our needs. The Indians use no weapons worth the name, and experience has taught me that it is far better to go among them with gifts than with guns. We have no time to waste at Paita.'

Pedro Fernandez understood from this that nobody had pressed him, but that he feared news of the piracies would be carried up the coast, in which event the Lieutenant of Paita might call him to account and prevent his departure. He controlled his rising anger, but 'Don Alvaro,' he said, 'you are the leader of this expedition, and it is your duty to take a long view of our needs, not to allow yourself to be brow-beaten by importunate fools who do not understand what they are asking.'

He excused himself, and went to tell Captain Don Lorenzo of the General's decision. The Captain was surprised and vexed at the report. 'Why, Pilot,' he said, 'I am pleased that you came to me rather than to the Colonel, who is in a mood to uphold Don Alvaro in all his fantasies. Since Don Bartolomé has taken off his Indians, we have now no prospect of watering here; but to suggest that the men go on half-allowance before the voyage has even begun in earnest, that is intolerable! Besides, if we are to maintain ourselves in those lands, the few arquebuses that we have are insufficient to keep down the natives. Within a few months of our arrival, half of them will be unserviceable, so that we cannot do without the seventy odd laid by for us at Paita. Come with me to the General, and I will talk him back into good sense.'

Between them they had no difficulty in persuading Don Alvaro to change his mind once more, which he did with many sage and sensible remarks, and others that were less to the point: yet he still endeavoured to justify his earlier decision by saying that there would be less waste if the soldiers knew that we were short of water, and that the consumption of salt meat, which was the cause of scurvy, would be reduced if the water-ration were halved; and, above all, that abstinence was delightful in the sight of God.

We sailed an hour later, but the frigate was sent ahead with orders to fire a warning gun if it should appear that news of our recent doings had reached the authorities of Paita. As it turned out, the Lieutenant, though well-aware of our depredations, thought it politic not to call the General to account but rather to hasten our sailing by every fair means. There were no royal ships in harbour, and his garrison was reduced by fever.

Chapter 6

WHAT HAPPENED AT PAITA

Quarrels broke out in each port we visited and as Paita, which lies two hundred leagues to the north-west of Callao, is one of the finest harbours on the Peruvian coast, so our finest quarrel was reserved for it. I was taking a nap shortly after our arrival in the early afternoon on the 22nd of April, when angry oaths and shouts echoed down the alley-way, and I drowsily recognized the Colonel's voice: 'A thousand pests and furies overtake you, tonsured billy-goat! How dare you poke your long muzzle into my affairs? What business is it of yours whom I send where, and upon what errand? I am the Colonel, and in all military matters I decide, direct and do what I please—subject only to the General's approval!'

A soft, urbane answer, the sense of which I did not catch, was cut short by a fresh volley of imprecations. 'So the sergeant came to consult you? Said that he was afraid of committing a mortal sin if he obeyed my orders? The Devil he did! When I hook him, I swear by Almighty God, I'll skin him like a ray; and as for you, how dare you abuse your sacred trust as confessor by making mischief between me and my sergeants? By Heaven, I'll carve you as I would a capon, you father of sodomites!'

'Peace, peace, my son!' cried the other in a bleating voice—and then: 'At your peril! Have you no care for your immortal soul?'

'Dear Lord!' I said to myself, now thoroughly awake. 'That must be the Vicar.' I tumbled from my bunk, naked but for a scanty shirt, to rush without knocking into the Great Cabin.

'Quick, for the love of God, Don Alvaro,' I pleaded. 'Out into the passage, at once, to prevent bloodshed and worse!'

The General, who was having his beard trimmed and telling his beads at the same time, gaped blankly at me. 'Why, if it isn't little

Andrés,' he said, 'with his shirt-tails flying! My lad, you look like the virtuous Joseph fleeing from Potiphar's wife.'

Doña Mariana burst into a loud laugh. 'You do the young wretch too much honour, brother-in-law. From the look on his face, I'd say that Potiphar has caught him in the act and is after him with a gelder's knife.'

In shame and confusion I snatched a damask cloth from the table and tied it around my waist, with a dumb appeal to Doña Mariana for pardon. 'Quick, Don Alvaro,' I repeated, 'there's not a moment to lose! The Colonel is on the point of martyrizing Father Juan.'

He leaped up, the barber's napkin still around his neck, and followed me to the door, which we reached in the nick of time. The Colonel, with raised fist and face a-glow, was advancing down the alley-way towards us. The Vicar, his silver cross raised high, retreated before him, step by step, feebly reiterating: 'Avaunt, sinner, avaunt!' As the door burst open, the good Father tumbled into my arms, almost senseless with terror. I pulled him in and sat him on a chest, leaving Don Alvaro to confront the Colonel.

All honour to the General: he showed no sign of fear but only a gentle sorrow. 'O noble Don Pedro Merino!' he exclaimed. 'How could you so forget yourself as to raise a hand in anger against our spiritual leader? Come, my lord, calm yourself and tell me what has so provoked you.'

The Colonel's fist dropped and he bowed in some confusion. 'Will it please your Excellency,' he asked, bubbling over with wrath, 'to instruct the Vicar that he has no right to meddle with military affairs? I ask this for his own good, because his impudence had almost led me to an act of sacrilege; you arrived in time to save him from death and myself from damnation.'

'My lord,' Don Alvaro replied softly, 'I know you for a pious and dutiful officer; it is only the chicha that makes a sinner of you. A horned Indian devil lurks in that cup of poison. Avoid it altogether, man, or practise decent temperance.'

'That is good advice, good advice indeed,' sighed the Colonel gustily. 'But once that little Indian devil has gained a foothold in my guts I have a right to expect my neighbours either to show Christian charity or give me a wide berth; the Vicar has monstrously exceeded his rights by persuading a sergeant to disobey my orders.'

'If you have the hardihood, my son, tell the General what the order was, and let him judge between us,' the Vicar gasped, his lips blue and his hands gripping the edge of the chest.

'What I may have told the sergeant,' the Colonel blustered, 'is not
to the point, and nobody's business but my own, least of all a priest's.'

Don Alvaro observed his embarrassment and used it as a handle
for controlling him; which he did effectually enough. While I returned to the Chart-room to pull on my hose, he summoned Captain
Don Lorenzo as a witness and reconciled the two men in his presence.
However, though they parted with professions of esteem and promised to forget what had taken place, the Vicar was vexed that the
General had not expressed greater detestation of the Colonel's impious
threats, and the Colonel nursed a resentment that Don Lorenzo had
stood by when he knelt to kiss the Vicar's crucifix and humbly asked
his pardon. Nobody, to this day, knows what the order was that the
sergeant hesitated to obey; many guesses have been made, most of
them crude and extravagant, but they are not to the point.

The Vicar returned to his breviary, the Colonel to his bottle; and
all was quiet once more. But less than half an hour later, trouble
broke out afresh. It so happened that Don Diego de Barreto's orderly
was wearing a bunch of coloured ribbons and a silk picture tied in
his cap, and another large bunch on his breast. The Colonel came
upon him suddenly outside a cabin and, fetching him a kick, asked:
'Tell me, mule, who's your drunken master, and when is he riding
you to market with the turnips?'

The soldier, taken aback, turned to revenge himself, but when he
recognized the Colonel, answered civilly enough: 'If it please your
honour, I'm Juan de la Roca, Ensign Diego de Barreto's orderly, at
your honour's orders.'

'And did the noble Ensign tell you to make a Christmas fool of
yourself, to the disgrace of your company, by dressing up in this
trumpery, contrary to regulations?'

"Yes, your honour, I have his permission; I should not have ventured otherwise. He knows that this is the Vigil of Saint Joseph, and
that I am from San José, beyond Cherrepé, where every loyal son is
now wearing the same finery for love of our patron.'

'Of all the saints in the calendar,' bawled the Colonel, tearing off
the ribbons and stamping on them, 'yours is the most repugnant to
me, and to any other man of honour! Have you never heard how he
rebuffed Our Lady when she was with child and had a craving for
cherries? Let me not catch you in carnival dress again, peasant, unless
on Shrove Tuesday, and meanwhile'—here he raised his stick—'take
that, and that, and that as a reminder.'

Captain Don Lorenzo stepped out of the cabin which he shared with his two brothers, and curtly asked the Colonel in what way the orderly had offended.

'Pray don't pretend, Captain, that you are ignorant of his offence,' said the Colonel, mimicking the other's Galician accent. 'I am aware that this insolent blockhead made a mock of his uniform with your connivance—tricking himself out like an abbess' lap-dog and then, to heap insult on injury, invoking the patronage of the repulsive Saint Joseph.'

'But before you took a stick to him,' said Don Lorenzo, restraining his anger with difficulty, 'would it not have been better to complain to my brother or myself of his terrible breach of regulations? In any case, the man is not on duty, and since we Barretos feel a peculiar devotion to Saint Joseph, I authorized him to wear these ribbons while he waited on us. We are at this moment celebrating the good Saint with cakes and wine, and shall be truly honoured if you consent to join our company.'

'I would rather eat turds with gipsies in a cave!' the Colonel roared, brandishing his stick again, and at that the cabin door burst open and Don Diego came rushing out and accidently jostled him. The Colonel, to whom action always came before reflexion, brought down his stick on Don Diego's head, making him stagger and nearly fall. Afterwards he pretended not to have known who his assailant was; but the Ensign now knew one thing which he swore never to forget, namely the weight of that loaded stick.

Worse was yet to follow. The Barreto brothers were bewildered and stood irresolute, but their sergeant had witnessed the assault, and when the Colonel raised his stick for another blow, ran forward and gripping his own beard, cried angrily: 'If your honour does not desist, I swear . . .'

The Colonel dropped the stick, drew his sword and lunged furiously at the sergeant, who turned and scrambled up to the half-deck as nimbly as a monkey, the point of the sword having passed between his legs and scratched the skin of his thigh.

'Halt that mutineer!' shouted the Colonel at the top of his lungs. 'I mean to spit him like a thrush!'

'To murder an unarmed man will earn you little honour, Don Pedro Merino,' said the Captain coolly, and the Colonel had the sense to sheathe his sword and pick up his stick, with which he stamped off to the Great Cabin.

I sat there with the General, writing at his dictation, but with frequent interruptions and amendments from Doña Ysabel, fulsome excuses to the Viceroy for what we had done in the past twelve days. He looked up with a weary smile. 'And what is it now, my lord?' he asked. 'So much noise came from the alley-way that I could hardly collect my thoughts. I hope that you have reprimanded the culprits, whoever they may be?'

'Indeed, your Excellency, I have,' answered the Colonel, quick to take his cue, 'and I beg your permission to have Sergeant Dimas, the chief offender, publicly flogged. I demand two hundred lashes.'

'That is the same sergeant, is it not, who complained against you to the Vicar?'

'The same mutinous dog! Just now, when I went to protest against the unsoldierlike behaviour of certain officers who were feasting in their cabin, an ensign dared jostle me and, when I defended myself, this Dimas put his hand to his beard and uttered threats.'

'If that is so . . .' said Don Alvaro.

'*If* that is so?' the Colonel shouted back.

'Since that is so,' Don Alvaro conceded, 'I can only grant your request. But what the sergeant did is one thing, and what my officers do is another. I am grieved beyond words that you should have come to blows with an ensign, and I trust that you will allow yourself to be reconciled to him in my presence before any vengeance is exacted from the sergeant. It seems to me that Dimas's offence is that he took his officer's part in a quarrel which he should never have been allowed to witness.'

Don Lorenzo, Don Diego and the third brother, Don Luis, had meanwhile sent a message to Doña Ysabel, begging her to come at once without attracting the General's attention; and when, after a brief absence, she returned to the Great Cabin, I could see that she was very angry.

'Don Alvaro,' she said, in her sweetest voice, 'I have come on my brothers' behalf, to plead for Sergeant Dimas. Like his namesake whom Our Saviour pardoned from the Cross itself he appears, in spite of what has been said against him, to be a man of courage and good principles.' But here her indignation broke through suddenly. 'He intervened to save my brother Don Diego from a brutal and unprovoked attack by the Colonel. If the sergeant is flogged, or so much as touched, the honour of my family will be involved.'

'And if this mutineer is not flogged,' shouted the Colonel, riding the high horse, 'I will resign my appointment at once and go ashore——'

'To a brothel, well-stocked with plump little ten-year-old negresses, you stinking satyr, where you'll swill chicha until you vomit!' interrupted Doña Mariana from her seat at the window.

'If you were not a noblewoman,' the Colonel replied, holding himself in gallantly, 'and if I were not a man of great refinement and consummate patience, so help me God! I would spill your brains on the cabin floor.' He flung his stick into a corner and marched out, slamming the door behind him.

The General wrung his hands. 'Now we are utterly undone!' he moaned. 'Doña Mariana, why in the name of the five wise virgins could you not have held your tongue?'

'And I suppose you wish that I had done the same?' Doña Ysabel asked contemptuously. 'My sister spoke like a true Barreto.'

'Light of my life,' cried Don Alvaro, catching her hands and kissing them with devotion, 'have nine years of marriage to me not taught you that the honour of your family is as dear to me as my own? Pray let the Colonel have his way this one time more; otherwise, he'll go ashore and carry a long tale to the Lieutenant. Then we shall not only be refused water and arms, but may even be detained in Paita for months until the Viceroy has considered our case.'

After swearing me to silence, Doña Ysabel motioned me to leave and I missed the remainder of their talk. On deck, I could hear the Colonel demanding with threats and insults to be put ashore in the skiff, and presently Don Alvaro emerged from the Great Cabin. I followed, and I heard him say in a low voice as he embraced the Colonel: 'Pray my lord, do not take offence at my sister-in-law's sharp tongue! I have scolded her well, and you may depend upon it that she will do heavy penance for those shameful words. Now I beseech you to remain with us. Did I not uphold your authority in the sergeant's case by ordering an immediate flogging?'

The Colonel protested that he would not stay in a ship where such small respect was paid to his rank and age, but I could see that he was somewhat mollified and would consent to remain. At this delicate point, however, the Chief Pilot came up, and begged the General to postpone the flogging. He explained that the sergeant had offered the Colonel no violence at all but only protested against his unprovoked attack on the Ensign.

'That will be quite enough, Sir,' said the General sternly. 'In

future, I shall thank you to confine your suggestions to naval affairs
and leave military decisions to the Colonel and myself.'

The Chief Pilot was not to be put off. 'You must either listen or
say goodbye to me,' he said. 'The whole forecastle will be in an
uproar if the sergeant suffers any further indignity. Already he has
been unmercifully punched and kicked across the deck by the Colonel's guards.'

'He put his hand to his beard, which is surely a sort of mutiny?'
said the General, wavering. The Chief Pilot pressed his advantage.
'Since not only the Colonel's honour is at stake but also that of your
brothers-in-law, it is your duty as flotilla-commander to call witnesses
and make a thorough investigation of the case, instead of allowing
one man to be at once prosecutor, judge and executioner.'

Don Alvaro beckoned to the Boatswain, who stood at a respectful
distance. 'Come, honest friend, what have you to say in the matter?'

'With all respect to the Colonel, your Excellency, and though it's
no business of mine, the Chief Pilot is not far out. If your honour
does not think twice, I warrant that by nightfall there won't be a
single seaman left in the ship who's fit to handle sail.'

Much discomfited, Don Alvaro turned again to the Colonel. 'My
dear lord,' he quavered, 'since it appears that my officers do not see
eye to eye with your lordship, you will perhaps not object to a formal
court of enquiry? When you have proved, as I have every confidence
you will, that you were moved only by a desire to maintain good
discipline, and that the right is on your side, then the punishment
will be dealt out to the full number of lashes, and all trouble-makers
silenced.'

But before he had finished this speech the Colonel had climbed
over the bulwarks and down a Jacob's ladder.

'And Sergeant Dimas?' asked Doña Ysabel, appearing at her husband's side. 'Is he not to be released now? The Chief Pilot spoke up
like a champion. Indeed, he seems to be the only officer on board,
with the exception of my brothers, who has spirit enough to decry
injustice.'

'Why, of course, my love,' Don Alvaro answered unhappily. 'The
sergeant is free as an uncaged bird.'

Yet he was still anxious to pacify the Colonel. As soon as Doña
Ysabel retired, he sent for Don Lorenzo and the Admiral, and begged
them to go ashore and use whatever arguments they pleased to induce
the prodigal to return. He pledged them his word of honour that, if

they succeeded in their mission, he would never again permit the Colonel to exceed his authority; though for the time being he held the fate of the expedition in his hands, he would not be in the least formidable once they had fairly left Peru.

They were ready enough to do as he asked, and though the Colonel had already sent the skiff back for his baggage, they followed him to his lodgings, to plead sweetly and submissively with him there; and the Admiral went so far as to say that the sergeant was being flogged at that very moment.

The Colonel soon gave way. From what I heard later, he could hardly have done otherwise, because the Viceroy had been on the point of sending him to jail for similar drunken excesses and had appointed him to the Colonelcy of the expedition at the plea of the Warden of Callao, with a warning never to show his face again in Peru until the King should have appointed another viceroy. That he never intended to leave the ship was proved by his not having ordered his nephew, Ensign Jacinto de Merino, whose guardian he was, to come with him. This was a fantastical young man, as great a fop as his straitened means allowed, who loved to torture the Castilian tongue with tropes and conceits until his meaning often escaped us, but held his uncle in such awe that he stood stiff as a post in his presence, never uttering a word unless in answer to a question.

Meanwhile, in the Chart-room the Chief Pilot took down his instruments and stored them again in his sea-chest. When he also removed the image of Our Lady of Solitude from the niche above the table, and wrapped her in a linen cloth, I asked him: 'Don Pedro, what does this mean?'

'I am throwing away a thousand pesos,' he said, 'and, who knows, saving my life. Since the Colonel is to be coaxed back, I am quitting, and no man's plea, however eloquent, will alter my resolve. When a voyage begins in disorder, it ends in chaos.'

I went straight to Don Alvaro. 'Your Excellency,' I said, 'I am here to resume work on the dispatch. But first, with your permission, I wish to tell you that I must resign my post.'

'You are resigning?' he asked incredulously. 'But why, little Andrés? Have I not treated you well?'

'Like a father,' I replied truthfully, 'but now that the Chief Pilot is packing his sea-chest . . .'

He leaped from the couch and ran into the Chart-room, where he threw his arms round Pedro Fernandez's neck and implored him to desist. 'Did I not earn the Colonel's displeasure on your account, by releasing the sergeant?' he asked.

'That may be so, your Excellency, but now you have sent for him again, and since he witnessed my intervention, there can be no room for the two of us in the same ship.'

'If you go ashore,' the General said bitterly, 'the whole crew will follow your example, and not even force will prevent them. Would you dash my hopes once more, at the last moment, merely for a private pique?'

'I can dissuade them from going; I need only mention your own world-wide reputation as a navigator. With you to plot the course, and the Boatswain to sail the ship, my poor pilotage will not be needed. To be plain, your Excellency, the *San Geronimo* has become a mad-house; I have decided to forfeit my venture.'

'Only an angel could please everyone in circumstances like these,' wailed the General, 'and I am a poor soul, full of faults, and wearied almost to death.'

He pleaded and coaxed in a voice of honey, but the Chief Pilot's mind was made up: he took his leave with courteous words of esteem and regret, and continued with his packing. When the chest was roped, he had it lowered into the skiff, climbed down the ladder, holding the sacred image under one arm, and waved his bonnet to us in farewell. I was sick to see him go, and though I had set my heart on this adventure, determined to abandon it also as soon as I had handed over my accounts to Miguel Llano.

When the skiff passed under the bows, a buzz of dismay went up and a sailor shouted: 'Ahoy, Pilot, where are you bound? Are you quitting the ship?' And another: 'To the Devil with all these comings and goings. Tell us fairly, Don Pedro, are you off for good? If so, not a man Jack will stay in this unlucky ship, though they hang us in a row from the main-yard.'

'Do your duty, men!' he shouted back. 'The Boatswain will be master, and the General is a far better pilot than I!'

'The General!' the first sailor scoffed, and spat into the sea. 'He may have been a good man in his day, but as anyone can see with half an eye, he's breaking up like an old hulk whacked against a reef. I'd rather have the Chaplain as Master!'

'Saint Nicholas be my witness,' another put in, 'Don Alvaro's not capable of navigating a wooden shoe across a washtub!'

The skiff reached the quay and Pedro Fernandez clambered ashore, when a procession of richly dressed personages wound across the cobbles, with smiling, affable faces. At the head, in red, gold and green, walked the Lieutenant of Paita, arm in arm with the Admiral; next came Captain Don Lorenzo and Don Luis, with the Harbourmaster; behind them followed the Lieutenant's suite and a group of Paita merchants who had come to give the flotilla a send-off with presents and prayers.

The Admiral, when he saw the Chief Pilot on the quay, with cloak and blanket over his left arm, and the statue under the right, called out gaily: 'Put down your burdens, friend, and pay your respects to his Excellency the Lieutenant. I have just been telling him that in you we have the boldest and most skilful pilot of either the New World or the Old, and that while you keep us on our course we have nothing whatever to fear.'

Pedro Fernandez brushed the compliment aside, but made his bow to the Lieutenant. 'I regret to report, your Excellency,' he said, 'that I have taken my leave of the General; should you have any use for my services in this port, they are freely at your disposal.'

A chorus of protest arose, and the Admiral asked him to explain this cruel desertion. Without heat, and choosing words that would give as little offence as possible, he explained that because of bitter quarrels between certain persons of high standing in the flotilla he preferred to seek work elsewhere.

'But, dear friend,' cried Don Lope, embracing him, 'thanks to his Excellency's generous intervention those differences are now a thing of the past. We are all reconciled, and henceforth the *San Geronimo* will be as happy a ship, even, as the galleon which I command. Look, what comes here? Did you ever see greater love?'

He pointed behind him, where Captain Corzo was assisting the Colonel's tottering advance, with as much tenderness as if he had been his rich and childless uncle.

'May it long continue,' the Chief Pilot returned drily. 'I shall not be present to applaud it.'

The Colonel came closer and when he saw Pedro Fernandez standing beside his baggage, shouted: 'What, Sir, are you deserting your ship? That is very bad, and ungenerous, too. Oh, the poor General, with all that he's suffered! And now, at the last moment, the Chief Pilot skips off and leaves him.'

'It is not desertion, my lord. I have cancelled my contract and forfeited my venture.'

'Don't chop logic with me, Sir. I have said that it's desertion! Upon my word, the Devil seems to be loose among us, trying his infernal best to destroy the glorious work General Mendaña has in hand. Let's all return to the flagship, and send the old goat-foot packing. By Saint Antony's sow, I swear he'll be sorely disappointed. He'll plot revenge and devise new tricks for setting us by the ears again, but to Hell with him, I say, and there let him fry! It's our duty now to hold aloft the standard of our Christian Faith, serving God and our King with extravagant deeds, though it cost us our heads.' He raised his stick as if it were a banner, waved it wildly, and fell in a heap on the quay.

Everyone but the Chief Pilot laughed; even the Colonel joined in the joke against himself. When the merriment had died down and he had been set on his feet again, Pedro Fernandez answered: 'My lord, let us value moderation and forbearance above extravagant feats of daring. You have been far too ready to use stick and sword against the troops under your command, and to shower curses on my hard-working sailors. I well know the damage that has been done and cannot think of resuming my post unless you swear that it will be repaired.'

The Colonel was content to answer with a grin: 'But my dear Sir, you surely don't expect forbearance and moderation from a Colonel?'

'I expect both from him, and on every occasion,' the Chief Pilot insisted, and then continued, using simple words, as if speaking to a child: 'Your lordship is still in Peru, from where my men will soon take you and your soldiers to the far-off Isles of Solomon; and while you go ashore there, they will stay aboard and look after the ships. Do you follow me so far? Well, if it has pleased your lordship to treat them like dirt, it may please them to sail off and leave you there to your own devices. And even if they don't play a bad joke on you, you mustn't forget that later still they'll be sailing back to Peru, for reinforcements and fresh stores. And the report that they take with them about our prospects will be no better and no worse than your lordship's treatment of them.'

'You speak clearly, Sir,' said the Lieutenant of Paita, 'but pray lower your voice, lest your ship-mates hear what is not meant for them. I am certain that our noble friend agrees with you in principle.'

The Colonel, however, was wedded to his own point of view. 'Not at all, your Excellency!' he exclaimed. 'This man pampers the crew, and unless he shows far greater firmness, he'll soon find them laughing at him. He must make them jump to his orders, not amble—why, it would have disgusted your Excellency to see the lackadaisical show that they put up on Friday evening, before the very eyes of the Admiral-General, too! And how did he take it? With a weak shrug, like Eli in the fable.'

Pedro Fernandez remained unsatisfied. 'Your Excellency,' he said, 'I have given my word that no man will ever persuade me to sail with the Colonel, unless he shows a complete change of heart.'

The Lieutenant was a shrewd and diplomatic man. 'Ah,' he replied, 'if it is a matter of keeping your word, let us say no more! But at least have the kindness to wait here and do nothing to aggravate this affair, until I am with you again.' He called for his barge and was soon drummed aboard the *San Geronimo*.

In the flagship everyone had been leaning over the bulwarks, listening to this exchange, and my admiration for the Chief Pilot led me to suppose that the troops were ranged behind him as wholeheartedly as the crew; but while the Lieutenant was below in the Great Cabin, several soldiers were loud in the Colonel's defence. The junta, lolling on the hatches at my back, spoke their minds with vigour.

'I'm with the Colonel all the way,' Matia said. 'That Dimas is a jumped-up valet and no more a soldier than I'm a wet-nurse. The Colonel gave him an order, and he ought to have obeyed it without question, though it was to cut his own father's throat. What did he do? Went whining to the Vicar. "Father, I have a tender conscience!" What right has a sergeant to a conscience? Let him leave such luxuries to his betters. "The Colonel has given me an order, and I fear for my immortal soul if I obey it!" Why didn't he go to the Chaplain instead, who was one of us once? Father Antonio would have cut him short: "An order is an order, my son," he'd have said, "and if the Colonel happens to be in error, what concern is that of yours? The confessional is always open to him. Do your duty, man!"'

'Yes,' said Juarez, 'he would have used those very words, and Dimas again proved his ignorance of good soldiering when he interfered in a noblemen's quarrel. Deaf ears, blind eyes, dumb lips, when officer falls out with officer: that's the first lesson I was taught as a recruit. Dimas has earned the strappado.'

'Hold hard, fellows,' the water-steward interposed. 'Maybe I'm only a seaman and can't follow you in matters of military custom. But do you hold that the Colonel was right to kick and strike the orderly for doing what he'd been given permission to do?'

'As to that, bully, has it never happened that a sailor got the rope-end for obeying a foolish order of his boatswain's? Had he been a good soldier, he'd have shielded his officer: he'd have said: "No, your honor, nobody gave me permission. I pray your honour's pardon; I've drunk a spoonful too much chicha." Mind you, I'm not saying that the ribbons were planted on the orderly to catch the Colonel's eye and make him snort and push up his tail; but he's had trouble enough with certain high officers—I'll not name them—and he intends to make himself respected. It all started with the General's Lady giving him a dressing-down from the quarter-deck the very moment he reported—of course, you can't muzzle a noblewoman; but that lady has a sharp tongue and the Colonel's skin is tender.'

'And then,' said Matia, 'then your knight-errant of a Chief Pilot took her part, and spoke up for the Boatswain, and I don't say that he was wrong there, Jaume, because seamen, too, have their pride. But he rubbed the Colonel the wrong way, don't you see? His lordship may be quick on the draw and a gay old dog, but his heart's in the right place, his purse is always open to any poor man, and he sees to it that we're well fed and armed, and never in his life has he offended a man without some provocation at least. If you ask me, those high officers should have known better that day than to offer the Chief Pilot their protection, and I honour the man for having refused it; to form a cabal against the Colonel is little short of mutiny and, for my part, I know where my duty lies. But when he pleaded for the sergeant just now, he committed trespass. The Colonel curses the Boatswain; very good, the Chief Pilot has a right to protest; but the Colonel kicks a soldier, runs him through, flays him, disembowels him, cuts him into steaks, and feeds him to the hounds, that's none of the Chief Pilot's business. He must be content to cross himself and pass on.'

'Your hand on that, Matia!' Juarez said. 'And the moral of it is: put skirts in a ship and troubles breed like lice.'

As he spoke, an ensign called the troops to attention, and the Lieutenant of Paita, with Doña Ysabel on his arm, returned to his barge. The General remained behind. On the quay, every hat was doffed to her, as she walked delicately over the rough pavement, and I have never before or since seen a woman look lovelier than Doña Ysabel did then, in the warm rays of the setting sun. Laying her hand lightly on the Chief Pilot's arm, she murmured: 'Come, my friend, we stand in need of you. Though no man will ever make you change your mind, I do not doubt that you will listen to a woman. I pledge you my word that the Colonel will cause no further scandal, either on the voyage or when we land in our Isles. Will you accept it?'

What could Pedro Fernandez reply? He knelt and kissed her hand in silence. Then, after thanking the Lieutenant for his kindness, he returned to the flagship and reported for duty. The Colonel followed a little later, no further attempt being made to reconcile them.

At Paita we filled eighteen hundred water-kegs and jars, and the Lieutenant handed over the remaining arquebuses, so that we now had two hundred in all. Of the three hundred and seventy-eight persons in the flotilla, no less than two hundred and eighty were capable of bearing arms; and the General contrived to find an officer willing to pay a couple of thousand pesos for a majority, to serve as second-in-command under the Colonel. His name was Don Luis Moran, and in my opinion it would have been wiser to let him stay ashore and keep his money—the grey, mean, spiritless creature, fitter to be an old lady's coachman than to command good troops.

Chapter 7

ON THE HIGH SEAS

Despite our urgent desire to be under way again, we found ourselves detained at Paita for nearly a month. The frigate was now leaking so fast that Captain Leyva refused to sail in her until she had been completely overhauled but, knowing that he would get no satisfaction from Don Alvaro, he went direct to the Lieutenant of Paita. Called to account, the General tried to brush the complaint aside as frivolous, and produced the *Santa Catalina's* clearance certificate, issued by the Harbour-master of Callao. The Lieutenant gave it a cursory glance and ordered a fresh inspection by his Harbour-master, whose report proved so unfavourable—in places her timbers were as thin as shoe-leather, and her keel eaten away by teredo—that the General complained bitterly that the caulking and other repair-work done at Callao had been scamped, and asked leave to exchange her against another frigate in the port. This the Lieutenant would not do, unless the difference in value were paid at once in hard coin; but the pesos could not be found. Since the frigate was needed for navigation among the island reefs where the galleons could not be hazarded, we were compelled to stay in port while 'The Holy Coffin' was unloaded, careened and patched.

Shore leave was granted to the officers, but neither to the crew nor the troops. A standing patrol of arquebusiers guarded the quay, who had orders to fire at anyone attempting to leave the ships. Even so, five young soldiers managed to desert by swimming across the harbour and one of them took with him an emigrant girl, towing her behind him on an inflated goat-skin. It was a wearisome and disagreeable time: the weather was torrid, no rain having yet fallen; the mosquitoes bit viciously; and we wasted a month's provisions. However, all evil has its term: and on the Thursday before Ascension Day the frigate was

repaired, reloaded, and we were free to sail, though one thing or
another prevented us from quitting port until the following morning.

On Friday the 12th of May, therefore, we stood out to sea, to the
sound of clarions and drums, the General grieving loudly that two
full months had passed since the day on which he had reckoned to
leave Peru. Yet he promised that we should make our first landfall in
eight weeks or less, if the winds were fair, and reach the Isles of
Solomon three weeks later, that is to say, in the last week of July;
and since the latitude of the Isles was well known to himself, it
would be a case of:

> Run on, caravel,
> Run down the parallel,
> And we'll strike land.

As we cleared the bay and watched the towering Chair of Paita
slowly diminish in the distance, a school of whales appeared and
sported between the ships. One huge bull, twice the size of the
Santa Ysabel, dived beneath her stern, and we held our breaths for
fear he might rise suddenly to the surface and strike us as we sailed
three cables' lengths ahead. He roared up, spouting a vast column
of spray, and Father Juan tried to appease his wrath by making the
sign of the cross at him, and chanting: 'O ye whales, bless ye the
Lord!', while the Chief Pilot, sensible of our danger, dissuaded
Manuel Lopez the Captain of Artillery from firing a gun at the malicious monster, as his wife urged him to do. The whale followed us
for a matter of two leagues after his companions had made off northward, and we sighted no other during all the time we were at
sea; they are uncommon in these latitudes, preferring cold water to
warm.

For the remainder of that day we were all in good spirits. The fair
breeze that had carried us up the coast was still blowing; but on our
voyage to Paita we had sailed north of the parallel along which it was
intended to run; and now steering south-west, we had the wind
abeam and made far slower progress.

At the General's order the ship's company had fasted since midnight, and mass was now celebrated; we were all much affected by
the solemnity of the occasion—wondering what might lie before us,
and musing on our families and friends whom we might never see
again. The Vicar preached an eloquent sermon, the gist of which I

entered in my journal while it was still fresh in my mind. He said
that the purpose of our expedition was to implant the Faith in the
isles of the South Sea; that whatever worldly glory or advantage
might accrue to us in the single performance of this task was only
adventitious. Thus harvesters who reaped a field might chance upon
a hare lurking in the patch that remained in the middle, and kill it
with a lucky sickle-cast; likewise, the warrior Saint George, riding
forth from Lebanon one day to preach the gospel to the infidels,
chanced to encounter a fierce dragon which he pierced with his trusty
lance, as a by-blow of his missionary zeal.

He then told us a story, for the truth of which he vouched, how
at Tumbes—not many leagues hence, where Pizarro landed and the
first place, after Panama, that our people settled on the mainland—a
priest went ashore, crucifix in hand, while ten thousand Indians stood
gaping. As he set foot on the beach, two great lions issued from the
woods and when he laid the cross gently on their backs they at once
fell down and worshipped it. Moreover, two great tigers following
them did the same, and by this sign gave the Indians knowledge of
the excellency of our Christian faith, which they thereupon embraced
one and all.

'This priest,' he continued, 'was a man of more than ordinary holiness, so much so that he kept his eyes always fixed on the sky, as if
the better to behold God's glory; and thus he avoided looking at
the women of that coast who went about naked. My brethren, faith
to work miracles with the help of God—as in the matter of the lions
and tigers—depends upon the strictest avoidance of carnal temptation. One day, the queen of a neighbouring tribe came to entice this
saintly priest. She was uncommonly white-skinned, with hair like
tow, so that you might have taken her for a German, and of most
voluptuous shape. She approached him stark naked, except for the
jewels about her neck and wrists, and said to him: "Father, I am a
queen and have come to greet you. Do you like what you perceive?"
Gazing up at the sky, he answered innocently: "Daughter, I like it
well enough." Said she: "I am all for your enjoyment, if you would
accept my love." The holy man trembled and bade her be gone,
saying that his love was for God alone and so should hers be also;
but she would not listen, and amorously wound her limbs about him.
Then, still looking heavenwards, he perceived a prodigious great striped
serpent in a tree and, as he cast the temptress off, it reached down and
twined its coils around her waist, and made to strangle her. Yet by

God's infinite mercy, she repented of her sins in good time to pour out a sincere confession of evil-living, though the monster had already half engulfed her, and died sweetly in the Faith.'

From this instructive tale it was but a step to the temptations that might befall us on our long and tedious journey, owing to the presence in the ships of many feather-headed females. 'I have heard it said,' Father Juan went on, with a shake of his bony forefinger, 'that the rhythmic rolling of a ship, once the stomach has accustomed itself to the motion, exercises a diabolical spell upon women, stimulating and inflaming their lechery; which is the reason why the heathen of old pictured their Goddess of Lust as emerging from the sea-foam. Now, the love of a man for a woman, my sons, is a thing that is natural; but none should look upon a woman save with the eyes of a brother, unless she be wedded to him with the blessing of the Church. For your souls' sake, therefore, beware lest you stumble and perish!

'As the blessed Saint Augustine writes: "If bodies please you, praise God and turn your love for them back upon your Maker, lest by enjoyment of such things as please you, you cause displeasure. . . . Stand by Him, and you shall be at rest. Whither go you in rough ways? Whither, I say? The good that you love is from Hell and can become good and pleasant only by His mediation. Since anything created by Him that is not loved as He designs is not rightly loved, rightly it will turn bitter in your mouths if you taste of it otherwise." Therefore, my sons, flee from the deadly sin of fornication, and from the still deadlier sin of adultery! If your flesh be proud, abase it by abstinence; be sparing with meat and wine; for the Seven Vices dance in a ring together and Lechery holds her sweetheart Gluttony by the right hand.'

He spoke much more in the same strain, to which the younger soldiers listened devoutly, but the veterans with ill-concealed impatience. The cook-room fires were burning fiercely behind their windbreaks and the large copper cauldrons already seethed with a rich stew of Lima beans, cabbage, onions, salt beef and green bacon. Juan de Buitrago said to me, sniffing the air hungrily: 'The proverb is right:

> "All good stews
> Have bacon cast in;
> All good sermons,
> Saint Augustine."

But, upon my word, it would need a saint to practise abstinence on an occasion like this, and if Gluttony is indeed Lechery's sweetheart, there will be many a deadly sin committed before the pages call out the middle watch.'

He had hit the mark: by nightfall there was not a sober soldier or sailor to be found in the whole galleon, and many naughty sights were seen; yet a pleasant humour reigned, and not a sword or knife was drawn. The officers feasted harmoniously at the common table under the quarter-deck awning. The Colonel was too soused to appear and his faction had decided to keep the peace unless their beards were pulled. Amicable toasts were exchanged, and Don Alvaro beamed upon us, making salty little jests; yet he hardly wetted his lips with the good wine, and ate no more than a crust of bread and a few olives.

As we sat at dessert, with doublets unfastened, in a happy mood, we were preached a second sermon, this time by the General. It concerned our dealings with the natives, to whom we came not as conquerors, but as ambassadors of Christ; not as takers, but as givers. 'Firmness tempered by kindness must be our rule. Let those lovely isles not suffer the fate of the West Indies,' he said, 'where, though the Cross has been firmly planted, innocent error has given place to cultivated vice. Alas, that this should have been inculcated by professed Christians who came among the Indians with fire-arms, whips and filthy lusts! I have heard it estimated by a sea-captain, that of the thirty million Indians inhabiting those islands when Columbus discovered them a century ago, a bare three million survive today—baptized indeed, but still uninstructed in Holy Doctrine, racked by disease and groaning under the lash. Let us show forbearance towards the islanders, even though we see them perform deeds of horror; let us remember that they are benighted in ignorance and that we, as men of enlightenment, have come to disperse this darkness for them.

'I remember well on my last voyage, at a place called Baso where our brigantine was building: we were hearing mass one morning, when the guards saw eight large canoes approaching, full of Indians hideously painted, with bows and lances. The sergeant made his report to me in a whisper; I crossed myself and retired, leaving the congregation on their knees. As the visitors entered the harbour, one of the guards would have discharged his arquebus at their Chieftain, who stood in the prow of the first canoe, brandishing his spear of palm-rib and ebony, but I seized the piece from him, and went down to the water's edge. The Indians hailed me as "Taurique," which in their language means "King," and invited me to enter the Chieftain's canoe; but I declined, and mass being over, I withdrew under a canopy where I took my seat in invitation to a parley.

'The canoes lined up a short distance from the beach, and the Chieftain displayed a joint of meat and some roots, crying: "*Nalea! Nalea!*", which is to say: "Eat! Eat!" Looking closer at the gifts, we were horror-stricken to see that the joint was the quarter of a boy, with a delicate arm and small hand! Presently an Indian dived from the canoe and left the gifts floating close to the shore, for one of us to retrieve. My negro fetched them from the water—did you not, Myn?—and when he was beyond range of their arrows, the guards asked leave to fire on the bloodthirsty cannibals; but I refused. "These people," I said, "do not yet know good from evil." To which my Colonel, Don Hernando Enriquez, replied: "Your Excellency, these people know it well enough, because they hunt their victims in neighbouring islands, rather than eat their own kinsfolk." The captains supported him in this, but "Christian brethren," I said, "that they abstain from eating their own families argues a certain mildness and love in them which can be turned to advantage. Before we make war on the savages, we should show them that they ought not to perform these iniquities; and until they have been thus instructed any harm that we do them will fall upon our conscience."

'I ordered a pit to be dug in the sight of the Indians, and Myn took up the joint—did you not, Myn?—and displayed it to them and laid it gently in the hole, while we averted our faces and made signs of disgust. They were surprised and cried in injured tones: "*teo nalea!*", "not eat," beat their drums and paddled away. But we had taught them that the eating of human flesh is loathsome to Christians.'

Doña Mariana, who had sipped a deal of Malmsey, made merry at the General's expense, and Doña Ysabel encouraged her with furtive nods and winks. 'Aha, brother-in-law,' she said, 'now I know why you fear to fatten yourself, and hold back from these excellent dishes: lest when you go in that habit among the Indians to teach them their Creed and Paternoster, they may not be led into temptation. But have a care! When the cunning rogues learn how sweet your tongue is and how tender your heart, they may cut them both out, and toast them on skewers for their infants to suck.'

Her brothers took up the jest, discussing who among those present would taste best if, provisions failing, we were forced to feed upon one another. Don Diego, the wildest of the three, cast me a wolfish glance, and said: 'Andrés Serrano yonder would roast crisp and cut tender enough, I swear!'

'You are right,' said Doña Mariana. 'Come, little Andrés, let me feel your ribs to learn how much fat they carry.' She reached over, thrust her hand under my shirt, and pinched me till I squealed for mercy.

'Hey, brothers!' she called. 'Why wait until provisions fail? This pigling is now at his best, and it would be a pity to eat him lean.'

They trussed me and made as if to carry me off to the cook-room, Doña Mariana crying that I was to be spitted clean and basted well.

Don Alvaro, meanwhile, showed displeasure that his own family were making mock of his words, and retired almost at once, leaving them to drink without restraint and to preach further sermons on very different texts. The Chief Pilot was the next to rise, pleading press of work, and at his instance Miguel Llano released me; but not before Don Luis and Don Diego had fattened me well, forcing me at the sword-point to swallow a great lump of figs and a trencher of bean porridge (which, they swore, went to make the best bacon) and swill a quantity of small beer; while Doña Mariana stuffed sugar plums into my already crammed mouth and nearly choked me. She then staggered off to the binnacle, where she rallied Pedro Fernandez for wearing so sour a look on a festival night. She snatched off his bonnet and declared that he would not have it back until he either changed his mood or justified it. Then he spoke of the grief that he felt, in sailing without news from his wife; and told her that when the order came to overhaul the frigate, he had sent a message to his brother-in-law at Lima, enquiring after her health; but no reply had come. The tender-hearted Doña Mariana gave back his bonnet and dropped a maudlin tear in sympathy.

The Chief Pilot was a man of serious nature; he spent an hour every day at prayer, but denied himself sleep rather than take time from his watches. He never diced or played cards, and was as regular in his habits as the pocket-dial he carried, constantly inspecting the ship to see that all was well, and reproving laziness or irregularity wherever he found it. I well remember his anger one morning when he discovered that some soldiers had driven nails into the foremast for the rigging up of a tent. Yet he went gently enough to Don Lorenzo with his complaint, telling him that even a small wound in the pine was liable to split it and allow rot to enter; then when a gale blew and the mast bent like a withy, snap! it would go where it had been weakened and leave us at the mercy of the waves. The Captain promised to punish the soldiers severely, as well as others who had been cutting wood from the upper works of the ship for frying their pancakes over.

Because the tent had been designed as their gaming house, the soldiers grumbled that the Chief Pilot had made the nail-hole an excuse for spoiling sport. When he became aware of their ill-humour, he asked a certain Sergeant Gallardo: 'If I took your sword and used it as a spit, would you be pleased?'

'I should be angered beyond measure, Pilot,' the Sergeant answered. 'Heat takes the temper from a sword: it might fail me in the hour of need, and lose me my life.'

Pedro Fernandez then said: 'Yet I care for this mast as you do for your sword; and were it to snap in the hour of need, not only I, but all of us might lose our lives.'

The Barretos respected the Chief Pilot's skill and courage, though despising him for his low birth and laughing at his religious fervour; for my part, the better I came to know him, the more I admired him. He agreed with the General and the Vicar as to the purpose of our expedition and the spirit of Catholic love needed for its success and, though not having voyaged to the South Seas before, he was nevertheless a sailor of long experience: he had circumnavigated Africa six times, twice on a voyage to Timor and four times on the Goa run, besides often crossing the Atlantic. It was his conclusion that the Isles of Solomon are the outposts of a southern continent, the land of Austrialia, as he fancifully called it in honour of the House of Austria, which must be of enormous size to counterbalance the Continents of the Northern hemisphere; otherwise, he told me, the earth would tip up and plunge to ruin. Austrialia must nourish many million souls, all ripe for conversion, and our settlement there would be the crowning achievement of a splendid century. Though the beginnings had been unpropitious, he hoped that God might yet turn the obdurate hearts in the flotilla to an awareness of His love and to mutual reconciliation, and thereafter inspire them to pass on to the Indians the sweet and wonderful news of mankind's redemption through the blood of Jesus Christ.

I did not contradict him; but during these last two months I had overheard so much unchristian talk from the soldiers and settlers, that I feared such a change of heart would be a greater miracle, almost, than that of the lions and tigers. They saw themselves already as great landlords, wearing silk clothes, ruffs and plumed hats, living at ease on their estates, while the Indians sweated in the fields and yielded them their pretty daughters to be honourably deflowered before marriage, as in Peru. 'We shall have to fight for our pleasures, friends!' they would say, slapping arquebus or sword-hilt. 'Pizarro's men landed in Peru with no titles of honour and no other advantage than their skill at arms; but it was this skill that made them rich, and will make us even richer, as gold is more precious than silver.'

The entries in my journal became fewer as we sailed farther, and increasingly concerned with the weather and Church festivals. We were ten days out of Paita, and the winds were still those of Peru, which at this season blow mainly from the south-east. Our course was W.S.W. and we ran a bare fifteen leagues a day. The ships were no longer followed by gulls or boobies, and we had sighted our last sail on the second day out. Corpus Christi was celebrated in fine style, with a candled procession around the ship, which was dressed with flags and coloured streamers; afterwards the soldiers performed a sword dance, and the pages another in the Sevillian style to honour the Most Holy Sacrament. The sailors worked and slept, the troops lounged on deck, playing at cards and getting in everyone's way; the settlers' children chased each other up and down the rigging, while their mothers sat, each with her gossip, mending clothes or making stockings wherever they could find shade. Trolling for albacores was a sport favoured by the officers, and one morning Don Luis caught two of large size; but most of the time they had nothing better to do than gamble, drink, sing songs and catches, and play tricks on one another. The supervision of their men they left to the sergeants.

The Colonel had not left his cabin: drinking too much aqua vitae and eating too little food had thrown him into a trembling delirium; he slept badly and was wakened by the illusion that his bunk harboured scorpions. He no longer recognized his comrades and grew frenzied; making a deal of noise, even at night, when absolute silence was the rule, lest a man should fall overboard and his appeal for help pass unheard. The General, at Doña Ysabel's insistence, had him gagged and bound; and when at last he sank into a deep sleep and then came to himself, he was so weakened that his legs would not obey him. However, he had no recollection of either the gagging or the scorpions; and the Chaplain, who was his sick-nurse, had thrown into the sea what remained of his aqua vitae, two whole gallons of it, so that there should be no relapse. He was slow to regain his health, but took kindly to Father Antonio, who humoured him in his whims and treated him with consideration. It came out that the good Father had served with him in the Low Countries, and now they lived their battles over again and grew as thick as thieves; so that the Barreto brothers conceived a suspicion of the Chaplain and reckoned him among the Colonel's faction, which was far from the truth. Don Diego circulated lying and wicked tales about him, of which the following may serve as an example. Father Antonio, playing at dice with the Colonel one Sunday, was called away to say mass in the frigate; and while administering the Holy Sacrament to an old woman, inadvertently gave her the dice in place of the Host. She, chumbling the bone in her toothless gums, cried out: 'Father, you have erred. Instead of Jesus's sweet body, you have given me God the Father, it is so old and tough.'

Day succeeded day, and we sailed on with only the wide horizon to gaze upon. I came to know every knot-hole in the walls of the Chart-room, every wild tale in the Purser's and the Boatswain's repertory, and could prophesy with exactness what dishes would be served on any given day. Next to me at the common table sat Juan de la Isla's daughter Maruja, who resembled her mother, a fat woman wholly given to gossip and gluttony, as a calf the cow. The Colonel's nephew was for ever paying Maruja far-fetched compliments, which were received by her with giggling laughter, and she regarded herself as already betrothed to him; but the mother insisted that she was as yet too young to think of marriage. On my other hand sat the merchant Mariano de Castillo, whose only conversation concerned money and profits, and who was well-dipped in the fat of usury. He could tell you to a hair how much loss there was in a measure of wheat from the waste of its winnowing and cleansing; or, to a crumb, how much more loss in a hundred dozen loaves, when you cut them with a knife rather than broke them with your hand. He was for ever quarrelling with the Purser, whom he accused of sharp practice, and how Don Alvaro had persuaded him to put his money into so wild a venture, I have never made out.

The pages were our time-keepers. They watched and turned the
hour-glasses in the niche of the binnacle and at each turn sang out:

> 'A good hour running,
> A better hour coming;
> The first now stilled
> The second a-humming,
> God knows how many good hours remain;
> Turn them, count them, turn them again!

'Hey, you there in the bows! Are you awake? Are you watching?'
Dawn came with their shrill chant of salutation, like the sound
of birds in the mating season:

> 'Glory to the dawn so red
> And the Cross whereon Christ bled,
> Glory to the Trinity,
> Very God in Unity,
> Glory to each Christian heart
> Of God's love that claims a part.
> Glory to this coming day,
> God has rolled the dark away!'

Then they would gabble a Paternoster and Ave Maria, and sing
out:

'Amen! God give us many such good days. Listen, General, pray
listen, your ladyship, listen Colonel, listen Master, and all noble lords
and dames: we wish you a fine and prosperous voyage! Sail on, sail on
cheerily! Now then, gentlemen of the aftercastle, and gentlemen of
the forecastle, good-day to you all, in God's name!'

at which we would rise to hear matins. When dinner time came
round, and the pages had laid the tables and brought the dishes from
the cook-room, they would cry:

'To table, to table! General, General's Lady, Colonel, Master and
all other noble lords and dames—listen! The table is spread, the food
is served, and the water is drawn for your Excellencies!

> 'Long life, long life to the King of Castile!
> On land and on water, our hearts shall be leal.
> An axe or a rope, now, for all the King's foes,
> (Amen, cry amen, or you shan't wet your nose!)
> The table is laden, that soon will be bare:
> Who comes not to table must forfeit his share.'

And at dusk, one of them would light the binnacle lamp and they
would all sing the responses to his lead:

> 'Hail to the hour: *of our dear Saviour's birth*
> Hail to Our Lady: *who bore Him on earth*
> Hail to Saint John: *who baptized Him one day*
> The watch has been warned: *and the sand slips away*
> God grant us good sailing: *and so we all pray!'*

They turned out the watches with:

'To quarters, to quarters, fine gentlemen of the new watch, to
quarters, to quarters! High time now to show a leg, so be brisk! Up,
up, gentlemen of the new watch! To quarters!'

We kept three watches: the Master's, the Boatswain's and the
Pilot's. Since the Chief Pilot was also the master of the *San Geronimo*
and had no assistant, this third watch was commanded by Damian of
Valencia, the Boatswain's mate, an excitable man who regarded
soldiers as idle vermin, cumberers of the earth, and sailoring as the
only honest profession.

Every day at noon we hailed the other ships for an exchange of
news and observations; every Sunday we hove-to for a couple of
hours and, while the Chaplain went aboard the frigate and the Vicar
aboard the galeot to celebrate mass and hear confession, the pilots
and high officers exchanged visits. On the third Sunday out, an
officer from the *Santa Ysabel* foolishly hinted to Don Diego that the
Admiral was lying with the sergeant's wife, and he, much incensed,
took the tale straight to the General. A grand commotion ensued in
the Great Cabin, with many bitter words cast about, some of which I
could not help but overhear. Doña Mariana made ready to board the
Santa Ysabel at once, to fling her rival over the rails and regain possession of her husband; but her sister held that Don Lope's adultery
was an affront which no woman of spirit should tamely accept, and
that the Admiral must come to her, not she to him. All that week
they talked the matter over, growing hotter every day, and on the
next Sunday Don Lorenzo and Don Diego went to the Admiral and
informed him that if he hoped to enjoy his wife when the Isles were
reached, he should send his concubine to another ship and beg forgiveness on his knees of the whole family. This he refused to do, bluntly
saying that ever since his beard sprouted he had not spent a week
without a bed-fellow; that it was too late now to learn continence;

and that his knees were far too stiff to bend to anyone but the King of Castile. Let his wife come freely to him, he said, and he would love and cherish her, and the woman could be her maid.

Don Lorenzo's answer, made in some heat, was that the Admiral could not have fully considered into what family he had married. To which Don Lope returned that, in accordance with the agreement signed by the General, he expected his wife to join him at the first island on which they landed; and that he would accept no fresh conditions imposed on their union either by her family or by any third party.

Don Diego then caught sight of the sergeant's wife, hiding behind the bed curtains, and asked her: 'Have you no shame, harlot, to desert your maimed husband and endanger your soul by adultery?'

'My lord,' she answered demurely, 'it is better to be well loved than ill wed; and I do no more than keep the Admiral's bed warmed for your honour's sister.'

They went away in a huff, without farewell, and on the following Sunday no visits were exchanged between the two galleons.

We had now reached fourteen degrees of latitude, still on a W.S.W. course, having run about five hundred leagues; but on Midsummer Day we changed course to W.N.W. because the winds had shifted, and gradually approached the ninth parallel, when our daily runs increased by five leagues. On the 30th of June, the day of Saint Martial, Father Antonio went to the General and offered, with the Saint's help, to cure his headache.

'My headache?' Don Alvaro asked in surprise.

'I mean by that,' he explained, 'your painful concern for the young women in the ship, whose unchastity you have been unable to curb either by threats or admonitions.'

'Why, Father, has a remedy been revealed to you from Heaven?'

'There is only one, my son,' said the Chaplain, 'namely marriage, a state sanctified by Our Saviour Himself, when He attended the wedding at Cana. Give the women leave to marry, and I warrant that though they have not baulked at fornication, yet they will be wary of the greater sin of adultery; but delay permission a little longer, and Miguel Llano's register of births will open with a fine blossoming of bastards. Few have the power to control their passions as you do, my son, and what young female is wise below the girdle? By expecting too much of your fellow-men, you have caused yourself unnecessary pain.'

Don Alvaro gave way at last, but he shrank from making a speech in a matter that went so much against the grain. Instead, at his orders, a parchment was tied to the mainmast on which he announced that since it was better to marry than to burn, such lovers as could not practise continence until the Isles were reached, should come to him and ask for his consent. He acted without Doña Ysabel's knowledge, who was ill-pleased when she learned of the notice. She said to her sister with a short laugh: 'Lovers indeed! It will be hard to decide who is in love with whom, when so many sluts are common to the whole ship's company. Don Alvaro would have done better to use the stocks and whip, as I advised him.'

According to Elvira, she then importuned the General to take off his friar's habit and ask Father Juan to release him from his vow; but he would not be moved. I carry in my mind a clear picture of his coming into the Great Cabin one morning with Juanito in his arms: the youngest of our emigrants, not yet a year old, the seventh child of a settler from Truxillo, named Miguel Geronimo. Don Alvaro in his Franciscan cowl, the thick skirts of his habit tucked up for coolness, looked for all the world like Saint Christopher bearing the Infant Christ over the river, and the marvellous tenderness in his eyes, as he crooned a foolish little lullaby, struck pity in my heart. It was plain that his childlessness gnawed at him, and when I stole a glance at Doña Ysabel, who was busy at her tambour-work again, I was aware that she nursed a furious resentment against him on this very account. Her face was momentarily disfigured by hate and shame, yet all she said was: 'As you love me, husband, take that filthy child back to his mother! He's crawling with lice and will bepiss us all.' The General sighed and meekly stole away.

During the next three weeks we celebrated fifteen marriages, but there were still some women left who preferred to stay single for a while, now that they had fewer rivals in their trade and could quickly amass a good dowry. So July passed, with only a single disaster. It happened on the ninth, the Eve of Saint Christopher, that Miguel Llano who had eaten tainted fish was seized by a violent flux. Doña Ysabel complained the next morning that he spent too long a time in the 'garden' of the Great Cabin, and had kept the ladies waiting, so the General made him go forward to the harness-tables overhanging the bow, which the crew used. These are dangerous perches when the sea is rough, and though that day it was no more than choppy, Miguel was out of luck. He had not been squatting there long, when a clumsy helmsman brought the ship to the wind, she was taken aback, and he in his weakness was jolted overboard.

This happened at a time when officers and crew were sitting down to their several dinners, and in the bustle his cries went unheard; presently the look-out at the cross-trees spied him struggling in the water, a cable's length astern, and gave the alarm. A sailor dived to his rescue, while the ship's company made a great noise with whatever came to hand, to keep off the sharks. Miguel sank once, and as he rose again, the bold rescuer grasped his collar and struck him between the eyes so that he should not struggle. At last they were both hauled aboard, amid cheers, but Miguel scarcely had any life left in him. The Boatswain lifted him by the heels to empty his lungs of water; the Purser tickled his throat with a feather to make him spew; Don Alvaro ordered a hot wine-broth to be poured down his gullet, and after that a cupful of olive oil, to keep the salt water from rotting his guts; and two sailors kneaded his chest and belly with oil. It was all to no avail: his lips paled and he was dying. The Chaplain came on deck, hurriedly confessed him and administered the Sacrament.

That night we buried Miguel Llano at sea. I was appointed to succeed him as the flotilla's registrar of births, marriages and deaths, and it was my sorrowful duty to open the death-ledger with his own name. He was a dry, quarrelsome man, who had not shown me much kindness; none the less, I prayed for his soul every night for a month or more, because I pitied his fate and had been the only one to gain from it.

Chapter 8

THE MARQUESAS ISLANDS

Every day at noon the Chief Pilot took the sun to determine our latitude, keeping us on a due westerly course of ten degrees fifty minutes south. When the high officers grew a little impatient because no land had appeared on the sixtieth day after our departure from Paita, he told them that they should not read the General's promises too close to the letter: we were now sailing more than three degrees south of the solitary Isle of Jesus, the only land that had been sighted on the former voyage before the Isles of Solomon were reached. He also reminded them that Don Alvaro had set out five months earlier in the year than we and thereby gained the benefit of fairer winds. We might have to spend many more weeks at sea; so far we had covered only eight hundred leagues of the fifteen hundred, and there was no saying whether we should sight even so much as a treeless rock before our arrival.

Ten days later, I happened to be talking to the Boatswain by the mainmast, when Ensign Juan de Buitrago sauntered up and joined in our conversation. We were discussing the event of the day—on a long journey even trivialities take on a look of importance—namely, the case of the General's negro Myn who, when climbing up to the half-deck, had been struck on the skull by a stone cannon-ball weighing nearly four pounds. The ball was not aimed at him, but had slipped from Don Diego's grasp while he played at catch with Don Luis. Myn crashed back on the deck, but sprang up at once, grinning and shaking his ears, none the worse for the pounding. 'What gentleman threw that walnut?' he shouted, and went on his way, chuckling to himself.

'Ay, Don Marcos,' said the Ensign, 'it is well known that negroes have thick skulls. But have you ever heard how remarkably ticklish they are? My grandfather Hermenegildo de Buitrago went with Balboa on the famous expedition to Darien, when the ocean across which we now sail was first sighted from the Peak of Pirri. In his droll manner he used to say to me: "Juan, my boy, if you ever have trouble with a blackamore, don't crack him on the head with your stick; he'll only laugh at you, roll his eyes and break wind. But tickle his hide with a feather and you'll have him at your mercy. That negro Nuño, now . . ."

'And off he'd launch into his story: "Balboa, you see, led us down from the peak, ragged and fever-ridden, through dense, thorny jungle; and when at last we came to the beach, he waded out, parted the water solemnly with his sword, and took possession of it in the King's name. But that wasn't enough, it seems. The priest who was with us insisted that the deed must be formally recorded, with the hour, the day, and the names of the witnesses entered, and full glory given to God. Balboa's secretary sat down on the sand, a parchment scroll spread on his knees, unstoppered his ink-horn, trimmed his quill and began to write at the priest's dictation. But his knees were thin and bony; soon he rose and said that he needed a table. 'Come here, Nuño,' says Balboa, 'you're a good Catholic and a loyal subject of the King, lend us your sweaty black back!' So Nuño knelt down, his hands on the beach, and the secretary spread the parchment on his broad shoulders and started all over again. But, God in Heaven, the negro's agony was a study for a sculptor: he was so ticklish that every stroke of the pen made the table pitch and toss like a cock-boat in a storm. 'Quiet, man, keep quiet!' said the priest severely. 'This is the most solemn hour of our lives: we are now entering the portals of history. Stop giggling like a drunken bridesmaid, you rogue; keep quiet, while I dictate, or it will be the worse for you!' The negro could not help himself: he wriggled like an eel in an oil jar and laughed like a hyaena. The secretary stood by with grave, melancholy face and pen poised, waiting for him to calm down. 'History!' cried Nuño, when he was able to speak. 'Reverend Father, how that blessed word does tickle Nuño's back!' At this the good priest lost his temper and took a hefty kick at the negro's buttocks; but the secretary, making a grab at the parchment, stumbled into him, and both went down. The solemnity of the occasion was ruined beyond repair. There, on the white Pacific strand, sprawled negro, secretary, priest, ink-horn and parchment—all upside-down." '

'Upside-down!' cried the simple-minded Boatswain delightedly.

'Upside-down, by the miraculous Virgin of Pilar! Ho! ho! ho!'

An uneasy feeling came over me that at some time or other, in a dream perhaps, I had already lived through this situation. I looked about me in sudden apprehension and there, not five paces away, stood the Colonel, very pale and resting heavily on his stick—his first appearance on deck for many days. It was only then that I remembered the tale of the Blind Girl of Panama, and understood why the Boatswain's words had rung so familiarly in my ears. The Colonel, his old resentment awakened by so perfect a re-enactment of the earlier scene, half lifted his stick and seemed minded to bring it down on the Boatswain's head, when a loud cry rang out from the topmast cross-trees: 'Land! Land ho!'

'How does it bear, man?' shouted Don Marcos.

'Two points on the starboard bow, your honour! An island, some ten leagues off!'

In great excitement, and unaware of the danger which he had so narrowly avoided, the Boatswain scrambled up the rigging and soon confirmed the look-out's discovery. The General was at once called away from his beads and ordered the flotilla to change course and make for the island. The look-out, amid cheers, went to the Great Cabin to receive his reward of three gold pesos and drain a goblet of the best wine.

Don Alvaro was overjoyed. He was convinced that we had reached the Isles of Solomon ten days sooner than he had promised, and at his desire everyone on board—soldiers, sailors, settlers and officers—went down on their knees and thanked God for His great mercy in leading us home, while the priests sang the *Te Deum Laudamus*. He named the island La Magdalena, because this was the eve of Saint Mary Magdalen.

That night there was more than the usual boasting and drunkenness among our soldiers, and I saw that they were no longer dicing for maravedis, or reals, as had been their custom, but for notes of hand: pledging themselves to pay, on being assigned their estates, so many pigs, serfs, or ounces of gold. I cannot say that the officers behaved in a more Christian manner; indeed, by their wild talk and riotous conduct, they might have been Sallee pirates making ready for a slave raid on Naples or the coast of Sicily.

When the pages had saluted the dawn, every man, woman and child ran on deck and all strained their eyes impatiently for a view of the land, though a smart shower of rain was falling. The men climbed into the shrouds and perched there like a flock of starlings. As the light broadened a cry of delight went up: there was the island, not half a league ahead of us, and it appeared to be inhabited. We steered for its southernmost point, and since no reefs nor rocks were showing, kept close inshore. The other vessels had orders to follow us at a respectable distance, and not to parley with the natives; for Don Alvaro was anxious, he said, to avoid unnecessary bloodshed.

Though not large, the island was by no means of contemptible size, perhaps ten leagues in circumference, well-wooded and en-grandized by lofty hills scored with ravines. Green palm-trees waved in the breeze, smoke rose blue from unseen villages, and the broad beaches were crowded with natives who shouted and blew whistles. The rain had ceased, and from behind a promontory to the east scores of small canoes shot out. Some held only three Indians, some as many as ten, but each was hollowed from a single tree-trunk, with a carved figure-head, its stern terminating in a narrow up-curved fin. I counted as many as seventy. They carried triangular white sails and were prevented from capsizing by outriggers on either side, in the form of log-floats secured by cane cross-pieces. But their crews did not rely entirely on sails: they also used broad-bladed paddles. The number of savages was perhaps four hundred, counting those who swam or were towed behind the canoes; and every one of them, though well-tattooed with designs of plants and fish, especially about the face, was as naked as he was born. Don Alvaro eyed them with attention and 'Myn,' he said to his negro, 'do you think that this is the same race of men we saw in our isles?'

'No, no, master!' answered Myn. 'These are white. Myn saw no white men in the Isles of Solomon; nothing but wild black savages with bushy hair and bows and arrows. Myn sees no bows nor arrows now. These must be Christians, very naked, painted Christians!'

'I agree with you, Myn,' said Don Alvaro, swallowing his disappoint-ment. 'This is not the same place, though none the less a happy discovery. All is different here; I would not say better.' He turned to the Chief Pilot: 'These islands have been given us for our refreshment and recreation; but our work lies ahead.'

The savages were indeed remarkably white: and so closely re-sembled Spaniards in shape and feature that the Captain of Artillery felt shame that his wife should see them stark naked, and sent her below at once. 'If they were monkeys,' he said, 'or African negroes, it would be a different matter, but it is shameful even for a married

woman to be confronted by such indecent sights.' Doña Ysabel and
her sister, however, hung over the poop-rail and watched the scene
below them without a flutter of their eyelids. The men were of graceful build: tall, muscular, clear-skinned, with good legs, slender fingers,
the best teeth that ever I saw, and long curly hair, some of it very
fair and arranged in fantastic coils and plaits.

'God's death!' I heard the Colonel cry. 'If these are the men,
their women must be beautiful indeed!'

I was standing by the side of the Chief Pilot, gazing with pleasure
at these novelties, when a small canoe came close under the stern: it
was handsomely carved and decorated with a shining inlay of pearl
shell. In it were three young boys who seemed to be chieftains' sons
and kept their eyes intently fixed on ours. One of them was about
ten years of age with elaborately dressed locks, as fair as any Dane's,
and angelic features in which beauty and nobility of spirit were so
happily reconciled that Pedro Fernandez clutched my arm and cried:
'Little Andrés, my friend, it strikes me to the very heart to think that
so lovely a child should be left to perdition, unbaptized and uninstructed.'

The other natives now paddled closer, pointing to the harbour from
which they had come and shouting in a language which none of us
understood; they used the words *atalut* and *analut* most often, as if
to invite us there. In token of friendship they brought us coconuts and
rolls of a doughy food, done up in leaves, which they called *tutao*
but which we did not relish, also fine ripe bananas and fresh water
in joints of bamboo as thick as a man's leg. These they reached up to
us but feared to come aboard, uncertain whether we were ghosts
or living men.

There was a sudden hoarse cheer from the soldiers when they
noticed two grown girls swimming well away from the canoes, and
behind them a cluster of perhaps twenty more: all mother-naked, with
slim waists and small, firm breasts, and not disfigured by tattoo marks,
except for a narrow blue ribbon on the fall of each shoulder. The
soldiers wildly waved their caps and shouted obscenities to which the
girls responded as though they understood what was said, and
made gestures of such lubricity that they would have inflamed the
passions of Saint Anthony himself. Don Alvaro soon put a stop to this
by-play; he told the Colonel to have two of the soldiers fastened
in the stocks; and then, forgetting in his indignation that he was
no longer on his estate at Guanaco, he abused the mermaids in the

language of Peru, threatening them with the lash and shaking his fist; after which he clapped his hands smartly and bade them be off. They turned and fled in a school, weeping for terror, and a long-drawn Ah! of disappointment broke from the crowd at the bulwarks.

The native warriors greeted our ladies in a very different fashion. They recognized them as women of a sort, but showed them no gallantry whatsoever. All they did was to point at them and laugh at their costumes, never in their lives having seen women wearing French hoods, starched ruffs and coloured clothes; their own were content, as we found later, with a short, plain skirt. It may also have been that they were surprised to see women afloat; their wives and daughters being forbidden so much as to rest their hands on a canoe.

Doña Ysabel flushed to the neck and said to Don Lorenzo: 'Pray, brother, order an arquebusier to load his piece with bird-shot and pepper the legs of these rude fellows. They must be taught a lesson in courtesy!' Don Alvaro, chancing to overhear this, intervened with great heat. 'Is this the way to carry the Cross among the heathen?' he cried to Don Lorenzo. 'Those are children of innocence! They laugh for affection, not insolence; and none of our ladies is under obligation to stay on deck if she feels offended in her modesty.'

She shrugged, sighed, and turned to her sister with a look that seemed to say: 'What is a woman to do when her husband is too devout to protect her honour?' Her brothers took the General's intervention very ill and gathered in a knot, talking in low voices, frowning and fidgeting with their sword-hilts.

Meanwhile the Boatswain, with jovial face and gentle words, had persuaded a native to touch the hull of the ship, by knocking on her side to show that she was solid and no illusion. With a little more coaxing he was persuaded to climb a rope and step on deck. This was a warrior of about thirty years of age, intricately tattooed, and wearing a beard of novel fashion: a strip had been shaved down the middle of his chin and the hair spread on either side in tresses threaded with dogs' teeth. He wore a tall head-dress made from the tail-feathers of a cock, a red flower over one ear, and an ivory disc with a spike stuck through the lobe of the other. I noticed that, like his fellows, he was circumcized. Soon he began to strut about the deck, juggling a couple of pointed sling-bolts with his left hand and twirling the sling, which was of plaited fibre, with the other, as if to show that he had no fear; though it was plain that we needed only to say Boh! and he would have leaped over the rails in terror.

The General, now seated in a chair over which a crimson cloth was spread, received him graciously, and handed me an old cambric shirt and a coachman's hat, with which I was ordered to clothe him. The Indian accepted these gifts with dignity, allowing me to button him in the shirt as though this were an everyday occurrence and, removing his head-dress, presented it to the General in exchange for the hat. When he jumped on the bulwarks and showed himself to his companions they laughed uproariously, but he did not lose his composure. He waved to them and shouted something in an urgent voice, as if to say: 'There are many fine things to be had here for the asking, and without danger.'

At this, some forty more clambered eagerly aboard and made us feel a stunted race by comparison: one warrior stood head and shoulders above Ensign Tomás de Ampuero, our tallest man, whom we had thought little less than a giant, and his feathered head-dress made him seem taller still. After some hesitation they began to walk about the main deck with great boldness, taking hold of whatever caught their fancy, but sentries had been posted to prevent them from swarming over the other decks. They appeared to be uncertain whether our soldiers were men like themselves, and kept peering closely into their faces and cautiously prodding their clothes with a finger.

One targeteer, to oblige them, opened his doublet and shirt and exposed his bare chest; another pulled down his stockings and rolled up his sleeves. Assured that we were human after all, they at once lost all fear and made themselves at home; indeed, it was as difficult to persuade them to go as it had been to coax them aboard. The General handed out a few more shirts and some toys, including a looking-glass which caused great awe and excitement; then the soldiers began to follow his example, but this proved to be a mistake. Our visitors called out loudly to their friends in the canoes to climb up too and collect their gifts.

'No, no, you greedy wretches!' cried the General, shooing them away. 'Be off with you all, quick! You have been well paid for your gifts. Boatswain, let no more come aboard!' He frowned at the natives, clapped his hands repeatedly and pointed at the canoes.

They laughed happily at his gestures but showed no signs of leaving us and took even greater liberties than before. Some of them invaded the cook-room, admired the pewter dishes and tried to steal them. The cook drove them out with a faggot, but not before they had snatched a flitch of bacon from a hook. Climbing into the long-boat with it, they cut off pieces with knives made from slivers of cane, which they stuffed into their mouths, laughing and chattering all the time.

Don Alvaro followed them there and spoke very severely, commanding them to hand over what was left of the bacon and leave the ship at once. When they continued to laugh and even thrust out their tongues at him he ordered a falconet to be fired with a blank charge. They watched the gunner ram his charge home and light the match, and flocked around him to see what new trick this might be; then the spark caught the powder and the piece went off with a roar, blackening their faces with smoke and filling their nostrils with its acrid stench. They leaped overboard with a great splash, frightened nearly out of their wits, like frogs disturbed by the pond-side.

Meanwhile some of the Indians in the canoes had made fast a finely laid cable to our bowsprit and bent another to the end of it, hoping to tow us to their harbour by vigorous use of their paddles; but when the falconet went off they abruptly let the ropes go. The only native now remaining in the ship was the boy whose angelic face had so moved the Chief Pilot. Having climbed into the bows by their cable, he was trying with a toothed club to knock a piece from the gilt scroll-work of the bowsprit pillow. This was reported to Don Diego who ran there, sword in hand, and shouted to him to be off; but the boy would not obey and clung to the harness-tables. Don Diego struck at him with his sword, wounding him severely in the hand, so that he cried out and dropped into the water. He was pulled into a canoe by a white-bearded man, profusely tattooed and wearing a shining disc of pearl shell on his forehead.

The old man showed indignation at the assault and paddled away to a larger canoe in which sat a stately warrior with beard and hair dyed in three different colours—white, red and blue—and carrying a sunshade of palm-leaves, who seemed to be their Chieftain. After much shouting all the canoes formed up in a half-circle about fifty paces away from us, while the old man glared at us fiercely, placed his hands to his chin, martially cocked his moustaches, and called on his companions to avenge the boy. At this they took their spears from the side-rests in the canoes, rose like one man and brandished them threateningly until they vibrated from butt to point. Others then loaded their slings and let fly a volley of bolts, while the rest paddled to within spear-throw, shouting discordant war-cries.

The Colonel, suddenly recovering his vigour in the face of the enemy, gave the order 'Present pieces!' in a firm voice, then 'Give fire!' Every man's arquebus was trained on the canoes; but the rain had wetted the powder and not a shot was heard. Meanwhile Sergeant Andrada had his front teeth knocked out by a sling-bolt and a number of spears whistled through the rigging or were warded off by the targeteers.

'Reload!' cried the Colonel, and pretty soon there was firing all along the bulwarks. The old man fell dead, the ornament at his forehead shattered by a well-aimed ball, and five or six more were killed, including the chieftain with the sunshade; several others were wounded.

In an instant all was confusion. Some of the savages leaped into the water; some tried to shelter behind their companions. The rest turned about and paddled away as fast as they could, with many collisions and much fouling of outriggers.

The General had watched the scene with despair. 'Ah, Don Diego, Don Diego!' he cried. 'Why did you wound that pretty boy?'

'To teach the imp manners,' Don Diego answered boldly, 'a lesson of which this insolent race stands in need. But, my lord, I think it exceedingly odd that you permitted them to insult my sisters. As you will have seen for yourself: give them a trotter, and they claim the whole sheep.'

The Vicar, who was too humble and unassuming to expect that the miracle of Tumbes would be repeated in his person, went to Don Alvaro. 'My son,' he said, 'I do not believe that these wild people are in a mood to receive the Cross. Let us sail on and leave them to ponder the moral of their greed and obstinacy. It may please Our Lord to fetch us this way again; but if not, there are souls a-plenty to save at the end of our journey.'

The General agreed with much sorrow, and though presently a canoe appeared with three old natives in it, one of whom waved a green branch and a white cloth in token of peace, he kept to his resolution. Gratefully accepting the coconuts which they brought, he declined their invitation to land.

We left La Magdalena in our wake, and soon sighted another island ten leagues to the N.N.W., which appeared to be smaller by two-thirds, with much forest and no high mountains; at its eastern end, not far from the shore, a large rock rose steeply from the sea. Because of the rock and in joint honour of the Colonel and the Chief Pilot, both of whom were called Pedro, Don Alvaro anticipated by a few days the feast of Saint Peter in Chains, and named our new discovery San Pedro. The Colonel expressed his thanks in flowery and well-chosen words, yet seemed offended that he was to share this glory with another. 'Let the Chief Pilot take the rock,' he said, 'and leave me the island.'

'I am content with that, my lord,' the Chief Pilot returned at once, as one who runs to strike back a tennis-ball, 'and may your lordship's barge never run against my rock!'

We passed San Pedro by, without so much as sending a boat ashore, having sighted two more islands five leagues to the north-west, separated by a narrow channel. The General named the smaller in honour of Saint Cristina, whose eve this was; the larger, more northerly, one he named Dominica, in honour of Saint Domingo, to whom he had made intercession at Lima. Both were beautiful isles with broad plains and high mountains and many plantations of fruit-trees, and they seemed thickly inhabited. Because Don Alvaro had undertaken to give the Viceroy's name to the first land of importance that we should discover, he called the whole group 'Las Islas Marquesas del Virrey Garcia Hurtado de Mendoza,' a resounding appellation soon shortened to its first three words.

Tacking on and off, we searched for a harbour on the coast of Dominica, which has a circumference of fifteen leagues, but did not find one. As we rounded its southernmost point, many canoes came to meet us, built in the same style as those of La Magdalena, and though their crews were darker-skinned, they too greeted us with cheerful laughter and kept their weapons in the rests. A herald stood in one canoe, waving a green branch and pointed to the land in invitation. We happened that moment to complete a tack and the ship was put about. The herald, thinking that we had rejected his overtures, looked offended and renewed his gestures with greater insistence, pacifically pulling down his moustaches, and making eloquent signs with his hands.

The General favoured his plea and told the Chief Pilot to launch the long-boat, first stowing in her bottom the tall wooden cross made by the carpenter that morning; but suddenly the wind freshened and since there was no headland behind which we could shelter, we sailed on, the herald yelling after us. The only close contact that our people made with those of Dominica was when the frigate, which had kept close inshore, was boarded by two natives who swam out to her. One of them was of huge stature and, seeming to despise the soldiers, roved the deck in search of a memento to take back with him. Nothing would satisfy him except Doña Ysabel's brindled calf, at which he gazed in wonder, there being no four-footed animals in the Marquesas Islands, except rats, pigs and small dogs. The calf was well grown and must have weighed nearly two hundredweight; yet he lifted it up by one ear and was about to carry it away when an arquebus was let off close to his ear. He fled empty-handed, whereas his companion had been given a sail-needle and, what caused him even greater pleasure, the Queen of Cups from an old pack of cards.

The common opinion of our soldiers was that these islands must be very fertile to breed such robust men and such graceful women, but were too small for our purpose. I heard Juan de la Isla, the merchant-venturer, remark to Don Alvaro: 'Your Excellency, this would suit me very well, if there were more elbow room; but when I remember that Pizarro's soldiers thought themselves ill-used if any of them was not awarded at least twenty-five thousand acres, I am glad that larger lands still lie before us.' He added, that since neither gold nor silver had been seen even among the Chieftain's ornaments, it might be concluded that none was to be had; and that we should spend no more time there than might be needed for taking on water and fire-wood, and whatever fresh fruit was to be found.

The General, whom the Chief Pilot had implored to grant the islanders the priceless gift of salvation, did not agree. He said that it would be greatly to our advantage, and to the King's, to plant a small settlement hereabouts, to be held as a base whither we could return if anything went amiss. The natives could be made amenable to Christian discipline, and with their help we might lay up a store of dry provisions and perhaps build a ship-yard, a rope-walk and a manufactory of sail-cloth; they were of a friendly disposition, quite unlike the warriors of the Isles of Solomon, who had greeted him everywhere with open hostility, and though these were good slings-men they seemed to have no knowledge of the bow. With this in mind he called the Colonel, who was now fairly recovered, and ordered him to go next day in the long-boat with twenty soldiers to find a harbour in Santa Cristina which could be used as a watering place; but not to permit them to use arms, unless they were provoked beyond reason.

Since the Chief Pilot was to be of the party, I asked and was given leave to accompany him.

Chapter 9

THE COLONEL SEEKS A HARBOUR

It was with some anxiety that I took my seat in the stern of the long-boat beside the Chief Pilot. The Colonel was in a wilful mood, and if he provoked the natives, a sling-bolt or a spear might kill me as effectually as any weapon of deadlier make. I had examined one of the spears flung aboard, which had passed through the skirt of the Chaplain's cassock and pinned him to the mizzenmast; it was tipped with the sharp spine of a sting-ray. As for the bolts, the spinning motion imparted to them by the sling made them travel point-foremost with sufficient force to spill a man's brains. I concealed my fears, however, and offered a silent prayer to my protectress, Our Lady Macarena of Seville.

Sailors of the Chief Pilot's watch rowed us towards the coast and when we came near enough to distinguish the faces of the islanders, who came running from all directions to gaze and shout, nine canoes appeared from the east and rapidly overhauled us. Their crews took up spears as soon as they saw us and circled around with cries of defiance; it may be that they had already been informed of the massacre at La Magdalena, which for such speedy craft was less than a day's sail away.

'Attention!' sang out the Colonel. 'Give fire when I raise my hat!'

In anticipation of such an encounter, the Chief Pilot had provided himself with a white kerchief; and now, not asking permission, he rose and waved it at the natives, who ceased yelling and laid their spears down. Happening to turn around, the Colonel saw the kerchief and in a grand passion asked Pedro Fernandez who, in the Devil's name, was commanding the expedition?

'None but yourself, my lord,' he replied. 'Yet I owe a duty to my unarmed crew, who must not be involved in needless fighting.'

'Drop that rag at once, sirrah, that badge of cowardice!' shouted the Colonel. 'These circumcized dogs have offered us force, and with force they shall be met. It would ill befit a son of Saint James to refuse a war-like challenge!'

He pushed his way down the boat, snatched the kerchief from the Chief Pilot's hand and flung it overboard then, standing insecurely on a thwart, supported by the sergeant, he gestured to the natives, cocking his grey moustaches and waving his sword above his head. 'Long live Saint James!' he cried ferociously.

They were surprised by our sudden change of front, but soon accommodated themselves to it. A tall, corpulent man with a white beard and sunshade, their Chieftain, shouted and brandished his spear fiercely in reply to the Colonel's threats; and thus the Devil was let loose. Sling-bolts rattled against the boat's side and the row of targes; the Colonel raised his hat; a volley rang out and seven natives fell dead. Of the rest, some leaped into the sea, while others paddled away at surprising speed. Among those who tried to save themselves by swimming was a man with a young boy in his arms, whose presence seemed to show that they had not sought us out with war-like intention; it is my belief that these natives were on their way home from the fisheries, because in the bottom of one canoe I caught sight of a seine-net glittering with small fish.

One of our soldiers, Sebastian Lejia by name, took careful aim at the man swimming on his back with the child held before him, and sent both down in a swirl of blood. I covered my eyes and crossed myself. The Chief Pilot jumped up in disgust. 'Who fired that shot?' he cried furiously.

'It was I,' answered Sebastian. Then, ashamed at what he had done, he lamely excused himself: 'Your honour must know that Hell receives those whom God has ordained to go there. Besides, I had my orders.'

With the Colonel's eye fixed balefully on him, Pedro Fernandez replied: 'A soldier must obey his orders, but since the man was in the water, why did you not fire above his head?'

'What? And lose my reputation as a marksman?' he asked.

'He had done you no harm,' said the Chief Pilot, 'yet with one shot you have robbed two precious souls of their chance of salvation. When you enter the gates of Hell, what advantage will it be that you can register yourself as a marksman? Our life on earth is brief; the life hereafter is eternal.'

'Beware of inciting my men!' growled the Colonel and went on to
declare that the soldier need have nothing on his conscience; God
loved frank dealing and straight shooting.

He then gave orders for the boat to follow the canoes into the
harbour where they had taken refuge. The Chief Pilot obeyed
grimly. As we rounded the headland, he took a shrewd look at the
anchorage and declared at once that it was not what Don Alvaro
had in mind.

'Are you saying this from a desire to quarrel with the Colonel?'
asked the Ensign-Royal, and pointed to a village in a green valley
facing us, as proof that the port was a good one.

Pedro Fernandez, keeping his patience, explained that the natives
possessed no anchors, but hauled their canoes ashore at the close of
every voyage; and that these, being of shallow draught, might go where
no galleon could follow. The rocks with which—as the Ensign-
Royal could himself see through the clear water—the bed of the harbour was strewn, offered no danger to canoe-men.

The Colonel grew very hot at what he called the Chief Pilot's
stubbornness, who in his turn showed his resentment so openly that
he was instructed to take us back at once to the *San Geronimo*,
where a double complaint would be lodged against him with the
General.

We returned in silence, not encountering any more canoes, and
Don Alvaro was called upon to mediate between the two angry
men; which he did judiciously enough. The Chief Pilot, he decided,
had been at fault both in displaying a flag of truce without the
Colonel's permission, and in correcting a soldier who had done no
more than his duty; however, to give his opinion on the safety of
an anchorage fell within his competence, provided he did not express
himself disrespectfully.

The Chief Pilot was not to be daunted. 'Is this a licence for the
shooting of little children?' he asked. 'Upon my soul, I never expected
to hear your Excellency condone so horrid a crime; nor do I care
who hears me say that plain murder was committed.'

'Choose your words with greater care,' said the General, 'lest you
force me to place you under restraint.'

'And would you place me too under restraint?' Doña Ysabel asked
from her seat at the window, speaking in her softest voice. 'I also
say that it was murder, Don Alvaro, and the Chief Pilot has shown
Catholic valour in refusing to countenance it.'

The General made a weak attempt at reconciliation, but neither party would budge from his views, and soon the Colonel left the Great Cabin with a slam of the door. When he reached his own quarters, a page informed him that he had nearly lost his little white bitch Carlotta; which made him angrier than before. While the whole ship's company had been watching the skirmish from the port bulwarks or shrouds, two canoes had approached unobserved from the starboard side and some impudent natives who, from their colour, were thought to be of La Magdalena, had climbed stealthily aboard to raid the deck. They stole a linstock, a sewing-basket, and a soldier's helmet, and might have escaped with their booty, had they not also tried to steal Carlotta. Now, the dogs of these islands, there called *au-au*, which resemble large rats with almost hairless hides and uncouth faces, never do more than whine or howl. When therefore one of the thieves unceremoniously picked up Carlotta by one ear to carry her off, and she bared her teeth and barked at him, they were dreadfully startled, jumped overboard with the linstock and the helmet, and escaped in their canoes before anyone could fire a shot at them. The Colonel took as a personal insult this attempt to kidnap the little creature, whom he had come to regard as his one true friend, and swore that it could be wiped out only with blood, and that he would never again leave her behind on a foray.

That evening Matia, Juarez and I discussed the day's happenings. I was able to do the junta certain small favours from time to time and had by now won their confidence.

Matia said, spitting into the sea: 'Sebastian's a mule; whatever that man does, he does it wrong. He had orders to fire but, missing the volley, he should then have saved his powder and shot. There's no sense in slaughter for slaughter's sake once the battle is over: show the enemy your strength but don't exasperate him. The Colonel would have given the son of a whore a good cursing, had the Chief Pilot not taken the words from his mouth. The day will come when Sebastian will wish he had that ball back in his pouch. I've known him for years now, patched pig that he is. He joined my company during the late troubles and the first time he set eyes on me he doffed his hat as if I were the Captain-General. "Could you, of your kindness, your honour, show me how to get a better shine on this breastplate?" he asked. "Why, yes, man," said I. "Soap it well, and then drop it into the bleaching tub." "My humble thanks," said he, "I'm anxious to be neat and carve myself a good career in the army."

But, Lord, it was the funniest sight of my life to see him soap that breastplate like a lady's shift; and afterwards he bleached it for three hours and hung it on a bush to dry.'

'Ay, he's a born fool,' said Juarez, turning to me, 'a priest's bastard if ever there was one. But thank God for fools; he brought a tidy package of coin with him from Lima, and three-quarters of it is already safe in our pockets. Only a simpleton like Sebastian would fancy himself as a pontoon-player; somehow, when he plays with us, his aces and court-cards fly off as if by witchcraft, and leave him all at sixes and sevens. . . . I wonder whether your honour has one more drop of that excellent Malvasia you asked us to sample last night? By the bread of God which He made in His own image and likeness, I never tasted better wine in my life!'

Next morning the Colonel was instructed to complete his mission and this time the Boatswain's mate with his watch took the party out. At Don Alvaro's request I went again, though with stronger foreboding than before. He had done me the honour of saying in private that I had a good pair of eyes in my head and would be more likely to render a faithful account of what I saw than either a soldier or a sailor, whose judgement might be warped by prejudice.

The Colonel led us back to the port which Pedro Fernandez had rejected, and we landed. How the ground seemed to quake under me, after the many weeks I had spent at sea, and how fresh and pungent came the island scents! Leaving three arquebusiers to guard the boat, the Colonel marched the remainder of his force up the beach and surrounded the village. This consisted of some forty narrow huts, spaced well apart, and thatched with palm-leaves, each hut being surrounded by a neat fence of canes and perched on a separate stone terrace. Large bamboo uprights, with wooden cross-pieces lashed to them, formed the frames; the roofs were less steeply pitched in front than at the rear, where they touched the ground; the doors, between carved posts, were very low and slid in grooves, but some huts had none, the whole front being open to the air. My eye was taken by a large decorated store-house, and an assembly-house fully fifty paces long.

The inhabitants laughed and chattered as though what we did were no concern of theirs, gazing at us with wonder and admiration; they reminded me of our peasants at home when army engineers come to a village and mark out an encampment. The Colonel posted piquets in the flanks and in the rear, and when the water-jars, which the sailors had carried up from the beach, were ranged in a neat row, he scratched a line behind them with the point of his stick. Then he clapped his hands and beckoned to the natives, who came shyly forward, men, women and children, to the number of about three hundred, and examined the jars with interest; they had never before seen pottery, all their vessels being of coconut-shell or gourds or wood. He made them a speech, with gesticulations several times repeated, to the effect that they must not pass across the line on pain of death, and that he required them to bring water to fill the jars.

They were a clean and friendly people; the foetid smell of unwashed bodies to which my nostrils had never wholly accustomed themselves in the forecastle and between-decks of the *San Geronimo*, was absent here. Their village was neat and well-kept, no rotting garbage littered the ground to breed flies, and many flowers and ornamental bushes had been planted about the huts. The elder women were tattooed from head to foot and I noticed several crones on whom the blue markings had faded to an ugly green; but the younger ones, like those of La Magdalena, had only narrow ribbons tattooed on their shoulders and three small dots on each lip, and were of a ravishing beauty. All wore short white skirts and, a few of them, flowing white cloaks as a protection against the sun, but shifts were unknown. They adorned their hair, cut short at the neck, with the fine scentless flowers which, because of their scarlet colour, we named 'cardinals.'

When the Colonel had finished speaking, the villagers ran off and presently fetched us coconut shells filled with water, emptying them into the jars; and large, intricately woven baskets heaped with delicious fruit, resembling apples, which they gave us to eat.

The soldiers were chagrined because the Colonel kept them from intercourse with the young women, who looked at them with dark, languishing eyes and tried to seduce them from duty. Their sergeant begged him to mollify them by recalling those sailors who had already yielded to temptation. He did so, and two or three who took their time about returning were afterwards soundly flogged by the Boat-swain's mate but thought this a slight price to pay for their pleasure. I heard one of them say, laughing: 'By the Virgin, our Pancha will have to get her corn in before the rains come. Once shore leave is granted, she'll be lucky to earn seven maravedis a week.' The girls were passionate and did all for love, unlike the mercenary women of Lima, whom they exceeded both in beauty and performance.

Several jars had been filled, a few cupfuls at a time, with much laughter and by-play, when the Colonel, growing impatient, ordered the natives to carry the remainder to the spring from which they fetched the water. Because of some superstition, they would not obey him: pretending to shiver, they made signs that we were to carry them there ourselves. The Colonel drew his sword and threatened them, whereupon they shouldered four jars and ran away, in the opposite direction, taking them to a hut with a high, steep roof, like an obelisk. We afterwards found this to be their temple, where offerings of food were made to an ill-carved idol with a bulbous nose and fat arms crossed upon his breast, who stood between two enormous wooden drums. I suppose that they carried the jars there to beg his permission to fill them at the spring, but the Colonel, seeing his order disobeyed, commanded a piquet to give fire. When the smoke cleared, we saw that one had dropped dead at the entrance to the temple and another was hit in the shoulder, the joint being shattered.

The villagers stood as if fastened to the ground, appalled by the noise of the volley and the screams of the wounded man; then, with one accord, they fled up the ravine like goats. By the time that the arquebuses had been recharged not a soul was to be seen, and the Colonel, laughing heartily, asked the Boatswain's mate to see that the jars, full or empty, were carried down to the boat.

He went to inspect the village, Carlotta barking at his heels. Being my own master, I followed his example and entered one of the huts, crawling in by the low door. When my eyes grew accustomed to the gloom, I saw that it contained neither stools, chests nor tables, but resembled a Peruvian slave barracks, except in its cleanliness. The front part was paved with smooth, flat stones, the back was taken up by a single long couch spread with dry grass and woven mats of varied patterns; a polished palm-log served for the head, another for the foot. From the roof hung parcels, wrapped in white cloth and secured by a line thrown over the ridge-pole; above the couch hung spears, javelins, clubs carved with human faces, and baskets of sling-bolts. I was loath to open any of the parcels or handle the weapons; these were savages, but enough injury had been done them already, without the addition of discourtesy. Moved by a sudden impulse, I untied the small crucifix which I wore around my neck and fastened it to a peg above the door, so that they should not be left with only evil memories of us.

In a small shed adjoining the hut, which served as a kitchen, I picked up a roll of *tutao* that had been baked to a rich golden colour; I tasted it and found it good, though somewhat tart. It seemed to me a food that would keep well and I took a piece of it away to show the General. Two hens, not unlike those of Spain, lay in a corner, their legs tied as if ready for the pot, and the fore-quarter of a black pig hung from a peg; but I found no evidence of cannibalism.

I went on to the assembly-house which, though much larger, otherwise closely resembled the hut I had just visited; here were gourds filled with a fermented liquor of agreeable taste. Next, I came to the store-house, raised on posts to keep out vermin; it contained a great heap of almonds, and piles of coconuts and turnip-like roots. Two emaciated old men, naked and completely bald, were dozing on mats at the entrance. They took no notice of me, being evidently senile, and I went away without disturbing them.

The Colonel found little to interest him in the village. He had gone to the temple, but seeing that the idol was adorned with neither jewels nor pearls and that the food offerings made him consisted of bread-porridge in plain wooden dishes, thought that this was a poor place, unworthy even of destruction. As he left he put the writhing native out of pain with a casual thrust of his sword, rallied the troops and, now that the water-jars had been dragged back to the boat and hauled aboard by the sailors, ordered us to re-embark. Carlotta's jaws were rosy with blood.

The noise of our volley had been heard on the flagship, and the General, fearing that we were in trouble, ordered the Chief Pilot to take the *San Geronimo* into the harbour at once; who though reluctant to obey because of the concealed rocks, could not dissuade him from his intention. With shortened sail and his most reliable man at the helm, he brought the ship in; but the wind died away under the land, a wave of unusual size caught us abeam and rolled us to within a lance's length of a sharp rock, with fifty fathoms of water close by. A yell of terror arose from all who saw the peril. Immediately the Chief Pilot let fall his foresail and it pleased God to send a breeze to fill it, so that the ship obeyed her helm again and stood off. Don Alvaro, convinced at last that the port was a bad one, ordered her to be put about, and was lucky to escape disaster; but the sailors blamed the Chief Pilot, declaring that he should have refused to hazard the ship, whatever his orders.

When we returned in the long-boat, the Boatswain's mate at once went to Don Alvaro and complained that his men were overworked, that they had been made to haul water-jars in addition to their labours at the oars, the soldiers not stirring a finger to help them, and that this was no way to treat seamen. Don Lorenzo took him up sharply, saying that the soldiers were excused all menial labour; since no natives were available, and since Don Alvaro had not taken advantage of the powers given him in his letters patent to bring out slaves for such purposes as these, the crew must see to the watering.

'Your Excellency,' expostulated the other, 'this is worse than the Egyptian bondage! My men have been on duty since dawn, they have broken their backs in hauling and heaving; and now their trick will be on them again before they have had time to breakfast or snatch a little sleep. Would to God, my father had apprenticed me to a tailor or a tinker! I warn your Excellency that no sailor will consent to haul water all day in this tropical heat, while soldiers take their ease in the shade.'

Don Alvaro was grieved. 'Friend Damian,' he said gently, 'every man to his trade. Surely, the soldiers' first duty was to guard you, and had they failed in this——'

But he would not be cozened by fine words. 'If it was their duty to kill unarmed men, who brought gifts and were ready to help us—if it was their duty to make the entire island hate us—then they have performed it to admiration. Now I've said my say, and I trust that your Excellency will forgive my rough speech; when I see injustice done, I denounce it.'

'Your feelings do you credit, my friend,' Don Alvaro answered soothingly, 'and I shall look for a remedy. But since it appears that the natives are disinclined to fetch or carry for us, except under threat of fire-arms——'

'You will pardon me again: one volley, and they fly screaming to the highest crag of their mountains, whence it would take a small army to dislodge them.'

'Well, then, since they cannot be persuaded even by force, we must sail on without fresh water or fire-wood. What we have left will suffice for the next few days.'

The Chief Pilot interposed with some heat. We had still some five hundred leagues to travel, which was well-nigh the width of the Atlantic Ocean from Spain to the Brazils; should the wind fail us, or should we be blown off our course by a hurricane, lack of water might undo us. Barely enough for a fortnight remained in the *San Geronimo* and, as for fire-wood, the soldiers were already chipping pieces from the upper works of the ship and the sergeants either could not or would not discover the culprits.

Don Alvaro spread out his hands in a gesture of helplessness: 'But, man,' he exclaimed, 'what are we to do if we cannot find a port?'

'Let us return to La Magdalena,' said the Chief Pilot, 'and take shelter behind the headland where the frigate anchored. I believe that if we treat the natives kindly, and do nothing more to exasperate them, they will gladly bring water in bamboo joints to the ship itself —the canoes we saw could have supplied the whole flotilla in one day, given the will. They are now aware that we can deal death at a distance; their last act was to send a flag of truce with an invitation to land. We might also persuade them to tow out logs suitable for burning.'

'I will not revisit La Magdalena!' he replied obstinately. 'I have sworn never to go back on my course until we reach the Isles.'

'Then why can we not search for another anchorage in this island?' the Chief Pilot demanded. 'Yesterday I warned the Colonel that the harbour he found was not suited to your purpose, yet back he must go to prove himself right and nearly lose us the galleon!'

'It would be better, my lord,' Don Lorenzo broke in, 'if you sent me instead of the Colonel. He has twice failed us now because he despises the Pilot's judgement.'

Don Alvaro was timid. 'Alas,' he said, 'while he obeys my orders, I dare do nothing to hurt his pride. He is a man quick to take offence and the common soldiers respect him.'

In effect, the Colonel went out once more, this time taking the Boatswain's watch; and within the hour they had entered a wide bay of horse-shoe shape, which the Boatswain pronounced a safe anchorage, spacious enough to shelter the whole flotilla. He found a bottom of sand at thirty fathoms near the entrance, in the middle at twenty-four, and at twelve close to the shore. This bay, which we called after the Blessed Mother of God—her name be praised!—lies in nine degrees, thirty minutes below the Equator, sheltered from all winds except the west, which does not, however, blow here. It is recognized from the sea by a steep, triple-peaked hill rising to the south, and by an overhanging cliff to northward. Wooded ravines converge towards the harbour and a smaller hill divides the beach into equal parts; from the northern side of this gushes a spring of good water, as thick as a man's arm, at a handy height for the filling of jars. Near by, a stream of equally good water flows past a village built on two sides of a square, backed by a plantation of tall trees.

Chapter 10

THE CROSS IN SANTA CRISTINA

After breakfast on the next day, the 29th of July, two companies of soldiers having already landed and taken up positions around the village, the rest of us went ashore with the General and Doña Ysabel, leaving only twenty men to guard the flotilla. We knelt down in rows on the beach, our faces to the east. Presently we heard the sound of singing. It was *Vexilla Regis prodeunt*, and along came the priests clad in rich vestments and bearing the elements of the Blessed Sacrament in a monstrance under a brocaded canopy; their acolytes were pages, two of whom swung censers while another displayed a silken banner painted with the likeness of the Mother of God. Myn, who had pleaded for this honour, led the procession, struggling under the weight of a wooden cross three times his height.

That morning, the Colonel had been instructed to land under a flag of truce and present the leading villagers with cloth and beads. The natives took courage from his kindness and, when they saw us performing an act of worship, participated in it from natural courtesy. Falling on their knees, their men in a row with our men, their women with ours, they showed respectful sobriety; and did exactly as we did, even to making the sign of the cross and singing ah! ah! in tune with the psalm. A native girl, who knelt on the right hand of Doña Ysabel, had such fine red hair that she wished to snip off a few locks as a keepsake, and stealthily drew a pair of scissors from her purse; but the girl cried out in alarm, so she desisted. The girl slipped away and was not seen again. It may be that her hair was dyed, or bleached with lime.

Mass being over, the same pious procession followed the Cross to the top of the knoll whence the spring flowed, Don Alvaro and his suite walking behind in order of precedence. It had been the General's intention that each officer's wife should accompany her husband, but since the presence of the Admiral made this undesirable, Doña Ysabel and the other ladies remained on the beach. When the procession reached the summit, a deep hole was dug in the turf, and Don Alvaro solemnly lowered the Cross into it.

Lifting his hand for silence, he declaimed in a high voice: 'Be witnesses the skies, the earth, the waters, with all the creatures that in them dwell, and all men and women here assembled, that in these islands hitherto hidden from Christian man, I, Alvaro de Mendaña y Castro, do now plant the Cross of Our Lord Jesus Christ, on which He gave His life in ransom for the whole human race, calling upon His name, the name of the Most Holy Trinity and that of the Blessed Virgin Mary! And on this day, the Feast of Saint Martha, in the year of Our Lord 1595, being present as witnesses all the military and naval officers, besides many noble ladies, I add this island, with its several sister islands, to the dominions of Christendom; with the solemn intent that every inhabitant of these parts shall in due process of time have the Word of God preached to him zealously and clearly.'

He then called for the Standard, which was in the keeping of Don Toribio de Bedeterra, the Ensign-Royal, and planting it beside the Cross, he continued: 'Be witnesses, furthermore, all lords and ladies here assembled, that I seize this island, now christened Santa Cristina, with its several sister islands, and take possession of them in the name of our sovereign lord Philip II of Castile, King of the Spains, to be part and parcel of his possessions in these South Seas, and to remain for all time his inheritance and that of his princely successors!'

A breeze caught the folds of the Standard, exposing the royal arms to full view, and we raised a resounding cheer. Our musicians struck up a lively march, to which the savages, who had advanced up the knoll as far as the guards would permit them, kept time with beating of drums and clapping of hands; and even imitated the tune on outlandish musical instruments of their own, such as single-stringed bows, jew's harps, flutes played with both the mouth and the nose, and wooden trumpets.

The General dismissed the troops and went down to the village, which differed little from the other that I had inspected, but had two well-paved streets and, standing a little apart, a tall-roofed building, protected by palisades, where an oracle was housed. He visited the assembly-house, where the Chieftain waited to receive him, squatting on his haunches at the entrance and flanked by aged councillors. This person won my admiration by his expression of perfect composure, inclined to severity; when Don Alvaro came up he did not move a muscle of his tattooed face, but scrutinized him with a steady gaze. He wore a head-dress of cock-feathers and drooping golden plumes; a heavy, tasselled kilt of dark-brown cloth; a wooden ruff encrusted with bright red seeds; two necklaces of large boars' tusks; anklets and bracelets made from the white beards of old men plaited on coconut fibre; and ear-rings of whales' teeth. His right hand grasped a tall carved paddle sharpened at one end for use as a spear.

When ceremoniously presented with a clasp-knife and a red cotton kerchief which bore the legend 'I serve King Philip,' he accepted these with a scarcely perceptible nod, neither deigning to examine them, nor expressing any sign of pleasure, and motioned to one of the councillors to lay them by. Then he asked many questions in a staccato voice, which the General was unable to answer, and having rewarded him with a carved whale's tooth, waved towards the huts, as if to say: 'This is your village, my lord.' He rose and entered the house, to signify that the audience was at an end; but one of his servants fetched a fine black pig for the General's dinner.

Seeing a garden not far off, from which a crop of roots had just been cleared, Don Alvaro walked over to it and, in the presence of the villagers, sowed three rows of maize seed; assuring them by signs that, if the plot were fenced against hogs and fowls, these would grow into strong plants and yield a hundredfold. They understood, smiled, rubbed their stomachs, and repeatedly cried *kai-kai*, which is their word for food.

So far, all had gone well; but the news of his intention to colonize this island with about thirty married settlers travelled from mouth to mouth and exasperated those whom it concerned. 'We didn't come to colonize this poor country,' they said. 'We volunteered for service in the Isles of Solomon; they and they only will satisfy us. The General means to abandon us here, so that when he reaches his goal he needn't part with the estates promised us, but can keep them for himself.'

While Don Alvaro was looking around for objects of interest, the Admiral approached him courteously to whisper something in his ear; but appeared by no means satisfied with the halting reply that he got. He turned on his heel, strode angrily back to the beach and, neither doffing his hat to the General's lady, nor granting Doña

Mariana even the solace of a smile, stepped at once into his skiff and was rowed to the *Santa Ysabel*. Those who stood by conjectured that a land now having been reached which was thought suitable for settling, he had asked that his wife might join him, but been met with either an evasion or a downright refusal.

Distressed by the Admiral's unseemly conduct, Don Alvaro retired to the flagship with such of the sailors as were now wanted for duty, leaving the ladies on the beach to eat their dinner of fruit and fried pork in the shade of leaning palm-trees. He instructed the Colonel that the water-casks were to be filled and several boatloads of fire-wood collected, but without compelling the assistance of the natives by either threats or force: if they could not be persuaded by gifts, our people must do the work—sailors and settlers first, then such of the soldiers as could be spared. The crew of the galeot might be exempted, because they were cutting and shaping timber for her repair; on the previous day she had fouled the bowsprit of the *San Geronimo*, and showed a ragged hole below the starboard rails.

Being assigned the task of setting down the General's speech for the archives of the Indies Council, I accompanied him aboard; but while he dictated to me in the Great Cabin, several shots rang out from the shore. I laid down my pen and looked at him enquiringly, in the expectation that he would return at once to prevent further bloodshed. But 'It is nothing,' he said uneasily, 'there cannot be a quarrel. Our people are only displaying their marksmanship. . . . I repeat: "with its several sister islands, and take possession of them . . ."'

He deceived himself, as usual, and I sighed for the poor Indians: besides stray shots, at least three volleys had been fired. Going ashore that evening, I found that a conflict had arisen between the soldiers and the natives, and the village was now quite empty. The trouble had begun when, tired of watching the casks being filled at the spring, the Colonel had gone off to a near-by grove, escorted by his negro, 'to pay a call on the fair ladies,' as he said, and left Don Luis Moran in command. The Major presented a pair of shears to a tall native named Terridiri, who was distinguished from all the rest by a green palm-branch worn upright on his brow, and by the long spear he carried, at the top of which a carved shark's head grinned with real teeth. The gift was made in the understanding that Terridiri, who had been seen to issue from the oracle-house and was evidently its priest, would make the villagers roll the full casks down to the beach and

help in the hauling away of whatever trees we might fell. He accepted
the present with an air of complaisance, whispered something to the
shark's head and, pretending to listen for a response, conferred a blessing on us; then he hung the shears across his breast by a cord of
plaited hair, and strolled away. His people were reminded of the
honour done to him, and urged to set about their task; but shrugged
their shoulders, smiled, and stayed where they were, importunately
holding out their hands.

The Major shook his head. 'Uai!' he said—this word, meaning
'water,' being the only one that he had learned—and pointed to the
casks. 'Uai,' they echoed genially, pretending not to understand
what he expected of them. At a loss how to proceed, since he might
not use force, he told his adjutant, Captain Diego de Vera, that he
must persuade the savages to fulfil their part of the bargain. When
one of them conveyed to the Captain in sign-language that Terridiri
had accepted the shears in payment for the blessing which the shark
conferred on the casks, he in turn made signs to the effect that this
was to no purpose: since they would not help us, they must return
the shears. He then sent two targeteers after the priest, who was no
longer to be found.

Our drummer beat a tattoo, and Captain de Vera announced in a
fierce voice and with much gesticulation that he needed the shears
at once; but what was everyone's business was no one's business,
and there the matter rested. Had I been in his place, I should have
taken my complaint to the Chieftain; but the Captain was a man of
little patience. Seizing a young boy whose richly carved adornments
and delicate skin showed him to be the son of some notable, he
bound him tightly to a tree (which made the child cry out for fear)
and offered to release him when the shears were handed back, but
not before. At this a warrior who stood near reached for his spear
and brandished it indignantly. The impetuous Captain roared out:
'Shoot that man!' and he fell dead, struck by three balls. The natives
ran to arms and battle was joined.

A sling-bolt hit the Major's scabbard, whereupon he hurried back
to the beach, shouting to all who cared to listen that he must retire
and protect the ladies. He left Don Lorenzo and Captain Corzo in
a hot dispute as to which of them should command the troops; for
Don Lorenzo was the senior captain of the flagship, but Don Felipe
held an independent command. Before the two could come to blows,
or involve others in their quarrel, the Colonel came running out of

the grove, incensed by this interruption of his gallantries. According to Matia, he was waving his sword, and at the same time fastening the points of his hose with the left hand. He pricked a native in the thigh, and his negro split the skull of another with his axe. One more volley was fired and the villagers fled, followed by our men who killed no less than seventy of them, including women and children, before they could take shelter in the dense woods. The Colonel pressed the pursuit almost to the mountain summits, where they entrenched themselves. Our people suffered no casualties, except that one soldier was lightly wounded in the foot by a barbed wooden spear; but it proved not to be poisoned and he could walk again within a week.

The work of watering and collecting wood continued; but the sailors grumbled ceaselessly at being deprived of native labour by the quarrelsomeness of the troops, who were now guarding the village against attack and offered no assistance. 'If these natives had fire-arms,' the Boatswain's mate said scornfully, 'or even poisoned arrows, such precautions might be needed; but, though strong and virile, they only play at war.' He added that these piquets were posted merely to excuse the soldiers' sloth.

During the next two days the villagers remained in their entrenchments, occasionally making the valleys echo with loud halloos, as if to discover whether we were still ashore; our people answered them with shouts. On the third day they sent down an embassy of old men, who brought presents of bananas and paw-paws to our advanced piquets and signed that they wished to forget what had passed, and be friends again. In proof of their sincerity they handed back the shears, and the Colonel, who was fetched to confer with them, thereupon granted them full pardon. 'It pains me,' he said, 'to think of you old fellows lying up there matless on the hard mountain top, and your pretty grand-daughters parted from their wardrobes. Come, men, be sensible, and accept the benignant sovereignty of King Philip.'

They went back to report their kind reception to the Chieftain, who soon afterwards led his tribe down to the outskirts of the village. When informed that the General was in the flagship and could not come, he agreed to treat with the Colonel instead. He was understood to ask why we did not accept his gift of the huts, which had been vacated for us with all their contents.

The Colonel wagged his forefinger at him merrily, and replied that we would take nothing from his people but food, drink and kisses, if they in turn were careful to take nothing of greater value from us; but whether the Chieftain understood this is not known, because the stern cast of his features never relaxed.

The truce was ratified by another exchange of gifts and the villagers returned to their huts as if no breach of the peace had occurred, but we could see that they held us in great awe. They brought their dead with them on litters, and from the lacerated cheeks and breasts of the women I judged that the halloos we heard had been part of the mourning ceremonies. The corpses' bowels were already removed and the skin punctured in many places to drain off the waters of the belly; old women now laid them in the sun and rubbed them with coconut oil for an Egyptian embalmment. In a dense wood, not far from the entrenchments, our soldiers had found a cemetery where coffins containing naked mummies were tied to the branches of trees.

'They are tamed for the present,' boasted the Colonel, 'but it might be well to remind them from time to time of their new allegiance.'

Our people now fraternized with the natives and took comrades with whom they exchanged gifts and conversation. They asked each other by signs the names of the earth, the sea, the sky, the sun, the moon and stars, and everything else within view; but the soldiers were instructed not to let any villager touch an arquebus or learn how to discharge it, lest he made perfidious use of the knowledge. The Chaplain had the shark-priest for his comrade, and intervened on his behalf when soldiers stole a joint of roast pork from the oracle-house: Christians being forbidden to eat meat that has been offered to an idol. These two took pleasure in each other's company and the Chaplain taught Terridiri, who had a wonderfully keen ear and a retentive memory, to repeat the Credo and Paternoster, and covered his nakedness with an old shirt; yet could not persuade him to relinquish his shark-spear.

He told the good Father that when men die they descend to a hell of three storeys, the lowest miserable in the extreme, the middle one tolerable, the uppermost exceedingly pleasant. Admission to the uppermost, he said, is secured either by death in battle, or by the sacrifice of a great many pigs. He also described a glorious heaven above the stars to which the souls of chieftains go to feast with their gods. In vain did Father Antonio try to undeceive Terridiri, by telling him of the true Hell and the true Heaven and insisting, with much emotion, that only the Cross could save from eternal fire: he smiled and said that the shark's head told him otherwise, and the

good Father, who had hoped to make a convert of him, was deeply
grieved by his obstinacy.

Terridiri asked leave to go aboard the flagship and speak to the
General, and this was granted. The Chaplain led him to the skiff,
which he entered with great satisfaction. Don Alvaro received him
cordially, offering him quince-conserve and wine; but he would neither
eat nor drink, because his idol forbade him. He admired the cows
and sheep, counted the sails, tapped and smelt the wood of the masts,
went below and noted everything with a care that we found surprising in a savage; and at last persuaded the shark's head to confer a
blessing on the *San Geronimo* which, he said, would now weather the
most violent storms and never sink or run aground. When he heard
that we were not to remain long in the harbour, he appeared downcast
and regretted that his duties at the oracle-house prevented him from
joining us. Terridiri was so grave and ecclesiastical in bearing, and so
closely resembled a certain canon of Seville, that I could not resist
a laugh: I saw him in my mind's eye, spear in hand and necklace
a-jingle, mounting into the pulpit of the Cathedral to preach a learned
sermon on the Fall.

It was the custom in this island that young girls were free to lie
with whomever they pleased, and our people took full advantage of
this. Only the married women, who were tattooed as lavishly as the
men, remained faithful to their husbands; but, as we learned to our
disgust, every one of them acknowledged at least two husbands who,
though abstaining from mutual jealousy, would combine to take
revenge on any lover that she might entertain without their knowledge. With such hospitality shown them, our troops should have
refrained from the least abuse; but the officers set a bloody example.
I was in the Great Cabin one morning, when Captain Corzo entered,
his greyhound on a leash, to report on the repairs to the *San Felipe*.
Afterwards he remarked to Don Alvaro that his hound was in fine
condition: he had gorged himself on the spoils of the first massacre.
'But this supply having come to an end,' he said, 'I went foraging
last night when my company was on guard, and now the larder is
replenished.'

'Ay, Don Felipe,' exclaimed the General, not wishing to understand the Captain's odious meaning, lest he should be obliged to
reprove him, 'it is well for a hound to gnaw a fresh bone now and
then; but I trust you recompensed the owner of the pig with some
gift of value?'

The Barretos sneered when they heard the tale and thereafter did as they pleased. The next day, Don Diego was in command of the standing guard in the flagship, when two canoes, carrying eleven natives, entered the harbour from the south. He told the soldiers to make no answer if they were hailed, but to light their matches and keep their pieces primed. The canoes stopped at some distance from the ship and the natives shouted and held up gifts of coconuts. Receiving no reply, they trustfully came nearer, and when they were at point-blank range Don Diego gave the order to fire. Two fell dead, the others turned to flee, but three more were killed as they paddled swiftly past the galleon on their way to the shore. Don Diego jumped into the skiff to give chase, and only three unwounded men reached the beach by swimming, whence they ran to the top of the triple-peaked hill. He seized the canoes, with one or two dead bodies in them, the rest having fallen in the sea, and went back to report that he had beaten off an attempt to surprise and take the *San Geronimo*. Don Alvaro was fain to believe this lie and delivered the bodies to the Colonel with orders to display them at the corner of the village street, as a demonstration of what savages might expect who attacked Spaniards treacherously.

When I went ashore it pained me to see the corpses hanging from the eaves of a house, because I knew too well on which side treachery lay: not one of the murdered men had carried arms. However, it would have been idle to give the General a truthful account of the skirmish: even if my word had been accepted before Don Diego's, a reprimand would have provoked him to even greater wickedness. My indignation increased when the Major offered his fulsome congratulations on the victory, swearing that these ugly shot-wounds would make a wholesome impression on the villagers, and so would wide gashes made by swords. He drew his own blade as he spoke, and hacked at one of the bodies, that of a large-limbed warrior; then he borrowed a lance and, charging from a little distance, transfixed its belly—'so hares may pull dead lions by the beard,' I reminded myself.

The natives came silently at night, cut down the corpses and took them away.

Our people had now occupied several huts in the neighbourhood of the spring; one served as guard-room; a second was used by the Colonel's faction; a third by Don Lorenzo's; a fourth by sailors who did the watering; and others by officers of the *Santa Ysabel* and the two smaller vessels. The Chief Pilot, scandalized by the killing of the natives, did not go ashore once while we lay off Santa Cristina; no advantage would be served if he fell foul of the Colonel, as might well happen.

His disgust at the cruel and unceasing slaughter was shared by our ship's officers. The Boatswain sat in the sailors' hut one morning when our gigantic Ensign, Don Tomás de Ampuero, entered and seeing an arquebus leaning against the wall, asked: 'What is this, friend Marcos?'

'Since the attack on the flagship,' the Boatswain answered, 'if such it was, the General has ordered me to take a weapon with me whenever I go ashore.'

'Is it charged?' asked the Ensign.

'There is no need,' he replied.

'Man, what sense is there in carrying an empty arquebus with you? Let me charge it.'

He took the piece and loaded it with powder and ball; then he reached for the Boatswain's tinder-box, struck a light, kindled the match and went to the entrance of the hut, idly aiming at a man some fifty paces away who, mounted on a wooden trestle, was engaged in scraping a coconut. He would have shot him, too, had not the Boatswain knocked the arquebus up just in time. The ball flew into a palm-tree and happened to cut down a couple of coconuts, which fell to the ground. The villagers cried out in wonder at this feat, not knowing that it had been accidental, and begged Don Tomás to shoot down a few more.

'What were you doing, your honour?' asked the Boatswain with indignation.

'Why, killing of course!' replied Don Tomás. 'I was diligently following the example of my seniors.'

'How can you be so ready to spill blood?' Don Marcos continued. 'What harm have these people done you? It is no proof of valour to play the wolf among lambs. Have you never learned what a foul and sinful thing it is to murder a body that houses a yet unredeemed soul? One day you will be taught that lesson; but by then repentance will have come too late.'

The Ensign was offended by this reproof and cried rudely: 'Baseborn sailor! Scum of Barcelona! Who made you a guardian of my conscience? Have a care, lest one day you lose your teeth or your tongue!'

'Have you never been told,' the Boatswain returned, 'that it is the duty of every Catholic, however humble, to reprove sin when he sees it, even in a person with more quarterings on his coat and a better education than you have to show?'

These words ended their friendship, and Jaume the water-steward who was present, said: 'There goes one who murdered flies when a child, and frogs and kittens when a boy; to my knowledge, he has already dropped half a dozen natives from sheer wantonness. This island is an earthly paradise where man, as you may see by his nakedness and ignorance of shame, has escaped the curse of Adam. He need not toil, because the soil yields in abundance and the climate is kind. I for one would be content to spend the remainder of my life among these happy people, if there were a priest at hand to confess me when I came to die and give me Christian burial. How can the Ensign bring himself to do murder in Eden? He should be locked up in a mad-house and whipped until his evil spirits fly howling away.'

Jaume spoke to the point: apart from the labour of kindling a fire by the brisk ploughing of a hard stick along the groove of a piece of tinder, or the hollowing out of canoes with adzes made of shell, no work demanding exertion was needed. Water flowed from a perpetual spring. Food hung from every tree; and not only fruit and nuts, but even bread: in the plantation behind the village grew hundreds of these bread-trees, as we called them. They have toothed leaves resembling those of the paw-paw, and the timber is admirable for all purposes. The fruit which, we were told, hangs on the tree for fully half the year, is a clear green when ripe, and the size of a boy's hand, not quite round, with crossed scales like a pineapple; a leafy stalk springs from its very centre. It has neither core nor pips, and almost every part of it is edible. The villagers cooked this fruit, which they called 'white food,' in a variety of ways and found it sustaining. The commonest was to roast it on the embers of a fire, peeling off the charred rind, before they cut it into quarters for the table. A great quantity of bread-fruit was harvested when the season was at its height, and they were pounded into the sour dough called *tutao*. Close to every hut was a leaf-lined pit filled to the brim with this substance, which was said to stay wholesome for many years; and we found a great pit common to the whole village, fully twenty feet deep—their provision against bad seasons.

I proposed to Don Alvaro that it might be well to buy a ton or more of this dough from the Chieftain, paying him with toys, cloth and

glass bottles, and to bake some of it into the golden cake which I had
shown him; the rest could be made into dumplings. He would not
listen to my suggestion, complaining that it was not Christian food
and that the troops were certain to scorn it; however, I invested a
set of brass buttons in the purchase of cake for my own use, and
stored it in a sea-chest which I had bought at the sale of Miguel
Llano's effects. The only provision that we did take away was almonds;
these were of moderate size, very oily, with an unjointed shell and a
loose kernel. Each man bought his own supply, some with gifts,
others with threats, according to his character.

The food most sought after by our people was pork with roasted
chestnuts, but they also took pleasure in sucking the sweet juice of the
sugar-cane. The chestnuts were the size of six Spanish ones, with
much the same prickly shell and a similar taste; the pork had a good
flavour, but only seven or eight hogs were brought for us to eat. The
breed was black and fierce, with coarse, grizzled hair, and not confined in styes, but tethered by a hind-leg to a tree. When the assault
was made on the village, the Chieftain had given orders that all pigs
should be set at liberty lest they fell into our hands. We were now
told that the noise of fire-arms had frightened them across the mountain; but the villagers could doubtless have recaptured many more,
had they been so minded. Some of our soldiers who went hog-hunting
one day, found the woods too thick for sport and came back empty-
handed. The natives had this manner of roasting a hog: they flayed,
singed and disembowelled him, and wrapped his carcase in a blanket
of green palm-leaves; being laid in a pit half-filled with red-hot stones,
he was then covered with layers of leaves and a mound of earth and
left until his flesh was tender in every part. Gourds and the turnip-
like roots which I had found in the store-house were roasted in the
same way.

On the beach outside the village, hauled up on wooden rollers, I
saw six long, well-made canoes. Each was hollowed from a single
bread-tree, with the addition of bow and stern pieces and a keel; they
were decked at each end, the planks being caulked with fibre and
pitched with gum. One of them measured thirty paces from end to
end, having a sixty-foot mast and seats for forty men, and all its parts
were securely lashed together with woven cord; I judged its draught
to be close on half a fathom. The outrigger was connected to the
canoe by planks, which served as a deck for storing food and trade
goods. I was given to understand that the islanders made long

voyages in these craft, visiting lands to the south and to the west, and were often away two months or longer; but when I enquired of my native comrade—for I had a comrade too, who had gone to sea in one of these vessels—whether they ever traded with a black, bushy-haired race of archers, he confessed ignorance that any such people existed; from which I concluded that we were still far from our goal. Myn, on the other hand, was told that frequent expeditions were made to the south, where battles were fought against black men who shot arrows; but this may have been said only to please him.

The health, vigour and friendliness of the Marquesan natives are proof that their climate must be very wholesome; we saw neither invalids, cripples, nor hunchbacks. The days were hot, the nights cool, but dewless—indeed, wet clothes left all night in the open were dry before morning; though I do not know whether this would be the case all the year round. Our Spanish climate being less lenient, as is well known, breeds men of a sterner sort: jealous, proud, suspicious, accustomed to labour and hardship, each man keeping one hand on his purse, the other on his weapon. When these people showed us kindness, we suspected them of perfidy; when they came for gifts and we withheld them, they thought ill of us, being themselves always ready to give us all they had; when we asked them to toil for us they declined, because that was not their custom.

The longer we remained among them, the worse grew the cruelty of our troops, who killed either as a demonstration against the General's plan to settle the islands, or for mere sport. The natives were cowed and, though they ceased to run away at the sound of shots, obeyed their Chieftain's order not to attempt revenge by use of arms. They kept out of our way as much as they dared, taking refuge in their part of the village, which the Colonel had placed out of bounds; but it would have wrung the heart of any man of feeling to see the grief which they displayed at the daily murder of their kinsfolk. The girls, who had been so ready to lie with our people, went about swollen-eyed and scarred by their own finger-nails, in no humour to think of love; so that, except for those who had been established in the huts now occupied by the officers and kept there against their will, none was to be had even by the lure of beads or mirrors. I do not know that any soldier was dishonourable enough to murder the native who was his comrade, yet for spite some murdered the comrades of others. In all, about two hundred islanders were killed before we sailed, and the most notorious of the killers was Sergeant Luis Andrada.

On the 4th of August, the galeot now being repaired and sufficient fire-wood and water shipped to satisfy Don Alvaro—though the Chief Pilot demanded more—the high officers were informed that next day we should weigh anchor; but this was to remain a secret from their men until the last. The news leaked out, however, and the troops took their final pleasures, not baulking at rape, sodomy and other enormities, until they were recalled and confined on board. At dawn, a party was sent to the top of the triple-peaked hill, there to erect three wooden crosses, visible from the sea. They were to cut another cross on the smooth bark of a tree, with the year, day, and the names of our four vessels; but Don Lorenzo, who was charged with this task, omitted the *Santa Ysabel* from the inscription because of the hatred he bore the Admiral.

As they returned, one Miguel Cierva, an unmarried settler, who had gambled away all he possessed and pledged himself deeply with notes of hand, straggled from the party and was not seen again. He was a smith by trade and a man of some piety. His desertion seems to have been unpremeditated—for he carried only his arquebus, powder and ball—a sudden act of desperation to be repented day and night when once he found himself alone. I have often wondered how he fared after our departure: whether the natives revenged themselves on him for their injuries; and whether, if they spared him, he found metal for working at his trade; and what he taught the natives; and, above all, how he managed to live without the comforts of religion.

We sailed immediately upon the return of Don Lorenzo's party. The villagers lined the beaches, watching us in silence, not knowing whether we meant to return, because we had not told them of our intentions. I was bitterly ashamed of all that had been done and left undone, and that night poured out my heart to the Chief Pilot. 'Ay,' said he, 'were I a Spaniard I should now be ashamed of the name, as often in the East Indies I was ashamed to own myself a Portuguese. In years to come when other ships touch at these islands, they can expect no friendly welcome and the message of God's love that might have been conveyed to willing ears will be rejected with scorn and hatred. I shall leave it to the doctors of theology to argue which is the greater sinner: he who licences crime, he who commits crime, or he who turns his back on crime when he has the power to prevent it. But of this I am assured: that for the necks of those who have sinned against these innocents a millstone is prepared that will sink them to the unplumbed bottom of the abyss.'

It was my opinion that had the General kept firm control of the troops from the start, there would have been no need for any bloodshed, and we could have made noble use of our stay, both in our own interests and in those of God. But Don Alvaro shut his eyes and stopped his ears to murder, and the Vicar held that since we were to resume our voyage so soon as the galeot was repaired, he should not attempt to convert any islanders at all. It had been his experience in the interior of Peru, he declared, that to impart the rudiments of Christian doctrine to the wild Indians and then pass on, was far worse than to leave them in ignorance: they would mix the true faith with their own superstitions and breed blasphemous new heresies, and having no priest to hear their confessions, would go astray like sheep without a shepherd. I did not presume to contradict Father Juan, who was a man of great knowledge as well as piety; but I grieved that so good a people should be lightly abandoned to their error.

Chapter 11

SAN BERNARDO AND THE
SOLITARY ISLE

When we were four days out from Santa Cristina, Don Alvaro announced at the common table that we could now expect to sight the Isles of Solomon at any hour. The Chief Pilot gasped and stiffened in his seat, but did not contradict him. As soon as the meal was ended, however, he drew Don Lorenzo aside and said that this was a misconception: Don Alvaro must be thinking of the distance which he travelled in an equal number of days on his first voyage, though by the agreed reckoning of all the pilots, five hundred leagues stretched ahead of us still and we were making less than twenty-five a day. The principal cause of our slow progress was that the *Santa Ysabel*, too light in ballast, could not keep the pace except at the risk of capsizing under a full spread of canvas; the frigate, too, was a slow craft. He therefore begged Don Lorenzo to see to it that the troops and settlers were sparing of food, fuel and water, as he himself undertook that the sailors would be; otherwise we should all suffer before the journey was over.

'You blow hot and cold, man!' said Don Lorenzo. 'At Paita you assured the crew that Don Alvaro's skill in navigation equalled your own; now you suggest that he is an ignoramus who can err to the measure of one league in every three.' He added, carelessly: 'Nevertheless, I will warn my sergeants to check the waste of which you complain.'

Whether he gave this warning, I cannot say; but if he did, it was disregarded. The chickens and pigs brought from Peru had by this time all gone into the pot, and the leavings of supper, hitherto set aside for them, were now tossed overboard, though they might well have been kept for breakfast on the following day. The water-steward reported to the Purser that fresh water was being used for

washing, strictly against orders, and that the supply had fallen low.
Don Gaspar carried the report to the General, who replied: 'Patience,
my friend! With God's help and a steady breeze from the east we
shall soon be at our journey's end.'

God sent us the wind we needed, but when we had covered a
further two hundred leagues on a W.S.W. course, and still no land
appeared, officers and men alike were grumbling openly at the length
of the voyage, for which they blamed the Chief Pilot; who, however,
behaved with exemplary loyalty towards the General. He would
answer all unkind words with: 'I am following my set course; I can
do no more and I will not do less.' Though he was ready to defend
himself against any charge of incompetence, none came; Don Alvaro
lacked the courage to admit his error and preferred to earn an undeserved reputation for patience by making no complaints and wearing
a resigned and injured look.

Doña Ysabel took Pedro Fernandez's part against his detractors,
especially those of the Colonel's faction, and now made a habit of
coming for a friendly chat to the Chart-room every evening after
vespers, accompanied by Don Luis; and it may be mentioned here
that Don Luis, who later made something of a name for himself as
a navigator and cartographer, learned the rudiments of these arts
from the Chief Pilot during our voyage. She treated Pedro Fernandez
with so much kindness, and showed such respect for his opinions,
that he told me one day: 'Andrés, when I remember how the General's
Lady behaved at our first meeting with the natives, I can only give my
thanks to the Virgin for having wrought such a change of heart.
Lately I have never seen Doña Ysabel without a book of devotion in
her hand and with her aid our affairs may yet prosper. Her brothers
pay attention to what she says, the Colonel fears her, and Don Alvaro
seldom opposes her wishes. She has great courage for a woman.'

'Yes,' said I, appearing to assent, 'she is a noblewoman of Galicia
and will go her own way through thick and thin; God grant it may
be a good one!' I had seen enough of the world to know that Doña
Ysabel was not yet old enough to turn devout, being then scarce
twenty-seven and at the height of her beauty, and suspected that her
kindness towards him was an off-shot of her enmity towards the
Colonel: whose head she desired on a charger, as the dancer Salome
desired the head of John the Baptist. In time of need, the Chief
Pilot might prove an ally of great worth to her because the crew
respected him. But still I could not understand why she should flaunt

before him Fray Luis de Granada's *Symbol of the Faith*, borrowed from Father Juan, a book which I had never once seen her read, though I was constantly called to the Great Cabin. Why should she trouble to feign piety for his sake?

The Barreto brothers, who had come to regard the expedition as a family enterprise and their fellow-officers as underlings or retainers, ceased to have things their own way, now that the Colonel was up and about again. Our meals at the common table were no longer eaten with even the pretence of cordiality. The General sat at the head with Doña Ysabel, the two priests, the Chief Pilot, the Major, and the Barretos. They conversed in Galician, and Pedro Fernandez used Portuguese, which comes very near. The Colonel sat at the foot with the Captain of Artillery and his wife, the Adjutant and the ensigns; these spoke Castilian. In the middle were the merchants with their womenfolk, who favoured the Andalusian dialect, and myself. Occasionally Don Alvaro addressed a polite remark to the Colonel, or to the Captain of Artillery who was a morose man, disliked by both factions; for the rest, head and foot might have been separated by a hundred leagues of sea, so little communication passed between them.

One day Don Lorenzo told a droll tale which reflected on the modesty of Castilian women and, a silence happening to fall at the foot of the table, Juan de Buitrago overheard it and took offence. He rose from his seat and, speaking in Galician to indicate the cause of his displeasure, asked Don Alvaro's permission to carry cup and platter elsewhere; the Adjutant, for the sake of solidarity, then made the same request. Don Alvaro pretended not to know why they wanted to leave and, instead of asking his brother-in-law to apologize for the blunder, said that it would be discourteous for them to rise before the ladies did, unless both had suddenly been taken ill. The Ensign replied that only for the ladies' sake would he consent to remain at a table where his countrywomen had been so grossly insulted by Don Lorenzo; and the Adjutant again supported him. Here the Colonel hammered on the board with the handle of his dagger, though not knowing what Don Lorenzo had said, and applauded them as fine fellows. 'A true gentleman,' he pronounced, 'is known by his readiness to ignore even the foulest insult when ladies are present, rather than alarm them by publicly boxing the offender's ears.'

Hardly had they resumed their seats, when Doña Mariana made a murderous jest, in Galician again, which set the head of the table in a roar and enraged Juan de Buitrago still further, he being the only one of the Colonel's faction who could understand it. Later, when we bade one another good-night, he would not give Don Lorenzo, who commanded his company, the customary salute, but took leave of him with only the slightest of bows. Don Lorenzo at once complained to the General, who reminded Don Juan that a junior officer is expected always to bid his seniors both good-day and good-night. Early the next morning, when the Adjutant and Ensign met Don Lorenzo, they cried with one voice: 'Good-day, your honour—by order!'

The truth was that the Ensign had recently received Don Alvaro's permission to marry Luisa Geronimo, the eldest daughter of the poor Castilian family to which the child Juanito belonged; she was his junior by more than thirty years, and he had already been forced to listen with patience to much crude though friendly raillery from the Colonel and from his fellow-ensigns. Don Lorenzo's story seemed to him one more shot fired at the same scarred target; but here, I think, he was in error.

At dawn, on Sunday the 20th of August, when we had put another two hundred leagues behind us, the cry of 'Land ho!' rang from the cross-trees. The look-out had his reward, though this was not the land for which we had come in search, but four small, low islands, set in a close square, with sandy beaches and groves of coconut-palms. The circuit of the whole group seemed to be little more than eight leagues; we came upon it from the east, but near approach from that quarter was blocked by extensive sand banks.

The General named the islands after San Bernardo, whose feast day it was, and announced at breakfast that he planned to work round to the west and despatch the frigate and galeot in search of an anchorage. Glancing around the table, he said: 'Doubtless none of you gentlemen will be sorry to stretch his legs on those new shores and drink a refreshing draught or two from a green coconut? I consider it my duty to plant the Cross here and take possession in the King's name. The islands are evidently inhabited; Captain Corzo sent word that shortly after dawn his look-out reported two canoes off the point to our south-west; they came out to reconnoitre but turned back at once.'

A murmur of assent went up from both ends of the table, and the Chief Pilot remarked: 'Our own look-out, who was posted higher than the galeot's, saw only two floating logs; however, inhabitants or no inhabitants, if your Excellency can find safe anchorage and a stream of good water, and if the troops are this time ordered to assist my people, a couple of days might profitably be spent ashore.'

Don Alvaro asked the Colonel whether, provided no attack threatened, he would set the soldiers to work beside the sailors; and he, to annoy Don Lorenzo, replied civilly that his soldiers would do whatever was needed for the common good. 'And by the Head of Lucca!' he added, 'if they cannot shift more water and wood in one morning than an equal number of bare-footed, loose-hosed sailors could in a week, I'll spit upon the rogues.'

Both Don Lorenzo and the Chief Pilot were nettled by this, but a landing would none the less have been attempted, had not the Vicar wagged his forefinger in dissuasion. 'My son,' said he to Don Alvaro, 'if you will listen to a priest who has lived many years longer in the world than any of the present company, you will not seek for a port in these islands, but sail straight on.'

'But why, Father Juan?' asked Don Alvaro in some surprise.

The Vicar spread out his hands in a gesture of impotence. 'Ah,' he replied with a shrug and a dry cough, 'the reason cannot be given. No, my son, it cannot be given even to you!'

He would say no more; but his words carried such an air of conviction that Don Alvaro yielded and we resumed our previous course, leaving San Bernardo behind us. Many were the guesses made at Father Juan's meaning. Some thought that he spoke as though he had been granted an angelic vision of warning; others, that he had been so grieved by the sins committed at our last port of call that he feared a repetition of them. My own view, which I kept to myself, was that he could not state his reasons without violating the sanctity of the confessional: I suspected that Doña Mariana had mentioned her determination to rejoin the Admiral when next they went ashore. I sat near Doña Mariana and saw her turn pale with mortification when Father Juan had his way, and choke back an angry protest; it was no secret that she was still much in love with her husband and hated this unnatural separation. If she contemplated any such action, the Vicar acted prudently, because Don Alvaro had undertaken to restore her to the Admiral only when the Isles of Solomon were reached; had she fled to him beforehand, her brothers would have tried to fetch her back by force, whereupon the Colonel and his faction would have made common cause with her husband and blood might have flowed.

The wind now settled in the south-east and we were treated to a few light showers, but the sea remained calm. Dense cloud masses seemed to promise land to the south; they were so fixed in their position that they seemed to be settled along the summit of a lofty mountain range, but when the General ordered a change of course to the south-west, no land was to be seen. We kept between eight and twelve degrees South, sometimes steering due west, sometimes north-west, sometimes south-west, according to Don Alvaro's fancy. The clouds alone diversified the scene, and were very fanciful in their shapes: one afternoon a lion appeared in the sky, white with a yellow mane and seemed to have three curs attacking it from behind. This group did not alter in shape or colour until dusk, and on the next morning we saw a cloud like a cowled head, with features not unlike those of Don Alvaro, but meagre and with gaping lips; which many of us took for an ill omen. That same day an altar appeared in the east, on which sat a toad; after two hours the cross of the altar broke apart, but the toad increased in size and ugliness.

By the 28th of August we had covered the appointed fifteen hundred leagues of our journey, and still found nothing; but on the following day we sighted a low, tree-covered island, surrounded by a reef of coral. It was about a league in circuit and seemingly uninhabited. Since no other land was near the General named it Solitary Isle. He ordered the frigate and galeot to sail inshore and search for a gap in the reef; the Admiral had been complaining of a great scarcity of water and fire-wood in the *Santa Ysabel*, which might be remedied here. The frigate, taking the lead, tried to enter a channel to the south, but soon we were loudly hailed and implored to stand off because the bottom was strewn with rocks. At one moment the lead struck a hundred fathoms, at the next only ten; and then no bottom was found at all. We changed course at once.

Dissatisfaction was brought to a head two days later, when the General tacitly admitted the unreasonableness of his hopes by placing the ship's company on half-rations of food and water. Wherever I went in the course of my duties, I heard grumbling from the sailors, who had hitherto shown exemplary patience: they complained that if the sergeants had done as the Chief Pilot advised and kept the troops from wasting food and water, we should not now all be hungry. 'Halve our rations, halve our work!' they growled, and began neglecting their orders or obeying them listlessly.

At the conclusion of his watch, the Boatswain gave one of the apprentices a fatherly lecture on the sin of sloth. The lad listened attentively enough and begged the Boatswain's pardon but, as soon as he turned to go, made a long nose behind his back; a gesture at which two of his companions laughed and capered. The Colonel happening to come up at that instant, took in the whole scene; he struck the offender with his stick and felled him to the deck. Then he pursued the other two, calling them prick-eared, long-tailed sooterkins, until they scrambled yelling up the shrouds.

The Boatswain's mate, who was now on duty, went to the Great Cabin immediately and complained that the Colonel had been assaulting the crew and interfering with naval discipline. The boldness of his speech was proof of how much esteem the General had forfeited by vacillations and obstinacy: 'This is intolerable, your Excellency! Let the Colonel do his duty as the King requires; and in times of war or rebellion we're at his orders. But, by God, he had better keep within the limits of his authority! Let him use that stick on an apprentice once again, and I'll not answer for myself. We're honourable men and won't be trampled down.'

Since no high officer was present, Don Alvaro allowed Damian's tongue to run unchecked, remarking only that if his men had been held in firmer discipline, the Colonel would have had no occasion to intervene.

'Your Excellency,' Damian retorted, 'I assure you that the worst behaved of our people is a saint compared with the best behaved of his. We work honestly for our living; we neither steal nor do murder. If the Colonel had repressed laziness and greed in his troops, we should not now be in our present plight; but he leaves them to the Major; the Major leaves them to the Captains and the Adjutant; who leave them to the ensigns; who leave them to the sergeants; who neglect them utterly. Since we left the Marquesas Islands they have not been on parade once, and the officers boast, quarrel and make trouble. There are too many of them in this ship—at least one to every five soldiers. Your Excellency alone could easily direct our affairs. Why waste food and water on them? We aren't going to Flanders or Italy where they might find useful employment, but to peaceful islands inhabited by friendly, ill-armed savages. What we need is not butchers in ruffs, but patient, industrious settlers who are prepared to win over the Indians by kindness and the force of Catholic example. Pray pardon my frankness, your Excellency!'

'I love frankness,' said Don Alvaro, 'but since few officers resemble me in this, have a care where you address your complaints. Especially, do not aggravate our troubles by offending the Colonel. There have been abuses and neglect, I grant, but you surely cannot wish me to cast my friends and relatives overboard for your private gratification? They have been commissioned for this expedition by His Majesty and are all of them men of birth. Go now, friend Damian! With the Virgin's help a remedy will be found for your complaints.'

The atmosphere of conspiracy thickened. The Barreto brothers tried to draw Don Alvaro into their faction by representing that the Colonel intended to massacre them all and usurp the command. With this end in mind they employed spies and tale-bearers, the most active of whom were Major Moran and the Purser; these would eavesdrop on conversations not intended for their ears and bring back their gleanings to Don Lorenzo, or to Don Alvaro himself, omitting, expanding and reshaping until the speaker would never have recognized his own words. Much the same was done on the other side, the Colonel's chief agents being Tomás de Ampuero and Doña Maria Ponce, the Captain of Artillery's wife, who was in love with Don Tomás; but I am bound to add that the Colonel acted in self-defence and was more plotted against than plotting.

The Purser also carried tales against the Chief Pilot to Don Alvaro, alleging that he was in conspiracy with the Admiral's pilot to steer for the Portuguese Indies, where they would desert the flotilla and go home by way of Goa; and that we had long passed the Isles of Solomon. Many of the soldiers and settlers believed this story; Don Alvaro himself half-believed it, yet if ever he came on deck at midnight to study the compass or the stars, he always found the ship on her true course. Pedro Fernandez, though knowing what was being said, and by whom, made no complaint: he told me that the Purser would in time be made to look deservedly foolish.

One morning, as I passed along the maindeck towards the forecastle, I forget on what business, Matia plucked at my sleeve and jerked his head toward some coils of rope where a group of young soldiers sat quarrelling and complaining. 'Hark how the rats squeak!' he said scornfully.

I stopped to listen.

'And don't forget, Federico—you owe me nine ounces of gold when we get to the Isles. I haven't your note of hand to prove it, but you pledged yourself before witnesses, and that's enough between messmates.'

'God bless your soul, man! When we get to the Isles indeed! We'll never get there! We've already sailed completely round the globe, well to the south of all known continents. Those Marquesas Islands are the last landfall we're ever likely to make now—unless we come up with them again on our second turn round the mill. Neither the General, nor the Chief Pilot have the least idea where we are. We'll sail on and on until the planks rot under us and the ship dives to the bottom, taking our grinning skeletons with her. That's what I meant when I said that the Sergeant oughtn't to shout at us as though we were on Viceroy's guard at Lima. There's no sense in scouring our breastplates twice a week when we're bound to die without ever needing them again.'

'That's nonsense, Salvador, and well you know it. Federico may be right about our having passed the Isles by, and perhaps one day we'll find ourselves in Cochin China among the yellow men, but the globe's a bigger pumpkin than you imagine. The Englishman Drake took three years to draw his knife around it, and he was no dawdler.'

'Well, it's much more likely that the Isles have sunk beneath the sea. Islands come and go, you know, at the will of God, and it's well-nigh thirty years since they were last seen.'

'You leek! Islands as large as those don't sink. You might as well say that Spain itself might be engulfed one day. No, take my word for it: the General and his people were bewitched. They saw sights and heard sounds that existed only in their addled brains—you've heard how hunger and thirst crazed them all on the way back, and how they sacrificed a snow-white parrot to save their Colonel's life. Snow-white parrot indeed! Who ever saw such a bird?'

'You're right, Sebastian. Those Isles were no more than a grand phantasmagoria; yet somehow the General managed to convince the Viceroy and King Philip himself that they existed. And now, because he wants to call himself a marquis, and make the fortunes of his Lady's family, he's dragged us here with half a dozen sacks of biscuit to perish in this waste of water——'

'And fish for those wonderful pearls, as big as pigeons' eggs, of which he brags! He saw children playing at marbles with them, he says, but was too tender-hearted to take away their toys! The devil of it is that his letters patent make slaves of us all: he can enrich whom he pleases and beggar whom he pleases, and there's no redress.'

'Why complain of the letters patent, man? They're equally a work of fancy. I'll say it again, and I don't care who hears me: the Isles of Solomon never existed!'

Matia strode angrily forward: 'Are you giving me the lie, Sebastian Lejia, you talbot? I was a seasoned soldier, who had fought in seven pitched battles and ten sieges, when you were still crawling about in the gutter with a bare backside, eating turnip-peel and mule droppings. Look at this scar—a lance-thrust dealt me by a Solomon islander! You dare say that I dreamed it, hey? By the pall and chin-cloth of Him who redeemed me, I'll make you swallow those words, you addlepate, you male washerwoman, you whoreson lump of dough with the frog's mouth!'

His hand flew to his dagger, but I restrained him.

'Easy there, friend!' I cried. 'When a man gabbles absurdities, what can his retraction of them be worth? Listen to me, gentlemen: it is beyond dispute that those Isles were reached, and to deny it would be both senseless and disloyal. In the Chart-room yonder is the ship's log kept by Hernan Gallego, the truth of which is confirmed by a sober account of the voyage, now in the Viceregal archives at Lima, written by the Purser Gomez Catorra. Moreover, I have myself handled the weapons and necklaces brought back to New Spain by Captain Pedro Sarmiento. Bleach your brains in the washtub, Sebastian Lejia, and then hang them in the shrouds to dry!'

This raised a laugh, and Matia's dagger stayed in its sheath; yet he had not finished with the dispute. 'Lads,' he said, stroking his grizzled beard, 'rations are short and the voyage is long, so listen to an old campaigner whose skin is laced with scars, but whose head and eyes are clear. These are the times when a soldier is tested: he keeps his arms clean and takes what comes his way. Avoid Sebastian like the plague: there's a cast in his eye, lies on his tongue and rust on his armour. Be men, and keep the company of men!'

Sebastian quailed under Matia's bloodshot glare, muttered something inaudible and slouched off. Young Federico asked: 'But, Matia, what do you think? You've made this voyage once before. Why haven't we sighted the Isles?'

Matia grinned, put a finger to his lips as though he were about to reveal a secret of the utmost importance and replied in a hoarse whisper: 'For one reason only: *because we haven't yet come to them!*'

Even the Chief Pilot was beginning to grow anxious. We had come something over sixteen hundred leagues, yet Gallego's chart placed the isles at less than fifteen hundred from Peru. At a mid-day conference the three other pilots presented him with a memorial to the effect that they had to bear constant complaints about the length of the voyage from their captains and lower officers, and therefore humbly asked for an explanation from the General, which they might pass on. The memorial absolved Pedro Fernandez himself from blame: the pilots stated that their dead-reckoning agreed with his, though they had taken the sun every noon for the past fortnight and we still kept in ten degrees South, where the Isles were supposed to lie. They added that according to a Portuguese chart found in the *Santa Ysabel*, we should now be scraping our way over the wooded mountains of Great Tartary; and that to judge from the sorry state of our hulls, the cartographer might not be far out.

Pedro Fernandez, who had not hitherto cared to raise the subject with the General, laid the memorial before him and asked what reply he should make. It happened that the Colonel and Don Lorenzo were both present, and Don Alvaro felt obliged to justify himself in their eyes. He rose angrily from his chair and 'Pilot,' he cried, 'have you no shame? There is a constant dinning in my ears of complaints from all and sundry that we are off our course and lost without hope. How do you, of all people, dare treat me so? First you go to Captain Don Lorenzo with mutinous hints that I am out of my mind, because I expected the Isles too soon; and now you complain that we have overshot our mark! Who is the Master of this ship—you or I?'

'I am the Master, your Excellency,' the Chief Pilot answered, raising his voice to show that he would not be brow-beaten, 'and I navigate according to the directions you gave me at Santa; you, who discovered the Isles of Solomon, should know where they lie. This is my first voyage in the South Seas, but I can run down a parallel with accuracy and my dead-reckoning is not challenged by any pilot of the flotilla.'

'Then why have you not done your duty and brought us to the Isles?' shouted Don Alvaro, whipping himself into a fury.

'Some of your officers, whose names I need not mention,' replied the Chief Pilot with great deliberation, 'allege that Gallego falsified his log at your orders. They say that you both made the distance from Callao appear much less than it is, so that the King should not think your discovery too outlandish for settlement. That opinion I leave for your Excellency's confutation. But it falls to you to explain why I and my three fellow-pilots, though following your instructions, have not yet sighted so large an archipelago. Pray, your Excellency, abstain from vague accusations and consider the matter logically. Concede either that, Gallego's dead-reckoning being at fault, he set down the wrong longitude; or that he hid the true latitude from you; or else, that errors of transcription were made by the secretary who put his log in writing.'

Here the Colonel intervened: 'Or, my lord, alternatively, that this Portuguese is a swindler and a knave, bent on leading us to destruction for the gratification of a private vengeance.'

'That, my dear Colonel, is by no means an impossible alternative,' said Don Alvaro, who was trimming his sails to any wind and cared little where it bore him. 'I know that the Chief Pilot has small love for you.'

Pedro Fernandez caught the eye of Doña Ysabel who was listening attentively and took courage to defend himself with spirit. 'Is it likely that I am bent on my own destruction as well as on his?' he asked. 'You assured me at Paita with tears in your eyes that I was the only pilot on whose skill you could rely; and greatly against my desire, but at the plea of your virtuous Lady, I consented to stay with you. On that occasion, too, I forgave the Colonel his trespasses, as I trust that God will forgive mine; and if you can believe that I nurse such mad resentment against him that, only to gratify it, I would lead four ship-loads of my fellow-Christians to their death . . .'

'Continue,' said Don Alvaro, hurriedly. 'The Colonel and Don Lorenzo will both agree on the justice of allowing you to speak in your defence.'

'Briefly then, my lord: Hernan Gallego may have committed an error in dead-reckoning. This is probable, because in his log he sets down the longitude of the Isle of Jesus, your first landfall, as being such and such, and then that of the Isle of Cristobal, which lies in the same latitude, as being such and such; but computes the distance between the two as less by two hundred and fifty leagues than is warranted by a comparison of their longitudes. The conclusion to be drawn from this entry is, that the Isles of Solomon, of which San Cristobal is one, lie at least sixteen hundred and fifty leagues west of Callao, perhaps even more; and therefore still ahead of us.'

'But, my friend,' protested the General, 'I reached the Isles in eighty days——'

Pedro Fernandez took him up quickly: '—with different winds, my lord, at a different season, and not slowed down by a lagging *Santa Ysabel*. Pray hear me out!'

When the General had subsided in his chair, he continued, confidently sawing the air with his hands like an advocate: 'I have heard it suggested that when at the close of the voyage Gallego was asked by your Excellency for his log and chart, he gave you falsified copies instead of the originals. But though it is common knowledge that he fell foul of you on your return to Peru, I cannot believe either that a man of his character would have stooped so low; or that a man of your experience could have been so easily taken in. At all events, he could not have also deceived his fellow-pilots, who knew very well in what latitudes they sailed. If, however, we are to suppose that they were all in the plot and that you did not trouble to check their readings, then it may well be that the Isles lie either higher than seven, or lower than twelve degrees South, and that we have indeed passed them by. The third alternative, namely errors in transcription, may be ruled out: it is unlikely that the same error would be several times repeated in the log, besides being shown on the chart.'

Here Don Lorenzo put in his oar: 'It is my firm belief, your Excellency, that we have unwittingly sailed through a gap between the islands and left them far behind. Once we reached fourteen hundred leagues, we should have cruised up and down until we found them. I do not pretend to understand navigation, one end of a backstaff being much the same to me as the other; but men of science, like our Chief Pilot, are often sadly wanting in common sense.'

'Captain Don Lorenzo,' said Pedro Fernandez, 'it would be better if you confined your remarks to military matters which you understand, and not accuse me of imbecility. To sail through the group without sighting even one of its islands would be about as easy as to walk along the maindeck without having to step over a dozen of your sprawled soldiers. Have we not said enough, your Excellency? By your leave, I will inform the pilots that Hernan Gallego is found to have underestimated the longitude of the Isles, and that with patience and fortitude we shall soon come upon them.'

Don Alvaro was no match for the Chief Pilot in a nautical argument, and ended the conference abruptly by taking up his beads and shuffling into a corner to pray.

Chapter 12

THE ADMIRAL'S FAREWELL

A change had come over the General. He was no longer a soldier in friar's garb, but rather a friar who by some freak of fortune had been put in command of troops. He ate and drank no more than a bird, spent the greater part of the night on his knees and when he rose, refreshed in spirit, seemed to float along the cabin floor, or soar up and down from one deck to another on invisible wings. His beads were always in his hands, and on his lips were the words of the psalm: *Ecce quam bonum, fratres*—'O, what a good and joyful thing it is, brethren, to dwell together in unity.' At the common table he would tearfully beseech us to make our peace with God and one another, to avoid open and secret sins, serving God and the King to the utmost of our powers. If he surprised two officers in a quarrel he would simultaneously seize their right hands and marry them in a clasp of friendship; and I verily believe that, if he could at the same time have compelled their lips to kiss, he would have done so. Having commandeered Our Lady of Solitude from the Chart-room, on the ground that the Chief Pilot had no right to keep so holy an image for his private orisons, he dressed her in silk clothes sewn by the ladies and set her up at the mainmast; and every day after matins he required the ship's company to sing the *Salve, Regina* in her honour. There was a holy gleam in his eye which made everyone say, whatever his faction: 'The General seems already to have taken leave of this world.'

He made it his habit to preach little sermons at odd times of the day. One morning before breakfast he held forth on the dangers of blasphemy, warning us that the road to Hell, a very broad, populous highway, was paved with 'O God's' and 'By Our Lady's' vainly uttered; and said that if an officer heard any such expression fall from a sailor's or soldier's lips he was to reprimand him gravely and, if the offence was repeated, bring him up for summary punishment. '*Carajo!*' I heard Matia mutter under his moustache, 'so our ration of oaths is to be halved too!'

The comments made by the Boatswain's mate on the slovenliness of the soldiers, though uncalled for, seem to have stirred Don Alvaro. He notified the high officers that he would inspect their troops every evening and watch them put through platoon drill; he trusted that their appearance would be as clean and soldierly as if they were expecting a visit from His Majesty in person. Every Saturday afternoon, and on the eve of every important festival, he had the ship dressed with flags and pendants while our musicians dispensed solemn music and the pages sang anthems under his own direction. Nor was this all: because the troops looked down upon the sailors he read them a lesson in humility by enrolling himself in the Boatswain's watch and sharing in all the most menial and laborious tasks. He was to be seen swabbing the deck, his habit girded up to his waist and his pitifully thin, white legs showing bare underneath, or perched astride a yard high aloft, helping to set an obstinate topsail. The soldiers thought him demented, the sailors found little to admire in his unhandy efforts, the high officers appeared to despise him. Doña Ysabel was too well-bred to rebuke him publicly for making a laughing-stock of himself, and must have known that to do so would only have encouraged him in his stiff-necked humility; but it is my belief that she hated him for the shame he caused her, and that nothing kept her nails from his cheeks, but the title and riches which she hoped to win by being his wife and sole heiress.

One Friday at noon the Admiral sent a message by his pilot, saying that he would esteem it a great kindness if the General could spare him a boat-load of fire-wood; the *Santa Ysabel's* supplies were exhausted and the soldiers burned whatever they could lay their hands on—spare masts and yards, chests and boxes, and even parts of the upper works. Don Alvaro sent the wood at once, together with a Christian message of love, which encouraged the Admiral to resume his interrupted Sunday visits. When, two days later, his skiff was seen approaching the flagship, Don Lorenzo and Don Diego immediately went to fetch Doña Mariana from the Great Cabin and, with brotherly solicitude, escorted her to the forecastle head, where they detained her in conversation until he had gone. The Colonel, on the other hand, greeted him warmly, offered him wine, and did all he could to show that he regretted the incident at Cherrepé; but the Admiral, though pressing his hand in gratitude, would not be cheered.

It was not hard to divine the reason for his deep despondency, namely that Father Joaquin, his own priest, had at last taken courage and refused him holy communion unless he put away the sergeant's wife. So much had already been told me in confidence by Pedro Fernandez, who got it from the pilot of the *Santa Ysabel*; the latest news was that the woman, finding herself shunned and hated by everyone but her protector, had fallen ill and in her extremity called for the priest to whom she confessed her adulteries, promising to reform her ways. Father Joaquin accepted her penitence and gave her absolution; but she was still not welcomed by her former friends of the between-decks and, with no one to nurse her, now lay at the point of death. Don Lope felt wounded in his honour, but his officers gave him no sympathy and he was too proud to make overtures of peace to the Barretos. In his interview with Don Alvaro, also, he made no mention of his private sorrows, though he complained bitterly of the anxieties attendant on his command. He had brought with him the master of the *Santa Ysabel*, to testify that he was not painting his picture in more dismal colours than truth required.

Don Alvaro beamed cheerfully at him, and cried: 'Courage, my friend! The faster we sail, the sooner will our troubles be over. Clap on more sail, man, and let your galleon prove that she has as fleet a pair of heels as the *San Geronimo*.'

The Admiral thrust the master forward, who explained at length (and Don Alvaro had already been told of this by the Chief Pilot) that the *Santa Ysabel* was very crank for lack of lead ballast, which until recently had been somewhat compensated by the weight of water and provisions in her hold; but these were now depleted and he dared not trust her under full sail. 'She has a thousand defects,' he continued. 'She's as wilful as a spoilt child and as obstinate as a pack mule.'

At this the Admiral began to weep, a thing that I should never have believed possible in so bold and lively a nobleman, and begged Don Alvaro not to let the flotilla part company with his ship. 'I never made a worse bargain in my life,' he said in a broken voice, 'than the day I exchanged the old *Santa Ysabel* for the present one; and I must humbly beg your Excellency's pardon for not having listened to your advice when you bade me be content with what I had. I grieve most for the unfortunate settlers whom I myself enlisted; should the ship capsize one dark and windy night and they drown, I would not attempt to save my life, but stay at my post and be sucked down with them.'

'Dry your tears, brother-in-law,' said Don Alvaro, 'and have faith in the all-seeing eye of divine Providence, for the Isles cannot be far off. If your ship is somewhat crank, that can easily be remedied. Fill your spare casks and barrels with sea water and you will soon have her in trim.'

'Alas, your Excellency, we have no barrels left, and the casks leak; they are warped from having stood empty so long.'

'A sad neglect! You should have sluiced them every day to keep the seams tight.'

'I did not wish to foul them with salt water, and fresh we could not afford.'

'And why not?'

'Only a hundred casks were left when we anchored off Santa Cristina. Today, God be my witness, we are down to nine.'

'To nine? A thousand red devils! You must be mistaken—how have you contrived to waste so much water? You left Paita with the same amount as we, and your ship is smaller than ours.'

The Admiral, making a noble effort, recovered his self-possession: 'Your Excellency forgets that the Santa Ysabel's complement is one hundred and eighty-two persons of both sexes; yours, only one hundred and twenty. Sixty extra rations of water amount to a great deal in three and a half months.'

'How three and a half months? You had the opportunity to replenish your casks at Santa Cristina.'

'Those that were still sound; but because of their larger numbers, my people had drunk far more than yours on the way, and therefore, do you see, we had emptied far more casks, and therefore far more had become unserviceable from disuse.'

'And you never thought of engaging a cooper to repair them?'

'There were three coopers with us when we sailed from Callao; now we have none.'

'You are mistaken, or why have their deaths not been reported to me?'

'They are still alive and plying their trade, so far as I know. You yourself turned them out at Cherrepé on a charge of immorality.'

'Ah, yes, I remember. Yes, that is so. And would you have had me keep them, to our souls' ruin? It is a true saying that one rotten apple will spoil the barrel.'

'But three coopers can repair a thousand spoilt barrels.'

'That remark is impertinent and unworthy of a Christian. Well, if you could not replenish the warped casks with water at Santa Cristina, you should have filled them with ballast.'

'They had already been broken up for fuel. You have no more than one hundred and twenty mouths; to provide soup for one hundred and eighty needs half as much fire-wood again.'

'O Don Lope, Don Lope, why did you not inform me of this earlier? I would have found a remedy.'

'I reported it to your Excellency three times, at intervals of ten days; on each occasion I was assured that we should soon sight the Isles and told to put my trust in God. Come now, Don Alvaro, to the point: will you of your charity give me twenty casks of water to moisten the throats of my people?'

Since the General knew that despite the wastage we still had four hundred casks or jars in our hold, 'yes' was on the tip of his tongue; but Doña Ysabel entered, and he reined himself in. Assuming a grave and portentous expression, he answered: 'Don Lope, I cannot assent. You have neglected your duty and must suffer the consequences.'

'Do you wish to sign my death warrant?'

'I have no notion what you mean, friend,' said Don Alvaro, reaching for his beads, 'nor do I intend to enquire.'

'May God forgive you and grant you better understanding before it be too late! My lord General, I bid you farewell.' He retired with a bow and a look of resignation, not unmixed with reproach.

'What did the knave want?' Doña Ysabel asked.

'Water, my love. He claimed to be nearly at the end of his resources.'

'You refused him water? But he has women and little children aboard.'

'He owns to having nine casks left. They will not go thirsty for a while.'

'In the Virgin's name! Women and children cannot sail the ship when everyone else has died of thirst. And why punish the whole company for the fault of their commander?'

'I cannot believe the Admiral. He is acting a part and has overplayed it with his tears and entreaties. Aware of your righteous anger against him, he now tries to trick us. He begs me not to abandon his ship, as though such a thought had ever entered my head. This can mean only that he has decided to run off when we approach our destination; perhaps the Vicar had wind of the plot when he warned us against landing on San Bernardo. Ships commanded by insubordinate officers have often deserted their flotillas. Did not the *San Lesmes* desert Loaysa on the expedition through the Straits of Magellan? Did not the *Santiago* and *Sanctus Spiritus* give Saavedra the slip in mid-Pacific? And did not Pedro Sarmiento try to steal the *Todos Santos* from me when I returned from the Isles of Solomon? You may be sure that the Admiral has far more water than he admits, though perhaps not enough to sustain his mutinous intention. I did well to harden my heart to his tears.'

Doña Ysabel considered. 'You are playing a dangerous game,' she said. 'It seems to me that you should go to the *Santa Ysabel* yourself to see how serious the situation may be, and if you find more water than he owns to possessing, arrest him. But beware of setting his officers against you; if things are left as they are, you will be suspected either of cruelty or of weakness.'

'I disagree at every point,' he said stubbornly. 'My refusal compels the Admiral to keep up with the flotilla; his ship is not so lame a duck as her master makes out. He too lied, to bolster the Admiral's pretences. As soon as his officers become aware of true distress on board the *Santa Ysabel* they will come to me; and I will give them satisfaction.' He took up his beads again to forestall further argument; in truth, he combined a dove's purity with the guile of a serpent.

When Doña Mariana learned of her husband's tragical farewell, she went on her knees before Don Alvaro and besought him to show a little Christian charity; but when she found that she could not soften his heart she said many vindictive things to which he listened with the look of a martyr. Then she turned sullen, and not all Doña Ysabel's lively rallyings could restore her natural good-humour.

The next day at noon when the Admiral's pilot came aboard, he begged Pedro Fernandez for a drink of water, complaining that he had gone without for twelve hours, and begged him to report the matter where it might best be remedied. Pedro Fernandez found Don Alvaro in a black mood. 'The trick is too clumsy to deceive us,' said he. 'Tell the pilot that in future we do not expect him to attend these conferences, which only waste our sailing time; he is to follow our pendant by day, and our lantern by night.'

Soon after this Doña Mariana fell into deep disgrace, her brothers treating her as though she had betrayed them. To judge from a hint that Don Diego let fall, she had for some time been in secret communication with her husband, the pilot acting as messenger, and planned to escape to him in the skiff; but the plot was now discovered. Certain it is that one of our apprentices was flogged until he fainted, and then flogged again, for a fault, not made public, that rumour named sodomy; I believe, rather, that he was the accomplice who should have stolen the skiff for her.

On the 7th of September the wind blew fresh from the south-east; but the *San Geronimo* made little way, carrying only her foresail without even a bonnet, because the Chief Pilot feared to draw away from the *Santa Ysabel* and thus tempt her master to make more sail than she could bear in safety. Our course was due west; and ahead of us, as evening fell, the horizon was obscured by a billowing black cloud of so strange an appearance that the General sent the galeot and frigate ahead to investigate it. They were to keep in close touch with each other and if they sighted land or reefs, or anything else, they were to show two lights, one above the other; and the signal of acknowledgement was to be two lights placed side by side. The cloud grew larger and larger, blotting out the stars of the western sky, and we began to sniff the air and ask one another: 'Don't you smell sulphur? Have we come to the Gates of Hell?' During the night the frigate fell back and we sailed on cautiously two cables behind the galeot, taking occasional soundings but never striking bottom. The Chief Pilot now concluded that the cloud must be the smoke of a volcano and, hailing the galeot, ordered her to change course to the south-west.

At nine o'clock we caught a glimpse of the *Santa Ysabel* not far astern of us; and at eleven a thick fog rose to port and blotted out the southern horizon. The soldiers swore that it smelled like a land-fog, but the sailors remained unconvinced until suddenly a smart shower of rain drew back the curtain, and land was plainly revealed, no more than a league away. 'Land ho!' rang out from the deck as soon as from the cross-trees, and a rush of people came up for a sight of it. The galeot's sails were reefed and for want of an anchorage she lay a-hull so as not to be driven inshore. We exchanged light signals with her and the frigate, which lay half a league off to starboard; but from the *Santa Ysabel* we could get no reply. This surprised us, because we had been making little way, and she should have been well within view.

The distant boom of surf on an unknown coast put us all in such fear of shipwreck that few dared go below; and a dense crowd of settlers collected around the long-boat. The Chief Pilot was busy with his log in the Chart-room, when about midnight Doña Ysabel and Don Luis came to him for reassurance. I was asleep at the time, but they could not have been there long, before I happened to wake and see Doña Ysabel's face very clearly in the light of the lantern swinging above her. She stood bent over the chart on which Pedro Fernandez had been plotting our position; but it was on his curly hair and strong neck, not the parchment, that her eyes were fixed. A greedy longing shone so plain in them that I shut my own quickly, lest she caught me watching her. I reassured myself: 'Nothing can come of this. He is far below her in station; and even if she were mad enough to declare her passion, he is a model of piety, loyal to a fault, and cares too much for his marriage to look at any woman but his wife.' Though I tried to put the matter out of my mind, it returned assiduously and filled me with worse dismay than I can describe. At last I fell asleep again, but the nightmare pressed upon me: I dreamed that the ship had been cast away on a reef, and that a rain of red-hot lava fell all about us. I stood by the mainmast, dressed only in my shirt, warning the Boatswain and the Ensign with frantic gestures that Doña Ysabel was in truth more dangerous than either volcano or rock; but they would not listen, and pointed upwards with puzzled looks to where Don Alvaro chattered like a monkey in the shrouds, alternately crossing himself with great devotion and hurling green coconuts at us.

God brought the dawn at last, and I awoke to the sound of many voices singing: the whole ship's company joining in the pages' salutation. I ran on deck and there, less than a league to the south-east, rose a round, wooded headland, very beautiful in the red light, and beyond it a long stretch of rocky coast. Close ahead of us lay the galeot; close to starboard, the frigate; but the *Santa Ysabel* was nowhere within view.

As day broadened we saw, thrust from the sea about eight leagues away, a sugar-loaf mountain so perfectly shaped that it might have been cut out with a knife; light smoke wreathed its summit, and there stood our volcano. The General sent the frigate to cruise around it, in case the *Santa Ysabel* might be lying becalmed under the land on its farther side. The galeot, at the same time, made for the headland to see whether she were anchored behind it.

While we waited for their return, the long-boat was got ready for hoisting out, the ship's guns loaded, decks cleared, and the troops paraded under arms. Don Alvaro ordered a public confession, and to set an example, was the first to enter a small tent that had been rigged up as a confessional, where he spent fully five minutes with the Vicar. Most of those who were watching wondered that so saintly a man could have so much to repent; the few who knew him better thought that he might well have remained a good deal longer. The Colonel entered next, and was out again almost at once; his sins never weighed heavily on his conscience and, besides, he had not yet forgiven Father Juan. He was followed by the Chief Pilot and the high officers in order of rank. The Chaplain meanwhile confessed the crew and the settlers in a second tent, and within two hours we had all made our peace with God, except for seven men who held back resolutely, despite the Vicar's entreaties and threats. Some, I suppose, had committed sins for which the proper penance was to surrender themselves and die at the yard-arm, and therefore postponed confession until they should come to a natural end; others were bad Christians and made light of all religion. Among these last was Matia, and when I reproached him for setting the younger soldiers a bad example, he asked me a riddle: 'Don Andrés, what black beast is it that never breeds true, grimaces from a tree-top once a week, and sings loudest at the death of its own kind?'

When I could not guess the answer he gave it me himself: 'A priest. Because none of the many bastards he fathers may enter the priesthood; and every Saturday at vespers he climbs into the wooden pulpit to preach; and he makes the greatest clamour at the funeral of another of the black-coated crew.'

'This is no jest,' I said severely. 'I am ashamed to hear such irreverence from your lips.'

'No, in the Devil's name, it is no jest, but dead earnest,' Matia answered, 'and why, being a man, should I confess to a beast?'

'God will teach you why in His own good time,' said I, turning angrily away. 'You have said today what He will be slow to forgive.' Yet for all that, I had a love for Matia Pineto: his pride had more of humility in it, and his savagery of gentleness, than he would ever care to admit. He accounted for his Catholic impulses in terms of military honour, and though he robbed with the right hand, with the left he was lavish. I prayed that he might one day embrace the Faith, not too late for absolution.

The galeot came back to report that the *Santa Ysabel* was nowhere to be found along several leagues of coast. The frigate had not yet returned, but we had little hope of better news from her. The sudden disappearance of our sister-ship caused alarm, and for a while was the only subject of talk. It seemed unlikely that she had capsized: when the frigate had last sighted her, an hour after we did, the wind was already falling light; nor could she have run on a rock and foundered, because then we should have observed her lantern signals and heard her distress guns. For the same reason it was hard to believe that she had been driven ashore; besides, we found no wreckage, not so much as a plank or a floating cap. Only one conclusion could reasonably be drawn: that as soon as land was seen she had slipped off and shaped a course of her own.

From this conclusion three different arguments branched. The Barretos said that for many weeks now the Admiral had been planning to desert us, though meaning to gain possession of his wife first, and that when he failed in this he went off alone; they agreed with Don Alvaro that his complaints of a water shortage, and of the unseaworthiness of his ship, were so many lies. The Colonel's faction, on the other hand, held that he was a loyal officer driven to desperation by Don Alvaro's studied cruelty and that, expecting no better treatment on land than on sea, he had made a bid for liberty. The sailors, who knew of the condition on board the *Santa Ysabel* from the crew of her skiff, thought that when Don Lope's final appeal was rejected by the General, he had said farewell in the foreboding that, when he returned, his authority would be defied. 'It's certain,' said Jaume, 'that their water was all but done, and that threats against his life had been made. Write him down in your ledger as dead, Don Andrés! His murderers, fearing the consequences of the crime, have deserted us and gone to seek their fortunes elsewhere.'

Doña Mariana seemed to share Jaume's view. She wept all that day without pause, and for several days more, saying that she was to blame for everything. By this she meant, I suppose, that had her determination to run away not been suspected, Don Alvaro would never have treated the Admiral so unhandsomely, and the officers of the *Santa Ysabel* would therefore have had no occasion to rebel.

Don Alvaro also shed a few tears; but he attributed the loss of the ship to the curse put upon her by the Canon at Cherrepé, and exculpated himself to the voice of conscience by loudly insisting that the exchange had been forced upon him by the Admiral himself. He conjectured that she had struck a reef at the very moment when the blinding rain squall struck us, and foundered without trace; the hand of God was clearly in it, he said, and we must not presume to question His justice.

The only other opinion worthy of record was the Chief Pilot's. He said sadly: 'She is gone, and none of us expects to see her again, even if she is still afloat. How or why she went is a question hardly worth discussing: but her loss is irreparable. She was carrying a body of respectable settlers, farmers drawn from the same neighbourhood, who might have brought our venture to a good issue. Those in the *San Geronimo* are not cut from the right timber, except for one or two; they are petty tradesmen, gentlemen's servants, miners, tapsters, rufflers, scoundrels and bullies. One cannot people a New Jerusalem with men of their quality.'

'No, not a New Jerusalem,' I said, trying to cheer him, 'but perhaps a New Rome. Was not Rome founded by bandits and enriched by rapine? Yet its later history has been nobler by far than that of Jerusalem.'

'Do not chop logic, friend Andrés,' he said severely. 'God's anger is heavy upon us, and rightly so. What good can come of our enterprise, now that He has shorn away the better part of our force?'

I would not give up hope yet. The *Santa Ysabel* might have gone off in search of water, with no intention to desert, and now be lying snugly at anchor in some bay, like the one we had found in Santa Cristina, that was not visible from the sea until one sailed close inshore. Yet I knew, as well as or better than anyone else, how much we would lose if she did not return. All the spades and mattocks of the expedition were in her hold; most of the hatchets, saws and chisels; the sulphur for purifying our ships in case of sickness; and, because Doña Ysabel had an unconquerable dread of fire in the magazine, all but four of our powder-barrels.

But enough of that for the moment. Canoes were already approaching; and every man's eyes turned towards them: a fleet of about fifty, led by a very large canoe with a short mast in the bows and a lateen sail of scarlet matting. All but four or five differed from those we had seen in the Marquesas Islands by being built of planks, not hollowed from logs, and by carrying no outriggers. Their bow and stern pieces were gracefully curved, either beaked at the top or crowned with what looked like a plumed casque, and decorated with red streamers. The canoe with the sail seated twenty men, the remainder no more than six, and some only one; the paddles were long and tapering. As for the natives——

The General summoned Myn. 'Myn,' he said solemnly, 'as you hope for salvation, tell me truly what you make of these men? Are they Solomon Islanders?'

There was silence at the rail while we waited anxiously for the response of our black oracle. 'By the Virgin Mary, Master,' he cried with a flash of teeth, 'those are the very fellows! Those are the heathen that eat men. Look, gentlemen! Look, they have black bodies and fuzzy heads; but beware of their arrows! Myn can smell the poison on them. We have come to the right gate at last, Master!'

Chapter 13

GRACIOUS BAY

Most of the canoe-men were short and black, with broad noses, receding chins and deep-set eyes which gave them a sullen look, though they were on the whole a cheerful people; a few were tawny and of middling size, with large, rounded noses, like the Jews. They carried bows, taller than themselves by a foot or two, polished stone axes, curved clubs, darts, and long, notched spears. Their nakedness was not so stark as that of the Marquesas islanders: a broad leaf covering the secret parts was secured around every man's loins by a string, and the elders wrapped a long white cloth tightly around their bellies. All were profusely tattooed in formal patterns, like those on the rims of Sevillian dishes, and some had circled their chests and upper arms with bands of cicatrices resembling large pock-marks. Since these patterns did not show up well on dark skin, they had resorted to further embellishments, such as bleaching their frizzled hair white, or shaving and dyeing one side of the head only; and the crew of the leading canoe wore small plaits, like a bullfighter's, tied with red ribbons. Their bodies were also streaked with red dye, and about their necks hung strings of small white beads, dogs' teeth, human teeth and what I afterwards found to be those of a gigantic bat; and they wore armlets laboriously ground from a great conch, and crescents of pearl-shell tied to the brow or beneath the chin. But what we found strangest of all was the deep hole pierced at the tip of every nose, into which a quill or a stick of curved shell was thrust, as if in continuation of it. Their nostrils were likewise slit as a convenience for the wearing of flowers, scented leaves, or gleaming fish-hooks of carved nacre. We saw no women either in the canoes or in the water.

They waved and shouted at us but, not much liking their outlandish appearance, our men returned the greeting half-heartedly and kept a tight hold on their weapons. Don Alvaro uttered a gay cry. 'Yes, you are right, Myn,' he said. 'Beyond doubt those are our hosts of long ago and, judging by the woven bags on their shoulders, this must be a part of San Cristobal; moreover, the latitude agrees exactly. I will now address them.'

He hailed the black fellows as they paddled chattering around us and, raising his hand for silence, exclaimed: '*Arra Caiboco Español. Arra Ago Itapulu. Teo Narriu! Teo Varia!*', meaning: 'I am a Spanish chieftain come across many leagues of ocean. You and I are brothers. Let us have no war and no fighting.'

None of them seemed to understand a word, and when they answered, Don Alvaro was equally at a loss. 'The people of this district,' he said in some vexation, 'seem to speak a different dialect from the one I learned in Estrella Bay. But no matter. Soon they will pick up a little trade-Spanish. . . . Come, my good rascals, let one or two of you climb aboard, and I will reward them with splendid gifts!'

A lean, old native stood in the bows of the large canoe. He wore fewer ornaments than his companions, but was evidently their leader. Pointing at the General with a grimace of disgust, and pinching his nose as if he smelled a corpse, he picked up a polished club and shook it menacingly. Word of his judgement upon us was passed from canoe to canoe, and presently all seized their bows, raised an echoing war-cry, and sent a flight of long, unfeathered arrows whizzing against the ship's side and into the sails. Don Alvaro stood at the taffrail, scorning all protection, and opened his arms wide in a gesture of friendship. Had the savages aimed at him, they would have stuck him as full of arrows as Saint Sebastian, for they seldom miss their man at thirty paces; but their anger was directed against the ship, not against our people.

'Give fire!' cried the Colonel, not waiting for Don Alvaro's orders, and every arquebus went off with a great roar. The leader and twenty more fell dead, many others were wounded, the rest fled, though sufficiently unabashed to fire a few parting shots. In the scramble to get away several canoes collided; one was stove in, but half the crew at once began bailing with coconut shells, while the other half paddled furiously in the hope of beaching her before she sank.

'If we look lively,' said the Colonel, 'we may catch that lamed hare.' He sent the skiff in pursuit with four arquebusiers, who killed one of the paddlers with their first shot. His companions jumped into the sea and were allowed to swim to safety; the canoe then sank, but not before our people had retrieved the weapons in it for the General's inspection, as well as a shoulder-bag full of biscuits. Don Alvaro sniffed at these, and said that they were made of baked yams, mixed with almonds and coconut and afterwards dried in the sun; he had eaten them in the old days, and it was yet another proof, if such were needed, that we had reached the Isles of our quest.

This point being now settled to his satisfaction, we stood on and off all that day, searching for a port. The frigate had rejoined us, but brought no news of the *Santa Ysabel*, which further depressed our spirits. Captain Leyva reported that the volcano's flanks, which were utterly treeless and dead, rose sheer from the sea, and that there was neither harbour, anchorage nor landing place to be found in all the three leagues of its perimeter. He had heard rumblings and explosions within, and seen sparks shooting from the crater at its peak, a sight to awe the boldest heart. On the western side a stream of molten lava flowed down from two large crevices and went hissing into the waves; to the south-east rose a lesser crater, but this seemed extinct.

After sailing for some hours along a coast that was everywhere rocky and steep-to, with only an occasional narrow strip of beach, we took shelter at dusk under some low cliffs at the mouth of a cove. This proved an ill-chosen berth: when the tide rose that night, the *San Geronimo* began dragging her anchors and drifted inshore. The sky was black as pitch, except for the distant red glow of the volcano, which made our peril seem the greater. Even our most experienced sailors took alarm: unnerved by the events of the day they yelled, prayed and swore indiscriminately. The Boatswain's mate was on watch and, confident that he could deal with the emergency, did not at first summon the Chief Pilot; but Don Alvaro came dancing along to lend a hand at weighing anchor. He himself raised the capstan-chant in a reedy voice:

'God confound—the Moors and Turks,
God destroy—their wicked works!
Stand beside us—God, for we
Do extol—Thy Majesty,
Do adore—Thy only Son . . .'

'For Christ's love, your Excellency,' shouted Damian, 'go rouse the troops and make them heave at these bars, while we hoist sail and wear her off the rocks!'

But he stopped his ears to Damian's plea and continued to exert
his puny strength at the windlass:

> '. . . *Damn the pagans—Everyone!*
> *Holy Peter—strong and great,*
> *Holy Paul—his busy mate,*
> *Holy Peter—Holy Paul,*
> *Intercede—to save us all* . . .'

Juarez, who had come up to find the cause of the stamping and
shouting, ran back to the companion-ladder and bawled down: 'Out,
gentlemen of Captain Barreto's company, out on deck! If you want
glory, here's a quick chance to earn it!'

They came tumbling up with weapons in their hands. 'Where's the
enemy, Juarez? It's as dark as the inside of a black dog.'

'The sea's your enemy! Bear a hand on the windlass, fornicators,
or you'll all be dead cocks and never crow again. We're fast drifting
on the rocks. Here you, Sebastian, and you, Federico, step lively!'

'Phoo, what a gipsy's trick to play on a man! Leave those lousy
sailors to follow their trade, and we'll follow ours.'

'You scabbed and shameless dogs! If I had my way, I'd nail you to
the mast by your ears!' But they stumbled below again.

By now all the sailors were on deck, yet much needed to be done
and time was running short. I found myself at the windlass in the
company of Juarez, four sailors, two apprentices, three pages, a
merchant and his negro, the Chaplain, Jaume the water-steward,
Juan Leal the old sick-attendant and Doña Ysabel's maid Pancha; all
heaving like Sisyphus at his stone. Pancha screamed to the Virgin of
Guadelupe to assist us; by whose grace we got the anchor a-peck
before it was too late.

Damian, meanwhile, was busy making sail, and his commands rang
loud above the hubbub: 'Oh, brave hearts, have out the fore
topsail, have out main topsail, haul home the topsail sheets! Let fall
your foresail, hoist up your fore topsail, hoist up your main topsail! Up
and loose the mainsail and set him!' There was no listlessness now:
the sailors knew well that they carried their lives in their own hands.
The sails were set in a trice, but as the helmsman put the flagship
round at the Chief Pilot's orders, she heeled over and shipped a deal of
water; I thought she would capsize but she righted herself nobly,
stood clear of the rocks, and forged ahead into the open sea.

The high officers, though aware of our peril, had not stirred from

their quarters; they would as lief have taken the reins from a coachman as demean themselves by doing sailors' work. It is both the
strength and the weakness of us Spaniards that we know our duty and
perform it exactly, each according to the station in life to which God
has called him. Once, when our late sovereign Philip II was seated
near the fire, he fell asleep; the fringe of his cloak caught alight
and was soon ablaze. Yet of the courtiers who were in attendance
none was of high enough rank to pull the cloak from his shoulders,
or beat out the flames, or even arouse him from sleep; it was
only by chance that a prince of the blood happened to pass and
rescue him from a fate properly reserved for heretics. It is this
formality that makes our soldiers the steadiest in the world and unconquerable in battle. The heretical English, on the other hand, whose
armies are a rabble, prove more than our match at sea, because the
same company of men, disdaining all honourable conventions, are
as ready to swing a cutlass or lay a falconet as they are to hoist or
reef a sail.

The next morning was wet, and distant thunder could be heard.
Don Alvaro went aboard the *San Felipe* and himself took her in search
of a port, ordering the flagship to follow at a cautious distance. He
disregarded an opening in the coast bearing south-west from the
volcano, but when towards evening he returned in despair, having
found nothing, the Chief Pilot reported that he had sent the long-
boat to explore it, and that no further search was needed. It was
the entrance to a sandy bay, small but ample for our needs and
sheltered from the prevailing wind; we entered and cast anchor in
twelve fathoms.

Among the trees at the back of the bay we could see thatched roofs,
gently pitched, with wide eaves; and canoes drawn up on the beach.
Don Alvaro liked the look of the place, which was well watered, but
when at his request the Colonel sent Sergeant Dimas with ten
arquebusiers ashore to take up a position from which to cover our
landing, the natives poured from the huts with weapons, not gifts,
in their hands. Arrows came flying so thick from a clump of canes
that the Sergeant, who had been instructed to refrain from attack
whatever the provocation, withdrew his men into a canoe-house on
the beach, and knocked holes in its sides for defence. By good fortune
no one had been hurt, and Don Alvaro, convinced that the savages
were massing for an assault, ordered the Captain of Artillery to fire
a couple of balls into their midst. The roar of the falcons and the

crashing of the shot among the canes settled the matter; they ran off, panic-stricken, and cast away their weapons. But fearing that they might presently regain their courage Don Alvaro hailed the long-boat, which was on the way back to us, and sent her to fetch off the soldiers. It was still light enough to get the flotilla safely out to sea, and soon the three ships were cruising slowly along the coast again, at a distance of two leagues. When next morning we stood in-shore, after being under way all night, there was cause to praise God for what far exceeded our hopes: a commodious bay sheltered from all winds, in a fertile and thriving region.

The General named this bay Graciosa, and very gracious it seemed to us; it runs N.N.E. and S.S.W., being at the western end of the island, south of the volcano. A closely cultivated islet, some four leagues long, lies across its mouth, having a narrow channel on one side full of reefs and rocks, and on the other a clear passage half a league wide; so that the circuit of the whole bay is no less than forty leagues.

The soldiers stood to arms all night, their matches lighted, because of the noise of drums, tambourines, and other wild music with which the natives seemed to be working themselves into a war-like frenzy against us; though, as I now believe, they were merely summoning ghosts and spirits to drive us away.

In the morning the beach was alive with sightseers, the news of our arrival having travelled around the shores of the bay, on which a dozen or more villages were built, and the bolder men ventured out in their canoes to inspect the ships. They were of the same race that we had encountered on the day before, though more peaceably inclined. Many wore red flowers in their hair and nostrils, and seemed rejoiced at our coming. We signed to them to leave their weapons in the canoes and climb aboard for presents, but they hung back grinning. At last a stately, grey-haired, tawny-skinned old man, wearing a head-dress of yellow, red and blue feathers and a great many armlets, some of conch and some of boars' tusks, approached from the nearest village. The crowd on the shore made way for him and cheered as he stepped into a canoe glittering with inlay of pearl-shell, took his seat in the bows and was paddled towards us. Without hesitation he climbed the Jacob's ladder, two attendants following him, and though he carried a bow in one hand and in the other a sheaf of arrows, his dignity was such that no one thought to disarm him. He stood on the deck looking about him with grave enquiry and presently made signs as if to ask who was our chieftain, using the word *Taurique*. A soldier took him to the quarter-deck, and when he ascended the ladder, what a resplendent figure waited to receive him!

The savage's surprise could hardly have been greater than my own. I blinked and rubbed my eyes but, yes, it was the General and none other. Satisfied that God and Saint Domingo had now brought him to the end of his voyage and of his vow, he had emerged from his Franciscan habit, as a butterfly from its chrysalis, and was now sunning himself in a gown of wrought velvet, a slight well-laundered ruff, a light-blue satin suit (the doublet stuffed with many pounds of bombast, the breeches puffed and slashed and fastened to his stockings by red garters fringed with gold), a red velvet hat with a white ostrich plume, and Cordovan shoes with large, shining buckles. Never have I seen the proverb that clothes make a man so plainly substantiated; gone was the friar, and in his place stood the haughty Marquis of Neira, His Majesty's Prefect of the Solomon Islands, taken in the act of granting his first audience; one foot advanced, and his right hand resting elegantly on the pommel of a sword of state.

The Chieftain approached at an even pace, laid down his weapons in token of peace and, though plainly astonished at the brilliance of the Taurique's costume, welcomed him as an equal. Don Alvaro in return clasped his hands, embraced him and made much of him. 'What is your name?' he questioned him. 'Who are you?'

Pointing to his heart, the Chieftain replied: 'Malope.'

The new Marquis politely repeated the name and introduced himself as Don Alvaro de Mendaña.

'Mendaña!' echoed the Chieftain. With a very pleasant smile he pointed to the General, and said: 'Taurique Malope,' and then to himself: 'Taurique Mendaña.'

'No,' said Don Alvaro, 'it is contrariwise—you are Malope, I am Mendaña.' But the other would have none of it; it was his notion that they had exchanged names in token of friendship and that henceforth each of them was bound in goodwill to the other by a tie stronger even than wedlock. He had spoken in a low voice, slowly and deliberately, without the gesticulations that we Spaniards use, though he underlined his meaning by signs. For instance, to enquire whether we were hungry he drew in his belly, assumed a woe-begone expression, raised his eyebrows and then glanced searchingly at us. To find out how long we had been at sea he pointed to the sky, drew a new moon in the air, held up his hand and doubtfully thrust up first one,

then two, then three fingers and, as it were, cast the months back
over his shoulder.

He was presented with a red butcher's shirt, a pair of old green
velvet gaskins, a leather belt with a brass buckle, and a looking-glass
in which to admire himself when I had dressed him in his finery—on
occasions like this the valet's duties always fell to me. He appeared
pleased, and gave the General two of his shell armlets in exchange,
as well as a carved porpoise tooth. His escort also received gifts:
horn combs, beads, little bells, snippets of taffeta and coloured cloth,
and a playing-card or two. They silently clapped their hands before
their faces, to express their delight; then they stuck the combs into
their corded hair, tied the beads and bells around their necks,
tucked the snippets under their armlets and, rolling the cards into
tubes, thrust them through holes in the lobes of their ears. About ten
natives in all were allowed to come aboard, and the soldiers treated
them kindly, consenting as before to tuck up their sleeves and roll
down their stockings to prove that they were men, not ghosts;
after which all were friends. They taught the savages to make the
sign of peace by crossing one forefinger over the other, to say *amigos*,
and to clasp hands. They also trimmed their finger-nails and toe-
nails with scissors, and shaved their scanty beards with razors. Of
course, every native wanted these instruments for himself, but we had
agreed not to cheapen their value by giving them away without a
handsome return, as had been done at Santa Cristina. We looked
closely for any golden trinket, but saw none; however, it was held
that the natives had not sense enough even to value precious metal,
let alone mine and smelt it.

The General decided to spend a few days here at anchor, and
next morning he took the Colonel with a few soldiers for a sail in
the long-boat. They made towards the entrance of the Bay, but on
their return that evening neither of them would comment on the
day's work. From their sullen faces we deduced a sharp disagreement,
and the Boatswain's mate, who steered the boat, told me that they
had landed on the rocky headland to the north and walked about there
for nearly an hour, gesticulating at one another.

All requests for shore leave were refused until Don Alvaro should
have assured himself of the friendly disposition of the villagers;
though this seemed evident enough. They came and went, bringing
us water for our daily use in coconut shells plugged with a stopper
of leaves, and showing sincere affection and goodwill. We were also

given bananas of several varieties, coconuts, chestnuts like those of the Marquesas Islands, huge three-sided nuts hard to crack but of a very sweet taste, other nuts of the size and shape of dates, cabbage cut from the crown of palm-trees, paw-paws and sugar-cane; also fish of many kinds (some taken by line, others speared with wooden tridents) and, what pleased us most of all—great store of roast pork.

On the third day Malope paid us a ceremonious visit escorted by fifty canoes which, while he was on board, waited in a ring around us. The villagers kept their arms out of sight, but the Colonel mistrusted them, and ordered thirty arquebusiers to line the bulwarks with weapons primed, in case treachery were intended. It so happened that Don Alvaro was at his devotions when Malope arrived and the Colonel, rather gruffly, told him to wait; but he either did not understand, or else thought that the Colonel had no right to interfere in a matter that concerned chieftains. He made some dignified rejoinder and continued on his way.

'Stop that fellow!' shouted the Colonel, and the sentry at the top of the companion-ladder raised his piece threateningly. Though no shot had yet disturbed the peace of Gracious Bay, Malope showed fright: perhaps he took the arquebus for a club, or it may be that news of our first day's encounter had reached him from farther along the coast. He fled like a stag, dodging from side to side of the deck to avoid capture—for several of us tried to detain him and assure him that no harm was meant—then leapt from the bulwarks, climbed into a canoe and was soon speeding shoreward, his numerous retinue following behind. As soon as he set foot on the beach, there was a rush of people towards him, and great chattering and laughter as if he were being congratulated on his nimble escape from an ambuscade.

That same evening the natives who occupied a group of huts close to our anchorage, retired to the village, taking all their possessions with them; an action which provoked the suspicions of the high officers, though to me it was patent that Malope had come aboard with the generous intention of inviting us to settle in his territory and was now offering these huts for our use. Don Alvaro decided to send an unarmed emissary to reassure Malope of our goodwill; these savages, he said, were too noble-hearted by far to attack a single man. He called upon the Colonel first; who scornfully refused to volunteer, saying that the only way to speak to these rascals was in the language of arms, and that with twenty good fellows he would undertake to pacify the Bay within a week. Next Don Lorenzo was invited, but he held that it would be worse than murder to send an unarmed man into that cannibal camp. 'If your Excellency wants to provide your heathen friend with a carcase for his spit, why not sacrifice our little Andrés? Did we not all agree some weeks ago that he would cut up better than any man present?'

'I am ready to go,' said I, a little nettled. 'I own to a high regard for Malope, and have no fear for my life.'

Almost at once I repented my rash offer, but Don Alvaro accepted it with alacrity and I was left with no honourable retreat; so the next morning, after a miserable night, most of which I spent on my knees, they rowed me ashore like a goose on its way to the Michaelmas Fair. When I stepped out on the beach, the first Spaniard ever to have done so, my knees were trembling, but I advanced with as much dignity as I could muster, calling in my heart on Our Lady of Seville. A crowd of natives, dancing joyfully, led me along the coast-road past orchards and yam-gardens, very well-kept, until we reached the village. At its entrance stood the assembly-house, where the war-canoes were also kept, to the number of seven or eight; it was thirty paces long, and its thatched bamboo roof rested on carved posts. One of these posts represented a shark standing on its tail with a man's body disappearing down the gape of its throat, the others were cut in the shape of chieftains. The ridge-pole and beams were painted with various designs in red: a fight between canoes, a fishing expedition, and warriors dancing obscenely before a devil with lank, striped body, a tail like a dog's and fishes in his hair. Pigs' jawbones hung in a row from the wide eaves and, from the ridge-pole, the shin-bones and shoulder-blades of a man, which caused me great apprehension. Twenty or more common huts were arranged in a circle around Malope's house, which at first I mistook for a temple, and the barn in which he stored his yams.

I was greeted by the assembled warriors with lavish hospitality, and though there was a rush to open my doublet and admire my white skin, and to take other familiarities with my person, at least no women were allowed in the assembly-house, or near it, so that I had no cause to blush.

Upon being asked my business, I said: 'Malope—Mendaña—*amigos*,' and drew a yellow silk kerchief from my pocket. Since this was a gift for their Chieftain they did not dare to touch it; but to conciliate them I distributed a few glass beads and playing-cards.

A meal was then set on the floor beside me: a large wooden dish containing boiled bananas, uncooked crabs and prawns, mashed turnips covered with coconut cream, a seaweed having the appearance of grapes, and cake made of sago-pith. I ate with relish, leaving only the raw seafood untasted, and between mouthfuls smiled back cheerfully at my amused hosts.

After I had done, they brought me an unripe nut of the sort that stains the spittle red when it is chewed, and which is called *buhio* in the Philippines. I accepted it with reluctance rather than risk offending them. They showed me how to bite off and spit out the top of the nut, which is the size of a large plum, then how to hold it sideways between my teeth, crack it open, dip it in powdered lime, roll it in a leaf, and chew. This leaf, being peppery, drowned the taste of the nut, which I presently swallowed, but this was a mistake—the natives spit out what they have chewed—and very soon my blood began to throb violently in my veins. I had a feeling of drunkenness and lost all fear of my hosts. I rose giddily, and asked to be led to the Chieftain. They took me around the village, telling me the names of the various huts, as though I would want to memorize them; showed me a pen full of fine pigs, and a good stone well with a boarded top and steps going down to the water. Every hut had a wall of loose stones around it, with an opening for a door and pots of flowers and sweet-scented shrubs standing just inside. The sides of the huts were weatherboarded and from the roofs rose little cock-lofts reached by ladders, where they stored their provisions.

At last we reached Malope's house, which was higher than the rest and had a façade decorated with red, white and black lozenges, set between wavy bands of red. Three human skulls were nailed outside to a post. As with the other huts, the only way in was by a round hole at waist height, provided with a shutter; but this one had a porch in front, raised level with the entrance, which was a chieftainly privilege. My guides hung back now, as I mounted boldly on the porch. I was kept waiting a little while and then shown inside by a hunchback with lime-bleached hair.

Some time elapsed before my eyes accustomed themselves to the darkness, but soon I became aware of Malope lying on a low platform behind a circle of cooking-stones, which formed a rude hearth in the centre of the hut. Three men and four women stood about him in attendance. Mats were spread on the floor, and I noticed a pair of large wooden drums in a corner and various weapons hanging from the roof; but otherwise the place was unfurnished, except for earthenware pots and wooden dishes.

'Malope—Mendaña—*amigos*,' I repeated. Raising himself on one elbow, Malope enquired after his brother. In answer I held my belly with both hands, groaned and pointed sadly to a sleeping-mat, my intention being to plead sickness as an excuse for the General's failure either to greet him yesterday or to come ashore today. Malope expressed his sympathy by kneading his own belly and groaning; then he sent a woman to fetch physic for the complaint—which proved to be a root of wild ginger. I smelled it approvingly, showed my gratitude by placing my hand on my heart, and then proffered the silk kerchief as a peace token. He accepted this with satisfaction, looped it through the lobe of his right ear, and handed me a frontlet of carved pearl-shell to take back to his brother.

He chewed *buhio* but, to my relief, offered me none. Presently he sent for a pale, plump young girl who came from behind a partition and seemed, by the profusion of her ornaments, to be his daughter. Most of her jewellery consisted of red and white shell beads, strung into patterns; but though weighed down with fillets, bracelets, anklets, necklaces and ear-rings, she wore no shame-fringe, being still a virgin; and here I must say that in this island virginity was as jealously guarded as in Spain, loose behaviour in a woman not being countenanced either before or after marriage.

Malope made me understand that if the General would give him one of his own daughters in exchange—for he knew we had women on board—a double wedding would be celebrated, with much pig-killing, which would unite their houses indissolubly. I clapped my hands in admiration of the girl's beauty, and promised to advise the General of the great honour intended for him but reported that, alas, he had been blessed with no daughters and was already married. When I tried to persuade Malope that a man could have only one wife, he silenced me with a frown, declaring positively that common men might have only one, but a chieftain must have four or five. In proof, he pointed to his own obedient harem. Unless I misunderstood him, he then offered to accept Doña Ysabel's cow in lieu of the bride, which would confer equal glory on his village.

I was giving him a goodbye when he pointed to my shoe-buckles and expressed the wish to tie them to his own naked feet. I prized those buckles, but feared to deny him, and so ripped them off; however, I thought it incumbent on me, as an envoy, to ask for a present in return, and pointed to one of his armlets. This he would not give me, saying that I was no chieftain, but when I left his house he followed me out and bespoke me one of equal size from a neighbour, who yielded it very grudgingly.

I returned down the coast-road with a jaunty step, and the savages escorted me in friendly fashion to the skiff. When I appeared in the Great Cabin with flowers and feathers stuck in my hat, and a redstained mouth, the Barretos mocked me and wanted to know how raw human flesh tasted; and though the General assured the high officers that they might now forget their suspicions of the natives, they would not listen either to him or to me.

The farther side of the Bay was ringed with bonfires that night, which were held to be beacons of war, because at dusk three canoes had gone up and down the coast at great speed, as though bearing an urgent message. The soldiers, chafing at the profound peace that had hitherto prevailed and longing for an excuse to use their arms, were greatly encouraged by this sight. 'The sooner the fighting begins, the sooner it will be over,' they said, 'and until we have conquered we shall make no progress with the settlement. Those naked fools treat us as equals, but they must be made to recognize that our arms and religion entitle us to be their lords.' At dawn the distant fires were still burning.

That morning a skiff put out from the galeot and some sailors went ashore to fill their water-jars at a stream on the farther side of Malope's village. They were going about their task heedless of danger, when a war-cry was raised from the bushes close by, and arrows whistled about them. Two men were wounded in the legs, and one had his arm transfixed by an arrow above the elbow, but all were able to escape to the skiff, where the soldiers who had been guarding it gave fire and thus halted the pursuit. It was feared that the arrows were poisoned, and two of the sailors, who thought their last hour had come, clamoured for extreme unction; but the wounds healed cleanly, and in a fortnight they were none the worse. The natives did indeed smear their arrows with the juice of an herb, but as a charm to guide them to their mark, not as a means of poisoning the quarry; sometimes, however, they dipped them into the putrifying guts of a corpse and this sort of magic, when we learned of it, caused us anxiety.

Don Alvaro, who had kept to his bed for the last day or two, was informed of the ambush and displayed righteous anger. When the Colonel proposed to take a punitive force to the scene of the incident and do as much damage as possible to the huts in the neighbourhood, he agreed. So the Colonel went ashore in high glee, with thirty men, and surprising the enemy as they came back for the last of our water-jars, fell upon them with lance and sword. He was a soldier of the old school, who preferred the clash of arms to the roar of guns; but the savages stood their ground so manfully and showed themselves so dextrous in the use of their spears that at last, dizzied by a blow on his helmet, he gave the order to open fire. Five natives fell to the ground and lay writhing, the rest fled. He pursued them to a group of huts by the shore, which he set on fire with his own hand, and then ordered his men to cut down a grove of coconut-palms in such a way that they would fall across the canoes drawn up on the beach; and when this had been accomplished and the coconuts gathered at ease, he laid a torch to the shattered canoes, took three pigs from a pen, and marched back in triumph.

Thus ended the first week of our visit to this island which, in honour of the piece of the True Cross displayed to us at Lima, Don Alvaro had named Santa Cruz. He now regretfully abandoned the notion that it was part of San Cristobal; but why so large an island should lie in the same latitude and yet have remained hidden from view on his first voyage, he could not well make out. We had covered more than eighteen hundred and fifty leagues since we left Callao, and it seemed impossible that San Cristobal should lie even farther to the west. Once more he suspected the Chief Pilot of perfidy and spoke slightingly of him behind his back.

Chapter 14

THE ERUPTION

Don Alvaro complained of weakness and a sensation as if of burning down the right side of his body, but had no fever and ate with an appetite. Doña Mariana spent a deal of time at his bedside, where she showed him more love than did her sister; and though it seemed strange that she should have forgiven him so easily, at first I suspected nothing. Then one day, in the Great Cabin, while chronicling Malope's visit to the flagship and mine to the village, I happened to set down this observation: that the natives had carefully collected their nail-parings and hair-clippings and thrown them into the sea for fear that we might make magic with them; and that Malope had likewise been at pains to dispose safely of his red spittle and the leavings of his buhio, dropping them into a box at the base of his roof pillar with a muttered prayer to the idol carved above it. At that I laid down my pen, seized by a sudden horror. I recalled that three days before, at the same hour, I had seen Doña Mariana drop her thimble and send it rolling across the floor with a covert motion of her foot, and that when I hurried to retrieve it she told me sharply that I was not her valet. She had let a minute or two pass by, then rose leisurely and groped for it herself, but kept her back turned towards me; though I guessed that she was picking up something else besides, I could not see what it was. It came upon me now that after breakfast on the same day Don Alvaro had been seated on the chest close to where the thimble went, trimming his nails. Had she been gathering what he let fall, before the pages came to sweep the floor?

I remembered fragments of gossip that had reached me since we left Callao, especially about the pack of Tarot cards that a witch in the ship was said to be using for divination. Elvira, who whispered the story to Jaume, did not give the woman's name but described the pack as though she had seen and handled it. She told him that when, at the request of a person of importance, two blind cards were drawn for Don Alvaro, the six of Sceptres turned up, which foretells failure of an enterprise in the midst of execution, and with it the Lightning-struck Tower, a card of great misfortune; and that when another two were drawn for Doña Ysabel, they proved to be the Ace of Cups, which marks the beginning of a love affair, and the Chariot, portending its triumphant conclusion. I guessed that the witch must be either Doña Mariana herself or her maid Inez, and that the person of importance could only be Doña Ysabel—who else would have asked for blind cards to be drawn for her and her husband? Also, Miguel Llano had told me in scorn and detestation, not long before his death, that he had surprised Doña Ysabel and her sister at the taffrail, two hours after midnight, courtseying to the full moon. 'All Galician women are witches,' he said, 'and all their menfolk stand in dread of them.'

Though I had only hearsay and suspicion to go upon, I would have wagered a thousand pesos to ten that Doña Mariana had kneaded the General's nail-parings, and perhaps also his hair-clippings, into a waxen image of him, to melt and waste over a candle. Her new solicitude was a cruel sham: an attempt to regain his confidence so that she could be the more easily revenged. But even if I were confronted with clear proof of her guilt, would it be my duty to warn Don Alvaro of the plot against his life? Fray Junipero, an authority on these matters, had taught me as a child that no witch has power over a Catholic while he meets his obligations to God and his neighbour— as Don Alvaro claimed to do; and it has always been my principle not to meddle in what does not directly concern me. Admittedly, my decision to do and say nothing was influenced by my secret dread of Doña Ysabel, who seemed to be conniving at the plot, if not actively furthering it; that she sheltered a sorceress who dealt out the seventy-eight cards of fate proved her readiness to ally herself with the powers of evil.

The Colonel led a second punitive expedition, this time on his own initiative, to a cluster of huts on a hill overlooking the scene of the previous day's skirmish. Going ashore in the long-boat just before dawn, he and his party of forty men contrived to surround the hill without alarming the natives and block every path that led to its summit. He then headed a charge, but meeting with no opposition at the approaches to the hamlet, fired the thatch of the huts to make the inhabitants bolt. Out they leaped through the door holes, first the women and children, then the elders, lastly the warriors armed with spears and clubs. A short, sharp fight ensued. The men, who numbered only seven, defended themselves courageously, scorning the great odds, and were cut down one by one until only a youth was left standing, his shield-arm nearly severed, who nevertheless darted through the ring and escaped. The Colonel restrained the troops from ravishing the women, though they regarded this as their right under the rules of war; he told them that soldiers must be chivalrous and take nothing from a woman that she does not yield freely, even if they have first widowed her. Two hours later he returned to the flagship with several wounded men and five dead pigs. 'Your Excellency,' he cried, striding into the Great Cabin and displaying the blood on his sword, 'we have taught these blackamores the folly of making an unprovoked attack. I undertake that they'll not sing so loud in future.'

'I am sorry, my lord,' the General complained, 'that you did not think fit to consult me before you set out.'

'Sage anticipation of orders is the duty of every field-officer,' returned the Colonel, thrusting out his chin.

'And of every pork-butcher, when Saint Martin's Day comes round,' remarked Doña Ysabel with a contemptuous glance at his naked sword, 'though that will not be for many weeks yet.'

Later we watched the natives lowering the corpses into canoes, each with its knees drawn up to the chin and a stone tied under them as a sinker. Among these were the corpses of three women, the widows of the fallen, who appeared to have been strangled. Their kinsfolk rowed them out a cable's length from the shore, freed them from the leaves in which they were wrapped, and threw them into the sea, where the sharks gathered for the feast almost at once. The islanders regard these creatures as divine and (though this may sound strange to Christians) if a man happens to fall out of his canoe and be pursued by a shark but climbs back to safety, his friends and kinsfolk will toss him out again to appease its rage.

In the afternoon Malope came down to the beach and cried across the water to us, his voice shrill with grief. He summoned the General with 'Malope! Malope!' and then beat his breast, exclaiming 'Mendaña! Mendaña!' He pointed to the smouldering huts, the felled palms and the shallows where the corpses had been sunk, and

then, so plainly that not even a child could have mistaken his meaning, he signed that it was not his people who had ambushed our
sailors, but enemies from the other side of the Bay. He strung his
bow and made as if to shoot an arrow in that direction, inviting us to
join him in a war of vengeance on the villains who had disturbed the
peace.

Don Alvaro's heart was touched: spreading his arms wide, he
invited Malope aboard, who however would not listen, for some
scruple that he had; nevertheless he came the next day and peace was
restored. The General gave him some red cloth in compensation, and
this infuriated Don Diego, who regarded the gift as a confession of
weakness. But Don Luis reproved him: 'Brother,' he said, 'Don
Alvaro is acting prudently. While we have Malope as our ally we
can make use of him in the subjugation of the neighbouring tribes.
Let us divide and conquer, as the Romans did.'

Don Lorenzo was not present at the time, having sailed in the
frigate with twenty soldiers to search for the *Santa Ysabel* once more.
His instructions were to cruise around the island until he reached
the position where she had last been sighted; then to steer W.N.W.,
which was the direction in which she would have driven had she
kept the wind dead astern and allowed it to take her where God willed.
When he returned on the afternoon of the 21st of September, which
was Saint Matthew's Day, we were shifting our berth to a more
convenient anchorage half a league beyond Malope's village. He
brought no news of the lost ship, but reported that he had circumnavigated Santa Cruz, a matter of a hundred leagues, and discovered
another bay due south of ours, equally commodious and with even
more canoes on its waters, also various islands of moderate size, all
lying within ten leagues of our coast. But W.N.W. of where we had
parted from the Admiral, many reefs stretched as far as the eye could
see, and he had not cared to hazard his ship among them. If the
Santa Ysabel had indeed taken that course on the night we lost her,
she must have been cast away; and so might we, too, but for God's
great mercy. This convinced most of us that the ship and our
comrades had perished, and the wise ones (but they were few)
understood that with the halving of our numbers we must be more
studious than ever to conciliate the natives, and that our settlement
must be founded on a far more modest plan that Don Alvaro's letters
patent provided. It is true that the great Pizarro when, marching
from Tumbes to Cajamarca, he seized the Inca of Peru and levied

tribute on his vast realm, had with him no larger forces than ours; but Don Alvaro was no Pizarro, no, not by much.

The new anchorage was close inshore, the bottom being mud at a depth of from twenty to thirty fathoms. About four hundred paces inland, nearly opposite our berth, a copious stream of good water vanished under some rocks before entering the bay, and about five hundred paces farther to the east a fair-sized river flowed. We had been warned by Malope that he exercized no power in these parts, and so soon as we cast anchor this was brought home to us by signs of open hostility all along the shore. That evening the ring of fires blazed again, and we heard roars as though of a bull-fight or carnival procession from a village which lay within falcon-shot beyond the river. The soldiers stood to their arms all night, and at dawn an army of about five hundred warriors trooped down to the beach, shouting defiance and sending great numbers of arrows, darts and stones in our direction; when these all fell into the sea, they waded in breast-high to shorten the range, but even so they could not reach us. They continued to shout and, with a splashing stroke to keep away the sharks, some swam out to our anchor-buoys, cut them loose and towed them ashore. Their name for us, accompanied by much spitting, holding of noses and turning of bare backsides, was 'The Amigos.' We wondered that they did not fight from canoes.

Don Lorenzo rushed into the Great Cabin to tell the General what was afoot. 'These docile subjects of yours will be running off with the Royal Standard next,' he cried indignantly.

'We had better teach them a lesson,' said Don Alvaro, sighing. 'They have no excuse to treat us ill, and if any of Malope's people are among them, that is no fault of ours.'

'May I take fifteen of my company out in the skiff to skirmish with them?'

'By all means; but tell the Colonel that you have my permission.'

Don Lorenzo reported to the Colonel, who had been on the point of setting out himself and now must needs stay behind. He loved to be in the forefront of battle and was one of those officers of whom it is said that they keep watch-dogs, but bark themselves. 'Go then, in the Devil's name, Captain Barreto,' he said, 'but look you, Sir, you are to do nothing rash!'

Among the party in the skiff were seven targeteers who, though arrows were discharged against them in a cloud (some tipped with flints, which was a novelty, and some with bone), protected their comrades so well that only two were wounded, both of them by glancing shots that furrowed their shoulders. Don Lorenzo held his fire and, as soon as he beached the skiff, leaped out against the enemy, sword in hand, followed by the targeteers in close order. The natives fought every man for himself, and the small Spanish phalanx was soon hard pressed. From where I watched at the taffrail, it was lost to sight among a huge crowd of howling savages, who danced in and out like bees at a swarming, while their leaders went forward to the attack, thrusting with their long spears and battering at the targes with their curved clubs.

The Colonel was wild with resentment. 'The lightnings of Sinai blast and shrivel that fool!' he shouted. 'He'll have all my best targeteers killed. Why in the name of Pope Joan doesn't he use fire-arms? For what other purpose were the accursed things invented? Sergeant!' he hallooed through his cupped hands. 'Hey, you there by the skiff, Sergeant Gallardo! Give fire at once, man, do you hear?'

The Sergeant heard and obeyed. Two or three of the savages fell at the first volley, several more were wounded, and the rest fled, leaving Don Lorenzo and his men panting, unhurt and alone on the field, greatly vexed that their sport had been spoiled.

'How dared you give fire without my orders, Sergeant?' cried Don Lorenzo, pale with rage. 'I had the fellows already on the run. You might have killed one of us with your volley.'

'Begging your honour's pardon,' replied the Sergeant, 'the Colonel shouted to me from the flagship.'

'This is my battle, not his,' yelled Don Lorenzo, forgetting in his excitement that he was addressing a mere sergeant, 'and it was the General, not he, who gave me my orders. The Colonel is no more than a spectator! Come, lads, let's go after the sons of bitches and cut the livers out of their black sides!'

The Colonel stamped his foot and ground his teeth. 'This is too much! It needed only that maravedi's worth to make up the full peso!' He bellowed after Don Lorenzo: 'Come back, you young fool! Come back at once, I say! By the seven boils of Job, if you weren't the General's brother-in-law, I'd clap you in the stocks. You're exceeding your orders and endangering my men!'

Don Lorenzo either did not hear or did not care to hear; he ran on. The Colonel crammed the long-boat with troops and leaped in after them. 'Row like demons, you red-capped scum!' he shouted at the crew.

The beach was deserted except for the arquebusiers guarding the skiff, and a little black boy, about three years of age, who sat and sobbed beside a canoe, rubbing his eyes with his fists; it is not known how he came to be on the battle-field. A trail of blood showed where the wounded natives had been carried off in their comrades' arms, or supported by their shoulders if they could walk. The Colonel sent his negro in haste after Don Lorenzo with an urgent message of recall, which he had no choice but to obey.

'Did my ears play me false, Don Lorenzo?' he asked, plucking at his beard, 'or did you indeed reprimand Sergeant Gallardo for obeying me?'

'I cannot answer for your honour's ears,' Don Lorenzo replied sullenly, 'nor do I recall what I said in the heat of fight, when you saw fit to interfere with my dispositions. The orders for this skirmish came from your superior officer, my brother-in-law, who has complete confidence in me.'

'Yet I can recall your words very well, and they were not only ill-mannered but damned mutinous. Hark ye, knave, while I am Colonel I will be obeyed, and since you have injured my honour in the hearing of the common soldiery, I need have no tender regard for yours.'

'Before you say anything that cannot be unsaid, Don Pedro Merino,' returned the other, very coolly, 'pray remember that I command this company and that any insult shown me will be resented by officers and men alike.'

'Rein in your mare, boy,' said the Colonel, 'or, by God's bones, I'll give her to another—saddle, bridle, bit and all! One more word, and I'll degrade you and appoint a less insolent officer in your place. Now get back to your quarters, and stay there!'

Don Lorenzo returned in the skiff, and the Colonel took thirty men in pursuit of the enemy, but too much time had been wasted; an hour or two later he reappeared without having come across a single armed native, though with a booty of ten fat hogs.

Doña Ysabel sat waiting for him when he entered the Great Cabin to make his report to the General. 'Oh, good day, Colonel,' she said in an off-hand manner. 'May I have a word in private with you, after you have spoken to my husband?'

He bowed low. 'You know me well, my lady. I may be a shaggy old soldier, but you can command me in everything, as the wild unicorn of the forests will tamely lay his horn in a virgin's lap and weep tears of joy.'

She took these words as reflecting on her enforced chastity, and walked out on the gallery, scarcely able to contain her rage. The Colonel turned to Don Alvaro, made a brief report, and then went after her.

Doña Ysabel opened the attack at once, not troubling to lower her voice; she must have intended Don Alvaro to hear every word. 'My lord,' she said, 'I am not ignorant of either your age, your rank, or your reputation in the field; indeed, it would be strange if I were, because you have so crammed these down our throats at table that often we feel like spewing them up, dinner and all. But they do not awe me: since my girlhood I have moved in far more illustrious company, and were you the Archangel Michael himself and commanded all the hosts of Heaven, I would still give you the same warning: that to insult one Barreto is to insult all! You bawdy old sinner, the sooner you are thrown to the sharks, the better we shall all be pleased. Understand now that I'll not tolerate any interference with my brother, while he is carrying out my husband's orders.'

The Colonel was plainly taken aback, but for once he controlled himself. 'Noble lady,' he said, 'your family pride does you credit, and the loyalty I owe the General prevents me from defending myself when you abuse me so cruelly; but I must be permitted to remind you that even a Barreto cannot alter our military laws and conventions. The orders given Don Lorenzo were passed through me, and therefore it was I who became responsible to your husband that he carried them out to the letter and, what is more, that he and his men returned safely to this ship. Your brother is a fine fellow, and it would be a thousand pities if he were cut down in the flower of his youth. Though I confess to having reprimanded him sharply for exceeding his orders, that was not only my right, but my duty: he must not be allowed to hazard his life needlessly. It is otherwise with myself, who am in a position to take risks that he has no call to take. What may be the end of a bawdy old sinner like Pedro Merino is no one's concern—unless his enemies are bent on hastening it, which is likely enough—but, by the Mother of God, his hope is to die by stroke of sword and not in bed, and if a mass or two be presently sung for his soul, the sharks are welcomed to the carrion.'

'You make no retraction and you offer no apology?'

'No, madam, to my deep regret it would be consonant neither with my honour nor with military discipline to do so.'

'His honour, says he! A plague on that, you soused black pudding, you hound in gaskins, you toss-pot, you turd, you beruffed tinker's ass!'

The Colonel stepped back a pace. I saw him through the door-way, gazing at her in shame and wonder: this was the language of the stable, not the Court. He had gone out to the gallery with a resolve to choke back the least discourteous word, however sorely he might be provoked; not so much (he afterwards said) because he feared to give the Barretos an excuse for revenging themselves, as because he sincerely repented his unchivalrous behaviour on that luckless day at Callao. Yet to stay silent under provocation was not in his nature and, in a firm voice, he replied: 'Well, madam, you have had your say, from which I understand that there is no room for you and me to sit at the same table, no, not though half a league of oaken board and a couple of hundred priests and merchants were to separate your seat from mine. But before I take my ruff and gaskins ashore, together with the maligned carcase which they adorn, permit me to sing you a farewell song in the most tuneful bray that a tinker's ass may command.' And, laying his hand upon his heart, he began at once in a cracked and throaty tenor:

'The witches of Corunna
    They come in black and white,
But Saint James with his sword-hilt
    Put them all to flight;
For the Devil, their master,
    Who on that cross did gaze
Broke foul wind at either end
    And swooned for amaze.'

He returned chuckling to the Great Cabin, informed the General that he was taking troops ashore to complete the pacification of the neighbourhood, and went off to his quarters, where with his page's help he packed his chest and cloak-bag, and made a bundle of what these would not hold. A trumpet sounded a general parade. He chose sixty men, half of them settlers and half serving soldiers, told them shortly: 'Lads, be merry, for today we shall make a start,' and sent them below again for their belongings. The boat made two trips and they were soon ashore.

Since he had taken the Adjutant with him, and all the ensigns except Don Diego, a profound though uneasy peace reigned at supper that night. 'Who comes not to table must forfeit his share,' said Doña Ysabel cheerfully. 'And what prodigious gluttons they were!'

she added, as though she did not expect them ever again to take their accustomed seats on the benches.

The burden of conversation fell on the Vicar, the Chaplain and the Chief Pilot. Father Juan spoke innocently of his joy that the great work had now been taken in hand. From his experience of savages, he judged that no second demonstration of our martial power would be needed, and that it was now possible to plant the Cross and spread the gospel throughout this spacious island. 'It is to be hoped that the General's health will allow him to go ashore tomorrow, since Don Lorenzo and the Colonel have gained so resounding a victory. His must be the honour of choosing the site of the church which, since he has named this island Santa Cruz, I propose to dedicate to Saint Veronica; but perhaps it will be enough at first to sanctify a native assembly-house. We could replace the idolatrous posts with plain ones, board up the front, and set the altar at the eastern end: a sacristy could then be added. Later, I hope to build a church in a style more pleasing to God, with room for a thousand souls, and take up subscriptions for an annual endowment. Ten thousand pesos should suffice for five years—when we shall be well on our feet. Don Lorenzo, where did you say that the General is to found the first of the three cities?'

'On the rocky headland at the entrance of the bay, your Reverence, the one that juts out towards the islet. He chose it because it commands a wide view of the sea, and because the absence of trees and bushes allows us a clear field of defensive fire. The air is salubrious and a small spring rises near by, sufficient for our needs if properly channeled. There are many other advantages besides . . .'

'But no harbour,' interrupted the Chief Pilot. 'It seems to me absurd to found a city eight leagues from the nearest anchorage, whatever the military merits of the site.'

'. . . for instance, that the islet lies handy and will be our orchard and granary,' continued Don Lorenzo, disregarding Pedro Fernandez.

But he persisted. 'If your honour will undertake to build a port on the landward side, using either cranes or conjuration—I care not which—to clear the bottom of its many rocks, and then heap them into a mole, I shall say no more. But it is rumoured that the Colonel, who visited the headland with Don Alvaro, raised the very same objection.'

'The General has the last word, Sir,' said Don Lorenzo coldly, 'as both you and the Colonel are apt to forget. If an artificial harbour be needed, doubtless he has made plans for its construction.'

'Heaven forbid that I should question either his authority or his resourcefulness,' replied the Chief Pilot, 'but it seems strange to me that I was not consulted before the decision was taken.'

'Come, come, Sailor! Land is land, and sea is sea. A matter of military strategy can be decided only by soldiers, and there is no call for you to dip your oar in here.'

Doña Ysabel made peace between them. 'In my opinion, brother,' she said, 'the Chief Pilot's objection deserves to be considered, even if it does coincide with the Colonel's. Don Alvaro's choice was not a final one, and if no site can be found in Gracious Bay to fulfil all military and naval requirements, perhaps the other bay which you discovered yourself will provide what we need. Now that our numbers are fewer, let our talk be more comradely.' She went on to ask Father Juan what form of ritual was used to purge a heathen place of worship of its devils and convert it to Christian use.

The Vicar launched into a learned discourse on exorcism, and made us quake with his horrific tales of black art and devil-worship; how certain Indians of Panama cut off the heads of Spanish soldiers and shrank their skulls by magic until they were the size of a fist. Yet a simple monk, barefoot and unattended, went boldly to their principal shrine, where these skulls were laid up, displayed the Cross to the sorcerers there assembled, and lo! a miracle . . .

As he spoke, and paused solemnly for emphasis, an immense roar was heard, like ten thousand barrels of gun-powder exploding together, and the ship shook and rocked at her moorings. We rushed on deck and stared at the huge, luminous cloud that towered over the northern horizon, in shape like a mushroom. Later we found that the volcano, which was called Tinahula and regarded as the abode of a fiery demon, had blown off its peak and filled the sea for leagues around with lumps of pumice. Whenever Tinahula is in eruption the natives believe that they have incurred the demon's displeasure, and this may have accounted for their meek behaviour during the next few days, while the volcano continued to rumble and breathe out flames and smoke.

It so happened that the Chief Pilot, in talk with the Ensign-Royal, had already expressed his disagreement with the proposed site and this was soon taken up by the other ensigns. So next morning the Colonel, who had spent the night in a native village, easily persuaded them to forestall Don Alvaro by founding a settlement close to our new anchorage, between the stream, the river and the sea. He posted piquets, paced out distances, and sent the skiff to the flagship with a request for tools, having resolved to begin work at once. The Purser gave him whatever axes, wood-knives, mattocks and spades could be found, but they were not many, and the only saws we had were owned by the ship's carpenters, who would not part with them.

The General had no notion of what was afoot, until presently Juan de Buitrago's father-in-law came to him, cap in hand, with a plea on behalf of the other married settlers. 'Your Excellency,' said old Miguel Geronimo, 'if we may make so bold, we cannot agree that the site chosen by the Colonel is a good one. We do not object to the soil, which is as rich as that of Andalusia: it will raise any crop we may choose to sow, as one glance at the native gardens will tell you. But, by your Excellency's leave, we think the spot unhealthy and fear that it may breed fever. I have six children, beside my married daughter, and should not care to live there with them. That the natives have not settled on the site is clear proof of its badness: why else should they have built their nearest huts a thousand paces away from good water? I have been deputed to ask your Excellency's permission to occupy some native village, where we can be safe from fever; but the Colonel is vexed with us, because we hold back when the un-married men are already employed, and therefore we humbly demand your protection.'

Don Alvaro sat up in bed. 'Is this indeed the truth? Has the Colonel set them to work so soon?'

'He has, your Excellency. They are felling trees with a will to build him a guard-house, and cutting posts and rafters, and trimming branches for thatch. But we oldsters are far from content, though he assures us that we must brush our fears aside for the sake of God and good King Philip, and that the valour of Spaniards will over-come all adversities.'

The General clapped his hands. 'Hey, Myn! Fetch me my second-best suit; I must go ashore and put a stop to this foolishness.'

'And none too soon, your Excellency,' put in Don Diego. 'Pray take a loaded stick with you of the same weight as the Colonel's.'

Chapter 15

A SETTLEMENT FOUNDED

As Don Alvaro re-entered the Great Cabin, Doña Ysabel asked him: 'How did your excursion go, my lord? Is the Colonel in the stocks yet?'

Her brothers being present, he displayed some embarrassment. 'Not yet, my lady,' he replied. 'There are a hundred and one different ways of killing a cat.'

'Some far swifter than others. It is better to dash out its brains than shut it in a barn and wait for the mice to pull it down.'

'In principle, I agree with you. But this cunning old tom is not to be destroyed out of hand. He showed me his usual deference and explained that, since I was sick, he had not cared to trouble me with matters of military routine—such as clearing the forest around the spring to deny the natives cover for another ambush against our watering parties, or using the felled timber to build a few huts for shelter and defence. Oh, no, the rogue protests, he never had the least intention of founding a settlement; that is my province, not his, and he would never presume—and much more to the same effect. . . . But did I not agree that it is wise in a season of squalls and great heat, to keep the soldiers healthily exercised? And that it is better to set them to a task of even temporary usefulness than allow them to become dispirited? "How dispirited?" I asked. "From waiting for your Excellency to choose the site of your island capital," he told me. "Yes, my lord," I replied, with a glance to wither him, "such exercises have their instructional value." '

'Yet he pulled the wool over your eyes,' Doña Ysabel persisted. 'You would have been well advised to arrest him at once, instead of listening to his lame excuses. And when he charged you with demoralizing the men by your delay, upon my life, I should have lost all patience had I been there! However, my disposition is not so tranquil as yours. What then? Did you order the work to cease?'

'Why, of course, my lady. It was discontinued while I called a council of officers, sergeants and representatives of the married settlers.'

'Caramba, a council! Instead of issuing his orders the Prefect calls a council?'

'At my age one learns that the longest way round is often the shortest way home. I would not necessarily be bound by the decisions of the council, and wished to gauge the strength of the opposition to the Colonel's plan.'

'And what did this wonderful council decide?'

'The Ensign-Royal and the Adjutant made the longest speeches. They moved that the work be continued, holding that short of abandoning Gracious Bay altogether, we must necessarily plant the settlement near its only good anchorage, and that there was thus no alternative to the Colonel's site. A couple of sergeants and all the married settlers disagreed. Old Miguel Geronimo contended that the place was unhealthy and that it would be better by far to occupy the village where they all slept last night, and adapt it to our needs; it is built on a hill, he said, and has a deep draw-well. A sergeant spoke in his support, declaring that a stockade and ditch, with guns mounted at the approaches, would make it impregnable. The Colonel took offence at the Sergeant's presumption and told him that he knew no more about the art of fortification than a thrush; but I allowed him to have his say.'

'That was Sergeant Dimas, was it not?'

'The same bold and honest man.'

'Yet you would have had him hoisted at Paita for coming to the rescue of my brothers.'

'That was never my intention, whatever I may have told the Colonel. Well, then I knew what I had come to discover. From the Ensign-Royal's words it was clear that the Colonel did indeed propose to found a settlement, not merely defend the approaches to the spring. On the spur of the moment I let him have his way; after recording my own preference for the healthier site on the headland. I put the matter to a vote and called for a show of hands. They decided in favour of continuing work by eleven against five. The Colonel was prudent enough to abstain from either speaking or voting; however, he has fathered the project and, as difficulties increase, the unwilling spirit of the minority will infect the rest and they will soon combine to make him the scapegoat of their follies.'

'Let me warn you once more, husband: you are playing a dangerous game. If the place proves to be a healthy one after all, the Colonel will get the credit; if the reverse, our people will be weakened by fever and blame you for not having silenced him. Besides, our provisions will not last for ever. You should have supported Sergeant Dimas's plea; that would have dealt the Colonel his needed rebuff and at the same time pleased the troops by easing their labours.'

'No, no! I could never in conscience authorize the seizure of a native village. What they may give us voluntarily, is welcome; but God will never let us prosper if we come here in the guise of thieves. We must conquer this savage people by love, not fear.'

'Surely you did not say so at the council?'

'Indeed, I did, in no uncertain voice.'

'By all the angels and archangels! And in so doing alienated the goodwill of the minority by leaving them no alternative to the Colonel's plan?'

'When his plan fails, as fail it must, I shall found our city in the place of my choice. Come my lady, I can speak no more; this outing has fatigued me almost to death. Send for Myn, tell him to make my bed and then undress me.'

The high colour of Doña Ysabel's cheeks and the restless snapping of her fingers told me that she was angered beyond words by his failure to discipline the Colonel; but, the Chief Pilot entering the room unexpectedly, she made a brave show of patience and ostentatiously fluttered the leaves of her pious book.

Next day, she persuaded Don Alvaro to send the remaining officers and soldiers ashore, except for the gunners and a standing guard commanded in turn by each of the ensigns. The settlers' families, who went at the same time, were to live in tents until houses should be built for them. The Barretos agreed among themselves to make things as difficult as possible for the Colonel, and to report at once to Don Alvaro if he showed the least sign of disloyalty. Doña Ysabel and her sister, the Chief Pilot, the priests, two merchants and myself stayed aboard the *San Geronimo* with Don Alvaro who, though he grew a little thinner and more haggard every day and complained of mysterious pains in different parts of his body, did not take to his bed again, but courageously fought the disorder with his shoes on.

The Chief Pilot, glad that he could at last move freely about the ship, set his men to swab and fumigate with rosemary the stinking quarters now left vacant. Carpenters patched the upper works where they had been stripped for fuel, and the sailors repainted the hull above the water line, but complained much of the stifling heat and, in their desire for the open sea, began asking when they might expect to be sent back to Peru. He could only counsel patience.

On shore, the Colonel showed himself as capable as he was industrious, and the natives did not attempt to interfere with his building. Every morning when I went across with the daily orders—for Don Alvaro governed the settlement from the Great Cabin while his Residency was being constructed—I noticed the progress made since the day before. A belt of forest was being cleared, though the want of axes and saws was greatly resented. To show his goodwill, Don Alvaro ordered the carpenters to give up theirs, which they did with ill grace, not yet having completed their repairs; he also found some old swords, intended for barter, which could be used as wood-knives. We had a blacksmith with us who undertook to beat out axe-heads from old iron in the galeot's ballast; but it was at last disclosed that the forge which figured in our list of stores had been left behind in Peru. Being a resourceful man, the blacksmith said that he could have made shift, if only the Purser had found him tongs, but without a pair of these to handle the hot metal, he was at a loss. It was a tradition of his craft, he told us, that God, foreseeing that no tongs could be made by man without the use of tongs, had created the first pair from nothing; and that Adam, to whom these were given, bequeathed them to Tubal Cain, the first smith to set up his sign. The General was grieved at the set-back and, after complaining loudly against the contractors, declared that Miguel Llano had never informed him of their failure to send the forge, and that the deficiency should have been made good at Paita.

Another lack was nails, and it was proposed to use rope instead; but the Chief Pilot would not release any from his own stores. He argued that the carpenters would eventually get their saws back in good condition, whereas once a rope had been cut to lash timbers together, it was of no further use to him. Let the troops, he said, twist what they needed from coconut-fibre, as the natives did.

Worst of all, we lacked provisions. Flour was running low, the salt beef had long been eaten and few beans or chick-peas remained. Though the soldiers did not relish the food of the island, except for pork and fowls—the natives kept fowls for the pot, of a white breed that laid few eggs and roosted high in the trees at night—Don Alvaro warned the Colonel that we must now live off the land and keep the rest of the flour in reserve. Since, however, he did not provide trade-goods to barter for victuals, the Colonel presumed an annulment of his strict rule against robbing the islanders.

Seven villages lay within about an hour's march of the settlement and foraging parties of from twelve to fifteen soldiers visited them frequently. The natives appeared to regard them as immortal beings who had harnessed thunder and lightning to their needs. At first, the approach of a party was the signal for flight, but later they remained quietly in their huts, and submissively gave what was asked of them; yet not by way of tribute, but because the natives of Santa Cruz consider it the height of ill manners to refuse any plea within their power to gratify. Sometimes a small gift was proffered in return for provisions, but not always, and seldom more than a battered button or playing-card.

It was usual for our men to come back from forage with half a dozen pigs or more, many bunches of bananas, and quantities of coconuts and yams. The natives themselves led the pigs, carried the bananas on long shoulder poles and trundled the remainder along in handcarts that our wheelwrights had made for the purpose; but might not enter the settlement lest they realized how few we were. From the camp gate, on which was carved a Saint Andrew's cross, in use here as a sign of *tambu*, or prohibition, many rows of tents could be seen, and thirty or forty huts already under construction. These would have sufficed to house hundreds of savages, and since the ships were still manned they must have greatly over-estimated our numbers. Only Malope's subjects, whom we treated as our allies and spared all tribute, were admitted inside; but this was after Don Lorenzo, representing himself as the General's eldest son and therefore of chieftainly rank, had gone to him wiith a demand for assistance in felling timber and building huts. Malope sent forty young men, commanded by his own son, who carried polished stone-axes and adzes of shell, and set about their tasks in a brisk and workman-like manner; they also taught our men the readiest way to twist rope from fibre (stripping it from the demajagua-tree as well as from the coconut) and how to lay thatch. Every tribesman was rewarded with a narrow piece of scarlet cloth to tuck into his armlet, which not only gave him wonderful delight but served as a passport and badge of friendship. Though to Spanish eyes one black-faced, sunken-

eyed native looks very much like another, spies and intruders were
kept away by this means; we could be certain that no possessor of a
badge would willingly surrender it to a member of an alien tribe.

Now, that everything seemed to be running on wheels, the Vicar
went ashore on the 8th of October, the feast of Saint Simeon the
Just. His chaplain had visited the settlement some days before to
choose a site for the church, which was to be built as soon as possible, though with accommodation only for two hundred persons—
our full number since the *Santa Ysabel* was lost. Father Juan, having
sanctified the precincts with holy water and led a solemn procession
around them with censers and banners, said mass for us and laid the
first stone of the chancel, dedicating it not to Saint Veronica, but to
Saint Simeon whom he did not wish to offend. The choir of pages
afterwards sang an anthem, 'I will go up into the House of the Lord,'
their voices ringing out sweet and clear; and hardly had they done
when a noise of laughter and singing arose outside the camp and
Malope's men, crying '*Amigos, amigos!*', approached at a run for
their daily labours.

The famous miracle of Tumbes recurred to the good Father's mind
and he hastily ordered a cross to be made of two wooden posts,
which Juan Leal the sick-attendant took up and carried towards
the gate, followed by the acolytes and the banners. At the Vicar's
desire the troops uncovered and bent their knees, whereupon the
natives devoutly obeyed their example and crossed themselves in
imitation. Having prostrated himself in prayer before the holy
emblem, he was then inspired to continue his progress through the
gate and down the coast-road, the tribesmen falling in at the rear. Our
musicians struck up a gay march and the cross was conveyed all the
way to Malope's village, where it was set up in front of the assembly-
house amid the plaudits of the inhabitants, who were overjoyed at
the honour paid them. Father Juan then preached a sermon upon
the Redemption, enacting the story of Christ's passion with gestures
of such pathos that he drew tears from my eyes, and the villagers
seemed to understand and suffer too. When we came away, we
left them all kneeling in a wide circle around the cross, except for
Malope and his sons who lay prostrated before it. Though the
Colonel was displeased that nearly a day's labour had been lost by
this interlude, the more pious-minded rejoiced that a beginning had
at last been made of the principal task which we had been sent to
perform.

The weather remained unsettled, and frequent falls of rain from the north-east swelled the river, revealing the marshy nature of the soil; the humid heat between squalls caused us such discomfort that we would gladly have run naked like the savages. Meanwhile the Barreto brothers obeyed the Colonel's orders with a show of alacrity and led many successful forages; but they had not forgotten what had been agreed with their sister. They began to complain in public about the work that they were required to do. Lorenzo would say: 'Upon my word, Diego, I cannot understand why our people have so tamely resigned themselves to settle this wretched spot! A child could have chosen a better situation; but the Colonel always acts without forethought and bears everything before him like a cataract.'

Diego would answer: 'Brother, you are right! There's fever-grass growing in rank tufts all the way from the guard-room to the river: an infallible portent of sickness. Besides, if the savages turn treacherous, we may expect attacks from all four quarters. The headland chosen by the General is not only far healthier but its only approach is by a causeway so narrow that three men could hold it against an army.'

Yet in trying to undermine the Colonel's authority they had done Doña Ysabel a double disservice. Those who rightly suspected that she had put these insubordinate words into their mouths became more attached than before to the Colonel, who cared for them like a father and never spared his efforts for the common good. But the ill-disposed took the complaint a stage further and began to ask themselves why they had left the rich and roomy province of Peru, where no man is poor at least in hopes, and come to this foetid and God-forsaken island at the farthest limit of the world, where no good prospects awaited them. True, they argued, the site chosen by the Colonel was bad, but the General by allowing his own choice to be overruled had confessed that no better was available. 'It is high time,' they said, 'to cut our losses and either continue our voyage to the gold-bearing isles—for this is plainly not one of them—or else admit failure and sail home.'

Juarez and Matia shared the opinion that the land was rich and salubrious; no natives had been found suffering from fever and the settlement was altogether free of mosquitoes, which always abound in unhealthy districts; the council had come to a proper decision, and this should now be loyally carried into effect. 'The right way to pacify this island,' Juarez told me one day, 'which the Colonel has in mind, is to station a few soldiers in each village. They'll depose the chieftains and take over their lands and privileges. It's the sword-hilt makes the best cross: that's what he says, and he's my cock! He'll keep a company at headquarters to reinforce any garrison that may find itself in trouble. But as time goes by the natives will be disarmed, converted and forced into serfdom; which will enable us to occupy more villages, and more yet, until the entire island is ours and parcelled into estates, and we can stuff roast pork every day of our life. The Colonel doesn't hold with fribbling. To make a parade of tender-heartedness, he says, is only to convince the black men that we're cowards.'

'But he must obey the General,' said I.

'Why, yes, Don Andrés, he knows his duty as well as any of us, but he needn't take the orders too seriously, do you see, because the General doesn't expect it; they're only issued to make good reading for posterity and as a sop for King Philip's conscience. Those large estates promised to us settlers: how will we ever get them, except by conquest? The General knows well enough that warriors who love their homes and gardens, and who outnumber us by more than a thousand to one, won't yield them without a fierce struggle. But first things first. Our present task is to secure our base, and the sooner that's done the sooner we'll be free to go out on garrison. If there's no set-back, by Twelfth-night you'll see me a chieftain with coloured feathers on my head, bracelets on my arms, and two or three little black wives bustling about me, those gay cardinal-flowers stuck in their ears and noses. They'll stir my soup, and scour my breastplate, and run their nails along the seams of my shirt—faith, Don Andrés, I've never been so lousy in my life, yet I haven't had time or patience to go a-hunting these ten days—and I'll own the largest herd of the fattest hogs in the South Seas.'

'Two or three wives, you circumcized Turk?' cried Matia. 'You're a glutton for trouble. Myself, I think little enough of the women here. Even if they weren't so devilishly black they couldn't hold a candle to the Marquesan girls. Now there was beauty and ardour for you! But these creatures seem to be a cross between pig and monkey, and they're tattooed all over, as close as a printed page.'

'I prefer them to your idle whores of Santa Cristina,' said Juarez. 'Under the bedclothes in the dark one willing wench is as good as another, and these islanders at least have their womenfolk under control. They don't allow them to frisk about all day in the bushes or the water; they keep them hard at work. I hold that woman, black, brown or white, is created for the service and pleasure of man. What's your opinion, Don Andrés?'

Not wishing to become involved in a theological dispute, I took my leave. I have always felt a certain reverence for women, like every Christian who adores the Virgin with all his heart. Her virtue and holiness have long atoned for the original fault of our Mother Eve; and since it is recorded that she was born without sin, lived without sin, became God's mother and at her death was received into Heaven as a creature already perfect—why, then only a fool would err with the heathen philosopher Aristotle who regarded the male as God's master-work, but the female as a by-work or prevarication. Though I have indeed known women whose deceitful and bloody-minded pride made them worse by far than the wickedest man alive, the female nature in general seems to me milder, more charitable and, though this may seem a paradox, less readily estranged from good principle than the male. The Devil showed great subtlety indeed when he tempted our Mother Eve first, and in the disguise of a talking snake. It is a common frailty of women to be deceived by novelties; but it is my belief that, had he gone to Adam instead, and persuaded him (with equal ease) to eat of the apple, Eve would have refused to share it. 'Drop that forbidden fruit at once, husband,' she would have cried, 'and run to make your peace with the Lord God, if you ever wish to lie with me again!'

I was kept more busily employed than ever since it had been realized that as the settlement grew so the value of the building plots would rise. Every householder had enclosed as much land as he could, by marking his claim with wooden pegs. It now devolved on me to survey and map the whole area, and to draft title-deeds after the General had reckoned how much land should go with each house, according to the owner's rank or the amount of his venture. All were dissatisfied with what was allotted them, the more so because Doña Ysabel had insisted that no one might sell, mortgage, or otherwise transfer his property. At the owner's death it might pass to his widow or children, or to a blood relation within three degrees, but was meanwhile inalienable; and should he leave no heirs, it would revert to the donor, namely the General or his successors in perpetuity.

Don Alvaro further instructed me to survey and distribute all arable land within arquebus-shot of the settlement. Every householder might claim a strip, its size again proportionate to his rank or venture, but would hold it on the same terms as his house plot and also be required to pay tithes to the municipality. These tithes, though destined to set up and maintain public services, seemed an intolerable burden on the land. Bitter disputes then arose about the privileges of citizens, and had to be settled by a constitution which Don Alvaro asked me to draft for his approval and which, when I had finished it, he tore in pieces and re-wrote with more insistence upon military and civil obligations than upon rights and privileges. He was thus obliged to appoint magistrates as well as Justices of the Peace; also a Factor, a Registrar of Mines, a Quartermaster-General, and an Overseer of Markets; and, as though I had not work enough already, he made me the Municipal Secretary, but never thought to increase my salary. I should have preferred by far the sinecure office of Registrar of Mines.

Few understood what the task of colonization implied: many a settler had imagined that he would go off with his gun and family in whatever direction he pleased and, once he had found a valley to his taste, might claim it as his own. There he would lord it over his black serfs in perfect independence, owing no further obligation to the General, unless it were to rally in his defence against English freebooters or native rebels. The soldiers had been ready enough to build a city that would later serve them as arsenal, market and fort; but when they learned that their liberties were more curtailed here than in Peru, and that the General regarded the island as his private demesne, not only denying them the freehold of their property but even reserving the right to withdraw the copyhold at will, they were disillusioned and downcast indeed. Some now complained that the land allotted them had not enough heart to grow maize or wheat, and that though an occasional yam-pudding with grated almonds was well enough, they did not intend to subsist on roots and nuts the year round.

Sebastian Lejia, who had some little skill with the pen and was what the troops call a barrack-lawyer (meaning a malcontent who tries to persuade his fellows that they are robbed and abused by their officers), borrowed paper, pen and ink from me one day on the pretext that he wished to make his Will, and then wrote out the following memorial for signature by his comrades:

We, the undersigned, being loyal and industrious subjects of King Philip II, are dissatisfied with the situation of this settlement, which has a thousand disadvantages, and therefore humbly beg our Governor, General Don Alvaro de Mendaña y Castro, to abandon it and find a more suitable site elsewhere in this island of Santa Cruz; or, if that be impossible, to fulfil his promise of taking us to the gold-bearing regions of his former discovery where he, in turn, will be free to enjoy the titles and privileges conceded him by His Majesty.

At Gracious Bay, the 13th October, 1595.

This memorial had been secretly prompted by Don Diego as a stab at the Colonel. But the last phrase, which Sebastian added on the advice of another, was directed against Don Alvaro: it was a sly reminder that he had adopted the title of Marquis prematurely and published a constitution for a city which he had no authority to build. Seven soldiers signed their names, but fearing that an example would be made of them unless many more did the same, they went from hut to hut that evening, soliciting signatures by promises and threats, until some forty more were on the paper. When Juarez refused to sign, they attempted to murder him, a little before midnight, by thrusting a sword through the side of the tent where his palliasse lay; but he had gone out to untruss, and when they heard him coming back, they mistook him for an officer and fled. He saw the slit in the canvas and took his arms and bedding to the guard-room, where he told Matia what he knew of the matter.

After matins the next morning, Matia went to Sebastian, where he sat at breakfast with his associates, and asked: 'Is it true, soldier, that you wish to quit this place?'

'Ah, welcome, comrade Matia! Will you sign our memorial?'

'I'm no comrade of yours. I asked you a question and will have an answer: do you wish to quit?'

'Why, certainly. What good can we accomplish here?'

'The good we came to do; and if you dare to interfere with me or my friends, as God is my life, I'll plunge my dagger into your heart! Keep your round robin to yourself, infamous washerwoman, or I'll set a stinking seal on it.'

Thenceforward they went after easier prey. One simple-minded soldier told me later: 'They came into my tent and asked me whether I'd care to be back in Lima, drinking chicha with my sweetheart in the street behind the Cathedral. "Yes," I said, "upon my word, so I would, comrades. I miss Teresa heartily."

' "Then sign your name to this paper," said Federico Salas. "It's a round robin."

' "What's a round robin?" I asked.

' "A circular charm," he told me, "to give every man his heart's desire."

' "I cannot write," said I.

' "That's no odds," he replied. "You can make your rubric at least." So he signed my name for me and, to gain my heart's desire, I scrawled my rubric underneath.

'Federico then said: "Now that you have signed, my lad, you must keep your piece ready. And if trouble arises between the Colonel and the General's kin, rally to the Colonel's side like a good soldier. But you're not to fire without orders."

' "When did I ever do that?" I asked. Then someone demanded whether my blood did not boil to see the General's Lady carrying enough money on her fingers and around her neck to keep us merry and idle for two full years. I told him that I had never thought of it.

' "Then think of it you must," he said. "That woman was created for mischief. But our plans are ripening quickly. If anyone cares to stay here, he's welcome. We're eastward bound for Peru and liberty!"

' "What does the Colonel say to all this?" I asked.

' "Never mind about the Colonel," said he. "You'll be told what to do in good time. Are you with us, comrade?"

' "If my officer gives me the order to embark and the Chief Pilot takes us," I answered, "I'll not lag behind."

' "To Hell with the Chief Pilot," he said. "We don't trust that hypocritical Portuguese. He's in the General's pocket. Martin Groc, the pilot of the galeot, is the man for us. He'll run us ashore somewhere on the coast of Chile, and we'll march inland to Potosi and make our fortunes there. No, we won't risk touching a Peruvian port."

' "Then when shall I see my sweetheart again?" I asked.

' "Oh, a pox on your sweetheart!" he cried. "You have signed the round robin, and that's enough for one day." '

The whole affair was utterly confused. The Colonel knew nothing as yet of the memorial which, though demanding no more than the abandonment of the half-finished settlement, was generally interpreted in a much larger sense. The signatories expected that Don Alvaro would take it as a personal affront and come ashore to censure the Colonel for having connived at it. After an exchange of angry words and recriminations, the Barretos would try to arrest the Colonel; which would be the signal for their death. The General and his Lady, demanding vengeance, would then suffer the same fate; whereupon the Colonel, having no authority to found a colony, would be forced to lead the expedition home again.

But all these were miscalculations, as will appear.

Chapter 16

THE COLONEL SPEAKS OUT

Here my cart begins to stick fast, so clogged in the mire of intrigues, feuds, enmities and suspicions that I shall have a troublesome task to drive the wheels through to firm ground by heaving and hauling at the spokes.

One afternoon the General suddenly decided to send the Chief Pilot back to Callao in the flagship; he was to carry the Viceroy a letter explaining why the Isles of Solomon had not yet been encountered—the reason Don Alvaro chose to give was that contrary winds had forced us off our course—and urgently imploring his help. If food, powder and tools were not sent us at once we must certainly perish, since without these we could neither maintain ourselves on Santa Cruz, nor continue our voyage to the Isles, nor even return to Peru. He dictated the despatch to me, very slowly to avoid errors, then signed and sealed it with trembling hands.

'Do you wish me to summon the Chief Pilot?' I asked.

'There is no need,' he replied. 'I shall be conferring with him soon enough. Meanwhile you might do me the service of spreading the substance of this despatch. In particular I wish it to be known—for the sake of silencing jealous tongues—that not enough flour remains to keep us all at sea for more than a month at most, even on halfrations. Understand, I give you no authority to divulge secrets of state, but if you forget for once to keep your mouth shut, I shall be far from taking it amiss.'

That evening I was seated in the Chart-room, when along came Ensign Tomás de Ampuero, who happened to be in command of the standing guard. 'Do you keep any liquor hidden away, friend Andrés?' he cried. 'I haven't a drop left to cheer my guts.'

'Only a small bottle of aqua vitae,' I replied, 'laid by against sickness.'

'Then for the love of the Virgin, open it,' he said. 'We're all sick men here.'

I poured him a noggin which he drank at a gulp. 'More!' he called, wiping his mouth. I poured him another, and he settled down to talk. 'What's new?' he asked.

'Oh, nothing,' said I, 'nothing whatever. All is old and threadbare. Except for one thing—but tell me, Don Tomás, can you keep a secret?'

'There's not a silenter man in the whole South Seas. You can take my word for that, Fat Cheeks.'

'Well, then,' said I. 'Strictly between you and me, the Chief Pilot is going back to Peru.' I quoted a few phrases from the despatch.

He flared up instantly, banging the table with his huge fist. 'If your friend Pedro Fernandez thinks to play that game,' he exclaimed with a foul oath, 'the standing guard will give him checkmate. You may take it from me that he'll never get the ship out of this bay; we would blow a hole in her bottom first. The General must be clean out of his wits. Aside from the folly of expecting fresh supplies of flour, beef and all the rest—his credit in Lima is more than exhausted—what in Satan's name is the use of sending that crocodile to explain why the Isles haven't been found? Who wants to find them now? From all I hear, they're neither better nor worse than this God-forsaken land. And does the General really believe that Pedro Fernandez will take the ship to Callao, load her, turn her round, and bring her back again? By the blood of January, I wouldn't, not if I were he: I'd never return to within a thousand leagues of this place. If he has the sense of a mouse, he'll head east, not west, and join his Portuguese friends in the Moluccas. That's what he was trying to do when we left the Marquesas Islands, until the General's suspicions made him swing south again; and that's how we sailed clear round the Isles of Solomon and came here instead.'

I filled his cup again, though I grudged the waste of liquor. 'Why, Don Tomás,' I protested mildly, 'you must not forget that our coming here is for the good of the natives. The King has ordered us to pacify and convert them, and it seems to me that we ought to obey. If Pedro Fernandez isn't sent back—and he's the only man capable of fulfilling the mission—how will the Viceroy ever learn of our straits and help us to carry on with our task?'

His face went as red as a cinder. 'The good of the natives!' he spluttered. 'Of those naked, black imbeciles! How can they be converted?

You deceive yourself. Men who have once supped on human flesh
are thrice damned and debarred for ever from the Eucharist; and the
depraved taste persists. Like Saint George in the song: "As they were,
so they are, and ever more shall be so." Even if this were not so, why
in Christ's name should we be condemned to death for the sake of
their salvation?'

'Come, my friend,' I said, a little sharply. 'Every Christian who
brings even a single soul to the font should count himself fortunate;
and many of these Indians show a strong inclination to virtue—old
Malope, for one.'

'Malope, Malope, eh? I wish I could stuff as many good beefsteaks
into my belly as that sly old wolf has stuffed whole men!'

He put the bottle to his lips without so much as a 'by your leave,'
and drained it. After he left me, I sat considering whether to report
his words to the General. I had kept to the letter of my instructions,
and come off the worse by nearly a pint of aqua vitae. I decided to tell
only Pedro Fernandez, who had just come in.

He heard me out calmly, but showed surprise both that the General
had not yet informed him of his intentions, and that I had been so
indiscreet as to broach them to the tall, tattling Ensign.

'You suspect me of an indiscretion?' I asked, piqued in my pride.

'Forgive me; I did not understand. But what can be the General's
object in spreading the news? We could never make that voyage,
and he knows it.'

'Don Alvaro has a very labyrinth of a mind,' said I, 'and sometimes,
by taking one turn too many to the left or to the right, he loses himself in its dark corridors and comes to strange decisions.'

He nodded agreement. 'This is a bad business, Andrés Serrano,
and what the end may be, God alone knows. But having allowed my
resolution to weaken at Paita, when I had already taken my leave, I
must now suffer the consequences. However, let me confess, that
were the scene to be re-enacted, and had I fore-knowledge of all that
has since happened, I should still be in two minds whether or not
to repeat my error. Of late, Doña Ysabel has played the part of
guardian angel with such gentleness and loving-kindness that it would
be base ingratitude in me to regret that I am here to serve her.'

He was blind to all her failings and schemings, and I had not the
heart to disenchant him.

Later that evening Don Alvaro told Pedro Fernandez in confidence
of a warning which, he said, had just come in from a well-wisher: that

a ship's captain, he might not say which, was plotting to set sail one dark night and desert us. But lest it should be thought that any person in particular were suspected, all canvas, from the flagship as well as from the smaller vessels, must be unbent, taken ashore, and placed in the guard-house. Since Don Alvaro did not mention the despatch, Pedro Fernandez concluded that the Ensign's drunken words had been overheard and reported, and that he himself, not Captain Corzo or Captain Leyva, was now under suspicion.

'At your orders, Excellency,' he answered, and glanced at Doña Ysabel, who darted him a covert smile of sympathy.

The truth was that, not having been consulted about the despatch beforehand, she now pretended to Don Alvaro that she had doubts of Pedro Fernandez's loyalty: an artifice which had the double object of disguising her passion for him and of holding him near her. I do not know what else she said: now that her design against the Colonel's life was hampered by a fear of losing Pedro Fernandez's good opinion, nobody could keep track of her lies, they were so many and devious. However, it was she who staged the set-piece in the camp which was intended to shock and startle Don Alvaro into taking summary vengeance on her enemy at last.

At her insistence he went ashore next morning to restore order, and no sooner had he entered the camp gates than the three Barretos ran to meet him, sword in hand.

'What does this mean, brothers?' he asked in alarm.

'What else but war?' Don Lorenzo answered.

'Yet I have been assured that the natives are in a fair way to pacification.'

'That is so; those woolly black lambs hardly dare to bleat now, but the war is on our side of the picket-fence. Our lives are in danger.'

'Explain yourself, pray!'

'Not in the hearing of the soldiers. Question the Colonel if you will, not me; he is on his way here. He never cares what he says, or to whom, or in what company.'

The Colonel sauntered up, and greeted Don Alvaro amiably with a magnificent sweep of his hat. 'Welcome, your Excellency!' said he. 'It is well that you have at last deigned to visit your infant city which, though of swift and sturdy growth, has infinite trouble with its teething.'

'So I am told: your company-officers even speak of civil war.'

'Ha! So the geese are in that field?' His hand went to his sword-hilt,

ready to draw in a flash. 'Then let me tell you that I know three
rogues, three accursed, tale-bearing, lying rogues, who wish to involve
me in a quarrel with you; and by God's wounds, I'll bear with them
no longer! Pray, your Excellency, accept a warning, that if you
either cannot or will not control them, one fine day they will be
found hanging in a row from a branch, with purple faces and pro-
truding tongues.'

'To whom can you be referring, friend?' asked Don Alvaro, feigning astonishment. He must have expected the Colonel to draw in his
horns and say, as many another would have said in the circumstances:
'I name no names, but by Our Lady, I have my suspicions, and I beg
your Excellency to stop your ears against these calumnies'—which
he would have countered with: 'Pray keep your suspicions to yourself,
Don Pedro Merino, until you can find just cause of complaint; when
I shall give you the satisfaction that is your due.'

Instead, the Colonel, with true Castilian candour, replied: 'Very
well, your Excellency, you force me to a public disclosure. I refer to
that damned rogue, and *that* and *that!*' And he pointed in turn at
Don Lorenzo, Don Diego and Don Luis.

The General was caught off his balance. 'Alas, your lordship,' he
quavered. 'You are mistaken, sadly mistaken.' Though his lips continued to move, not another word came out and large tears ran down
his cheeks and glistened in his beard. Had the Barretos then shown
courage and leaped at the Colonel as one man, Doña Ysabel would
have succeeded in her intentions, his murder passing for honest man-
slaughter in revenge for a triple insult; but Don Lorenzo looked to
Don Luis, who in turn looked to Don Diego, who stood irresolute.

The moment passed. Up ran the Colonel's nephew who, seeing
swords in the Barretos' hands, drew his own and stepped in front
of his uncle. The Colonel pulled him back by the collar of his coat.
'Put up your blade, Jacinto, lad!' he cried harshly. 'That these Galician
pot-boys have the ill manners to display naked steel in their General's presence does not excuse the same in a person of birth and
breeding.'

Several other officers then approached, and he turned again to
Don Alvaro. 'Your Excellency does well to weep,' he said. 'By God,
I should weep too, were I kin to such a mischievous crew of liars—
cowards who would not dare steal a crumb from a cat, who seduce
the common soldiery and go hand in glove with pirates and murderers.' (Here he glowered at Captain Corzo, who stood beside the

Barretos.) 'With the sole exception of your Excellency, who towers head and shoulders above me, I care not a f—ted fig for any of your clan, from the greatest to the least. Henceforth, indeed, I shall treat them like the dirt under my feet, because they have not even had the spirit to uphold their honour like gentlemen. I shall say more: again with the exception of your Excellency and myself, there's not an officer or soldier present who has the least desire or intention to stay in this island. It is I alone who keep them at their posts; and God knows that, but for me, your Excellency's honour would lie in the dust. Who speaks of civil war? Criminals in the pay of your fine brothers-in-law have been peddling a memorial about the camp. Last night they tried to take revenge on certain old soldiers who would not sign it, by a dastardly raid on their quarters; but a dog gave the alarm and all took to their heels. At the same time three masked assassins' —and here he looked at the Barretos shrewdly up and down—'tried to enter my house by way of the kitchen, but the negro came out against them with his axe and routed them. Well, what now, Sirrah?'

He stood defiantly waiting for Don Alvaro's reply; none came, but only more tears. The Barretos sheathed their swords with a single swish and snap, and led him away; while the Colonel returned with firm steps to supervise the troops who were raising an embankment beside the river.

Don Alvaro presently recovered his spirits sufficiently to inspect the Church and the Residency, both nearly completed, also the kitchens, the work-shops, the guard-house, the store-huts and the other buildings. He praised the Barretos for their industry, awarding them all the credit for what had been well done and, after eating dinner in their hut, went with them to the embankment to watch the work.

Sergeant Dimas saw him coming and ran forward to beg the favour of a private audience. The Colonel flamed up at this overt breach of discipline and yelled after him: 'How dare you take such liberties, Sergeant? How dare you desert your post and wander off to address the General without my leave?'

But he feigned deafness and stood bowing and scraping before the General.

'Pray continue with the task you have in hand, Colonel,' said Don Alvaro.

The Colonel called his men to attention and doffed his hat, but complained in a loud aside to Captain Leyva who was with him: 'Is

this not an ugly sight? If any rascal may carry his complaints direct
to the General, my men will lose all respect for me.'

Don Alvaro took Sergeant Dimas aside to hear whatever he may
have had to disclose and, afterwards pressing his arm affectionately,
was heard to say: 'No, no, the time is not yet ripe. Wait a little longer,
my friend.'

The troops sympathized with the Colonel, who would never have
injured the honour of his subordinate officers by allowing their men
to come directly to him with their confidences. He returned to the
working party and, ignoring Don Alvaro who stood with the Barretos
at some distance, poured such abuse on Sergeant Dimas that his ears
reddened and his hands twitched.

On the Thursday, when Don Alvaro came ashore again, it pleased
the Colonel to disguise his resentment by treating him with obsequious correctness. Every salute was an insult, and the more Don
Alvaro tried to avoid his attentions, the more sedulously were they
pressed upon him. He bore with him that day, but on the Saturday,
spurred on by Doña Ysabel, who gave him no peace, he plucked up
courage and told the Colonel breathlessly, as one who repeats a message quickly before it is forgotten: 'Pray, your lordship, let us have no
more of this mummery. For all your hat-doffings and leg-scrapings
you are a disobedient officer, and I must hold you solely responsible
for all the loose talk now running round the camp. You pamper the
troops and allow them to vent what nonsense they please.'

'I pamper the troops, your Excellency!' cried he in astonishment.
'On the contrary, it is I who insist on their respecting you as the
King's representative in these lands. As for the loose talk, it began in
the Great Cabin and was transplanted to the settlement by your
egregious brothers-in-law.'

'That is not so. First, you made the soldiers discontented by over-
riding my wishes and setting them to work at a foolish and thankless
task, and now you teach them to mock me.'

'To mock your Excellency! By your good leave! As for the foolish
and thankless task, it is true that you have not overwhelmed me with
gratitude for all that I have done . . .'

But the General had turned on his heel with a virtuous expression,
and gone off; thinking, I dare say, that this time Doña Ysabel could
not reproach him with having shirked the issue.

That afternoon the Colonel sat in his house, brooding fiercely on his injuries and drinking the palm-wine which his negro prepared for him. Suddenly he kicked over the joint-stool and stamped off angrily, shouting to himself as he went. He looked for the General everywhere and at last found him in the Church (now wanting only the pulpit), kneeling at the altar rails and with no companion but myself. He announced his approach with a loud cough, and then asked the favour of a few words in private. Don Alvaro rose quietly to his feet, placed a finger to his lips, and 'Remember where you are, my lord,' he whispered.

The Colonel burst into a laugh that echoed about our ears. 'Your Excellency is admirably pious,' he said. 'But until this building has been dedicated to Saint What's-his-name tomorrow, it can claim no greater sanctity than the guard-house of the camp-jakes.'

'Hush, man, how can you say such things? Do you not see the crucifix on the altar?'

'The guard-house also boasts a crucifix.'

'And the precincts have been well sprinkled with holy water.'

'Ay, and so have the jakes,' returned the Colonel. 'Just now I saw Father Antonio emerging . . .' And he choked with laughter, wonderfully pleased with his own wit. But seeing the General about to go, he barred his way with outspread hands, saying: 'No, your Excellency, you cannot leave me yet; this business will not wait. To please you, I'll lower my voice to a whisper, but by the griefs and sorrows of Our sweet Lady, it comes most unnaturally to me.'

Don Alvaro, recognizing from the stink of his breath and the thick tones of his voice that he was far gone in drink, would have brushed past him and escaped, had he not feared to provoke violence. "Unburden yourself, friend,' he said resignedly, sitting down on a stool, 'and by your leave, we shall keep Don Andrés with us to take a record of your business. He is a discreet young man.'

'Discreet or indiscreet,' the other replied in a roaring whisper, waving his flask in circles, 'I care not a rotten almond! Now, Don Alvaro, you know well that your Lady called me a hound. An old hound she called me, and I'll not quarrel with that. I confess that I resemble an old hound with scarred coat and torn ears, a terror to all curs that dare pick a quarrel with him. Hound, your Excellency, is not altogether a term of reproach, since every gentleman values the comradeship of his hound, next only to that of his horse; and who ever saw a hound, unless he were hydrophobic, so wanting in chivalry as to turn and maul the bitch that snapped at him? But your

Lady did not stop at "hound." No, by the God Who redeemed us all, she did not stop there, but abused me foully, and in your hearing, and even made as if to pull the hairs from my beard. Yet I never raised my hand to her, now did I so, your Excellency?'

The General shook his head gravely.

'No, I was the A *per se* of chivalry! A soused black pudding, she called me, and worse names, not easily forgotten even by you, Don Alvaro, who seldom burden your memory with what irks you.'

'Why have you withheld your complaint until today?'

'Complaint! By my father's sword, which was exceedingly long and well-stained with the blood of infidels, I have not come with a complaint, but with a warning! We Merinos are from Castile and always vault a gate instead of creeping along the fence until we find a breach through which to squeeze. And now I will tell your Excellency plainly though, at your own desire, in a whisper: your Lady, Doña Ysabel, is a sorceress no less wicked than the infamous Eutropa who encompassed the death of numerous gallant knights in the *History of Palmyrin!*'

'Bah, my lord, you have read so many such romances that your imagination is besotted, and you see ogres, dwarfs, sorceresses and the like lurking behind every hedge. My wife a sorceress! Put a guard upon your tongue and have a care what you say next, Don Pedro Merino!'

'Then I must speak more plainly still: she is a common witch!' He raised his forefinger in solemn warning: 'Not only is she seeking my destruction in complot with her brothers, but yours too in complot with her sister! If nothing be done to prevent her, the carrion birds will soon be pecking both at your eyes and at mine.'

For a moment Don Alvaro gaped at him stupidly. Then he groaned, his hand flew to his heart, and his face went the colour of a deal board.

At this I stepped forward and charged them with tears to say no more, and to forget what had already been said; as I engaged to do myself. But Don Alvaro would have fallen from the stool had the Colonel not caught him. Together we laid him gently on the floor, undid his doublet and shirt, pillowed his head on a cushion, and put the flask of palm-wine to his lips. Soon his colour returned, whereupon the Colonel took his leave in the same hoarse whisper, assuring me that all was forgotten, and tiptoed away.

About an hour later I supported Don Alvaro step by step to the guard-house, where he lay down on the arms-chest but was so weak that we had to raise his feet upon it. When Captain Leyva, whose company had the guard that day, asked him what was amiss, he moaned: 'You are all against me, I cannot tell why. Whatever could be done to conciliate you, has been done; and I have worn myself out in your service. But whom can I trust? Each has a different aim and desire from his fellow; none respects the orders of His Majesty who sent us here. The Colonel defies me openly.'

He was still muttering in this piteous strain when Captain Corzo entered, followed by the Chief Pilot come to satisfy himself that his sails were not being borrowed by the sailors to patch their tents; but the Barretos did not appear. Captain Leyva nodded sagely but in silence, lest any word of sympathy he let fall might be turned against him; it was his principle to remain neutral in every dispute until it should be plain which side was the stronger. But Captain Corzo who, though mistrusting the Barretos, inclined naturally to their faction from his hatred of the Colonel, swore by the Rood of Saint Denis that Don Alvaro had no cause to be troubled. 'Are we not all your Excellency's servants,' he cried, 'and willing to go with you to the end of the world?'

Don Alvaro smiled wanly. 'You have already done so, my brave friend. And now that you are here, will you show me faithful service?'

'That is understood, your Excellency—is it not, gentlemen?'

The Major was seen to assent, and the Chief Pilot expressed his loyalty in eloquent phrases. Don Alvaro appeared to be somewhat reassured and, when the sun had dropped behind the islet, Pedro Fernandez and I supported him to the skiff, where we found the Barretos waiting for us.

At supper that night Don Lorenzo gave his sisters an account of the morning's quarrel. 'I have already heard Diego's report of that interlude,' said Doña Ysabel. 'Well, what happened then? I am told that the Colonel was seen leaving the Church at about two o'clock and that afterward little Andrés brought my husband half-fainting into the guard-house.'

'I know nothing of that,' said Don Lorenzo.

All eyes turned to the General, who hung his head, pressed a hand to his brow and begged Doña Ysabel not to question him on the matter.

'Alas, husband, are you still so weak?' she cried. 'But here is Andrés for your spokesman; he will tell us what the drunken Cyclops did to you.'

Don Alvaro, preferring to tell his own story, fortified himself with a little wine. It was instructive to hear with what facility he intertwined lies with truth: I felt that I could never trust him again, his words carried such perfect conviction. So much of the talk as concerned the Church and the whispering, he repeated with accuracy, but then he represented the Colonel as having complained: 'You came without warning, surrounded by your armed kinsmen like a man who goes in fear of his life.'

He continued: 'My answer was: "And if I did, Don Pedro? You know that I had need of them." He let that pass and accused me of betraying the troops—betraying them, if you please—by not bringing out more axes and wood-knives. "God's passion," he said, "your Excellency is wasting good troops in a land where neither God nor the King can be served by their presence." "His Majesty himself must be the judge of that," I said, to which he replied: "By my father's sword, I care not a rotten almond either for you or for your viperous Lady, who abused me so foully! I am a plain-spoken Castilian and give you fair warning that, if she tries my patience further, the carrion-birds will soon be pecking both at her eyes and yours."'

Doña Ysabel laughed aloud. 'You mimic the Colonel to the life, my lord,' she said. 'But did he complain of any particular abuse?'

'Yes, that you called him a hound, and in my hearing. He may have said more, but indignation overcame me and I fainted away. Then with much tenderness Andrés revived me and led me to the guardhouse.'

'Well, if I had not taken him down, who else would have dared? Not you, for one, my dear lord.'

We went ashore next morning, the ladies as well as the men, to assist at the dedication of the Church, a rite performed with solemnity and great feeling by Father Juan, though the soldiers were sparing with their expressions of joy. Afterwards Don Alvaro, swaying in his walk, took formal possession of the island. He must have heard of the contents of the round robin, because when he planted the Royal Standard, he referred to 'this island of Santa Cruz, the most westerly of the Isles of Solomon over which King Philip has graciously appointed me Prefect.'

The cheers that greeted the conclusion of the ceremony were neither loud nor unanimous, and I caught muttered oaths from the settlers who stood near me, and then these words in a woman's voice:

'His Majesty is welcome to our island; I wouldn't give a cracked maravedi for it.' This drew a burst of smothered laughter.

As I sat down to record the General's speech for the archives of the Indies Council, Pedro Fernandez came to me, and said: 'Friend Andrés, to preserve my reputation as a pilot, and Don Alvaro's as a geographer, pray change the word "westerly" to "easterly."'

'No man living can seduce me from my duty,' I answered with mock severity. 'When I come to that sentence, I shall make no omission and no addition; and yet I undertake to meet your wish. An o placed before *este* [east] is but a zero, a thing of no account: and if the word be read *oeste* [west] I need not answer for the error.'

The Colonel, true to his undertaking to forget what had happened in the Church, now desired Don Alvaro to approve plans for a stockade which should serve as a refuge for the women and children if ever the settlement were attacked. It was to be built on a knoll in the only position from which covering fire could be directed against the beach. Don Alvaro rejected his plan, because these were the grounds of the Residency and Doña Ysabel, who had gone to her brothers' hut after viewing them, proposed to build a pleasance on that very knoll. Instead, he pointed to other sites as being more suitable, but the Colonel tore his arguments to shreds and left him at a loss for a reply. Though agreeing that the building of a stockade was a matter of some urgency, he postponed his decision until he should have attended to a vexatious crop of disputes about title-deeds, rights of way, the upkeep of fences and the like; and in the end returned to the flagship without giving it. No doubt, he hoped that the Colonel would take his silence for consent and raise the stockade on the knoll; which would be a fair excuse for arresting him.

That night, just before dawn, trumpets blew, drums rattled, and the whole camp seemed in an uproar. The Colonel's voice could be heard bawling: 'To arms, to arms! Every man to his post. Make ready to receive them!' Yet no yelling of savages could be distinguished. It was the Chief Pilot's watch, and in the absence of the Captain of Artillery, who slept ashore, he ordered the master-gunner to let off a falcon that stood ready trained against the nearest village along the coast; first tilting the barrel a little upwards so that the ball should whiz harmlessly over the huts. The roar of the discharge brought the General running on deck in his night-shirt, sword in hand, and with chattering teeth he asked what, in God's name, was afoot.

'To judge from the shouting,' Pedro Fernandez answered, 'the natives were about to attack the camp. I fired the falcon over their heads as a reminder that you keep a watch-dog.'

We listened attentively. Women were screaming in the village, and shouts of confusion and dismay arose from the camp. Presently a canoe appeared in the darkness and Don Alvaro sang out: 'Standing Guard, prepare to repel boarders!' But it was only Don Diego, who climbed on deck half-dressed, trembling with fear and unable to give a coherent report. 'The Colonel wants to murder us all,' he sobbed, 'you and me and my brothers and sisters, and Captain Corzo, too— I came to warn you.'

He had, in effect, run away and left his brothers to their fate. Soon afterwards the noise in the camp died down, as if an order for silence had been given, and the Ensign-Royal's voice came clearly across the water: 'Ahoy, Officer of the Watch, do you hear me? The Colonel's compliments to the General and will he send powder and match at once? *Powder and match!*'

'Pay no attention,' Don Diego pleaded. 'That's Toribio de Bede-terra. He's in a plot to decoy you ashore and then cut your throat. I fear my brothers are already dead.' And he began to weep again.

'Where is Don Jacinto Merino, the Officer of the Guard?' asked the General. 'Is he also in the plot?' But no one seemed to know what had become of him.

When day broke, the master-gunner was sent ashore in the skiff with half a barrel of powder and a few yards of match. He was in-structed to shout 'All's well' if he found the Barretos alive, but other-wise to remain silent. We waited in great suspense, and presently a reassuring halloo floated back.

Later we learned that our fears had been groundless: a young sentry, frightened by the noise of branches scraping against some posts, had turned out the guard, crying 'The savages are upon us!' The Colonel had then sounded the call to arms, but no natives were seen and the subsequent shouting arose from his discovery that the arquebusiers of Captain Corzo's company had run out of powder and match. The affair ended in catcalls and cheerful laughter; but the tale of Don Diego's cowardice was carried ashore by the master-gunner and spread through the huts.

Chapter 17

THE MALCONTENTS

An apartment in the Colonel's large new house was lent to
Father Antonio until the vicarage should be completed, but the Vicar
still slept on board, in the cabin vacated by Juan de la Isla. One day,
on his return from mass, he entered the Chart-room with a more than
usually grave face and, understanding that he had private business
with the Chief Pilot, I kissed his cross and left them together. Afterwards, Pedro Fernandez told me: 'The Vicar came to warn me that
the troops have decided to leave the island. He cannot tell me where
they want to go or whom they propose to take as pilot, but he is certain that they will use force if need be. I implored him to go ashore
again and persuade them to remain at their posts, because of the duty
we owe to the natives. "For my part," he said, shrugging his shoulders,
"I should be glad to stay in this island, a few years even, preaching
to the heathen. But, my son, if God should rule otherwise . . ."'

'We have hardly been here a month,' said I with indignation, 'and
it has come to this already?'

Pacing up and down the narrow room, he burst out: 'Oh, what a
toppling tower of confusion we have raised on the ashes of ambition,
discord, avarice, vanity and vindictiveness! Soon we shall all be buried
under its ruins, friend Andrés, unless we keep steadfast faith with
God and the King. I have not yet told you that yesterday afternoon
someone tried to kill me as I stood by the mizzen. The shot came
from the thickets beyond the beach. Another was fired at the frigate.
I do not know what bird was aimed at; it may have been Francisco
Frau, the pilot. But by God's grace both bullets went wide.'

'Why should they want to kill you?' I cried, aghast.

'Who knows?' he answered, thrusting out his underlip. 'Perhaps so
that their friend Martin Groc of the *San Felipe* may succeed me as

Chief Pilot? Since we left Callao I have made many enemies, from the Colonel down to the Purser, and their number grows daily. Because I ordered the master-gunner to let off that falcon, the Captain of Artillery now hates me; though I did it not from love of meddling in military affairs, but to shield the officer of the standing guard, who was revelling between strange sheets. Had the General caught him, a bloody murder would have been done.' He did not disclose the name of the woman, but it was whispered that Doña Mariana was already consoling herself for her widowhood and anticipating a third marriage.

Don Alvaro wilfully ignored the dissident spirt ashore, hoping that it would cause the Colonel trouble and humiliation. He felt safe in the Great Cabin under the protection of the ship's guns, and the standing guard were picked men: should the troops take up arms, he would step ashore as their protector, display the Royal Standard and clap the Colonel in irons. But he had not reckoned with the general hatred felt for the Barretos which inclined most of the malcontents to the Colonel's side.

The Colonel, for his part, did nothing. Conscious of his own rectitude and devotion to duty, and careless of the future, he left the General to beat out the forest-fire that his brothers-in-law had mischievously lighted. It was enough that the troops were still steady on parade and worked well under his orders.

But Pedro Fernandez was convinced that the flames were spreading fast and it greatly troubled him to find even the Vicar standing by, his hands resignedly folded. I told him: 'It is not Father Juan's duty to intervene in a matter that concerns military discipline, unless his good offices are sought by both Don Alvaro and the Colonel. While they remain at loggerheads, nothing at all can be done. This is a fever that must reach its crisis before we can hope for improvement.'

'I disagree with that,' he cried. 'I undertake to pacify the men in half an hour, if Don Alvaro will but give me leave!'

'In my opinion,' said I, 'it can do only harm to pay attention to the grumblings of a few hot-brained fellows. I saw no sign of rebellion when I was ashore yesterday. While they continue to obey their officers . . .'

But despite my urgent dissuasions, he went off to the Great Cabin.

Doña Mariana sat there alone, fanning herself wearily. 'Where is the General?' he asked her.

'In the larder,' she answered. 'My dear sister is busy proving to him there that we cannot afford to feed more than our immediate family. The sums which he has hitherto deducted every week from salaries or ventures no longer cover the value of the food brought with us, since it cannot be replaced. She says that the priests must henceforth subsist on the endowment of the Church, and that the rest must fend for themselves. Perhaps she will plead for an exception to be made in your case; or, perhaps, she will not. But don't stand there, cap in hand, man! Here's a chair; sit down and amuse me for a while until they return. You must have plenty of time on your hands, now that the sails are in the guard-house and you need not trouble your head with the Day's Work. Tell me something to make me smile; you cannot imagine how bored I have been since my brothers went ashore. Tell me the first thing that comes into your mind!'

He sat down reluctantly. 'These are bad times,' he said. 'I fear that I am in no mood for jokes and lively trifling. But since you command me . . .'

'Let us talk about love,' she said. 'Love is the most fruitful topic in all nature; how the sparrows used to chatter about it under the eaves of our house at Corunna! And here, half a world away, four-legged bats squeak and fret in the same strain under the mangrove-shade beside the river. Have you noticed the amorous little creatures, hanging head-downwards like black pears from the branches, five hundred at a time? . . . Tell me, Don Pedro, when did you first fall in love?'

'By your leave, my lady! To confound the love of man with the lechery of bat and sparrow is to dishonour our Creator. But, since you ask me, I have never fallen in love but once in my life: she was far above me in station, the youngest daughter of a Licentiate, and the most virtuous and beautiful woman of all my acquaintance. The Virgin be praised, she returned my affections and her father did not despise my suit; within six months of my declaration we were married, and in course of time a son was born to us, now five years of age. That is all I can tell your ladyship about love.'

'You are fortunate indeed,' said Doña Mariana. 'I wish that the bright history of my heart were equally uncheckered—and, I dare say, my sister wishes the same. You cannot conceive, friend, of the distress occasioned to a woman of rank, whose husband lives and who has her reputation to preserve, when without either reason or warning Don Cupid lets fly a barbed arrow and lodges it deep in her heart. What remedy has she? To disclose her passion would be imprudent; to con-

summate it, disgraceful. Should she make confession to a priest? But
to do so would be to present as a mortal sin what is as yet a mere
misfortune, to add penance to her pain: no harm is done unless, by
word or sign, she acquaints the loved one with her condition, and thus
makes him suffer sweetly with her. She must either grieve in silence,
slowly burning to death, or rashly give vent to her passion, and burn
in everlasting Hell. Picture her torments: there she stands, shifting
her weight from foot to foot, not daring to go, unable to stand still.
Pity her, fortunate man for whom the path of love has always been
spread not with noxious thorns but with wholesome and innocent
daisies. As for myself, I thank the Saints that my great loss has been
sufficient grief to me: that I have not since been plagued by the
pangs of alien and unrequited love.'

Pedro Fernandez understood well enough that she was not speaking
in generalities but acquainting him with Doña Ysabel's condition.
The mingled horror and elation of this discovery, which however
he dared not admit as the truth, sent his mind so fast adrift that he
could not find a word in answer. Doña Mariana eyed him closely, with
a cruel smile.

He had by no means recovered from the shock when the General
entered with Doña Ysabel herself, and it was with difficulty that
he recalled the mission upon which he had come. He rose quickly
and made his demand, not in the speech he had prepared for the
occasion, but with words chosen at random and uttered in an unsteady voice.

Don Alvaro observed his confusion and, at once suspecting that
it proceeded from a bad conscience, cut him short: 'I wonder, my
friend, that you dare come to me with so preposterous a request.'

The Chief Pilot, recovering the thread of his purpose, asked in
what way it could be considered preposterous.

'The troops would never listen to anything you might say in
favour of this island or myself,' he was told. 'They are determined
to follow their own foolish course, in which the Colonel encourages
them, and your appeal would only add fuel to the flames. I forbid
you to go!'

Nevertheless, Don Alvaro recalled him later and gave him permission to do as he asked, though on conditions. It is likely that Doña
Ysabel had meanwhile enlarged upon the perils of our situation,
saying that Pedro Fernandez's dislike of the Colonel would keep
him loyal for the present, and that it would be advantageous if he

could convince even a few of the mutineers (as it pleased her to call them) that they had been misled.

The Chief Pilot, guessing that she had pleaded his cause, prepared to go ashore next morning, with the ardour of a knight who rides to tourney, his mistress's glove tied to his helmet. I asked leave to witness the proceedings, and this Don Alvaro granted me. The truth was, that I could not bear to stay behind in fear of what might happen to Pedro Fernandez, should he rouse the soldiers' rage by too ingenuous a summons to loyalty.

As we stepped ashore, Tomás de Ampuero strode towards us.

'You are bound for Peru with despatches, are you not?' he asked the Chief Pilot derisively. 'Would you do me the kindness of taking a message at the same time?' He turned his back on us and made as if to break wind.

Next, the Major sidled up, with the face of a man who fears the worst, and muttered: 'The sky has an ugly look, gentlemen. I dare not think what may happen.' With him was Captain Corzo who, when Pedro Fernandez told him of his mission, remarked: 'You are a bold man, but I'm uneasy for your sake. The soldiers have threatened to kill you.'

However, we did not pay any great attention to either of these officers, knowing them for what they were.

We arrived at the guard-house, where Pedro Fernandez revealed his business to the Adjutant, who remarked drily: 'The Colonel will be exceedingly vexed that you have come to address his men, as though he were incapable of controlling them himself. My advice to you is: avoid any encounter with him, take the men out of earshot and cut your speeches short—if you can.'

The rumour soon ran through the camp that the Chief Pilot had brought a message from the Great Cabin, and before long we were surrounded by an excited and curious crowd.

'I have been sent by the General,' Pedro Fernandez announced in a loud voice. 'Follow me to the Churchyard, and I will address you there.'

'Why doesn't he come himself?' someone shouted.

He disregarded the question and went on. When we reached the Church porch, he turned, and held up a hand for silence. The soldiers gathered around under the shade of the monstrous ferns that grew there, interspersed with the low, leafy trees which we called yellow-dyes.

Here is my chronicle of the proceedings, set down the same night. Let it be read as a scene from an unfinished cloak-and-dagger tragedy, entitled *The Isles of Unwisdom*. I warrant that the Admiral's famous namesake, Don Lope de Vega Carpio, has written many a less lively one for the Madrid stage.

SCENE: *Before the Church of San Simeon. Enter the* CHIEF PILOT, *with* ANDRÉS SERRANO, *Sergeant* JAIME GALLARDO, *the settlers* MIGUEL GERONIMO *and* MELCHIOR GARCIA, *the soldiers* SALVADOR ALEMAN, SEBASTIAN LEJIA, FEDERICO SALAS, GIL MOZO, JUAREZ MENDÉS, MATIA PINETO *and others.*

THE CHIEF PILOT, *one arm akimbo, the other raised oratorically:* Gentlemen, I am at your service. Pray air your grievances one at a time, and I will attend to them fairly, as I have been empowered to do.

A LOUD BABBLE OF VOICES: God damn you! Is it true that you're off to Callao? What for? You treacherous rogue, do you think there's one man here trusts you to come back again?

THE CHIEF PILOT: One at a time, gentlemen; one at a time.

A VOICE: As the parrot used to say at the bawdy-house! (*Loud laughter.*)

SERGEANT GALLARDO, *shouting above the din:* A pox on you all! Listen to me! The Chief Pilot is the most honest and well-meaning man in the flotilla, I'll stake my life on it. But what does that profit us? Listen to me, brave hearts!

SHOUTS *of:* Silence for Sergeant Gallardo!

SERGEANT GALLARDO: If he reaches Peru in safety and gives a fair account of our situation, and asks for help, the Viceroy will laugh in his face. How could he do otherwise, when he learns how this expedition has been bungled? It would need a glib liar—indeed, a very Ananias—to persuade the merchants of Lima to throw good money after bad. Because he is an honest man the Chief Pilot will fail us. He won't even be able to come back with the empty ship, because the Canon of Panama will distrain upon it for debt. I vote, lads, that the General be warned against sending the *San Geronimo* to Peru, unless in consort with the *San Felipe* and the *Santa Catalina*, and with all of us on board.

SHOUTS *of:* Long live Jaime Gallardo! That's what we all say!

THE CHIEF PILOT: I thank you, Sergeant, for your good opinion of me. But what is this buzz about a voyage to Peru? The General has not spoken one word about sending me there.

GIL MOZO, *an orderly:* A lie! Don Tomás saw the despatch with his own eyes. Ask your fat friend whether he didn't.

ANDRÉS SERRANO: Gentlemen, upon my word, Don Tomás has done nothing of the kind; and though the General did consider sending back for help, he soon found this impracticable, and had all the ships' canvas carried ashore.

THE CHIEF PILOT: Now that this misunderstanding has been removed, let me hear your grievances.

MELCHIOR GARCIA, *a settler, peevishly:* Does your honour imagine that we came here to till the soil? There's a million acres of good land in Peru, had we wished to turn farmers. But we sold our businesses at a loss to follow General Mendaña to the Isles of Solomon and make our fortunes in the gold-mines there.

THE CHIEF PILOT, *righteously:* No, you volunteered to serve God and King Philip, and our declared object has always been to convert the heathen and pacify these islands, not to mine gold. (*Boos and catcalls.*)

MELCHIOR GARCIA: That is not to the point. Our obligations are to ourselves, not to the savages, nor is this island one of those mentioned in the King's orders. The soil is bad and couldn't be worse. We refuse to stay here, and you may tell the General so. Either take us to the Isles of Solomon, or back to Peru, or else to some other part of the world where there are Christians. (*Loud cheers.*)

THE CHIEF PILOT: Why do you say that the soil is bad?

MELCHIOR GARCIA: It yields but a few wet roots. This is no soil for corn.

THE CHIEF PILOT: Confess, man, that you never were a farmer! Are you complaining because you cannot harvest today what you sowed yesterday? Don Andrés, do you know this settler? What was his trade when he joined us?

ANDRÉS SERRANO: He is Melchior Garcia, thirty years of age, unmarried, a native of Lima. I have his record in my book. After his company was disbanded he had no better trade than begging at the street corner; and for charity's sake the General equipped him as a volunteer. He has left little behind him that he can regret. (*Cheers, boos and laughter.*)

THE CHIEF PILOT: I know many more like him, who could not look the New World in the face and have sailed to a still newer one. How do the Peruvians commonly pass their lives, if not in ceaseless struggle for a livelihood? And how many of them manage, even after years of toil, to provide for their old age by hoarding a potful of silver pesos? Confess, gentlemen! At home you were rich in hope only; but here you have a God-given chance to convert that hope into reality. A plot of virgin ground costs you nothing, a trencher of wholesome food is to be had for the asking, and it is but a fortnight's labour to raise a snug cottage. Work then, and provide for yourselves. One day, when you have banished the wolf of want that has been howling at your doors, you will be free to indulge in such curious pastimes as mining for gold and diving for pearls. One day, but not now. (*Ironical cheers.*)

FEDERICO SALAS, *a young soldier:* No, not now, and not for another twenty years, I'll be bound. We'll be old men before we see that day. And meanwhile, there's not a wine-shop nor a pastry-cook within a thousand leagues.

A RAUCOUS VOICE, *singing:* The wine-shops of Lima,
                 For soldiers in luck
                 Are full of good Malmsey,
                 And —— —— ——
(*Roars of laughter.*)

THE CHIEF PILOT *to* FEDERICO: So you expected to find everything ready for you to the last merry detail? A city with churches, inns and shops, and your own house handsomely furnished—the table laid, a cellarful of choice wines and WELCOME in foot-high letters chalked on the door? Is that it? How do you think Toledo, Seville, Rome and the other great cities of the world came to be? They began as a few huts raised by resolute men, whose successors benefited by their labours and blessed their memory. Little by little, stone and tiles replaced wattle and thatch, until the rude beginnings stood crowned with the glory of cathedrals and palaces.

MIGUEL GERONIMO, *an elderly settler:* Do not listen to a few lazy rascals, your honour. We all wish to work, but who can till without tools?

THE CHIEF PILOT: The soil here is loose enough to be worked with wooden spades, until we can send for iron ones.

GIL MOZO: And I warrant that you're looking forward to fetching them. When I see you digging your own patch with a wooden spade, I'll trust you.

THE CHIEF PILOT: You do me an injustice. All the labour of steering

you across unknown seas, of plotting the course, of straining the eyes
at night for signs of reefs or rocks was mine alone . . .

A BABBLE OF VOICES: But why did you bring us here? These aren't
the islands you were told to find. Take us off again!

THE CHIEF PILOT: Gentlemen, I beseech you! You are gnawing
at an old bone; but here is a new one to try your teeth upon.
Know then, that you are asking the impossible. We came here with
following winds, and while those persist we cannot return unless we
sail many hundreds of leagues northward, across the Line of the
Equator, to catch winds of the contrary kind. We have not enough
food for so protracted a voyage, even if one man in three were left
behind; and for want of water-casks and jars we should die of thirst
long before we starved. Besides, the ships are unfit for any such
enterprise. We cannot careen them here, and their rigging is two
parts rotten and not to be trusted in more than a capful of wind.

GIL MOZO: Then we are in irons here! Yet I would as lief drown
in a hundred fathoms of salt water, as rot in this fever-hole. For
God's love, take us off at all hazards!

THE CHIEF PILOT *with flashing eyes*: That is against the General's
wish, and to oppose him is to be disloyal to His Majesty.

SALVADOR ALEMAN: Take back those words, sailor! We are not
disloyal.

THE CHIEF PILOT: I shall not take them back. Refusal to work
the land seized by the General in the royal name is no less than
disloyalty. Seduction of a comrade from his duty is more than disloyalty: it is plain treason.

SEBASTIAN LEJIA, *arquebusier*: Tell me, your honour: is it treason
to sign a memorial which humbly asks the General to abandon his
settlement, and take us where he has been ordered to go?

THE CHIEF PILOT: If the memorial asks for that, and that only,
it is not treasonable. But remember that it was God who lifted the
curtain of mist and showed us this island; otherwise, we should
have been cast among the reefs. And since He gave it to us, we should
be content to remain for a time and sustain ourselves on His bounty.

SEBASTIAN LEJIA: Yes, for a time! But what then?

THE CHIEF PILOT: Then the General will decide what is to be
done. Meanwhile, I have this message from him: that he intends to
search once more for the *Santa Ysabel*. It is not impossible that she
may have reached the Isles of Solomon before us. According to my
computations they lie only a few score leagues to the westward.

SALVADOR ALEMAN: Not one of us will say no to that—if the General goes himself.

THE CHIEF PILOT: He cannot be expected to do so; his health is feeble and he dares not expose it to new risks. He and his Lady will stay here to animate you until the search vessel returns.

GIL MOZO, *laughing loudly:* Oh, isn't he the cunning rogue? He persuades the General to load the galeot with our remaining stores and send him off to pilot her! Sailor, you stand self-convicted: tell me, if the wind blows fair for San Cristobal, how will you come back? With oars?

THE CHIEF PILOT, *patiently:* The General will send whom he pleases, and the search vessel, by continuous tacking, should be here again within a month. Whoever pilots the ship will, no doubt, be accompanied by some high officer—in whom the General trusts . . .

GIL MOZO: But who, being ignorant of navigation, can easily be hoodwinked!

A new crowd of soldiers arrive, released from night-guard. THE CHIEF PILOT *calls for silence and delivers his speech with noble gestures:* Gentlemen, hear me out! You are not the first subjects whom King Philip has sent on wearisome journeys to advance the frontiers of his vast realm. How often has a fistful of brave men held an entire province against the opposition of countless foes! Day and night they have defended lonely outposts against attack, thirsting, hungering and without rest: prepared to eat dogs and cats rather than disgrace the honour of Spain by surrender.

A VOICE: There are no dogs or cats here. Have we your honour's permission to eat bats and rats instead? (*Loud laughter.*)

THE CHIEF PILOT, *ignoring the interruption:* They fought on with no hope of rewards—or none to equal those that here await us. There is no need to starve on Santa Cruz. The soil is rich, the seas teem with fish, the natives are generously inclined. We are the fortunate ones! How many thousands would give all they possess for the opportunity that is ours: to be pioneers in a rich, unknown land, to win fame and fortune by bold development of its resources! Let it never be said of us that we baulked at the ditch, or refused to leap the wall. Time is no matter. What odds, if we do not reach our destination before May?

FREDERICO SALAS: What odds, if we never do? What odds, if we choose to put to sea without waiting for next May?

THE CHIEF PILOT, *with passion:* Then we shall have earned infamy as traitors to God, to King Philip, to the General and, what will perhaps sting most, to ourselves!

Traitors to God: if on such tenuous grounds we abandon the lovely work of saving souls with which Our Saviour charged us, and leave in the clutches of the Devil those whom we set out to rescue.

Traitors to the King: if we desert a secure base from which we might stud his imperial crown with still richer jewels of discovery—for the vast Southern Continent of Austrialia lies at our doorstep.

Traitors to the General: who waited six-and-twenty years and sold all he had to equip this glorious enterprise.

Traitors to ourselves: because wherever we might sail we could not hope to escape the King's vengeance. No civilized port within three thousand leagues acknowledges any sovereignty but his. If we forced the General to come with us, he would denounce us as mutineers to the nearest Royal Governor; if we marooned him here, news of his whereabouts would be demanded, and the truth exacted from us by the thumb-screw. We should be left to rot in prison for years, until the King had decided upon a punishment consonant with our treachery! (*A hush.*)

SERGEANT GALLARDO: Those are brave words, sailor. But it appears to me that the longer we stay, the worse our predicament. You admit that the ships' rigging is two parts rotten. By May it will be wholly rotten, and the hulls so eaten away with teredo that they will founder at their moorings. We shall be trapped without hope of escape. And though, in God's good time, His Majesty may graciously remember us and send a vessel to our rescue, what chance have we of being found? No one knows where to look for us, and it is plain that the General himself does not know where we are. There is nothing for it but to sail at once, taking all the ships and as many of the able-bodied men as our supplies permit.

THE CHIEF PILOT: Do you expect us to leave our women, children and old people behind?

SERGEANT GALLARDO: Yes, if need be. The priests can protect them until our return.

THE CHIEF PILOT: There speaks the careless bachelor! And where should we go? To New Spain? The General took that route on his first voyage but, as the survivors will tell you, he sailed early in August and did not make port until late January, suffering terrible hardships on the way and losing scores of men from starvation.

SERGEANT GALLARDO: No, not to any port of the New World. Let it be the Philippines. Martin Groc says that they are only half the distance away, and that the winds would favour us.

THE CHIEF PILOT: That voyage also has its difficulties. We cannot count on finding a chain of islands that will supply us with water and fresh food. And in any case we must wait until a last search has been made for the *Santa Ysabel*. If she is found, there will be no need to send for tools and powder.

SERGEANT GALLARDO: And if she isn't found? What then? Our one hope is to make for the Philippines. For water, let us seize a few canoes, fill them, plank them over, and caulk them well.

THE CHIEF PILOT: How would you get them into the hold? On deck the water would soon rot.

SERGEANT GALLARDO: Then use coconuts or joints of cane.

THE CHIEF PILOT: So ho! Ten thousand coconuts and a thousand joints of cane; which the sailors would have to collect, trim and fill, because soldiers consider such tasks beneath their dignity! And what about provisions?

SERGEANT GALLARDO: We could make shift with native food—yam-biscuit and pork for the most part. There are still hundreds of villages where we haven't yet foraged.

THE CHIEF PILOT: And what assurance have you that your biscuit will not corrupt as quickly as the pork?

SERGEANT GALLARDO: We will take that risk.

APPLAUSE and CRIES of: To the Philippines!

FEDERICO SALAS: The city of Manila is civilized!

THE CHIEF PILOT: Yes, thanks to the stout hearts who founded it two generations ago! But is it not far better to stay in Santa Cruz, and rival them in riches and honour, than trail off with sheathed sword and sloped arquebus?

FEDERICO SALAS: Where the King and the Pope live, there is honour; not in Manila, still less here.

THE CHIEF PILOT: We are wasting words. Come, gentlemen, re-consider your views, and if you have a petition to make, submit it in the proper manner through your officers. The General will not stop his ears to just complaints; but he has been greatly offended by news of a round robin that has been circulating . . .

A VOICE *from behind a tree-fern:* At the instigation of his double-dealing Lady and her cowardly brothers!

THE CHIEF PILOT: That is an infamous lie. Who dares to traduce Doña Ysabel?

THE VOICE *again:* Long live the Colonel! Death to the Barretos!

THE CHIEF PILOT: There speaks the tongue of mutiny.

SEBASTIAN LEJIA: Oh, leave the fool to his preaching, comrades! Anyone who cares to stay is welcome; but we're resolved to go, and nobody shall stop us.

SEBASTIAN LEJIA, FEDERICO SALAS, SALVADOR ALEMAN, GIL MOZO *and the other original signatories of the round robin run off to their huts and presently return with their swords, whispering fiercely together.*

FEDERICO SALAS: There stands the man who brought us here, and by all the angels in Heaven, doesn't he deserve to die?

SEBASTIAN LEJIA: I, for one, would gladly drink from his skull.

The veteran MATIA PINETO *crouches down behind* SEBASTIAN, *whom his confederate* JUAREZ MENDÉS *suddenly pushes in the chest. He tumbles backwards.* MATIA *and* JUAREZ *quickly disarm him.*

SEBASTIAN LEJIA: Help, comrades, help! God confound you, Matia! Give back my sword! I'll be even with you one dark night!

MATIA PINETO: Steady, lads! The first fellow who interferes, I'll stick him like a hog.

(*They fall back sullenly.*)

(*To* THE CHIEF PILOT): Pray forgive the interruption, your honour. It was only the washerwoman being sent about her business.

THE CHIEF PILOT: I thank you, soldier, but I have done. God save the King!

(*A tucket sounds. Exeunt omnes with cheers and counter-cheers.*)

Chapter 18

A FORAGE WITH MALOPE

When the Colonel heard that Pedro Fernandez had gone to the Churchyard to address the troops there, he was on the point of calling out the guard to disperse the meeting; but Juan de Buitrago dissuaded him. 'My lord,' he said, 'would that not be to play into the hands of your enemies? The Chief Pilot claims to be an emissary of Don Alvaro's. With all respect, I counsel you to lodge your protest at the Great Cabin before you take action ashore.'

'By God, you are right,' said the Colonel. 'I'll go at once.'

'May I be permitted to escort your lordship?' asked the Ensign. 'The Barretos might be lying in ambush.'

'No, by your leave, I'll take Carlotta. She's a very terror to rats.'

I heard the sequel from one of the pages. Doña Ysabel ran to the Great Cabin, crying: 'Good news! The Colonel is delivered into our hands. He's on his way here in the skiff, alone, without even his negro to protect him. Quick, my lord, call for the Boatswain and tell him to tie a noose at the end of a long rope and have six men ready below the mizzen-mast!'

'No, my lady, no!' said Don Alvaro. 'That would not agree with my honour. Had he brought his friends with him, the horse would be of a different colour. But since he comes alone, I dare not offer him violence: besides, I have not yet sufficient evidence that he is fomenting mutiny. Be patient only a little longer and let us hear what he has come to say.'

'Have you so soon forgotten his threats against your life and mine, and the lives of my brothers? Leave the task to a Barreto, my lord, since you dare not despatch him yourself. I will strike him down myself.' She snatched a chopper from its hook beside the fireplace.

'Put that back, my lady,' he said, 'if you wish to keep my love.'

Almost at once the Colonel entered, and the conference took place behind closed doors. Here the strand of my story is broken; but it is known that he returned cheerfully to the camp, the bloody climax of the feud once more postponed.

He arrived at the gates as the meeting broke up. Disregarding the Chief Pilot, who offered him a courteous salute, he shouted to the troops: 'Stand fast there, my lads, I have a message for you from the General!'

At the sound of his voice, the Ensign-Royal and Tomás de Ampuero came out of their tent. 'Get the men into their ranks, Don Toribio,' the Colonel ordered. 'Christ save me, how my belly ached as I came up from the beach! The rogues were crowding around that sailor like women in the market-place haggling over a great codfish. And you, Don Tomás, pray fetch him back; I want him to hear what I say.'

Pedro Fernandez and I turned about and stood a little apart, while the troops were marshalled in threes and called to attention. The Colonel went down the lines, followed by the ensigns. Finding seven men armed with swords, which was against the standing orders of the camp, he swore roundly and sent them under escort to the guard-house, there to await a flogging.

He glanced scornfully at the Chief Pilot, as if to say: 'Watch me, and learn how to address troops!', and then began in a rasping voice:—

'Gentlemen, I'll not waste my time or yours with flatulent oratory, but give you the gist of the matter in three words. It has come to the General's notice that you're discontented, that you dislike this island, and that you want to go to a better. SILENCE IN THE RANKS THERE!'

He paused, glaring at them and, when all was quiet, proceeded:

'The General accused you of being mutineers, but I defended you. I told him that you had neither mutinied nor shown signs of doing so. "Mutiny," said I, "is when troops run amok with drawn swords, crying: 'Death to the rogues!' That will never happen while Pedro Merino is in command," I said. "Thank you, my lord," he replied. "I love those who come out frankly on my side." "And I thank your Excellency," said I, "for your declaration of trust." Then he informed me that you had written down your grievances, and that if the document were presented to him in the proper way, namely through your company officers and myself, he would give it his earnest consideration —as was his duty.

'Well, gentlemen, let your officers have the paper, and if it is drawn up in suitable terms, I shall transmit it to him. Meanwhile, let no soldier under my command, whatever his rank, utter a single word that smells of disrespect or, by God's bones, I'll hang him higher than Haman, though he were my dearest friend; the General's honour, and with it that of our good King, has been entrusted to me. But, hark ye to a word of warning! Spies and tale-bearers abound—I need not name them—who call me traitor because I speak up for you and swear that you're honest men. Some, whispering behind their hands, even charge me with inciting you to rebel—as though I would stoop to so nasty a crime, or as though you would listen if I did. Beware of the sneaking rascals!

'One last thing: before we can consider leaving these shores, all the islands near by must be searched for the Admiral's ship. To do otherwise would be cowardly, her commander being a bold and much-maligned nobleman, and her men our comrades and brothers.

'Now, if you have any questions prepared, out with them!'

One shouted one thing; another shouted another. He silenced them with a roar, swearing that he had not a hundred tongues to answer a hundred foolish questions thrown at him simultaneously.

Don Tomás then stepped forward to ask whether he might speak first. The request being granted, he said: 'Some of us, your lordship, don't trust the Chief Pilot to go in search of the *Santa Ysabel*. If I undertook the mission myself, could I count on your lordship's support?'

The Colonel looked him quizzically up and down. 'It is comical enough,' he said at last, 'when a sailor harangues the troops like Alexander his Macedonians—but when a soldier plays the sailor . . .' The rest was lost in general laughter.

'Let the Colonel go himself!' cried Sergeant Gallardo.

'What? I?' he exclaimed with a grimace. 'I cannot tell port from starboard, and the very sight of an astrolabe makes my head spin round. Yet someone must go; and whoever is chosen must be a man of confidence.'

At this, Pedro Fernandez asked leave to speak to the Colonel in private; the Ensign-Royal searched his clothes for concealed weapons and finding none, brought him forward. 'Don Pedro,' he said, 'being no less loyal to our King than your lordship is, and as ready to lay down my life for him, I have listened to you with joy. Yet I take it ill that you have permitted Don Tomás to speak of me as though I were a traitor.'

The Colonel apologized handsomely and in the hearing of all. 'I thank you, Sir, for your goodwill, and beg pardon for the injury of which you complain. We have had our differences, but though I often question your prudence, your loyalty I have never doubted. You say you are ready to die for King Philip; why, so am I, by the bowels of Christ! Your hand on that, Don Pedro! So long as I serve His Majesty, I care not a snap of my fingers what my end may be.' They clasped hands, and the troops cheered.

Thus the rift between the two services was at last repaired, and had it not been for Doña Ysabel's unappeasable rancour, all might yet have gone well with us. The unrest of the troops sprang solely from their sense of discord in high places, but for which Sebastian Lejia and his rascally friends would never have made a single convert to their way of thinking.

We took leave of the Colonel and returned to the flagship, where Pedro Fernandez happily assured Don Alvaro that the troops were now amenable to discipline and that the Colonel, though vexed at what had been said against him, showed no disloyalty.

Doña Ysabel, seeing that her position had sensibly weakened, resolved that it must be now or never. She followed Pedro Fernandez to the Chart-room and said in the sweetest manner imaginable: 'Dear friend, you have done Don Alvaro and me a service today for which we will always be grateful. Would you do me another?'

'I am your devoted servant,' said he, with visible emotion, kissing the hand she held out. 'Only command me!'

'Then ask my husband's permission to take the long-boat in the morning and collect food from the villages beyond the usual range of forage. If you can bring back half a boat-load of pork, nuts, biscuit and the like, it will smooth his path when he goes ashore to arrange matters to his liking—which will be in two days' time, if God wills.'

'I am always at your call,' he answered.

'Ah!' she sighed. 'Had I but more friends of your mettle, I should be happy indeed. . . . And Andrés shall go with you. The General is taking a purge tonight and will not need him tomorrow.'

'Am I to be given troops?'

'As many as you ask.'

Her plan was to keep him out of the way—and myself too, as the chronicler of the expedition—while she took her revenge on the Colonel.

The General gave Pedro Fernandez his consent, the Colonel accommodated him with a sergeant and twenty men, and we embarked next day, about an hour after breakfast. We rowed past Malope's village, waving in salutation, and continued for another half-league until we came to a group of canoe-houses. There we hailed some men who were building a war-canoe, but they ran off shouting. After a short deliberation we landed and entered the village that lay near, from which the inhabitants had fled, leaving behind only one lame man and a child disfigured with ringworm. The pen before the Chieftain's house was empty of pigs, and though we might have climbed into the cock-lofts and helped ourselves to the villagers' yams and coconuts, it was pork that we most needed. Setting four arquebusiers to guard our boat, the Chief Pilot led the way up a path that, winding inland, promised to bring us to the yam-gardens. He warned the soldiers to carry their pieces at the ready.

This was my first passage through virgin forest, and its grandeur overawed me. The older trees were immensely thick and tall, their tops arching one hundred and fifty feet above our heads and shutting out the sun, their boles smothered with ferns and creepers. Not a breath of wind stirred as we went forward, but all was damp and oppressive, smelling of decay, and the green light sicklied our cheeks. Some trees had flung out drooping branches at the height of a house, which took instant root where they touched the earth and formed substantial buttresses. Others were set about, half-way up, with pendant fronds of fern. Fearing snakes, we stamped the ground as we walked, to scare them; but saw none. No fruit offered itself for the plucking, and no flowers bloomed, except at one blessed spot where a towering almond-tree had fallen and, bringing down others in its ruin, had let in the sunshine. Here a small herd of pigs crossed our path, crashing into the undergrowth before we had time to fire. Otherwise the forest seemed untenanted, though we heard countless pigeons cooing unseen in the branches high aloft. When we had marched for ten minutes or more, daylight shone at last at the end of our leafy tunnel and we came upon the gardens, laid out on the slope of a hill. These also were deserted, and we stood at a loss, wondering where to try next, until presently we heard the report of an arquebus, and then another, whereupon we returned at a run, cursing and gasping for breath.

To our relief we found that all was well. The shots had signalled the arrival of Malope, who was waiting for us on the beach, the green

gaskins tied round his head like a turban; he had followed us in his
war-canoe, which was escorted by one of smaller size under the command of his eldest son. When I went forward to make the Chief
Pilot known to him, he recognized me, pointed to the silver buckles
tied to his feet and smiled as he said slowly in good Castilian:
'Friends, let us go to dinner.' It was a phrase that he had been taught
by his son, with a few more of equal usefulness, such as 'Give me
that,' 'Halt, enough,' 'What do you call this?' and 'To the Devil with
it!' He then invited us by signs to follow him to a place where pigs
and coconuts abounded, and ordered the small canoe ahead. We were
grateful for his leadership, and soon came to another village, hardly
distinguishable from the one that we had found deserted. There Pedro
Fernandez asked Malope to hail the inhabitants and assure them of
our goodwill, which he did very readily, arranging with them that a
store of provisions would be gathered together against our return.

On we went, and he performed the same service for us at two more
villages. As we came away from these, he signed that the next, which
lay behind a small headland, was not well-disposed towards his tribe,
and that we should be wise to send an armed party across the neck of
land to surprise it and compel it to civility. This was done, but the
villagers, seeing that our party consisted of only nine men, ran to arms.
The sergeant, following his instructions, fired an arquebus in the air,
at the sound of which they yelled and fled away to launch their canoes.

Our boat had now come in view round the headland and fear of a
volley prevented them from embarking. Pedro Fernandez, leaping
ashore, asked them for pigs. They stood irresolute. After a while they
reluctantly fetched one, together with a few bananas and coconuts,
but when he asked for more, brandished their arms again and,
fitting arrows to their bowstrings, took cover behind trees and huts.
Recognizing Malope, they reminded him with shouts of the truce
agreed between his tribe and theirs. He stood looking from us to
them, as if in doubt where his duty lay, until Pedro Fernandez caught
hold of his arm and threatened him with a dagger—not meaning to
kill him, but presenting him to the enemy as one who acted under
duress. 'Tell them not to shoot,' he cried. 'If they do, *pu pu!*' and
snatching a lighted match from an arquebusier he made as if to fire.

Malope appreciated the delicacy of the situation, and was not
offended. He dropped his weapons and, showing no signs of fear,
went alone to the Chieftain's house. There he conferred for a little
while, after which he came back to tell us by signs that before three

o'clock—it was now a little past noon—our provisions would be laid outside the assembly-house. Meanwhile, women brought us a quantity of coconuts, ready opened, also ripe bananas and paw-paws, and drew us water from their well, smiling hospitably. As we ate and drank, a troop of small girls came up shyly and, after whispering together, danced naked for our entertainment. They performed such obscene and lecherous antics as would have disgraced a brothel of Panama; but the novelty of the show tickled the men, who laughed and cheered and cried 'Olé, olé!' Only Pedro Fernandez was offended and turned away his head.

The Chieftain's son then emerged from his father's house and, asking for gifts, was presented with a silken cap and a goat-bell. Overcome with delight, he invited us to go with him on a raid against the islet across the bay, where together we might kill numerous men and pigs; and Malope engaged himself that we should do so before the month was out. At last they found us two more pigs, a dozen bunches of bananas and more than a hundred coconuts, which we piled into the long-boat.

The Chief Pilot and I walked back along the coast with most of the soldiers and three native guides, until we came to the first of the friendly villages where food had been promised us. The long-boat and the canoes went ahead. Gaily-coloured flowers and blossoms grew in profusion beside our path, and the guides constantly pointed to some mean herb, to give it a name and inform us, for the most part unintelligibly, of its singular virtue or bane. Noisy white parrots flew everywhere, and we saw a pair of kingfishers and a flock of canaries; besides very ugly green tree-lizards, poisonous centipedes and a monster rat. A bird with crimson feathers sat perched on a branch thirty yards from the path and one of the guides, coveting its plumes, asked us to shoot it for him; but Pedro Fernandez prudently forbade this, lest a miss should betray that the arquebus is no weapon of precision.

After an hour's march we came to a stream close to the village where Malope—who always required us to address him as Mendaña—was waiting for us. When we had slaked our thirst he beckoned, and made signs, first snapping viciously with the thumb and forefinger of his left hand and then beating upon it with his right fist; from which we understood that some beast had its home near by, and that he wished us to join him in hunting it. Nothing loth, we accompanied him up the stream, until we reached a deep pool, where a crocodile of huge dimensions could be descried at the bottom. He set one of his men with a barbed spear to stir up the reptile, which was twice the length of a man, and it soon showed signs of resentment and swam downstream, belaboured with clubs and thrust at with spears, to take refuge in another pool; whence it was again dislodged and went on, never uttering a sound, though disabled in a foreleg, and somewhat stunned. We harried it from pool to pool and, before it could escape into the bay Malope, who had hitherto been a spectator of the hunt, leaped into the water with a cry and seized firm hold of its horny tail. His sons followed his example, the other men beating the brute about the neck with clubs, until with a yell of triumph it was hauled on the bank, growling and snapping at a stake that they had thrust between its ferocious jaws. The sons kept their hold on its tail, and the father battered its neck with a pointed rock. But since it was so long in dying, Pedro Fernandez thrust an arquebus down its throat and fired. It leaped high in the air, scattering the hunters and, horribly rolling its eyes, expired to their great satisfaction.

Federico Salas was with us, released from the stocks, after a good flogging at the hands of the drummer. He now came forward, took his dagger from his belt, cut out the crocodile's eyes and wrapped them in a leaf.

Pedro Fernandez innocently asked him why he did so. He smirked as he replied: 'I shall present them to a person of importance.'

'May I ask to whom?'

'To whom other than Doña Ysabel? A crocodile's eyes, as your honour must know, are the most potent aphrodisiac that God in His wisdom ever bestowed on impotent man. The General's Lady has but to dress them for his supper, and by midnight he will be a raging satyr, and she a contented woman before dawn.'

His comrades echoed his loud guffaw and added many more crudities, by no means respectful to the General or his Lady.

I had seen Pedro Fernandez angry often enough, even enraged once or twice, but never before had he shown such sudden and uncontrolled fury on so slight a cause. 'I spit upon you, filth of the gutter!' he screamed. 'And upon any others who dare insult our noble protectress.'

The soldiers stood in amazement. To add to the comedy, all the natives but Malope fled terror-stricken into the forest, and he, misreading the cause of the altercation, snatched the crocodile's eyes from Federico and laid them at the Chief Pilot's feet.

'I'll be even with you one of these days, you long-nosed son of a whore!' growled Federico at Malope.

'Back into your ranks!' shouted Pedro Fernandez, regaining command of himself. He sheathed his dagger and abruptly ordered the advance.

We continued along the path to the village, where bananas, sugar-cane, coconuts, almonds, yam-biscuit and the rest were laid out for us in great heaps; also two more pigs and a pile of palm mats. The natives sat quietly in the assembly-house beside their war-canoes, which they had decked with greenery and white cloth in token of peace. Malope, ascending a little mound to show his importance, received the gifts on our behalf with a short speech of praise, then turned to us, and said: 'Forward, forward! Friends, let us go to dinner!' And at a word from him the villagers took up the victuals and carried them to the long-boat; it was a sight worth seeing, how a hundred of them filed along the coast-road, their burdens swinging at the ends of poles balanced on their shoulders. We embarked and rowed on to the next village, and the next, until we had fourteen pigs and more food than could be shipped with ourselves still remaining aboard; so the canoes towed the long-boat and we travelled on foot. At last we reached Malope's village, where we were taken off in a pair of war-canoes. 'Embrace my brother Malope,' said he in parting, and handed Pedro Fernandez a package done up in leaves and tied with native thread. 'Friends, let us go to dinner!' he explained.

As we approached the flagship, Federico and Sebastian were muttering together that they had not come all the way from Peru to be sent under command of a sailor on piddling and disgraceful errands.

'And is this one of them?' Pedro Fernandez cried, his anger flaring up again. 'To bring back a boat-load of fine provisions that have cost us no more than a few words of thanks to Malope?'

'Those painted cannibals!' Sebastian replied. 'Only let us get at them with sword and shot; we'll soon teach them to respect Christians.'

'May God forgive you for those words!' said he.

Doña Ysabel praised us when we came aboard, and called Don Alvaro out of bed to admire the day's spoils and help her divide them among the troops, the crew and the Great Cabin. While Myn was clothing him, Pedro Fernandez handed her the package, saying that Malope had sent it as a gift for his brother to eat; and she laid it by. Before the distribution was made, she offered Pedro Fernandez a

whole pig as his perquisite, but he refused to accept more than a
sailor's share, stammering that the pleasure of serving the General
and herself was ample recompense for his labours; to which she replied that no lady was ever blessed with a more faithful servant.

That night, when the General had retired, she came to the Chart-
room and said, hesitating a little, as though in modesty: 'Tell me,
friend Pedro, how came Malope to send crocodiles' eyes to my husband? I have not yet told him of the unkind gift; he would be ashamed
to learn that even the savages of this island are acquainted with his
sad affliction.'

Pedro Fernandez blushed red as brick. 'I must have mistaken his
meaning,' he blurted out. 'I did not know what the package contained.
No doubt it was intended for me.'

'Take them then, by all means,' she answered, keeping a straight
face, 'though I should never have suspected that you, too . . .' And
not troubling to finish the sentence, she thrust the package into his
hand. 'Now come with me,' she said.

The Chief Pilot followed her shamefacedly to the Great Cabin,
where Don Alvaro beckoned him to sit on his bed, and told him that
he had that morning determined forthwith to rid himself of the
incubus that had sat so long astride his breast, choking out his life.
But, as he went ashore, Myn had rolled up his sleeves, jigging up and
down, and foolishly cried: '*Olé, olé!* Now for the black puddings!
Myn will bloody his arms to the elbow.' Some soldiers who stood by
had looked up angrily—'Oho,' they said, 'so the General comes with a
martingale for the old war-horse, does he? Did you hear his negro's
words?' He had then chastized Myn before them all and, after a brief
visit to the guard-house, returned to the flagship. 'It had come upon
me, my wise counsellor, that I should henceforth do nothing without
your approval.'

'Your Excellency pays me great honour. But what did you propose
to do?'

'I was about to put the Colonel on trial for his life.'

'Indeed! Upon what charges?'

Don Alvaro counted on his fingers: 'First, that he has spread disaffection; second, that he has threatened to hang my brothers-in-law;
third, that he has disobeyed my orders on more than one occasion.
Fourth, and worst . . .'

'As your Excellency knows, I have no cause to love the Colonel
but, his speech to the troops yesterday being no less loyal than my

own, I confess that I praised him for it, and we concluded a truce.'

'You are easily deceived, my open-hearted friend. No sooner had you gone than he addressed them again, in a very different strain, warning them to be prepared for swift action. Doña Ysabel has been given precise information about his latest plot. He means to lead armed men into the Church while we are at prayer next Sunday, to seize and murder her brothers and herself, and force me at the point of his sword to sign the order for a voyage to the Philippines; but before we arrive, he will secretly poison me and give out that I died of a fever.'

'Oh, the damnable wickedness!' cried Pedro Fernandez. 'To think that I offered the monster my friendship!'

'You will stand by us?' Doña Mariana asked, laying a trembling hand on his arm.

'Upon my life, I will,' he said breathlessly.

'Tomorrow,' continued Don Alvaro in a hoarse whisper, 'after an early breakfast, I intend to take you and four other trustworthy men ashore with me. My brothers-in-law will be waiting at the gates and, supported by them, I shall seek out the Colonel, and command him to accompany me to the flagship. If he resists, force will be needed. It may well be that Myn's folly has come to his knowledge and that he will be on his guard.'

'You can trust me to the death.' And Don Alvaro feebly gripped his hand.

Yet in the Chart-room that night Pedro Fernandez was low-spirited. Deep in his heart he knew that what awaited the Colonel was far less than justice, but he silenced his conscience with a reminder that the Colonel had shown no mercy to the innocent islanders of the Marquesas, and with a protest that Doña Ysabel was incapable of deceit.

He began to tell me of his childhood in the Rua Nova at Lisbon: how his father, who was a sailor, had once engaged for the Goa voyage and bound him to good behaviour until the ship was home again—' "And for every evil deed you do in my absence, lad," he warned me, "your mother will drive a nail in this plank; and for every nail I find on my return, you may expect ten sweeping strokes of the birch."

'That summer I fell among bad company, and by Christmas Day five large nails stood to my discredit; but at New Year I was granted a change of heart. My mother, pitying me, and sensible of my reformation, had drawn the last nail out again before the feast of Saint Peter in Chains, when my father came back. Thus I escaped the birching, yet wept bitterly when she showed him the plank with the nail-marks scored in the soft wood.'

'Why have you told me this, friend Pedro?'

'As a parable of the soul's weakness. How often since then have I not fallen into error? Though after confession and penance my sins have been forgiven me, still the nail-marks show in the plank!'

I had an inkling of what was in his mind: no ancient sin confessed and atoned for, but a new sin, which he dared not acknowledge as such even to himself. 'Yes,' said I. 'Who is free of fault? A sin committed in the imagination weighs as heavy in God's scales as though it were committed in fact; did not Our Saviour point to ocular adultery . . .'

'No severer words ever left His lips,' he broke in, as if to prevent me from saying more. 'Yet did He not pity the adulterous woman and show her mercy?'

Chapter 19

MURDER

Shortly before dawn a clamour was heard from the beach: 'Ahoy there, Officer of the Guard! Lend us the long-boat!'

Don Jacinto Merino, who had the guard again, went to the Great Cabin to report the matter. 'O! O!' shrieked Doña Ysabel. 'They have murdered my brothers and now they come to murder me. For the love of all the Saints, deny them what they ask!'

'Feign deafness, Don Jacinto,' said the General, equally alarmed, 'until we can make out who they are.' They shouted four or five times more, and then silence fell.

When it grew light, the beach was seen to be deserted, but an hour or so later thirty soldiers marched out of camp. Don Alvaro hailed them, ordering them to stand fast until he had conferred with their officer. They obeyed, and he went hastily ashore in the skiff, accompanied by Don Jacinto, the Chief Pilot, myself and some servants.

'Who commands you?' he asked the men.

'At your Excellency's orders,' answered the Adjutant, stepping forward.

'And your errand?'

'We are bound for Malope's village. He must take us up the coast in search of more provisions.'

'But Malope collected a boat-load of food for us yesterday!'

'So he did, your Excellency. Four pigs and half a dozen bunches of bananas were allotted to the camp; the greater part remained in the *San Geronimo*. The Major told us to borrow the long-boat and have it filled again, but since no one answered our shouts, we decided to borrow canoes from Malope instead.'

'I should have been ready to lend you the boat,' the General said,

'if I had known in good time, but no matter! See to it that the troops
do no damage in the village.'

'You can trust me,' replied the Adjutant with a disagreeable smile,
'not to make black puddings without your Excellency's permission.'

Don Jacinto then asked leave to join the party, which included
Juan de Buitrago and the Ensign-Royal; and Don Alvaro agreed that
a sergeant might take over the standing guard until he returned.
The Adjutant gave the order to march and they went off, singing
briskly:

> 'Keep in step: three by three,
> Every man: knee to knee,
> Every lance: at the trail,
> Keep in step: without fail,
> And it's *Sús! Sús! Sús!*

> 'For the cranes: as they fly
> Keep in step: through the sky,
> And Peru: cannot thrive,
> Cannot thrive: or survive
> Without *Sús! Sús! Sús!*

> 'Keep in line: by the flank,
> Every man: in his rank,
> Serve the King: till you die,
> Keep in step: so will I,
> With a *Sús! Sús! Sús!*

The mill of justice could now grind without further hindrance.
Captain Corzo walked at Don Alvaro's right, armed as usual with a
long wood-knife, and the Chief Pilot at his left, carrying no weapon;
behind followed two targeteers, and Myn twirling his axe, chuckling
to himself and smacking his thick lips. To disguise the nature of our
mission, I had been instructed to bring a pile of papers with me, and
my ink-horn.

The Barreto brothers met us at the camp gates. 'He marked out
the stockade yesterday,' Don Lorenzo reported in low tones, 'and on
the site that you forbade him to use. Since daybreak the troops have
been felling trees; now they are off duty until Malope's men arrive
to help them, and he has pitched his tent by the spring. He is about
to breakfast there alone. The Captain of Artillery has come over to
our side; Captain Leyva is likely to follow his example; of the remain-

ing officers only Tomás de Ampuero is dangerous, and he is still in his tent. The Chaplain is saying mass in the Church.'

'I am heartily relieved that this is open rebellion at last,' said Don Alvaro. 'Let us go to the spring. Pedro Fernandez, pray take a message to the guard-house: I wish the Captain of Artillery to stand by in case of need.' This was a sleeveless errand; Don Alvaro lacked the courage to carry out his project with the Chief Pilot's eyes upon him.

We walked on slowly towards the spring, Captain Corzo sharpening his wood-knife on an emery stone as we went, Myn cutting gleeful capers, myself trailing glumly in the rear. When we came in sight of the tent, Don Alvaro turned to me. 'Andrés,' he said, 'I shall wait here while you tell the Colonel that he is wanted on a matter of urgency.'

'I should consider it a kindness if you chose another messenger,' I answered. But Don Diego pricked me covertly with his dagger, and forward I went, smothering a cry.

The Colonel sat in his tent on a tree-stump, clad in shirt and hose, eating pig's fry and yam-pudding from a scarred pewter platter. Cross-legged on the floor, hunched over a tall book, a page was reading aloud to him. Outside, his negro tended the fire, fanning it with a palm-leaf; a second panful of pig's fry sizzled on a trivet.

'My lord,' said I, gently.

'Hush, man!' he answered with a frown. 'Do not interrupt the sweet flow of *Palmyrin.* I would not for the world miss the end of this marvellous encounter. Continue, Pacito! Nay, lad, go back to the beginning of the sentence once again.'

Pacito read:

'The Knight of Death on the next morning came forth before his tent, attired in black armour whereon was painted in divers places the semblance of a woman's face descried through shrubs . . .'

'That would be the sorceress Eutropa,' the Colonel commented knowingly, his mouth full of pudding. 'She lay thus in ambush, to the ruin of many a noble knight.'

'And in his shield was figured a knight of sorrowful aspect surrounded by many deaths, who all fled from him: the whole so naturally portrayed as moved the beholders to fear of those ugly anatomies, and compassion of the man. He sat upon a dark flame-coloured horse, leaning upon his lance . . .'

'My lord,' I repeated, 'loth as I am to disturb you, I must tell you that the General is waiting outside and wishes to see you on urgent business.'

He sprang up and ran from his tent, without even a hat, to pay his belated respects; but when he saw so many of his enemies gathered around Don Alvaro, he called over his shoulder: 'Quick, Pacito, my baldric, also my loaded stick!'

Pacito closed the book, marking the page with a straw, and ran to do as he had been told. The Colonel fastened the baldric over his shirt, and stepped forward with a low bow. "Good-day, your Excellency,' said he. 'Pray pardon my disarray, but you have come without warning. Will you do me the honour of sharing my poor breakfast?'

Don Alvaro fetched a deep sigh. He shut his eyes as if in prayer, then grasping his sword he screeched: 'Long live the King! Death to all traitors!'

Don Diego's orderly, Juan de la Roca of the coloured ribbons, had crept behind the Colonel like a snake. Now he rose, seized him by the shirt collar, and crying 'Long live Saint Joseph!', stabbed him with a dagger in the mouth and the right breast; Sergeant Dimas, closing in from the other side, struck him with a Bohemian knife and left it sticking in his ribs. The negro started to his feet, intending to help his master, but Myn pushed him down and stood over him with his axe.

'Oh, gentlemen!' gasped the Colonel, his mouth cruelly gashed, and a red stain spreading fast on his fine cambric shirt. Horror and incredulity at so shameful an assault could be read in his eyes. His hand went slowly to his sword, but before he could draw, Captain Corzo was on him and nearly severed his right arm with a slashing blow of the wood-knife.

He gave a great cry and sank to his knees. 'Enough, enough!' he moaned. 'Send for the Chaplain!'

'There is no time for that,' said Don Lorenzo, smiling brutally. 'Make a good act of contrition and have done!'

As he lay writhing on the ground, his lips formed the prayer: 'Jesus, Maria . . .'

I stood as though petrified in horror, feeling a very Judas for my part in the vile business; when Leona Benitel, a good woman who had been washing for him at the spring. hastened up, pillowed his bloody head in her lap and helped him to die in peace. Stroking his forehead, she whispered: 'Patience, my son! Christ in His mercy will forgive your sins and avenge you.'

Don Diego, who was to have been a leader in the work of butchery, still hung back, but Captain Leyva, to show that he favoured the stronger side, drew his sword. 'I will put this traitor out of his agony,' he cried, and ran him through the heart. He shuddered and died, and Leona screamed: 'May the wrath of God fall upon such cruel Captains!'

Don Alvaro came up to apostrophize the corpse, which he did with such melancholy sorrow as I could not think forced or insincere: 'Alas, poor madman; why did you tear up your Catholic commission and take service with Satan, dying too soon for repentance?'

At his orders the Royal Standard was unfurled, the drum sounded, and he called out: 'In the name of King Philip! Vengeance has overtaken Don Pedro Merino. Be warned by his fate! A general pardon is hereafter extended to all who were privy to his plot, if they will swear a new oath of fidelity.'

Meanwhile, the Chief Pilot had gone to the guard-house, where Don Luis met him, saying: 'Justice has been done.'

'But the trial? There has not been time for a trial.'

'He resisted arrest,' was the answer.

Hearing their voices, Tomás de Ampuero and Gil Mozo, his orderly, came out of their tent and asked what was afoot. 'Nothing of interest to you,' replied Don Luis, drawing his dagger and running at him. He aimed for the heart but, the Ensign throwing himself backward, he struck too high and the dagger lodged in his shoulder. 'Me? What have I done?' he called out in pain and indignation.

Don Luis drew his sword, but Pedro Fernandez courageously stepped between the two men, and asked: 'What is this? Would you kill a man without provocation?'

Gil Mozo had run off towards the beach and Don Tomás made for the Colonel's house intending, I dare say, to take shelter with the Chaplain. All three Barretos were hard at his heels, but with his long stride he might have outdistanced them, had he not tripped over a tent-rope and fallen heavily. He was slow to rise, and Don Lorenzo lunged at him as he crouched on hands and knees. Now that the Ensign was mortally wounded, Don Diego plucked out the dagger and planted it squarely between his sagging shoulders.

'Death to the Barretos!' shouted Sergeant Gallardo, emerging from another tent, sword in hand, and making for Don Luis. Don Luis retreated, but Sergeant Dimas appearing suddenly, cried: 'Come, traitor, and meet your doom!'

'Traitor, is it?' Gallardo replied in a fury. 'If your cut-throats will allow me fair play, I shall spit that lie on the point of my blade, you damned coxcomb!'

They were evenly matched and fenced savagely, forwards and backwards, with sword and dagger, until Gallardo's sword broke and he fought on with the stump. He called for another, but nobody took pity on him, and presently Dimas ran him through the lungs; when he fell spouting blood, and expired unconfessed.

The Drummer came up with the Colonel's blood-stained clothes, the perquisite of his office, and asked: 'Why, lads? Was this Gallardo another of the traitors?' When they swore that he was, the rascal stripped the corpse to the buff and even wrenched the silver Saint Christopher from about its neck.

As I left, to search for the Chief Pilot, my foot struck the point of the Sergeant's sword, lying in the grass. I stooped and thrust it into my doublet, intending to mount it in a carved handle for use as a dagger; and when that night I examined the broken edge, I saw that it had been filed half-way through.

I told Pedro Fernandez indignantly of the Colonel's fate. 'May his soul rest in peace,' he said, as he crossed himself. 'Murder was never Don Alvaro's intention, I have his Lady's word for that.'

'Where are you going now?' I asked.

'Wherever I can save life.'

Men were roving about the camp with drawn swords and howls of 'Long live the King! Death to all traitors!'; now was the time to wipe out gambling debts, or settle old quarrels. I heard the names of Juarez and Matia shouted, and then some said: 'Let's be avenged on those card-sharping knaves at last; they were always loudest in the Colonel's praise.'

'Quick!' said I to Pedro Fernandez. 'To the veterans' hut! The men who saved you from death two days ago are in danger.'

We ran off together, to stand with our backs against their door. Up came the rabble, yelling 'Make way, there! Death to all traitors!', and a rough soldier scattered my papers in the mud. I rushed to retrieve them; but Pedro Fernandez would not budge, even when Don Lorenzo arrived and ordered him to be off.

'These men are loyal,' said the Chief Pilot, 'and I am proud to own them as my friends. Have a care what you do!'

'Kill them, kill the traitors!' the cry went up.

One man raised his arquebus, aiming at Pedro Fernandez, but another knocked it up. 'Fool,' said he, 'if you kill the Chief Pilot, how shall we ever get home?'

In the face of death, Pedro Fernandez took some almonds from his pocket and juggled with three of them, not letting one drop. 'Hey pass!' he sang out, like a mountebank. 'Can anyone present keep four in the air? Hey pass! Hey pass! Look now, brave hearts! Hey pass!'

The soldiers laughed against their will and cried 'Olé!' His calm disconcerted Don Lorenzo. 'Come away from that door,' he commanded, 'if you would not die.'

'Have a care,' the Chief Pilot repeated, his eyes on the four almonds which were rising and falling like the waters of a fountain. 'Don Alvaro has proclaimed a general pardon.'

'Not for these rogues! Only Saint Peter and the Devil could save them from our vengeance!' He drew his sword and advanced threateningly.

Suddenly the door flew open and out rushed three women, one armed with a ladle, another with a broom, a third, half-naked, with a club in her hand, of the kind used by the natives for pounding yams. They set about the rabble with a will, screaming abuse at the tops of their voices, and drove them off. Don Lorenzo's sword was sent whirling through the air, and Don Luis ignominiously felled with a smart blow of the yam-pestle. Yet such is the nature of women that they burst into tears so soon as victory was won, wringing their hands and tearing their hair. They mourned for Sergeant Gallardo as an honest gentleman, but also for the Ensign, complaining bitterly that love had undone him: which was the truth, since the Captain of Artillery's friendship had been bought by the Barretos with a promise to kill his wife's lover.

Captain Corzo marched up with four men, decapitated the corpses and stuck the heads upon stakes outside the guard-house, as the General had given him leave to do. Don Diego had placed himself under the Royal Standard, as the position of greatest safety; and that other coward, the Major, anxious to gain the credit of having struck a blow or two for his King, strode off to the Colonel's tent. There he found Pacito hugging *Palmyrin* to his breast and weeping, and the negro philosophically eating the unfinished breakfast. He drew his sword against the negro, who defended himself with the skillet and escaped;

so he went for the page and dealt him a cut on the head, slicing the scalp. To Leona Benitel's young son, who was helping her to lay out the Colonel's corpse, he did the same, and then chased the boys towards the Standard, under the folds of which they took sanctuary. Don Alvaro thanked him for his zeal, but implored him to spare their lives.

The long-boat was now seen approaching from the flagship, crammed with loyal sailors, all armed in one way or another. In the stern sheets stood the Vicar, as bellicose as any, with a rusty halberd in his hands. They scrambled ashore and the Boatswain's mate, who was in command, exclaimed fervently: 'We have come to die at our General's side!'

Don Alvaro smiled at them. 'Welcome, honest Damian; welcome, reverend Father!' he said. 'But the flame of rebellion has already been snuffed.'

'God be praised for that!' Damian answered. 'However, by your Excellency's leave, we will stay until the foraging party returns.'

Captain Corzo then rowed to the flagship to announce our victory to Doña Ysabel. Enlarging on the heroic part that he had taken in the subjugation of the Colonel, he brought her and Doña Mariana back and escorted them to the guard-house. The ladies' appearance had a calming effect upon the men who, recognizing Doña Ysabel's hand in the day's business, greeted her with obsequious cheers. Don Alvaro ordered them to pile arms, and hurried forward to receive her congratulations.

Federico, the most active of the true rebels, thought the moment opportune for sauntering out from the thicket where he had lain in hiding. 'What cheer, comrades!' he remarked carelessly. 'Has anything happened since I went away to cut amaranths?' As no one paid him any attention, he slipped into the crowd and escaped arrest.

Don Alvaro then kissed Father Juan's cross and asked him to celebrate a mass of thanksgiving in the Church, which he was glad to do. The troops were paraded and marched off to brisk and merry music. The rest of us followed in no order. After the benediction, the good Father, ignorant of the vile circumstances in which the executions had taken place, mounted the pulpit and begged us not to be scandalized by what we had witnessed, since it was for the safety and well-being of all. 'If thy right foot offend thee,' he intoned, 'cut it off; or if thy right eye offend thee, pluck it out—thus Our Saviour bade us.'

The troops fell in again and were dismissed outside the guard-house. The baggage of the victims was then brought to the Barretos, who divided the contents among themselves in truly fraternal love. Work was not resumed, the fatigue-men being allowed to roam idly about the camp until their dinner hour. Don Alvaro remained praying in the Church and did not come to eat with us. For myself, I could not swallow a morsel.

At about two o'clock a look-out on the knoll reported that the advance-guard of the Adjutant's expedition, now on its way back, were approaching in two canoes. Don Alvaro was summoned and at once bade the trumpeter sound the Rally, so that the new arrivals should be given no warning of what had occurred; the three heads were also taken down from the stakes, and the Standard concealed.

A sergeant marched up and saluted. 'What is new, friend?' asked Don Alvaro.

He answered: 'We have brought back three good pigs, your Excellency, and bad news of Malope.'

'Three pigs? That is not much. . . . But what of Malope?'

'He is dead.'

'No, no! It cannot be. Oh, Father Juan, did you hear those words? And you had such good hopes for his conversion. Alas, the poor soul, summoned so hurriedly to his Maker!'

'Hurriedly indeed, your Excellency!' the Sergeant said in a grim voice. 'One of our people murdered him!'

'Ah, God help us! Who was the wretch? Who dared commit so foul a deed . . .' He could not continue, for emotion.

'It was Sebastian Lejia. We marched to the village, where Malope asked us to come to dinner in the assembly-house. We seated ourselves in a row and food was served, while the Adjutant and Malope's son planned a raid upon Orchard Islet. We were laughing and talking in perfect amity when, without warning, Sebastian rose, thrust the muzzle of his piece against Malope's right pap, and fired. He tumbled back, gurgling, and Salvador Aleman put him out of his misery by splitting his skull with an axe.'

'Alas, the fault was mine!' sobbed Don Alvaro. 'I should have recalled the foraging party while I had the chance. What happened then?'

'The savages shrieked and fled. Juan de Buitrago drew his sword and threatened Sebastian, who was defiantly recharging his arquebus.

"That was the work of a devil, not a man!" the Ensign shouted at him, but he answered boldly: "I did right to kill the infidel. He was not trustworthy; only yesterday the Chief Pilot was forced to draw his dagger on him. Who else wants to die?" However, Captain Diego de Vera had him disarmed, trussed up, and put into a canoe under guard; my men are now bringing him here.'

Don Alvaro sank down upon a drum. 'Now we are utterly undone!' he groaned—a phrase often on his lips. But this time he buried his head in his hands and swayed from side to side.

When Sebastian arrived, with a hang-dog look, he was sent to the guard-house and fastened in the stocks. The main-party were now straggling towards the armoury, to replace their weapons in the racks, as usual; but the General had ordered Don Luis and some sailors to hide behind the back door; they were to bind and gag them one by one as they emerged. This was done expeditiously and in silence. The Adjutant and Sergeant Andrada, who brought up the rear, were also disarmed, and Don Alvaro had them placed in the stocks beside Sebastian. They gazed about them in wonder, not knowing what to think until they spied Pacito nursing his wounded head in a corner, fettered to a post. When they asked him with their eyes what had happened, he ran one finger across his throat and began to weep again; which caused them much apprehension.

Next the Colonel's nephew returned, in company with the Ensign-Royal; but neither of them was molested. Doña Mariana had pleaded for the life of her lover, and Father Juan for that of Don Toribio, who was related to the Bishop of Lima on his mother's side. 'Here at least are two faithful servants of the King!' announced Don Alvaro, rising feebly from his seat.

The rear-guard arrived under the command of Juan de Buitrago, and were in their turn overpowered outside the armoury, but Don Lorenzo manacled the Ensign and marched him off between four arquebusiers to a sentry-box at the other side of the camp.

'Why do you treat me like this?' he asked indignantly.

'The Colonel is dead, and a general pardon has been offered to his associates,' Don Lorenzo replied.

'Then why these manacles?'

'Your enemies have sworn to kill you. You are in safe custody.'

The Ensign's young wife, already with child, had been weeping silently for hours, and now ran shrieking after him between the huts and bushes, until she fell in a faint.

'Was that Doña Luisa?' asked the Ensign in anxiety. 'Let someone at once assure her that no harm will come to me.'

'Wait behind this tree, and I will go myself,' answered Don Lorenzo. 'Shoot him, if he stirs,' he told the escort. Then he went to the Colonel's house, where Father Antonio could be heard praying for the souls of the dead; his voice came in gasps, as though he were wrestling.

'You are wanted,' Don Lorenzo announced brusquely, as he strode in. 'And you had best come at once.'

Father Antonio did not rise from his knees. Reading murder in the other's proud, flushed face, he answered: 'What if I refuse to wade this muddy river, my son?'

'Then I will drag you through it by your skirts.'

'Captain Barreto—since you will not call me Father, I cannot call you son—remember that I am a priest! In the name of the One God, I adjure you not to add sacrilege to murder. . . ."

'Come with me, I say!'

A black face peered in at the window. It was Myn, who had taken advantage of the disturbance to slip off in search of loot.

'Myn, my son,' Father Antonio cried, 'if you are a good Catholic, come to my help!'

Don Lorenzo did not carry his cruel game further. Before the negro entered, he said mildly: 'I intended no violence, Father. But pray come with me to confess one who is about to die. Upon my honour, this is all that will be required of you.'

'Your honour?' he asked, investing the words with a garment of scorn. Then he rose, hurriedly washed his hands, robed himself, took what he needed from the chest which served as his sacristy, and followed Don Lorenzo out. 'Stay by my side, Myn,' he said, 'and guard me.' Myn shouldered his axe obediently, and they went off together.

The Chaplain found Don Juan laughing and jesting with his guard. 'Well met, Father,' he said. 'Now I shall know what has happened during our absence. These men seem afraid to open their mouths.'

Father Antonio replied: 'Murder has been committed, my son. The Colonel has been cowardly stabbed to death—in the presence of Don Alvaro.'

The Ensign struggled to cross himself, but the manacles hindered

him. He said, in deep grief: 'May God pardon his faults, which were
many, for the sake of his cruel end, which was undeserved!'

'And Tomás de Ampuero has been hunted and cut down by the
General's family.'

'They must have caught him alone and unarmed.'

The good Father did not answer.

'And what next?'

'Now, my son, they intend to kill you.'

'Ay, that was always their intention. They know that I esteem them
less than three bugs on the wall of a brothel jakes.'

Father Antonio reproved him: 'Hush, man! This is where quarrels
end: I have been summoned to confess you. You are to die at once.'

'Despite the General's pardon?'

'That did not avail Don Tomás. Are you ready?'

'With you to confess me, reverend Father.'

'Dear son, if you wish for absolution and eternal life, I implore
you to hold nothing back. Repeat after me the *Confiteor*.'

The Ensign knelt obediently and when he had done, 'Father,' he
muttered, 'I accuse myself of having sinned in the flesh . . .'

'Captain Barreto,' said the Chaplain, 'pray withdraw your guards
to a respectful distance. . . . Now continue, my son!'

When the Ensign had done, Father Antonio was heard to say:
'Those are grievous sins, my son! Do any others press upon your
conscience?'

'One only, Father,' he answered, raising his voice. 'A sin which,
though it seemed trivial at the time, has brought more evil in its
train than all the others together. At Callao, four days before we
sailed, by the mainmast with Don Andrés and the Boatswain . . .'

'Say no more!' said the Chaplain. 'I overheard your words and I
witnessed the sequel. Yet you were not the first with that mischievous
tale: thirty years ago, when I served under the Duke of Alva, the
same blind orphan girl was lodged at Brussels, above a goldsmith's
shop; and I doubt not, she had been at her tricks long before in
ancient Rome and Niniveh and Sodom. Come now, dear son, make
a good act of contrition. . . .'

He gave him absolution and administered the sacrament.

The Ensign, wonderfully refreshed in spirit, asked the good priest
to comfort his widow. His last words were: 'Let the negro be my
executioner. I would not have this murder weigh on the hearts
of my own arquebusiers.'

At a sign from the Chaplain, Myn stepped quickly forward and, before Don Lorenzo could intervene, swung at Don Juan and struck off his head with two sure blows of the axe.

At the guard-house, the General was waiting impatiently, not knowing what kept Don Lorenzo so long.

'Pray pardon the delay, your Excellency,' said he, running up. 'Which of these three traitors is to be judged first? Shall it be the Adjutant?'

'And why not?' cried the Major. 'I'll bring the rogue before you with all my heart.' He hurried into the guard-house and dragged out Captain Diego de Vera, as a butcher would a ram.

Don Alvaro looked around him dubiously. 'What do you say, friends? Is it to be death or pardon?'

Next to the Colonel, the Adjutant had been the best-liked officer in the camp, and such a hum of 'Pardon, let it be pardon!' went along the ranks, that the Barretos dared not press for the extreme penalty. He was ordered to kneel and take an oath of fidelity to the General, after which his sword was returned to him and he was freed.

Then Sergeant Andrada was brought up for trial. He knew that Don Alvaro had held him in abomination since his boast that he had killed more Indians on Santa Cristina than any other man, and therefore expected no mercy. 'At your service, my General!' he said. 'If this head must fall, let us be quick about it!' The Major, tugging at one arm, tried to hurry him off to the executioners, but Pedro Fernandez pulled him back by the other. 'Why this indecent haste?' he protested. 'For the love of the Virgin, let the sergeant be given a fair trial!'

Don Alvaro walked away to avoid an appeal for clemency, but Doña Ysabel, wishing to earn Pedro Fernandez's gratitude, went after and persuaded him to relent.

The Sergeant fell on his knees, and was allowed to take the oath; but as he rose, he saw Don Diego with the Colonel's loaded stick in one hand, and in the other a halberd on which was stuck the Colonel's gashed and pallid head. He covered his eyes to hide the streaming tears, and 'Alas, noble old man!' he cried. 'Is this the end of your long and faithful service to His Majesty? Sweet Christ, what a royal reward! A dastard's death, and your grey locks wagging from the summit of a stake!'

'Honestly spoken, by God!' the Colonel's nephew burst out, unable to contain himself. 'No one with a spark of honour in his breast, or of pity in his bowels, but must weep with you!'

'Silence, sirrah!' cried Don Alvaro. 'Have you no sense of obligation to those who interceded on your behalf?'

'I thank them all sincerely,' he said. 'But I also thank the man who has dared to speak aloud what is in every heart.' He turned to embrace the weeping Sergeant, and the troops gave him subdued applause.

Sebastian Lejia, still in the stocks, induced one of his guards to call the Chief Pilot who, coming to him at once, enquired what he wanted. 'They tell me, your honour, that you have saved Sergeant Andrada's life. For God's sake, do the same for me!'

'Why should I take your part? In cold blood you murdered our noble benefactor, as in cold blood you murdered the man who was swimming with his child off La Magdelena.'

'In either case I did no more than what I was told, your honour. Then my orders came from the Colonel, now from a person whom you hold in high esteem; but do not ask me for the name. And I swear to your honour, by sweet Jesus who redeemed us all, that my undeserved death will bring a dozen more in its train. . . . The General's Lady will thank you for your good services,' he whined. 'Only yesterday she gave me permission to marry her under-maid Pancha.'

Pedro Fernandez little knew what a Devil's bargain had been struck between Doña Ysabel and Sebastian: Pancha was to be his reward for the murder of Malope. I myself did not at once suspect her part in this infamous crime, though aware of her talent for deceit and double-dealing, because it seemed to go altogether against her interests.

Sebastian was released from the stocks along with Salvador Aleman, and they were taken before Don Alvaro. Salvador's life was spared when he pleaded that he would have dealt a comrade the same merciful blow to end his agony. Sebastian kept silent. The General himself now had him fast by the collar. 'Here is the vilest assassin of our age!' he said. 'A man who, without warning, instigated by the Devil, shattered the generous breast of our innocent ally Malope. Is there a man so lost to shame dares plead for him? You shall be strangled, villain!'

The Chief Pilot doffed his bonnet. 'Your Excellency,' he said, 'I beg you to lay no further victim on the altar of justice. The Colonel is no more, and those whom he misled have returned to obedience.

This man acted under orders; it would be unjust to hang the dog and
let his master go free.' He assumed that it was Don Lorenzo who
had prompted the crime, because he had often been heard to say
that we should wage indiscriminate war on all the natives and wrest
the island from them by force of arms.

Don Alvaro must have guessed what was in his mind. He relaxed
his hold on the prisoner and complained petulantly: 'Mercy is very
well, friend. But how am I to avenge Malope's murder, if I spare this
man's life?'

'Enough blood has been shed,' answered Pedro Fernandez, 'and
your Excellency must remember how few we now are. Send the
heads of the Ensign and the Sergeant to Malope's village, as if they
were those of the murderers. The savages will know no better.'

The General glanced at Don Lorenzo, who said quickly: 'The Chief
Pilot is right. This man's orders must have come from Juan de
Buitrago, who has already paid for the crime.'

Then he yielded, but instructed the Chief Pilot to take Sebastian
out of his sight, before he repented of his clemency; and, having said
this, he fainted clean away. His actions that day reminded me of
a dying candle-end, that flares up suddenly before it sputters to final
extinction.

While Doña Mariana and I were reviving him, Pedro Fernandez
called four sailors and sent Sebastian to the flagship, where he confined him in the forecastle on a diet of biscuit and water. The crew,
still feasting on the food that Malope had given us, were outraged
by his deed. That night they mixed salt with the water in his pitcher,
and brought him almond-shells to eat. Nor would they let him go
to sleep, but continually prodded him awake, shouting: 'Why did
you kill Malope, you fiend? You ought to be hanged, drawn and
quartered!' It was a novel pleasure for seamen to have a soldier in
their power, especially one who had always looked on them with
scorn.

The next morning Sebastian sent for Pancha, who presently peeped
in at the door. His face lighted up, and he told her: 'Sweetheart, the
very day that I'm released, I'll marry you; I have Doña Ysabel's consent.' But when she spat at him and put her arms lovingly around the
neck of the gaoler who had been his chief tormentor, and let him
fondle her bosom, he turned his face to the wall and sobbed.

Chapter 20

THE ECLIPSE

A light breeze blew from the direction of Malope's village, and carried with it the sound of distant lamentation, so lugubrious and prolonged that it made our hearts sick. Don Alvaro, trembling with anxiety, ordered the head of Juan de Buitrago to be taken there in placation; he had learned that on the death of a chieftain his kinsmen always demanded a victim to escort him to the other world— the murderer, had his death been violent, but otherwise (since no chief was believed to die naturally), an enemy suspected of killing him by magic. This unpleasant task was entrusted to the Adjutant, who went off with Don Jacinto and twenty men; but no sooner had the villagers sighted the long-boat, than they broke and ran into the woods, still wailing loudly. He shouted after them, displaying the Ensign's head on a stake, but as they paid no attention, he landed and marched to the village.

To demonstrate their ecstatic grief, the bereaved tribesmen had felled scores of young fruit-trees, trampled down the flowering plants in their yards and even mutilated the carved posts of the assembly-house. Into the pen which usually housed Malope's pigs, every man and woman had cast some weapon or adornment as a parting gift to the soul of their Chieftain, including several of the red badges they had received from us. The soldiers would have entered the pen to pocket the carved shell frontlets and the armlets of boars' tusks, but the Adjutant prevented them. 'It is unlucky to rob the dead,' he remarked. Nevertheless, he had scarcely turned his back before they stole Malope's own ornaments from the wooden altar beside the house on which they had been placed. The Ensign's head was then nailed under the eaves, and Don Jacinto climbed in by the entrance-hole to see whether any of Malope's widows were still in residence, to

whom the General's condolences might be conveyed. He found the
house empty. The hearth was cold, broken spears littered the floor
among strewn banana skins and the rinds of other fruit, and on the
platform where Malope used to sleep lay a coffin, shaped in the
figure of a shark, which contained his corpse. Only the lower half of
his face was visible, all the rest had been covered with nettles pressed
down upon it by heavy boards, which was the islanders' way of
keeping a body from corruption while it lay in state.

The wailing cry of *ulo, ulo* sounded dolefully from the woods, and
the Adjutant crossed himself and led his men back to the boat. All
that day and night, with brief breaks, the mourning rang in our ears
like an accusation.

Jaume the water-steward came to me with a dejected look, and
asked: 'Don Andrés, have you heard what is being said about the
General's health?'

'I know that he is very sick. He has given me no writing to do since
the day the Colonel died.'

'Or the day that Malope died.'

'The same, but what of it?'

He came closer, and whispered: 'They're saying, Don Andrés, that
Malope changed names with him as a safeguard against treachery:
by the magic of sympathy, any disaster coming on Malope would
involve Don Alvaro too, should he be concerned in it.'

'What a preposterous notion!' said I. 'In any case, whoever gave
Sebastian his orders, you may be sure that it was not Don Alvaro.'

'I agree with you,' he returned. 'But if he's heard the rumour, as
Elvira tells me that he has, and if he believes it, as she assures me
that he does—why, then mark my words, he'll never rise from his
sick-bed. It's on his mind that he did not threaten death to any man
who harmed Malope; and now he complains of searing pains in his
right breast, where the ball struck Malope, and of a headache fit to
split his skull. Not for nothing does he come from Corunna, where
every child is raised in terror of witchcraft, and the very priests are
alleged to be in league with Satan.'

'And are there no witches in Majorca?' I asked, laughing. 'I have
heard Galicians swear that black magic is unknown in their province,
but that Majorca and the other Balearics are raddled with it.'

'Well, I won't deny that we have our wise women. My own uncle,
a cobbler in a mountain village, was house-bound for more than ten
years; his wife, jealous of the baker's daughter, had laid a spell on the

doorstep which he could never cross without falling down in a faint. She did him no other injury, though, and when she died he stepped over the threshold in safety, went down the street and made straight for the baker's house. But the witches of Corunna don't use their spells merely in self-defence.'

I did not contradict him. 'Friend Jaume,' I said, 'let us say no more about black magic; to do so is to increase its power for evil.'

He nodded and, after a pause, said casually, as though changing the subject: 'The Chief Pilot has a wife and a child, has he not?'

'And loves both of them dearly,' I answered, rising to go. So Jaume entertained the same suspicion of Doña Ysabel as I did! When I considered the matter carefully, however, it occurred to me that Doña Mariana was, after all, no witch, and neither was her sister, though they might both be acting the part to terrify Don Alvaro. Doña Mariana's by-play with the thimble must have been intended to attract, not to divert, my attention: had she wished to pick up the General's nail-parings unobserved, she need merely have sent me off on an errand. She had been counting on me to spread the tale. The gossip about the Tarot-cards was surely also meant to reach Don Alvaro's ear and depress his spirit. Now both sisters were disseminating the monstrous and irreligious tenet that he must die because it had pleased a rude pagan to change names with him.

'I will tell him the truth about Doña Ysabel,' I decided. But I learned that, when the Vicar had asked that the three other heads should be removed from public display and given Christian burial alongside their trunks, Don Alvaro though granting his plea had deliberately withheld the order to carry it into effect. As a result, the heads had been left lying about the camp and, by the morning, hungry dogs had stripped them clean of flesh. 'Carlotta, too, had her share,' said the sailor who brought me the news. I shuddered at such heartlessness and refrained from making my disclosure.

The mourning for Malope lasted for a week. On the third night after his death great fires were lighted, and we doubled our sentries in expectation of an attack; however, none came. That evening Sebastian's gaolers relented and gave him the fresh water and biscuit that was his due, but he would neither eat nor drink; and when on the seventh night the wailing suddenly ceased he was at death's door. The Chief Pilot summoned the Vicar; Sebastian was confessed, received absolution, and died like a martyr. They buried him beside the headless bodies of the Colonel, Don Tomás and Sergeant Gallardo, none of whom had received any such consolation; he also held an advantage over Juan de Buitrago, whose trunk had been despitefully thrown to the sharks.

Major Moran was now the senior officer ashore, but did not venture to assume command for fear of offending the Barretos. He stayed in his hut, while they did as they pleased; and presently the General, who was weakening hourly, appointed Don Lorenzo his deputy both on land and sea. That Malope's men no longer came to help us, was made an excuse for discontinuing work on the stockade, though Doña Ysabel now gave leave for raising it around the knoll. Instead, the troops were set to complete the Residency, our only building of two storeys, with the utmost speed. When one side had been thatched and floored, Don Alvaro was carried ashore on Myn's back and laid in his bed; the negro told us later that he weighed no more than a child.

One evening Don Lorenzo came to the Great Cabin and asked permission to capture twenty native boys, who were to be trained as guides and interpreters; and Don Alvaro granted this. An hour before daybreak a sergeant and twenty men set out in the long-boat to the most distant of the villages where we had foraged with Malope; but though landing stealthily in the half-light, they were met by a shower of arrows. The Sergeant's instructions were to take no fire-arms ashore, but to cajole the boys with gifts and sugared words; which explains why no officer volunteered to lead so large a party. Since surprise had failed, the troops withdrew; the Sergeant was the last to leap into the boat, and his courage was rewarded with an arrow wound through his hand, which afterwards mortified and cost him his life. Seven others were hurt, two of them severely, before the boat drew out of range. The savages pressed their pursuit in canoes until, outstripping our people and disembarking close to the jetty, they ran along the beach towards the camp gate.

Don Lorenzo sallied out with drum beating and pendant flying, but he disdained to use fire-arms, and another seven soldiers, of whom he was one, were wounded without loss to the enemy; who would have broken into the camp, had the gunner of the galeot not fired a falconet over their heads and put them to precipitate flight, just as the long-boat hove in view. Painfully drawing the arrow out of his foot, Don Lorenzo then hailed the boat and, when the wounded had been brought ashore, sent it back again to the village under another sergeant. This time the men were ordered to burn down the canoe-houses and do whatever damage they pleased; but he sent them off in such a flurry that, though he issued them arquebuses and ball, he forgot to dole out the powder, and they returned two hours later with eight more wounded.

These three victories, in which they had not lost a man, so elated the natives that they prowled around the camp all night under the full moon, taking cover behind bushes, and whenever a soldier came within range, they loosed an arrow or slung a stone at him. (On Santa Cruz, the use of slings was confined to chieftains and their sons, who were tawny, of larger build and of nobler appearance than the rest.) The camp-jakes being close to the picket-fence, several men were shot at as they went to untruss and two hit, one of whom was Salvador Aleman. He was found dead in the dung-trench, his gaskins pulled down to the knees and an arrow sticking in his belly; the ghost of Malope seemed to be exact in his vengeance. The other man was blinded in one eye by a sling-bolt, but is still living and keeps the Inn of the Adoration in Lima. Since the enemy did not show himself, no arquebuses were let off: partly to husband powder and lead, but mainly because unaimed shots would soon teach the savages to despise the sound of a discharge.

That was the disastrous 14th of October, the day on which we also had first warning of the plague that was to cost us so dear. It was not a malignant fever, of the kind that has given Portobello, Panama, San Tomé and many another port so sinister a reputation: none of the sufferers died suddenly, as in those places, a few hours after the earliest signs of sickness had appeared. Some lingered for weeks and even months, according to the strength of their constitutions; others, like myself, threw off the attack after a few days. Its symptoms were dizziness, a sore throat, a high fever by night with evil dreams and delirium, by day a terrible lassitude and so feeble a stomach that even wholesome food tasted nauseous; and in most cases the infection descended from the throat to the lungs on the second night.

Father Joaquin, who had brought with him a basket of the renowned febrifuge called Jesuit's bark, was lost in the *Santa Ysabel*; with warmth, care and a decoction of this bitter physic, the fever need have proved fatal to none of us. I do not think that the site was much to blame; though it is clear that the unaccustomed diet, the sudden fall in temperature at night, the frequent showers after which the soldiers let the clothes dry on their bodies, the dampness of the

ground on which they slept—disdaining to make themselves plat-
forms as the natives did—all these were inimical to the health of any
Spaniard who was not made of stone. But it came to me that while
the Colonel had kept his men sternly disciplined and actively employed, none had shown the least sign of sickness; that, in effect, the
plague sent upon us was what the Italians call *la influenza*, which they
ascribe to mysterious planetary influences, rather than to bad sanita-
tion or the proximity of putrid marshes. It is often the sequel of widespread disaffection or crime or public disaster, or a long war that
neither side has the heart to continue; and I attribute my own recovery to the care I had taken not to participate directly in the wicked
events that I chronicled.

The first death occurred on the 17th of October, the vigil of Saint
Luke the Evangelist, which was a sorrowful reminder that we had no
physician; and the victim was none other than Father Antonio.
His passing caused profound grief to all, except the Barretos, but
especially to the Vicar, who had given him his viaticum. He lamented
piteously over the Chaplain's corpse and, with eyes raised to Heaven
and tears streaming down his cheeks, cried out in my hearing: 'O
Lord, my God, how heavy is the punishment that Thou hast visited
upon my sins! Hast Thou left me, Lord, without a priest to whom I
can make my confession? O Father Antonio de Serpa, how fortunate
is your lot! How gladly would I change places with you, caught in
this most miserable plight: though I am empowered to absolve the
sins of every man in this island, yet none may do the like for me.'
Staggering about, his face hidden in his hands, he refused to be con-
soled, though Pedro Fernandez and Juan de la Isla implored him to
calm himself. Presently he dragged himself to the Church and there
wept uncontrollably before the altar, praying for Father Antonio's
soul and extolling his virtues; and at last went out into the Churchyard and, calling for a spade, dug a deep grave with his own feeble
arms.

That night, when the moon rose in the east, it was in full eclipse,
which caused great consternation: I heard it whispered that this was
an occasion when witches were at liberty to do whatever evil they
desired, and that the spirit of a great personage would have quitted
its body before the next moon-rise. No sentry went on duty without an amulet about his neck and a comrade to stand by him; and at
daybreak a buzz spread through the camp that as a certain officer left
his tent to untruss by starlight, he had seen a naked woman with a

branch in her hand bewitching the Residency. I gave little credence to this rumour, but another, that Sebastian's corpse had been disinterred during the night either by hungry dogs or by witches, Myn solemnly confirmed for me.

The bell tolled for the Chaplain's funeral, and its ominous sound, together with the tales of black magic that reached Don Alvaro's ear by way of the maids and pages, struck terror in the sick man's heart. Assured that he must die before the day was out, he summoned Don Luis to his bedside, also Captain Corzo, the Adjutant, two of the merchants and myself, and dictated to me his last Will as follows:

At Gracious Bay, in this Christian Island of Santa Cruz, on the Feast of Saint Luke, 1595, in the presence of my secretary Andrés Serrano, and the witnesses Don Diego de Vera, Andrés del Castillo, Juan de la Isla, Don Luis Barreto and Captain Felipe Corzo, I, Alvaro de Mendaña y Castro, Marquis, Prefect, Governor, Captain-General and Lord Chief Justice of the Isles of Solomon, being now at the point of death, do herewith publish and declare my last Will and Testament.

First: I devise and bequeath my soul to God.

Item: I order that the public bequests required of me by law etc., etc.

Item: I order that my body shall be buried in the Church of Saint Simeon the Just, in the said Christian Isle of Santa Cruz, and that Father Juan de la Espinosa shall officiate at my interment, and that on the same day, or failing this, on the following, a mass shall be said over my grave, for which he shall be paid the customary fee from my estate; and that twenty further masses shall be said for my soul in the same church, or failing this, elsewhere, and that the fees shall likewise be charged to my estate.

Item: I nominate Doña Ysabel Barreto, my lawful wife, as Prefect of the Isles aforesaid. And to give effect to this my Will and Testament, I appoint as my executrix and executor the said Doña Ysabel and the Licentiate Father Juan de la Espinosa aforesaid; to whom jointly I assign whatever powers are needed for the carrying into effect of this my last Will and Testament and the disposal of all the goods which I have brought with me to these shores; of which I herewith appoint the said Doña Ysabel to be sole heiress and owner, as also of all other goods, chattels and possessions that are now, or may in due time become known and recognized as mine; together with the hereditary Marquisate, conferred on me by our gracious Sovereign Lord, King Philip II, which she shall hereafter enjoy in her own right, and the other titles and distinctions with which it has pleased His Majesty to honour me, excepting only the Captaincy-General.

Item: I appoint and nominate as Captain-General of the forces at present under my command, Captain Don Lorenzo Barreto, my wife's brother.

Item: I revoke and annul all other Wills and Testaments, etc., etc.

I closed his wasted finger around the quill, and he signed his name with the utmost exertion; the usually well-contrived rubric wavered unrecognizably. Then he sank back exhausted on the pillows, and sent for the Vicar, to whom he made a long, fervent confession, also repeating the *Miserere mei* and the *Credo* after him. Yet even when he had received absolution and the Blessed Sacrament, he still seemed troubled in his mind and begged that the room and everyone in it should be well sprinkled with holy water, and the Crucifix taken from the wall and placed in his hands. With this request Father Juan complied, but neither Doña Ysabel nor her sister shrank from the drops, as they would surely have done had they been witches, and both of them made a great show of Catholic devotion and of tender sorrow for the dying man. Nevertheless, his last words, whispered a few minutes before noon, were: 'Set a guard over my corpse, Father; nail me firmly in my coffin; bury me deep!' And then, with a wintry smile: 'At least Almighty God will have my soul, not they!'

Some may doubt that the General died for the reasons here given, or suspect that Doña Ysabel hastened his end by a slow poison, but numerous instances may be adduced of men becoming their own executioners through superstitious fear. Particularly I recall the fate of a French gentleman, my nearest neighbour at Seville who, having killed a compatriot in a duel about Saint John's Day, was cursed by the widow in this form: that he would die when the last apple fell from the tree under which the fatal blow had been struck. This tree was within view of his bed-chamber and he took the words so deeply to heart that he fell sick and every morning counted the apples remaining on the boughs. 'Alas, Jacques,' he would say to his servant, 'only five are left,' or, 'Only three are left,' and grew daily weaker. The devoted servant sent into town for a china apple which, under cover of darkness, he fastened to a twig; then, though winter-gales blew and the rain poured down in torrents the apple neither fell nor rotted. My ailing neighbour was greatly encouraged by the seeming miracle of its hanging there so staunchly on the bare boughs: he recovered his appetite and strength and at Epiphany, the day being sunny and dry, he rose and walked in the garden to view the fruit that had saved his life; but becoming aware of the fraud, he suddenly put his hand to his heart and died all at once, before even a priest could be called to his soul's aid.

We buried Don Alvaro the same evening, with as much pomp as our reduced circumstances permitted; the coffin, swathed in black cloth, was carried to the Churchyard on the shoulders of eight officers. The soldiers followed at the slow march, in accordance with the usage prescribed for such occasions: their arms reversed, the colours trailing, muffled drums beating slowly and mournfully, and the fifes wailing loud and shrill. Myn had dug the grave next to Father Antonio's, and there the Vicar consigned dust to dust. A farewell volley was fired, and the pall-bearers returned to the Residency, to offer their condolences and homage to our She-Governor, or Governeress, who had not thought fit to display herself at the grave-side.

Don Alvaro had always treated me with a consideration that fell only a little short of generosity, and I should have grieved more for him if sorrow had not been crowded from my mind by anxiety for the future. Our situation, which three days before seemed hopeful enough, had suffered a catastrophic change. Now that so many officers and men were wounded or down with fever, we could not send out large foraging parties without dangerously weakening the garrison, and small ones would no longer suffice; moreover, since Malope's tribe had turned against us, our number and dispositions had ceased to be a secret. The savages grew bolder and invested the camp even by day. Green amaranths, which the soldiers called Christian vegetables (that is to say, familiar and wholesome ones), grew in a patch not far from the gates, but whenever a small armed party marched out to cut some of them, native marksmen were lying in ambush among the tree-ferns, and several more of our people were wounded on these errands.

With men succumbing to their injuries, and three of the settlers' children dying of the flux—they had eaten rotten fruit—and the fever spreading swiftly, until not thirty soldiers were fit to parade, our case was bad enough; yet, I dare say, had the Colonel and Juan de Buitrago and the Chaplain been alive, they would have contrived between them to put new heart into the men and show them that all was not lost— no, not by a great deal. But Doña Ysabel shut herself in the Residency; and Captain Lorenzo's wound confined him to his quarters; and Major Moran was an object of scorn to all; and the Adjutant was still under suspicion; and Captain Leyva lay sick; and Captain Corzo had retired to the galeot as to a healthier place. Where then could the troops look for leadership?

The Vicar in his pious zeal made our case look gloomier by far than it was. He perambulated the camp, with none to check him, crying: 'Repent! Come hither and repent! Make your peace with God, my sons! He has sent this plague upon us, as upon the Israelites in the Wilderness, in just punishment for our sins; and I verily believe that not one of us will escape alive, many though we are. The islanders will triumph over us and possess themselves of our arms and all else that is ours. If for a single fault God has chastised a whole kingdom, what may he not do here?'

Fear for his own salvation had unmanned the good Father, yet he did his utmost to save the souls of others. 'Consider,' he cried, 'the case of King David who destroyed Uriah the Hittite that he might lie with his widow: how when he confessed, God gave him a choice of three penances. Here we have offended in a hundred worse ways than David, yet not repented, so that God's wrath is kindled against us, and the naked and bloody sword of His justice swings free. Sickness, war, famine and discord stalk among these huts. O, cleanse your hearts, my sons, cleanse your hearts! I know a sergeant who has confessed but once in his life, and a drummer who cannot say whether he be Moor or Christian. Open your eyes, and perceive the filth in which you wallow!'

I was now lodged in an upper room of the Residency and, one morning from my sick-bed, I heard Matia, who stood guard below, complaining to Jaume against the Vicar. 'Were he not a priest, I swear I'd strangle him with my own hands. A priest should cheer his flock in sickness and in danger, not hasten them to their graves. O, that Father Galvez were with us again; never in my life shall I sail to these South Seas again unless with a Franciscan!'

'You are unlikely to have the chance,' said Jaume. 'And this Father Juan is a saint. He told me today that a single drop of the blood shed in Christ's passion was enough to wash away the sins of infinite worlds.'

'Oho, so you went into the confessional?'

'I confessed and, God be praised, he absolved me!'

'O, Jaume, Jaume, to think that you have been gaffed at last! But I'll not ask absolution from a priest who makes cowards of my comrades.'

After vespers I heard the Vicar preaching. The camp was quiet, except for howling dogs and the smothered shrieks of a woman in delirium, and his voice came clear through the open windows of the Church:

'. . . And I will recount another notable and proven miracle, vouched for by a worthy priest of my acquaintance who had a cure in the West Indies. A nobleman, poor in virtue but rich in the goods of this world, lived fast-rooted in grievous vice. He would ride with lance and dagger into the city of Havana where, gritting his teeth and gazing fiercely into the Heavens, he would cry: "Hey, God the Father! Come down and fight with me, and let us see which of us is the better man!", with many other blasphemous and indecent expressions. This sinner was one night walking up and down a dark apartment of his magnificent mansion, rosary in hand, muttering I do not know what foolishness, when a woman's voice, as sweet as a chime of bells, spoke from the floor: "Don Bassanio"—for that was his name—"why do you not put that rosary to its proper use and pray with devotion?" Astonished and awed, he reached for his tinder-box, struck a spark, lighted a candle and looked about him. He was alone in the room.

'Searching further, he found on the floor a coloured picture of the Virgin, which he took up and laid against the wall, supporting it with both his hands, while he knelt and piously told his beads. At this juncture, two tall negroes appeared from nowhere, blew out the candle, stripped him stark naked and flogged him with slave-whips. They flogged him and flogged him, as he continued with his devotions, until he was nearly dead and fell fainting to the ground; whereupon a supernatural light pervaded the room and the same gentle voice said: "Go, villains, go! Leave this soul which is not yours—my Son has granted it to me through His mercy and my prayers." Instantly they vanished, the light passed out by the door, and the rich man crawled after it and lay down on his bed. He sent for a friar, who asked in wonder why he had been summoned in the middle of the night.

'The stricken sinner related his experiences, displaying his bruised and bleeding back, and begged urgently to be confessed, for the first time in eight-and-thirty years. The friar bade him be of good cheer, and console himself with the thought that God had generously pardoned even worse offenders. And he began the recital of his sins— not omitting one, for they were all fixed in his memory—which lasted, with brief intermissions, for no less than seventeen days; and at the end, observing his perfect contrition, the friar absolved him with a light penance. But so weak was he that he fell a victim to fever on the very day his penance was completed, and died like a saint.'

Thus Father Juan saved many a strayed soul with authentic and comforting anecdotes and, the better to fulfil his obligations, came to live ashore in the house of Captain Leyva, who had now succumbed to the plague.

For a week I was too sick even to keep my journal, and meanwhile many events occurred which can be reported only in brief, the details being lost. The natives continued to ambush our people whenever they left camp or strayed near the picket-fence, and we had three more men killed and ten wounded. Malope's son was their leader, and the soldiers blamed Sebastian, though dead, for the tactics that our former friends now adopted. It appears that in the assembly-house, just before the murder, he had taken up an arrow and driven it in turn against his helmet, corslet and tassets, boasting to the natives that they were proof against their weapons; so now they aimed at our eyes or legs.

General Don Lorenzo gave orders for a few of the sick to be hauled out of bed and sent on guard, and thus contrived to detach a sergeant and twelve fit men for a punitive expedition against Malope's village. They took the long-boat and, everyone running off at sight of them, they looted the huts at their ease and then burned every one to the ground.

This action alarmed the villagers who were our nearest neighbours on the other side, and they sent us a deputation under a flag of truce. Don Lorenzo hobbled out to meet them at the gate, but they retired when they saw his escort of arquebusiers. He called to them ingratiatingly, and asked: 'Why do you not bring food as you used to do? We are your freinds.'

Their leader replied, with eloquent gestures: 'Halt, enough! Malope—Malope *amigos—pu pu!*', meaning that he did not understand why, if we were such good friends with Malope, we had shot him dead. 'What do you call this?' he asked, pointing accusingly to the thick smoke that drifted across the bay from the burning village.

Don Lorenzo explained that the murderer had been punished and his head nailed to Malope's house, whose sons were ill-advised to pursue their vengeance. They next asked after 'the Taurique,' meaning Don Alvaro, and were told: 'He is asleep.' Given presents from a chest of trade-goods, the property of the Colonel, they went off well-content, and both that day and the next came to the camp-gate with generous offerings. The food that they now brought was doubly welcome, because for the past week we had been forced to feed the sick with flour from our scant reserves. Throughout our stay in Santa Cruz, no native ever refused us hospitality or showed bad faith; yet how did we treat them in return?

In my register the deaths now exceeded the marriages and births, being, respectively, forty-one against eighteen and two. Though it was clear that we could not maintain ourselves ashore without inviting utter disaster, Doña Ysabel let it be understood that she would regard as mutinous any further talk of leaving the island. It seemed to me likely that she would postpone until too late the necessary decision—not that I much cared what became of me, so dulled were my feelings and intelligence—when the aggrieved soldiery would surely murder her and all her family. If that time came, I should not lift a finger to aid them.

Chapter 21

THE SETTLEMENT ABANDONED

Don Lorenzo did what he could for the welfare of the troops despite his wound, which was now purulent, and on the day after the General's funeral he ordered the Captain of Artillery, with ten convalescents, to take the frigate in renewed search of the *Santa Ysabel*. They were away for a fortnight and, though following their instructions to the letter, found no trace of our lost comrades. Captain Lopez brought back a heap of pearl shells from one of the low islets to the north-east, but no pearls; also eight handsome, light-coloured boys, who were of no use to us as hostages, nor even as interpreters, because they spoke an altogether different language from that of Santa Cruz. Some charged him with vicious inclinations, but it is my belief that he acted from pure stupidity. On their arrival the boys speared a score of fish in the bay, which they divided among themselves and the officers; but a few days later the novelty of their new circumstances palled on them. Having robbed us of a good many toys and trifles, they stole a sea-going canoe from our neighbours and sailed off home.

An equally foolish affair was Captain de Vera's seizure of three women, with six children, as hostages from the village beyond Malope's. Since they refused to eat, their husbands were allowed to visit them daily, but always came accompanied by a flock of relatives who clamoured loudly for their release, shouting and wailing outside the guard-house and the Residency. After a week of this, Doña Ysabel wearied of the farce and set them free, at the Chief Pilot's request.

Meanwhile, the fever had spread to the flagship, where the master-gunner and two of the standing guard died, but so far none of the crew was affected; and then to the smaller vessels, where nearly all the sailors fell sick, and fifteen died. A constant shifting of quarters

now followed, those ashore hoping to recover their health on ship-
board, and contrariwise. I was up and about again, though unsteady
in my walk, and liable to shed tears of pure weakness at the least
excuse. The forlorn aspect of the camp shocked me; the troops filthy
and unkempt, no longer ashamed of their stained and rusty armour;
heaps of refuse flung to rot outside the huts; all cultivation abandoned;
the neglected dung-trenches giving off a foul stench.

The only officer whose spirit had not been tamed by the common
misfortune was the Chief Pilot: to show that he still had faith in our
enterprise he even offered to bring his sailors ashore and set them to
planting yams and maize. One day the Ensign-Royal went to visit
him. I cannot say whether he was acting disinterestedly, or whether
he had been deputed by others to say what he did; at all events, he
warned Pedro Fernandez to cease his meddling unless he cared to be
stabbed or strung up, or find himself, at best, marooned on the island
for which he had conceived so strange and morbid an affection.

'So you have returned to your old way of thinking?' the Chief Pilot
said sadly. 'I had hoped that the Colonel's cruel fate might have
taught you prudence. Here we are, Don Toribio, serving God and
the King to the best of our ability, and no man who, having put his
hand to the plough, looks back . . .'

Don Toribio cut him short with: 'So you are still singing your
old song of *Keep in step! Sús, sús, sús!*—behaving more like a soldier
than ever the Colonel did—and weeping for the heathen whom we
have cheated with false hopes of salvation? Your piety is commend-
able, but since there will be no priest to watch over their souls' welfare
once they are baptized, it seems to me more pious to let them be. At
present, unless I am ill-instructed in Christian doctrine, they have a
limbo prepared for them after death, which is a tolerable enough
state, compared with the Purgatory and Hell awaiting the baptized
who die in sin.'

'How do you mean: "there will be no priest"? Is not our Vicar
willing to preach and baptize here for as many years as God grants
him life?'

'Your intelligence is out of date. Father Juan has himself drawn up
a petition to Doña Ysabel in which he sets out many unanswerable
objections against clinging to the settlement, and every man ashore
who can hold a pen has put his mark or name to it. Then was then;
now is now. Much has happened since the Colonel was executed, and

the Vicar having come over to the side of reason, no signatory need stand in fear of the Governeress's vengeance.'

'Did he take this step of his own impulse?' Pedro Fernandez asked in surprise.

'I dare say that Captain Corzo prodded him a little; and also that he was not sorry to be prodded, for the great longing that he has to be with birds of his own black feather. But it is all one: the paper bears his name at the head, and tomorrow he will read it to your crew.'

Not more than nineteen soldiers were still capable of bearing arms, and most of these had the fever on them so that they could go on sentry duty only during daytime. The two veterans made a name by going about their work in soldierly style, when their comrades had abandoned themselves to despair: Juarez stood guard on thirteen consecutive nights, and Matia on fifteen. They held that a close sympathy exists between a soldier and his equipment. 'Let your helmet rust and your head will ache; leave your corslet unscoured and the pain will go to your lungs; neglect your sword, and strength will drain from your sword-arm.' When the petition was offered them for signature, they refused even to look at it, saying sourly: 'We are ignorant soldiers; we know no Latin.'

Father Juan coming to the Chart-room, begged the Chief Pilot to sign and persuade his crew to do likewise. He answered that since his offer to grow crops was taken in such bad part by the troops, he had little sympathy with their petition; he would read it to the sailors, but nothing more.

The Vicar understood from this that he was displeased, but remarked shrewdly: 'My son, if I thought that your reasons for wanting to stay in this island were wholly pious, I should praise you. . . .' With that he left, having been called away to the forecastle, but while still in the waist of the ship he suddenly cried out: 'My head, my head! O God, shield me!' and clung to the bulwarks. He was taken below to Juan de la Isla's cabin, where it was found that he had the fever strong upon him.

Pedro Fernandez went ashore to fetch him his bedding and baggage and warn Doña Ysabel that mass would not be celebrated for several days at least. From a desire not to intrude upon her grief, he had paid her only a single brief and formal visit since Don Alvaro's death; but on this occasion he hoped to be granted a longer audience. He found her dry-eyed and dressed from head to foot in black, which enhanced the beauty of her golden hair and milky skin. 'A Governeress must not give way to grief,' she told him with a sad smile, 'though her heart bleed inwardly.' When she learned of the Vicar's affliction, she offered to feed him from her own table, but did not seem much concerned at the news, remarking merely that God's purposes could not be gainsaid.

He was about to take his leave with a deferential salute, when Doña Ysabel restrained him. 'Dear friend,' she said, 'you have witnessed the courage with which I face my cruel bereavement. Can you, too, steel your heart to hear ill news that concerns you nearly?'

Pedro Fernandez answered that he could, since her lips would take the sting from any misfortune they might report, were it ever so great.

'Then listen, friend Pedro,' she said, tightening her grip on his sleeve. 'Some hours before my sainted husband died, he made me a weighty disclosure: that in Callao, on the evening when we should have sailed, a letter reached him from your brother-in-law, the confessor of the Clarissas in Lima, to the effect that your wife had died peacefully in his presence after receiving the sacraments. The funeral was to take place the next morning, and you were desired to attend it. Your poor wife having passed beyond mortal help, the General thought it right to withhold this message from you, because your services could not be spared. He told me that it had often been his intention to break the news to you, but feared to unsettle your mind already loaded with the cares of navigation; besides, he had destroyed your brother-in-law's letter, lest Miguel Llano should read it, and was ashamed of the deceit.'

Tears started from Pedro Fernandez's eyes and his large frame was shaken by sobs. He had loved Doña Ana with the extravagant devotion that deep-sea pilots often feel for wives from whom they are parted for years at a stretch. But presently he managed to control his grief, as if Doña Ysabel's courageous bearing set him an example, and sighed as he crossed himself devoutly: 'May her soul rest in eternal peace! The Lord has given; the Lord has taken away—blessed be His name!'

She bent forward and tenderly touched his brow with her lips. 'Alas, dear Pedro, I pity you! I know too well what bitter pangs you suffer.'

Still weeping, he fell at her feet, but she raised him up, imploring him sweetly not to give way to his grief. Then she added, what she had omitted before, that his brother-in-law had undertaken to rear the motherless little boy, and care for him well in his own house.

When Pedro Fernandez took his leave, somewhat comforted by her kindness, she bound him, for her sake and that of the whole expedition, not to let this great loss prey upon his mind to the neglect of duty.

'Now that my sainted husband lies under the sod,' she said, 'and my three brothers have all taken to their beds, you are the only man in whom I can place reliance. It is a common accusation against us Galicians that we keep ourselves to ourselves and distrust even our neighbours, let alone strangers; yet when we are shown true friendship by an outsider, which he proves by frequent acts of devotion, why, then we admit him freely to our close circle, and keep no secrets from him, and all we have is his.'

He trusted and believed her. Having spent most of that night on his knees, praying for his wife's soul, in the morning he thought it his duty to forgive Don Lorenzo for the murderous threats he had made, and be reconciled to him. In the wing of the Residency which had been made over to Don Lorenzo as Captain-General, he found Doña Mariana alone in attendance upon him. He was now past the help of physicians, stretched on his bed as stiff as a linstock, except when a spasm seized him and he groaned dismally like a felon on the rack. His face was set in a fixed grin, the corners of his mouth drawn downwards and backwards, and his forehead dripped with sweat. A stout rope had been hitched to a beam above the bed, and Doña Mariana told the Chief Pilot, amid tears: 'Only with this, and the help of two strong men, can we turn him on his side.' For Don Lorenzo's twitching grin spelt neither mirth nor defiance: it was the horrid *sardonicus risus*—the spasmodic cramp of a man in the agony of lock-jaw.

'How goes it with you, my lord?' the Chief Pilot asked in a voice of commiseration.

'I am dying, Don Pedro,' he answered indistinctly through clenched teeth, 'and I fear, without shrift.' After a pause, he was understood to say: 'Ah, Death, in what a wretched state have you overtaken me!' Then he turned his eyes to the crucifix at the foot of his bed, and muttered: 'Lord, have mercy on me, a sinner!'

Pedro Fernandez offered to fetch the Vicar, for which solicitude Doña Mariana thanked him tearfully. Glad to be able to forget his own sorrow in the service of others, he returned to the flagship, and entreated Father Juan to confess Don Lorenzo, who had not another hour to live.

'No more have I!' whispered the Vicar. 'Nevertheless, let him be carried to my bedside, and I will do even as you ask.'

'Alas, reverend Father, that is impossible.' And the Chief Pilot explained the predicament.

'I cannot come to him, my son. My strength fails.'

'God will renew it,' said the other, adding that no young man should be allowed to die without confession, and be cut off in the midst of his sins; nor, indeed, should anyone else while a priest was at hand.

'You are bent on killing me,' groaned the miserable Vicar. 'Can you not see that I am unable to stand on my feet? Have you no mercy? But do as you please, take me where you will: it makes little odds when or how I die.'

He suffered himself to be wrapped in a blanket and then lowered into the skiff, and from the jetty Pedro Fernandez carried him on his own back to the Residency. There he confessed Don Lorenzo, as well as four other dying men who had been borne into the sick-room, and administered the sacrament. When he had done, he was taken tenderly back to his cabin, their thanks and blessings ringing in his ears.

Early on the following morning, the 2nd of November, Don Lorenzo died, worn out by his convulsions, one of which was so violent that it tore apart the muscles of his belly. May God pardon him! Doña Ysabel grieved deeply at his passing and gave him the same funeral honours as Don Alvaro, though his cortège was a pitifully small one, and for want of a priest the Chief Pilot read the Burial Service. The Captaincy-General was now extinct, Don Lorenzo having omitted to nominate a successor.

The whole de la Isla family was swept away. During the last week of October Don Juan's devoted wife and daughter had died of the fever in great uneasiness of mind; now he himself, too late to benefit from the Vicar's last administrations, confessed his sins directly to his Maker, and met death with so cheerful a heart that already he seemed a pilgrim on the highroad to Heaven. This honourable and gallant man had never uttered a single word in regret of the blind bargain that he had made by venturing in these Isles; being altogether unlike his fellow-merchants, the brothers Castillo, whose curses and laments concerned little else. Both Diego and Luis Barreto, who received constant attention from Doña Ysabel's servants and were supplied with sustaining and dainty foods, threw off the fever quickly enough, and Don Diego succeeded to the command of his brother's company.

Andrés Castillo died next, followed by his brother Mariano and Doña Maria Ponce. By this time the savages had ceased their war on us, though knowing very well in what a cleft stick we were caught, and that ten determined men, coming at night, could easily have overpowered our sentries and taken possession of the camp. Whether it was fear of our artillery, or fear of catching our fever, that held them back, or whether they pitied us, must remain a matter for conjecture; at any rate, they continued to leave substantial gifts of food at the camp-gates, for which we paid them with the clothes of those who had died. Yet, notwithstanding this amity, the Colonel's nephew was found one morning on the beach, half in and half out of the water, an arrow stuck through his heart; and a wound at the back of his head as though he had fallen against a jagged stone. Since no vengeance was required from the natives, I suspected that the two Barretos, jealous for Doña Mariana's honour, had lain in wait for him one night, stunned him with a club, and then thrust the arrow into him by hand. She took the news calmly—how could she do otherwise?—but suffered the more.

On the 5th of November, Doña Ysabel moved back to the Great Cabin, pleading that the Residency held memories of the General's last hours, and of Don Lorenzo's, too poignant for her to bear; yet the demon of lust still spurred her to crime. She had allowed three days for Pedro Fernandez's grief to assuage, and now opened a covert attack upon him; having in the meantime seen him often and spoken sweetly and piously of their common bereavement. On the fourth evening, she said: 'My friend, if I am not mistaken, it is God's will that we should at last abandon our mission to these islands, and leave the hopes and prayers of my poor husband unfulfilled; very soon we shall be without a priest. But for this, though abandoned by all except the very few, I should stay to the bitter end. You, I know, will never desert my cause, whatever may happen, now that, like myself, you are left alone in the world. I could not truthfully say as much for anyone else, no, not even for my own brothers.'

Pedro Fernandez assured her that he was deeply honoured by her confidence in him, which was not misplaced, and that he held her in higher veneration than any woman alive, or any man either, except it were His Majesty the King and the Holy Father at Rome; but sorrowfully agreed that, if the Vicar did not recover, it must be as she said. 'Nevertheless, my lady, this need not be our last visit to your domain. You are Don Alvaro's sole heiress, and one day, having fitted out another expedition, better equipped, as well manned, stronger in the Faith and in every other way, you will return to resume the task which you laid down; and on that day I undertake to sail with you.'

He told her of his ambition to discover the great southern continent of Austrialia, of which the Chinese claimed to have knowledge, and his zeal to begin the work of converting its teeming millions: 'Then, my lady, you shall be Vicereine, and I (if you will not despise one of low station) will command your fleets.'

She brushed away a tear, assuring him that he was more to her than all the grandees of Old Spain, but that—more was the pity—the resplendent prospect he laid before her could never be realized. Although she was fit to wrestle with and overcome the difficulties of setting a new expedition on foot, as she had done before—'and I confess,' she sighed, 'that my husband was more hindrance than help when I was working on our joint behalf'—one stumbling-block only barred the way: that Don Alvaro had left no male heir.

'I verily believe,' she continued, 'that if I could present myself before His Majesty at Madrid and, falling at his feet, beseech him to confer the Captaincy-General upon my infant son by Don Alvaro, he would not hesitate to do so. Then every door would fly open and all purse-strings be loosed, a thousand bold knights would clamour to sail under my pendant, and I should once more be Governeress of the Isles of Solomon; and you, friend Pedro, for your faithfulness, would be my son's trusty guardian. In due course, with God's help, you would make me Vicereine of Austrialia—what a sweetly-sounding title—and Holy Church would reap the richest harvest of souls since its foundation. But, alas, these are fond dreams! Because of Don Alvaro's saintly continence, no heir waits in my womb for posthumous birth. The King will despise the suit of a barren widow, and this island, and all the rest, will be relinquished to the claws of him who held them before we came.'

She rose and hurried away, as if to vent her grief in private—having a very nice sense of the tragical.

By this time, the sick troops had straggled back aboard the *San Geronimo* in the hope of being confessed by Father Juan before he died, and only the Ensign-Royal, Sergeant Andrada and twelve healthy men remained in the camp. They lived together in the guardhouse, protecting the sailors who filled what was left of our casks

and jars and then trundled them on handcarts from the spring to the
jetty. Since fuel was also needed, several huts were pulled down, and
the timbers sawn into convenient lengths. The natives watched this
activity from a distance and, seeing that we were about to take our
leave, treated us to a chorus of derision, but otherwise kept the peace.

On the 17th of November, the sails being at last back in the ships,
the Ensign-Royal hauled down the flag, marked the remaining buildings with the Cross of Saint Andrew to protect them from the
savages, and came aboard the flagship with his men. Doña Ysabel
had given orders that all dogs must be left behind because of the
scarcity of provisions, and it grieved us to watch the faithful animals
course along the beach in a pack, yelping and howling reproach-
fully at us. Only one dared leap into the sea and swim out to the
San Geronimo. It was Carlotta, the smallest of them all, and though
some would have shot the poor creature, or let her drown, she was
taken aboard and soon found a new home in the forecastle, where
the sailors made much of her.

Thus we abandoned the settlement, even before it had been
decided where to go next, or how. The ships were in a ruinous
condition, and none of us had the least notion by what means they
were to be victualled. The Chief Pilot asked Father Juan to approach
God for guidance, which he did with much feeling. 'O Lord,' he
pleaded, 'hearken to the prayer of Thy dying priest! We have sinned,
and Thy hand has chastened us. Oh, forgive us our trespasses, inspire
our leaders with wisdom and waft us all safely to a Christian port!'
Then falling back exhausted on his pillow, he said between a sigh
and a groan: 'My son, I am spent, I can do no more. Send Andrés
Serrano; I must make my last Will.'

This was a simple business, because the good Father had little to
bequeath, except the five hundred pesos of his venture for which
nobody would now have given him even five in good silver, and because all went to the Bishop of Lima, to be distributed among the
Cathedral clergy. Sergeant Andrada and two soldiers were ordered to
watch at his sick-bed in turn, and about midnight one of them, who
was something of a scholar, read aloud to him from Fray Luis de
Granada's *Symbol of the Faith*, which heartened Father Juan greatly,
so that he renewed his hopes of living. At dawn, the Chief Pilot came
to feel his pulse. 'Reverend Father,' he said, sadly, 'the time is running short.'

'I know it, my son,' he answered. 'God be praised: we shall soon be on our way, leaving behind us this corner of Hell that has cost us so dear.'

'Alas, Father, do not deceive yourself. It would be well if you prepared yourself for the journey from which none return.'

'Why did you not warn me sooner?' he groaned. 'I felt so little pain that I thought I was treading the road to recovery.' Calling for a crucifix and grasping it with both hands, he prayed in anguish: 'O eternal Father who sent me here, I know not what I ought to do or say! Where is there a priest to stand by me in this hour of need? Soon my power of speech will fail.'

Almost at once his death agony came upon him, yet his lips formed the words: 'Father, into Thy hands I commend my spirit,' and with that he expired.

There was talk of a burial in the Churchyard, but nobody cared to return to the camp once our last distasteful goodbyes had been said. On the pretext that the natives might desecrate his remains, it was decided to bury them at sea.

That day the wind, which ever since our arrival had blown from the east and south-east, suddenly backed to the north. It was not a gale, nor even a half-gale, but with the help of huge waves which came rolling through the mouth of the bay, it sufficed to break three of our four cables; and the fourth, being only a slight one, appeared altogether too weak to hold a vessel of her size. The rocks were close, and as the Chief Pilot could not hope to avoid shipwreck by hoisting sail, he warned us that we must be prepared to take to the boats. Matia made a grim jest of the matter. 'Have no fear for the ship, your honour,' he said. 'Terridiri blessed that cable with his shark's head off Santa Cristina, and prophesied that she would never run aground. Besides, is this not the only one of the four that was not sprinkled with holy water when we left Callao?' He was indignantly silenced and threatened with a flogging, but his words went the round of the ship and the superstitious soldiers, no longer having a priest to guide them, took his blasphemy for sober truth. Even so, the cable did indeed hold fast, for which mercy the Chief Pilot and I, at least, thanked Him from whom it proceded; and the wind veered again to east.

Early next morning, Sergeant Andrada approached Don Diego, who now exercised the greatest authority in the flagship after Doña Ysabel, and said: 'Your honour, I dreamed last night that you sent me ashore on Orchard Isle across the bay, and there I found enough pork and biscuit to victual your whole company for a month.'

'Go to it, Sergeant!' replied Don Diego. 'Take the long-boat and every fit man you can muster, and we shall see whether you are as good a dreamer as the patriarch Joseph.'

'But what will be my reward?'

'A tenth part of all you bring back, and for that I pledge you my word.'

Sure enough, he returned before noon with five large canoes in tow, laden nearly to the gunwales with yam-biscuit, which he had found hidden in some thick bushes overhanging a creek, and twenty pigs; he claimed that he had slaughtered at least one hundred in all, but lacked the means of transporting them. His comrades told us that he had led them straight to the creek, pretending to be guided by a divine instinct, and secured the canoes; and thence to a village near by, where a large pen full of pigs was found, as if in preparation for a feast. There, though hospitably received by the Chieftain and given ten pigs and many coconuts, he asked for more, and when this was refused, fired on his hosts without warning. He killed a score of them, and every pig in the pen, though aware that the long-boat would hold no more than twenty. The villagers fled and were chased out of sight until a pit-fall opened in the path, when three of our men tumbled through upon sharp stakes; their shoes saved them from being impaled, but even so a targeteer came out with an ugly gash in his leg.

Andrada, a bloody-minded man who had hated all natives since the loss of his front teeth, seemed by no means the kind of person whom God would bless with a revelation. When I pressed my enquiries, Juarez told me the truth, namely that the village nearest to our camp was allied to the one on the islet, and that all its pigs and biscuit had been sent across the bay by night, to prevent our seizure of them; and that the Sergeant had wormed this secret from a woman hostage by dangling a string of glass-beads before her.

Sergeant Andrada was duly awarded two pigs and three sacks of biscuit for his pains; one pig he sold to the Purser for five silver pesos, the other he kept for himself. After the troops had been well fed on chitterlings and black puddings, the carcases were salted down; but since Don Diego refused to give the crew any part of the spoils, Pedro Fernandez was forced to go foraging himself. This proved an adventurous excursion. That same day he took the long-boat back to Orchard Islet, accompanied by twenty sailors and half a dozeñ soldiers from the frigate. They landed at a village less than a league from the scene of Andrada's misdeeds and, despite a flag of truce, were met with a shower of arrows and sling-bolts. A couple of shots fired above the enemy's heads soon routed them, and our people entered the village, but found only a few baskets of biscuit and no roots, except those used for the making of an orange dye. They pursued the natives up a hill to a small fertile plain, planted with yams and every sort of fruit-tree, where the sailors cut large bunches of bananas and felled three palms for their coconuts, and also found a store-house crammed full of biscuit. After another blood-less skirmish, they succeeded in carrying off the whole of this valuable booty, and stowed it aboard the boat; which the Chief Pilot then sent back to the flagship. He ordered the crew to rejoin him as soon as they might; in the meantime he would have taken his party down the coast to collect more provisions from a certain palm-covered head-land, where he would wait until he was fetched off. Striking inland again, and meeting with no opposition, he worked his way round to the point; and there felled a score of trees, gathered almonds and coconuts, and cut a quantity of palm-cabbage, which is good against scurvy.

The long-boat had not returned by late afternoon, and the party chafed at the delay. Pedro Fernandez, fearing that it had been inter-cepted and captured, led them back along the coast towards their original landing-place, in the hope of finding a canoe which could be sent to the flagship with news of their whereabouts. The men, how-ever, were convinced that the boat had reached the *San Geronimo* in safety, and that Don Diego had persuaded his sister to sail away with their victuals, leaving them marooned. Nothing that the Chief Pilot could say would persuade them that this was a foolish notion. In the end he grew indignant, swearing that even if sufficient sailors remained in the ship to work her, or any officer capable of shaping a course, Doña Ysabel would never have assented to so mean a proposal.

They marched wearily along the shore until sunset, when they rested awhile and then pursued their journey; but, the path fading out, they had to force their way over jagged rocks and through slimy mangrove-marshes and thick forest that seemed never to have been disturbed since the day of its creation. At one place they were obliged to make a detour, wading up to their middles in the sea. By midnight they could go no farther, because two of the soldiers convalescent from fever fell down in a faint; but at about cock-crow they heard shouts and saw the lantern of the long-boat, which had been cruising in search of them. The wind had been contrary, and the crew were in no condition to use the oars. The Chief Pilot embarked his men with joy, though they were utterly fatigued and, after retrieving the cabbages and nuts, regained the *San Geronimo* as dawn broke.

He slept for five hours, but was then summoned to a Council in the Great Cabin, of which the proceedings are attached.

Nothing else of moment took place on that day, the last we were to spend off Santa Cruz; but when night fell, Captain de Vera went ashore with six men to disinter the General's coffin, which he did without being molested by the natives, and carried it down to the jetty. Juarez Mendés and Matia Pineto were of his party. They had asked leave to be the last to quit the island, an honour that had been conceded to them by the Ensign-Royal when the flag was hauled down. This was granted, and they re-embarked; but upon their hailing the galleon, Don Diego told the Captain to take the coffin aboard the frigate, and said that this was Doña Ysabel's order. I could readily believe it: though she wished to fetch the corpse to Manila as a means of scotching any rumour that Don Alvaro had died an unnatural death, to sail in the same ship with it was a very different matter.

PROCEEDINGS OF DOÑA YSABEL'S COUNCIL

On board the *San Geronimo*, lying in Gracious Bay, the Island of Santa Cruz, on the 18th of November, 1595.

Those present were: Doña Ysabel Barreto, Governeress of the Isles of Solomon; Major Don Luis Moran; Captains Don Diego Barreto, Don Felipe Corzo, Don Diego de Vera, Don Manuel Lopez; Ensigns Don Luis Barreto, Don Toribio de Bedeterra and Don Diego de Torres; also the Chief Pilot, Captain Don Pedro Fernandez of Quiros, with Martin Groc, pilot of the *San Felipe* galeot.

Doña Ysabel opened the proceedings by stating that it was her intention to quit Santa Cruz without delay and shape a course for San Cristobal, one of the Isles of Solomon, in a last attempt to find the *Santa Ysabel* galleon. Should this be granted, she would then do what appeared best for the service of God and His Majesty. If, however, the search proved fruitless, she would make for Manila in the Philippines, there to refit her flotilla, engage priests, recruit settlers and, returning to the said Isles, continue to fulfil His Majesty's orders. She now called on the military officers to express their opinion at the wisdom of these proposals.

Major Moran and the three company-commanders abstained from comment. Captain Lopez enquired in what direction San Cristobal was held to lie: whether to the east or to the west.

When called upon for a reply, the Chief Pilot considered that it would be disrespectful to the memory of Don Alvaro to maintain that the Isles of Solomon lay to the westward, and therefore begged to be excused from giving an opinion. Upon Captain Lopez's objecting to this that the Council should not be kept in the dark about matters of such importance, he proposed that a W.S.W. course be followed until a latitude of eleven degrees South were reached and that, if no land had by then been encountered, they should proceed on a north-westerly course to the Philippines.

No other officer having any comment to make, the proposal was put to the vote, carried unanimously, reduced to writing and signed by all present.

Doña Ysabel next desired the Chief Pilot to report on the sea-worthiness of the flotilla; who stated that the flagship's bottom was foul and much of her rigging decayed, and that the *San Felipe* galeot and the *Santa Catalina* frigate were in no better condition, besides being dangerously undermanned because of the sickness. He advised the abandonment of the smaller vessels, after stripping them of sails, cordage and the like and transferring their crew and cargo to the *San Geronimo*.

Doña Ysabel asked Captain de Vera, commander of the frigate in place of Captain Alonzo de Leyva deceased, and Captain Corzo, commander and owner of the galeot, whether they were in agreement.

Captain de Vera replied that he would obey orders, but thought that it might be advantageous to keep the frigate for the navigation of waters where the flagship ought not to be hazarded. Captain Corzo, rejecting the proposal outright, declared that 'it would be rank cannibalism for the galleon to feed on the carcases of her sisters'; he then alleged that the Chief Pilot had depreciated the *San Felipe* spitefully and wished to rob him of a ship worth two thousand pesos at the least.

The Chief Pilot said that Captain Corzo overrated her value: if the flagship ever reached Manila, he undertook to find him a better vessel for two hundred pesos.

The Governeress asked the company whether Captain Corzo should be ordered to abandon the *San Felipe* for the common good; to which he himself replied: 'I still carry my wood-knife.'

Ensign Don Luis Barreto stated that it would be a great injustice to deprive the Captain of his command after the loyal service he had rendered; but for him, the Colonel would still be alive and crowing, and the Barretos thrown to the sharks.

Since the Chief Pilot would not retreat from his view, no agreement could be reached. Doña Ysabel then ordered that Captain Corzo should keep his ship, and upon Don Luis's assertion that Captain Leyva had made a nuncupative Will bequeathing him a third-interest in the frigate, granted his plea that this vessel too should be allowed to sail.

A proposal was put forward by Captain Don Diego, supported by Major Moran and Don Luis, that the sick in the *San Geronimo* who had not yet reached the crisis of their fever should be transferred to the *Santa Catalina*: thus the health of those who had so far escaped infection would be protected, and others who were still weak would not be kept awake at night by their delirium.

This was resisted by Captain de Vera, who said that he would not have accepted his command, had he known that the frigate was to be turned into a floating lazar-house. The Ensign-Royal, who was under orders to sail with him in exchange for Ensign Don Diego Torres, made the same objection. The Chief Pilot remarked that, though his own task would be lightened if the proposal were accepted, he regarded it as cruel and uncatholic. He pleaded that the sick should not be deprived of the few comforts that could be provided for them in the flagship, such as shelter from the glare of the sun, rain and night air, and forced into the frigate where they would have to lie on deck.

At this juncture Captain Don Diego absented himself, but returned almost at once.

Major Don Luis Moran suggested that an old sail could be rigged on the *Santa Catalina's* deck as a protection against the elements, and said that the sea breeze was far healthier than the foetid airs of a forecastle.

The Chief Pilot objected that any such contrivance would interfere with navigation and that the sudden fall in temperature at sunset, always accompanied by an increase of fever in the patients, would prove fatal in most cases. He appealed to Doña Ysabel's charity.

It was ordered that the sick should remain in the flagship.

Doña Ysabel desired the Chief Pilot to find crews for the two smaller vessels, also food and water proportionate to their numbers, and further to provide their pilots with charts and sailing instructions; both of which duties he undertook to perform.

The Chief Pilot then asked permission to absent himself from the Council, on the ground that he had heard a man cry out for his help. This was granted, and business was suspended until he returned, when he informed the Governeress that Sergeant Luis Andrada, allegedly on instructions from Captain Don Diego, was lowering the dangerously sick into the long-boat for transference to the frigate.

The Governess ordered the mistake to be corrected at once; whereupon the Council was dismissed.

Chapter 22

NORTHWARD ACROSS THE EQUATOR

When we set sail for San Cristobal on the 18th of November, our people shook their fists at the retreating shore and shouted ten thousand imprecations at the inhabitants, as though our stay there had not been sufficient curse to them already. We had ninety-one souls on board the flagship, and the two smaller vessels carried thirty more. No canoes put out to speed us on our way with arrows or sling-bolts; which showed prudence, because the ships' guns had been charged and gunners were standing ready with lighted matches. The wind blowing fair from the south-east, we cleared the Bay without difficulty, but the *San Geronimo's* gear was so rotten that the falls carried away no less than three times while we were hoisting the long-boat aboard; and though I am no sailor, I could see that not much of a gale would be needed to strip us of every stitch we carried aloft. We dropped the Vicar's body overboard as Santa Cruz sank below a horizon red with angry flashes from the volcano Tinahula. Three of the sailors who had taken part in the forage now showed signs of fever, and a fourth had poisoned his foot by treading on a spined sea-shell.

Our course was W.S.W. On the 19th the Chief Pilot took the sun and found that we were in latitude eleven South. Meanwhile, the Boatswain and another four seamen had fallen sick, which left us only five healthy men besides the Boatswain's mate; the remainder of our crew of thirty having been distributed between the *Santa Catalina* and the *San Felipe*. Damian grumbled that we were mad to plod on, close-hauled, in search of San Cristobal which, even if it could be found, promised us no better hospitality than we had abused in Santa Cruz—why did we not turn and run free for the Philippines? The Chief Pilot was vexed with him until suddenly the mainstay—that stout cable running from the maintop to the foot of the foremast to take the strain of sails—broke like a thread and the mainmast was sprung at the step. Then he was converted to Damian's view, whom he sent to supervise the splicing of the mainstay, but confessed that he would not give the mast a three days' warranty; and this happened when we were still some nine hundred leagues from the nearest Christian port.

At his urgent representations, and having no strong hope of finding the *Santa Ysabel*, the Governeress, though with some reluctance, agreed to make for Manila. Don Luis, Captain Lopez and certain other officers, well apprised of the danger we were in, helped her to bear down Don Diego's opposition who stubbornly refused to credit that anything was amiss with our ship and still had dreams of enriching himself for life at King Solomon's gold-mines.

On the 20th of November, therefore, a north-westerly course was shaped and when it became known for what port we were bound, the news had better effect than any physic. The crosses in my register, now forty-seven, did not increase in number for a while, the Boatswain and all the sick seamen making a swift recovery. That night at the common table Pedro Fernandez remarked that we could not be far distant from the vast Island of New Guinea, the northern coast of which he felt an inordinate ambition to chart, and that he refrained from doing so only at Doña Ysabel's command. The truth was: certain clouds sighted that day far ahead of us on the port bow seemed to him piled along the crest of a high mountain range—the Isles of Solomon, at last, stretching north-west through nearly five degrees of latitude! But to quiet Don Diego, who might have insisted that we should turn and land, he took advantage of his ignorance and beguiled him with talk of New Guinea, which lay some two hundred leagues farther west.

Doña Mariana, worn out by the care of nursing her brothers and by hidden grief for Don Jacinto, fell an easy victim to the fever. She had always been wild at heart and possessed most of the faults of her family, namely pride, greed and duplicity, but was not altogether bad and, had a priest been by, might well have turned contrite and died devout. But many unconfessable sins weighed heavily on her conscience, and she began to conceive a hatred for the sister who had tempted her into evil and who now, for fear of taking the infection, kept away from her. She wondered bitterly whether the Chief Pilot was hooked, or already drawn out of the water.

For a week past, Pedro Fernandez had been in so strange a mood, alternately blithe and glum, amiable and quarrelsome, that on the evening after we sailed I accepted the Purser's offer to rent the cabin in which the Vicar had died. It was airy, with a good bed, and had the advantage of a padlock fitted on the door by Juan de la Isla. I did not doubt that Don Gaspar had been told by Doña Ysabel to make me this offer; my removal from the Chart-room would clear the way for her.

It was not until many months later that I learned the details of what happened that same night. About three hours before dawn, when her maids were asleep, she stole into the Chart-room, wrapped in a long black cloak, and softly closed the door after her. Pedro Fernandez started up and, the lantern burning dim, drew a dagger from under his pillow, mistaking her for an assassin sent by Don Diego. 'Ah, Pedro, no!' she whispered. 'Would you kill the one you love best?'

Half-asleep, and overcome by confusion, he whispered back: 'Forgive me, my protectress, my angel, my one hope!' She gently took the weapon from him and laid it out of reach, then came to sit on the bed. He pressed his lips to her hand, unable to conceal his emotion.

'Is it so with you?' she asked, trembling. 'So it also is with me.'

He made no reply, but stared at her, wild-eyed.

'I have a hunger to speak with you, my love,' she said, 'but my teeth are chattering for cold. For God's sake, let me come into your bed.'

Since he did not answer, she shed her cloak and, clad only in a silken shift, slipped under the coverlet between him and the wall, and 'Take me in your strong arms and comfort me,' she said. 'I am lonely and chilled to the marrow.'

He embraced her as reverently as though she were a wonder-working image, and said: 'Let this never be accounted a sin. Heaven knows that I love you with all my heart, and that I would never do you wrong; it is a joy beyond expression that I can at last tell you so face to face.'

'Pedro,' she breathed, 'when the year of my widowhood has elapsed, will you marry me? We shall both be free then, as free as air, and this kiss is a token that I am yours for ever.' She pressed her lips to his.

He returned the kiss, weeping for wonder.

'Am I not beautiful?' she asked presently. 'Don Alvaro despised my beauty.'

'God forgive him!' he answered. 'He must have been stark mad.'

'Feel this smooth, tender belly,'—here she seized his hand—'nay, do not shrink! Was it not cruel to deny a living soul houseroom here? And these firm, round breasts, was it not a sin to deny them their natural function?'

He trembled, and was nearly over the edge of the chasm, but made a valiant effort to regain his footing. 'In the Virgin's name, let me go!' he said between clenched teeth. 'Being so virtuous yourself, you cannot guess how sorely my flesh is tried.'

She released him, and lay sobbing as though her heart would break; until pretty soon he thought better of his resolution, hugged her close to him again and assaulted her with passionate kisses, which she did not resent.

It was as though he had seduced her, yet she gloried in what had been done, declaring that they were now one flesh in the sight of God, and that unless He had intended this, He would never have smoothed away the difficulties that beset them; and that she was the happiest woman alive. He, though by no means convinced, took courage from her shining eyes and answered that, at the worst, theirs was a venial sin and could be remedied by honourable marriage at Manila, and that the statutory year ordained to prevent a widow, already with child, from lying with a new husband did not touch their case. And 'My love,' she said, 'if, as a fruit of this night's pleasure a son be born to us, he will be rightful heir to the Marquisate. You will have raised up seed for your brother, as Our Saviour did not forbid, and by this means we shall fulfil the desire nearest our hearts, which must redound to God's greater glory.'

He consented in this false and heretical reasoning. They kissed, clasped, and comforted each other until dawn, agreeing to meet again next night at the same hour; but she warned him that meanwhile she would treat him with scorn and severity, the better to conceal her love from watchful eyes, and would continue to do so until they reached Manila.

Her maid Elvira, becoming aware of her nightly absences, grew alarmed. She confided in none but Jaume, whom she asked to give the Chief Pilot this secret warning: that if the Barretos discovered what visitor he entertained at night, he might expect cold steel between his shoulders, and who then would bring the flotilla safely into harbour? Jaume came covertly to me, as being intimate with Pedro Fernandez, and asked me to pass on the message; but pretended that it concerned a conspiracy to seize the ship. 'Their lives are their own,' said I at once, to show him that I was not deceived, 'and who am I, to warn him against keeping a mistress? What hope have I of convincing him that there is danger? If he does not feel the indecency of lying with her so soon after the funeral of her husband, and so soon after receiving news of his own bereavement, he must be infatuated indeed.'

'Then you will not intervene?'

'I do not think so. To keep silence is dangerous, I agree, yet to speak seems more dangerous still. He believes whatever she tells him, as though she were a fifth Evangelist, and would be far from thanking a well-intentioned friend who sought to acquaint him with her true character. If I tell him no more than that his amour is discovered, he will pass the news on to her and cite me as his informant; and she, to cover her tracks, will find means to silence me for ever. Let me be frank with you, Jaume: in the pursuit of her ends Doña Ysabel is capable of any baseness and, what is more, she holds us all in her power. Has Elvira discussed the affair with her friend?'

'With Belita? No; Belita knows nothing. Don Diego and Don Luis now share her fraternally, so she is never to be found in the Great Cabin between midnight and dawn. Elvira confided only in me.'

'Then tell her that her secret must not travel any farther. It is safe with us two, but unless she cares to be pushed over the taffrail one moonless night . . .'

'You are right, Don Andrés,' he said. 'Well I dare say, the Devil had better have his fling.'

We were now making about twenty leagues a day, and on the 27th of November the look-out sighted a floating tree-trunk and a large tangled mass of river weeds, among which, when we came up with it, we saw almonds, half-burned thatch and a couple of snakes. Pedro Fernandez took the sun and, for Don Diego's benefit, reported that we had already reached latitude five degrees South; but we were still in latitude seven, cruising wide of the northernmost Isles of Solomon. The wind had veered to the south-west, bringing squalls and showers, which proved, he said, that New Guinea was not far distant. A heavy ground-swell met us head-on; the ship began to pitch sullenly, and then to roll as another array of toppling waves struck at us from starboard. This buffeting strained her timbers and aggravated our sufferings; but it also discouraged Doña Ysabel from further nightly visits to the Chart-room, for even the most passionate love finds its match in sea-sickness. Thus we passed by and left the Isles of Solomon unvisited and even unsighted. No white man has set foot upon them to this day and their position remains a secret known to few.

The winds grew variable, and sometimes ceased altogether, but the swell persisted disagreeably; our daily run decreased to eight leagues or less as we approached the Line, which we did not cross until the 13th of December. Saint Lucia, whose day this is, heals sore eyes and restores dim vision; when her sun arose, the skies were clear, the air quiet, the sea smooth, but not the keenest-sighted man in the world could have descried the least sign of land on the cloudless horizon.

Pedro Fernandez expected Doña Ysabel to show him marked disdain, and for a while the harsher her words, the more he rejoiced. When she discontinued her nightly visits to the Chart-room, he guessed that sea-sickness was the cause, and pitied her. But she recovered and still did not come; and though they might happen to be alone in the Great Cabin, her manner towards him remained as cold and severe as a judge's who tries a man for his neck. He did not grow impatient, supposing that the flowers were upon her, but she continued to hold him at arm's length, and what could he do? Having pledged himself not to reveal their secret by word, look or act, he waited discreetly upon her pleasure.

Jaume and I noticed the alteration in him. He looked like one who has been smuggled into Heaven by the back-door and then thrust out of the window without warning, to fall head over heels through space, like Vulcan in the fable, and never know when he will strike the hard earth. It may well be imagined that he did not complain to me or to anyone else. He had work in abundance to occupy his mind and keep him from brooding, being both pilot and master of a ship that was undermanned, ill-provisioned, and unseaworthy in the extreme. He took his place at the common table among a dwindled company consisting of the Governeress, her two brothers, Major Moran, Captain Lopez, Ensign Torres and myself. Luisa, Juan de Buitrago's widow, should have been with us or, at least, allowed her dole of food, being now great-bellied; but Doña Ysabel owed nothing, she said, to the relict of a proven traitor, who must be content with her former humble station.

Never before or since have I eaten in such disagreeable company. With Doña Mariana keeping her bed, there were no jokes, no raillery, and very little talk, except when Don Luis lamented that he dared not face his creditors in Peru and must perforce push his fortune in

China or the Spice Islands; or when Don Diego found fault with
the dinner—to which his sister always replied that if he ate a trifle
less he would relish it the more. Occasionally, one of the Barretos let
fall a spiteful remark, directed against the Chief Pilot, at which the
Major and Ensign Torres would break into sycophantic laughter; but
Captain Lopez, the Chief Pilot and I took our meals in silence.

At last one morning, when I was in the Great Cabin, making an
inventory of Doña Ysabel's private stores at her dictation, Pedro
Fernandez entered, looking glum and playing uneasily with the bonnet he held in his hands.

'I am busy, Pilot,' she said.

'I must speak to your ladyship about the galeot,' he said, staring
straight ahead of him.

'Pray address me as "Your Excellency." What is amiss now?'

'The *San Felipe* has been behaving strangely these last two days.
She keeps away, and will not acknowledge our signals.'

'But why?'

'Three days ago, when her pilot came aboard to compare bearings,
he saw that our mainmast was sprung. He must have told Captain
Corzo that we are unlikely ever to reach the Philippines. If we were
left disabled by the fall of our mast, do you see, he would be in honour
bound to stand by and rescue us.'

'Oh, is that how he shows his gratitude? Very well: wait for the
galeot to come up, and hail her. Say: "Her Excellency's orders:
Captain Corzo is to keep position half a league astern, on pain of
being declared a traitor." '

'And is that all?'

'In God's name! What more do you want, you great oaf, standing
there with your mouth agape, sighing and twiddling your greasy cap?
What in the world has come over you lately? Are you sickening for
the fever, or have you fallen in love with that idle strumpet Pancha?
Begone, man, before I lose my temper! Leave me to finish these
accursed accounts. Andrés, how many jars of oil remain, did I say?'

'Seventeen, your Excellency,' I replied, 'besides the one in current
use.'

'May I be permitted to have a word with you in private?' Pedro
Fernandez asked urgently.

'No you may not. Andrés here is a very oyster for discretion. If
you have something to say, out with it quickly, and then be gone.'

He looked at her in dumb appeal, swallowed, bowed, and retired.

Not long after, I heard him hail the *San Felipe* and deliver his message through cupped hands. When evening fell, Captain Corzo stood on another tack, and by morning was out of sight. The frigate still struggled along, on our port quarter, her present pilot being a common seaman who was unable either to read a chart or use a cross-staff, so that her one hope of survival lay in following our lead.

We were beginning to feel the pinch of starvation: the biscuit and salt pork brought from Santa Cruz were now expended and the daily ration had been reduced to half a pound of mouldy flour and a gill of stinking water, full of drowned cockroaches. Our cook mixed the flour with sea-water and kneaded it into griddle-cakes, which he baked in the hot ashes. Soon ensued such trials that I can scarcely trust myself to write of them. Crimes were committed against nature, as when a grown man stole a pannikin of water from a dying child. Two sick soldiers and one woman went mad and had to be secured in irons howling and gibbering, lest they injured their neighbours.

Doña Ysabel never ventured forward. An armed guard was posted to keep soldiers and crew from troubling her with petitions, and she had all the artillery, arquebuses and powder brought aft, so that if they attempted to mutiny, the people of the aftercastle would have the whip-hand of them. Everyone in the vessel was awarded the same ration, but she thought it advisable to give her guards and servants double. The Chief Pilot and I were shown small consideration. At the common table only the Barretos ate what they pleased: the rest of us were asked to pay famine prices for everything set before us. We were sold flour at six pesos a pound, and oil at twenty pesos a pint, Doña Ysabel either accepting cash or deducting payment from our ventures; but reckoning their worth at only one real to the peso. My modest venture of three hundred pesos and my arrears of pay, which amounted to another thirty, would not go far at this rate, but I was still in fair health and escaped the scurvy which, not long after we crossed the Line, began to show itself among the crew in ulcers on feet and legs. 'Don Andrés can live on his fat like a bear in wintertime,' jeered the Major.

My death-ledger sprouted new crosses. Hardly a day now passed but a corpse or two was thrown overboard: in the month that began on Saint Lucia's Day, we disposed of twenty-nine, including two young women and five children. The soldiers and settlers lived in indescribable filth, all pride, hope and affection gone, and the moan of 'water, water!' sounded everywhere. If I passed through the ship on an errand

to the forecastle, men would loll out their swollen tongues, and point
to them, like Dives appealing to Lazarus; and women with shrunken
breasts would hold up for my pity little children that were wasted to
mere anatomies. Alas, for Juanito, Don Alvaro's nursling; he was a
sturdy child and took long to die.

Pedro Fernandez went about in a daze, doing what was required of
him by force of habit, yet doing it well. He seemed now resigned to
Doña Ysabel's unrelieved cruelty as to something altogether inex-
plicable, and it was only when she discarded every pretence of charity
and revealed herself under her true colours, that he knew how things
stood between them: she had cast him off like an old shoe and her
former protestations of enduring love proved utterly worthless and
insincere. Yet he was slow to accommodate himself to the change
and still tried to find excuses for her shameless avarice and neglect of
Christian principles.

Rigging and sails had now grown so rotten that the crew were
unequal to the labour of splicing and sewing; carpenters, pages,
negroes and all other available persons, except soldiers, were pressed
into this necessary service. The bowsprit-pillow, loosened when in
collision with the galeot some months before, now broke adrift almost entirely, hanging down to starboard and taking the bowsprit
with it; so that the spritsail, with all its gear, fell into the sea, and
none of it could be recovered. The mainstay carried away a second
time, and our only means of keeping the mainmast in position was
to improvise another stay: by using the remains of one of the hemp
cables that had betrayed us at Gracious Bay and the back-stays, which
Pedro Fernandez and the Boatswain's mate unrove for the purpose.
Not a yard but was canted downwards, owing to parted lifts and ties,
and for three days or more, a sail might be seen left lying on deck
because no one had either strength or heart to hoist it again with a
rope that had been spliced three-and-thirty times. The Chief Pilot
had the topsails and the mizzen unbent and used them to patch our
two courses, which was all the sail we now carried. The ship was so
open in her upper works, that when we sailed close-hauled, the water
ran in and out, flooding the between-decks. Only the beams kept her
afloat: they were of the excellent Peruvian timber called *guatchapeli*,
which seems never to warp or rot.

The wickedest man aboard was Don Diego, who ate and drank as
freely as if he were a guest of the Viceroy's; and the most virtuous by
universal consent was Juan Leal the sick-attendant. This venerable

old fellow himself caught the fever, but rose from his palliasse on the third day in order to minister to his companions. He bled them, cupped them, made their beds, emptied the night-buckets, and either coaxed them through the sickness by words of simple cheer, or helped them to a good death and piously committed their bodies to the deep. In Chile, thirty years before, he had been a soldier and still wore something of a martial air, despite his tunic of sack-cloth, his bare feet, and the ragged gray beard that swept to his waist. Nobody saw him sleeping and he seemed to live on air. The Purser conceived an admiration for Juan Leal and stole water and food from Doña Ysabel's larder, which Matia and Juarez, who took turns to stand guard at the foot of the companion-way, would convey to him for distribution to the sick. He did the same, at their insistence, for Doña Luisa; agreeing with them that it would be a pity should Juan de Buitrago leave no heir to his valiant and soldierly spirit.

The wind blew from the north-east and kept in that quarter for a full month. We shipped a deal of water from being forced to sail on a bowline, and there was no remedy but to man the pumps for an hour at the beginning of every watch. To collect the men for this task and make them perform it called for much exertion on the officers' part, even when double rations were promised as an incentive. Some slipped off and hid themselves; others defiantly refused to work; others, again, lay down and feigned sickness. They had to be thrashed into obedience.

On the 16th of December, when we were in latitude three degrees South, the Chief Pilot went to Doña Ysabel and asked her in the name of Christian charity to relieve the dangerously sick; he had a list of some thirty men and women in his hand. She replied that she could spare no food, but he shot her so grim a look that she relented and undertook to find them a daily ration of pease-porridge helped out by a half-jar of honey and the scrapings from a lard-tub, while these lasted, and every afternoon a mug of water with a little sugar in it. But still we had not travelled more than a third of the way to the Philippines.

On the following day, Captain de Vera closed with us, and as we drew abreast, shouted that the Ensign-Royal had leaped overboard in a fit of madness; also, that the ship was leaking like a sieve. He asked for a loan of three sailors to assist his crew, who were worn out by working at the pumps.

The Boatswain's watch were sent aboard the frigate to keep her dry while the master-carpenter found and plugged the leaks; but he reported that not all the shipwrights in Old Spain could do anything for her, she being so worn out that he could poke his finger through either of her sides as easily as through cheese. Pedro Fernandez then begged the Governeress to abandon the *Santa Catalina* and take off her crew, with all the stores and gear. She gave him a plain 'no!' for answer, without an explanation or excuse, and dismissed him. After she had time to reconsider the matter, he went to her again and informed her that the frigate was doomed; and that with ten more seamen, an extra sail and more cordage, the flagship would have better hopes of reaching Manila. 'No!' she repeated, this time adding: 'I do not trust Captain de Vera: he was in the plot to murder me and I cannot conceive why my husband spared him. Doubtless, he murdered the Ensign-Royal because he would not take part in a new attempt on my life.'

The truth was that she feared to bring Don Alvaro's corpse aboard, yet dared not let it remain in an abandoned ship. So the Chief Pilot went to call upon Captain de Vera, and told him: 'I have pleaded with Doña Ysabel to find room for you and your men in the *San Geronimo*, but she distrusts you. Why not approach her yourself? If you stay on, that will be the end of you.'

'My friend,' said Captain de Vera, 'only one thing prevents me from following your advice: namely my honour. I would rather be sucked down into the abyss than ask the least favour of that she-wolf, that witch, that murderess, or even be found in the same vessel with her.'

'Those are intemperate words, my lord. However, if you are too proud to plead, bring your people aboard at midnight, with what stores and gear you can assemble. We shall welcome you like brothers, and Doña Ysabel will never dare to send you back.'

'Pilot, you have my gratitude for your good offices; but I know her better than you do. A woman who found it in her heart to kill her own husband by playing on his superstitious fears will have little pity on me. If I am to board the *San Geronimo*, I must come either armed, and throw her and her brothers into the sea—for which I should have to hang in Manila—or else unarmed, and suffer a like fate here and now. No, I prefer to stay where I am; the frigate may yet make port, or we may escape in the skiff to some island.'

A little before dawn we lost sight of the *Santa Catalina's* lantern, though the air was clear, whereupon the Chief Pilot eased off the sheets and waited for her to come up. Don Diego raised a furious outcry: this was no time to delay the navigation, and unless the frigate had passed us by during the night, she was away on a tack of her own. Upon Pedro Fernandez's declaring that it would be a crime to abandon a sister-ship on the high seas without a capable pilot to guide her, he answered that now it was God for all, every man for himself and let the Devil take the hindmost. Towards evening the Governeress gave the order to make sail again, which could not be disobeyed.

Memories of her husband's fate revived in Doña Mariana's heart as she lay dying, and though she had been avenged on Don Alvaro for the part he had played in it, she now saw the history of the quarrel in a different light. Doña Ysabel must have feared that at Don Alvaro's death the Admiral would succeed to the Captaincy-General and Governorship of the Isles and that his children would eventually inherit the Marquisate—a misfortune which she was determined to forestall; she had therefore persuaded Don Alvaro to bind him for a while with the chains of marital chastity, and in the meantime plotted against his life. Thus, even if Don Lope had not dallied with the Sergeant's wife, he would before long have been either murdered or executed on a trumpery charge, to prevent the consummation of his marriage. Perhaps he had been warned of this by Father Juan, who could be shrewd enough when it pleased him, and therefore sailed off on his own as soon as Santa Cruz came in view. 'What a generous fool I have been!' Doña Mariana sighed, 'first to play pander in Ysabel's seduction of the Chief Pilot, then to help her into widowhood, and now to keep silence while she is got with a posthumous but legitimate child! The Virgin grant that it may be a girl, and crooked at that!'

She confided these thoughts to Pancha, who was now her maid (Inez having died), and promised to bequeath her a golden necklace if she would give a message to the Chief Pilot. He was to be told the reason for his recent ill-treatment, namely that Doña Ysabel, being now with child, had no further need of his amatory services; also that the tale of his wife's death was a fiction, derived from information which he had himself volunteered on the day we left Paita and that, for all that was known, Doña Ana might be safe and well. He would be handed a sealed letter a week after his arrival at Manila, the existence of which would meanwhile provide for his safety, if he did as he was instructed, etc., etc.

I wrote Doña Mariana's Will at her dictation and two of the pages witnessed it. Apart from the necklace for Pancha, a reward for faithful nursing, and two hundred pesos in silver to provide masses for her soul, she left all she possessed to Don Fernando de Castro, a nephew of her first husband's, who was at present stationed in the Philippines, and also made him her executor; no Barreto benefited under her Will or received the least mention. She was wasted to a thread, and no longer had hopes of recovery, but did not seem disconsolate at the prospect of death. She passed away early next morning, without a prayer or a complaint, only Pancha and I being at her bedside. When I brought the news to Doña Ysabel, she asked to read the Will, which I had with me; after perusing it, she remarked that her poor sister's wits had been addled for many weeks, and handed it back to me with a melancholy shake of her head.

Chapter 23

HUNGER AND THIRST

On the 23rd of December, while on a nor'-nor'-westerly course, we sighted an island some three leagues off, towards which we steered in search of a harbour and provisions but, the wind suddenly dropping, were unable to reach it before dark. Although the sea appeared to be clear of reefs, the Chief Pilot refused to hazard the ship by too close an approach, and ordered her to be put about. The seamen pressed him to sail on, pleading they were in no condition to perform the least unnecessary task; but the Boatswain and his mate agreed on the wisdom of standing off until daybreak, and between the three of them they put the helm down, let go the foresheet, and about we went.

At dawn we stood in to our position of the night before, and a look-out was sent aloft; who cried in alarm from the masthead that he could see nothing but reefs to the north, west and south as far as the horizon. We had entered a vast trap, baited with the island, and saw little prospect of escape: the only opening was to the east, but the wind blew north-easterly and we possessed no after-sails with which to clear the point of the reef by working to windward. However, a few of the sailors, aware of our peril, bestirred themselves, while Damian took the helm and slowly wore the ship round at Pedro Fernandez's orders. She had so little way on her that, cleverly as the sails were managed, we doubted whether she would ever get free. It was three o'clock before we made open water again, and the reef had been close enough for us to distinguish the smallest crabs scuttling about on its coral. Pedro Fernandez gave credit for our salvation to Saint Anthony of Padua, to whose shrine he had vowed a pilgrimage if he should ever escape with his life.

When the islanders saw that we did not intend to visit them after all, they came out in canoes to expostulate; but by this time the reef lay between. They mounted upon it with sorrowful shouts and gestures, from which we understood that they had already prepared us a feast and that we must not disappoint them by leaving it untasted. All were men: naked and robust, with long, loose hair. One canoe doubled the reef; its single occupant yelled, pointed at the island, and held up coconuts and a sort of bread which he made a pretence of eating. When we beckoned him to come aboard, he declined and hung back; upon which Don Diego, for sport, shot at him with an arquebus, but missed. This island, which we did not trouble to name, lies in six degrees North, and seems to have a circuit of about thirty leagues; it is low, round and densely wooded, but we made out clearings and cultivated patches. Pedro Fernandez took it to be one of the large and scattered group which the Portuguese call the Barbudos, meaning 'The Islands of the Bearded Men.' That evening the lookout reported four islands to westward and a number of isolated rocks, some to port, some to starboard, some ahead; but we put our trust in God and continued on our course. So passed Christmas Eve of the year 1595.

The pages had ceased to sing their familiar ditties; matins or vespers there were none; and our only spiritual comfort was the daily *Salve, Regina* croaked to Our Lady of Solitude, who still presided at our sprung mainmast; though her silken finery had rotted in the sun and rain and the gold leaf had peeled from the Infant's locks, she smiled hopefully down at us and seemed to promise salvation if we endured to the end. But the sailors no longer set much store by their lives. They told Damian that neither God nor the King required the impossible of them: they would rather die once than many times and might as well close their eyes, fold their arms and let the ship go to the bottom.

'This is where I drop my rope-end and take up a whip,' answered he, 'though I once prided myself that my tongue had sufficient lash to it. Neglect your duty, lads, and by God, I'll soon bring you howling to your knees, you asses, you eunuchs, you soldiers!'—which was his word of greatest contempt.

An apprentice said sobbing: 'If you won't let me die here in peace, cruel Valencian, I'll leap overboard.'

'Then the Devil will take you, body and soul!' Damian replied.

'What do I care? Hell can be little worse than this.'

Pedro Fernandez, coming up, looked at the men with compassion.

He seemed calmer now that he had been disillusioned about the
Governeress yet at the same time given renewed hope that Doña Ana
might still be alive. One of the sailors, a good top-man when in
health, told him: 'Your honour knows better than anyone that it isn't
heart we lack, but muscle. While we starve, you dine at the common
table. Earn our love by going to Doña Ysabel; ask her for food.'

'But how would you pay? You have no money and are entitled to
none until we dock at Manila.'

'That is so, but we're entitled to our rations—substantial ones, too.
We aren't greedy, your honour, but it's common knowledge that
there's still plenty in her private store: oil, wine, lentils, flour, sugar
and all. She fattens three pigs with the left-overs from her table, and
has water and meal enough to keep her brindled calf in good coat. It's
downright evil to throw to beasts what would support the lives of
Christians. Doesn't she know that she's slowly killing us? A week ago
the Colonel's white bitch went into our pot and, though she had
tasted human flesh, we ate her, head, guts and all.'

'Brave hearts, I have pleaded with the Governeress over and over
again, but she will not listen.'

'Then tell her we'll give pledges for anything she cares to sell us.
She can deduct the value from our pay when it's due. We shan't
quarrel with the price—the higher she pitches it the better we'll be
pleased. If we take our case before the Governor-General, he's bound
to tear up our pledges and try her for usury.'

'You talk too much, man! Nevertheless, I'll go to her once more.'

'Tell her,' the apprentice called after him, 'that the day will come
when she'll need our help, and then we'll remember how she's treated
us.'

He knocked at the door of the Great Cabin and was admitted.
Doña Ysabel was glad to see that his manner to her was now curt
and distant. Lately she had feared that he might shame her in her
brothers' presence by hints at what had passed between them; if that
happened, she would be forced to clap him in irons as a madman and
continue the voyage with no better pilot than Don Luis. She deigned
to unbend a little and even to smile frostily at him as she asked:
'Well, friend, and what do you want of me?'

'Food and water for the crew, if it please your Excellency.'

'I have already four times refused that same demand; tell me something that I have not heard before.'

'Very well: until today I have vainly appealed to your charity, now
I appeal to your love of a bargain.'

Doña Ysabel raised her eyebrows and laughed. 'Come, this promises to be interesting. What is it you offer?'

'Your life, in exchange for a few victuals. My men cannot be made to work even with whips. They will all be dead by New Year's Day unless you feed them, and the ship left to drift up and down with the tides.'

'You rascal! Your duty is to serve me, not to curry favour with that scum.'

She watched him closely, to reassure herself that he contemplated no revenge, but he answered scornfully: 'You can count on me to keep my station and do whatever I am ordered, within reason at least.'

'In that case, you will kindly hang a couple of the ring-leaders from the yard-arm, as an example to the rest.'

'And leave myself even fewer men? I said "within reason," your Excellency. My task is to sail this ship wherever you direct, but I must have a crew.'

She sent for the Purser, whom she instructed to fetch two small jars of olive-oil and have them taken forward under guard. Then she told Pedro Fernandez: 'Henceforth you may eat with the sailors whom you love so dearly: I cannot afford to feed pilot and crew as well.'

The next day, while the griddle-cakes were cooking on the ashes of the galley-fire, the junta played a game called 'Let's all be cooks together.'

'Who'll be the cook?' began Juarez.

'We'll all be cooks together!' the others replied in chorus.

'But I dispose,' said he. 'Yesterday Jaume fobbed us off with a meagre Majorcan bread-soup, though I was hungrier than Our Saviour on the mountain-top. Today it'll be preparation-stew, such as Cathedral canons eat on Shrove Tuesday to give them a good shove through Lent. Last night I remembered to soak the chick-peas and the salted pig's face. It's Matia's turn to do the marketing: hey, take this list, and a negro with a big grape-basket! Jaume, light the fire, and fetch me two great earthenware pots—if you bring me copper or iron cauldrons, I'll lop off your ears, so help me God!'

'Since I'm to be the errand-boy,' said Matia, 'and Jaume our scullion, you must turn butler and set good wine before us.'

'With all my heart,' he replied. 'I spoke with the vintner this very morning. Off with you, laggards!'

'Here now, old cock,' said Jaume after a pause, 'are your pots, well-rinsed, and firmly set on the trivets. I bought the fuel at the breaker's yard—ship's timber that burns a salty blue—I'll blow the flames and fan them with my hat, so! Ah, here's Matia again; how the negro trembles under the weight of his basket! Quick, man, unload, we're ravenous. What luck?'

'I have done well, bullies,' answered Matia. 'Praise me! Finding no capon in the market, I chose a tender young turkey of twenty-five pounds' weight; and then had to double my other purchases to keep the proportions true. But no matter; we can now invite Don Andrés to join our feast, if he'll eat with common soldiers.'

'I am honoured, gentlemen,' said I. 'But do not let me stand idle. Let's all be cooks together!'

'Then you may provide the afterclap,' Juarez told me. 'A little marzipan of Sicily with candied cherries. Meanwhile stand over the flesh-pot and remove the scum with this ladle. Hey, lads, is that turkey not yet gutted? . . . Look alive, now stuff it with chestnuts, bread, and its own liver! So, so! I begin with the beans and the pig's face. Into the left-hand pot with them.'

'Here comes the turkey to keep them company,' said Matia. 'It's as fat as the King of France's daughter. And four fine steaks.'

'And a slab of green bacon,' Jaume chimed in, 'with a head of garlic and two little Chile peppers. Don Andrés, your ladle! We'll let the pot boil at a wallop for as long as you might say a Credo, a Paternoster and a *Salve, Regina*; then it must simmer with a gentle heat, well-stirred, for a matter of five hours. But, Lord, I had nearly forgotten the red sausage! Come, lads, a game of pontoon while we wait! The winner disposes at tomorrow's banquet.'

'How time flies!' said I, pointing aloft. 'It's past noon already.'

'So late, my lucky lads?' cried Juarez. 'Hurry the vegetables! Here are turnips, carrots, cabbages, celery, hare's ear and red amaranths. Scrape, scrape, cut, cut! Jaume, throw them into this colander and rinse them in the stream!'

'At your orders, my Lord Chief Butler! Meanwhile, Matia, you prince of all adulterers, chop me this garlic and slice these onions, and weep copiously for your sins. A few sweet potatoes would not come amiss, nor a generous shield of pumpkin.'

'Here's our right-hand pot bubbling,' said Matia. 'No, it's too full! Jaume, lad, fling away half the water! Is there salt? Now cast in the vegetables in due order of precedence: first my Lord Garlic and my

Lady Onion, then the good knights Sir Carrot and Sir Turnip, then Dame Cabbage and the rest—the valet Lettuce can wait till the last.'

'With your permission,' I ventured courteously, 'let me add two sharp-tasting Ronda apples, thinly sliced, also a touch of saffron. And what say you, Juarez, to a sprig of rosemary?'

'No, never: keep your rosemary for the Devil's funeral! But I'll thank you to remember the cuckold's friend, Goodwife Parsley. Stay: bruise her in the mortar first!'

Both pots were kept well-stirred and their seething contents frequently tasted from the ladle. While Juarez saw to the wine, which was the very best Malaga, the rest of us took hold of a huge, boat-shaped silver dish, ready warmed and, having strained the vegetables dry, spread them over it. We then laid the turkey amidships; the pig's face on a coil of sausages in the bows; the beefsteak and bacon in the stern. Lord, how the junta ate and drank, sniffing the savoury steam with widened nostrils! The mouldy, bitter griddle-cakes, set reeking before them in a breastplate, were transubstantiated; and so was the nauseous water in the pannikins at their sides.

When they had done, I said: 'Why, gentlemen, I almost forgot the afterclap,' and rose to fetch it from my cabin. To their amazement I returned with marzipan of Sicily, as I had been ordered to do, cut each a generous slice, and took my leave quickly to avoid being questioned or thanked.

The gift was *tutao* cake from Santa Cristina which I had hitherto kept securely locked in Miguel Llano's sea-chest. My string of brass buttons had bought me half a hundredweight of that hearty confection. One-third of it I now set aside for charity, and another third I kept for myself. The remainder I presented to Pedro Fernandez, who was loth to accept it, until I told him severely: 'This is for the Chief Pilot, on whose health our lives depend, not for one Pedro Fernandez, a shiftless and talkative Portuguese.'

The soldiers and settlers complained no less than the crew; though they had little to do but keep alive. When Jaume brought up their morning's ration of water, Sergeant Andrada supervised its distribution with drawn sword; and the Chief Pilot likewise stood by when the sailors' ration was drawn.

On the day after the Governeress had doled out the oil, Myn went below, an empty pitcher on his shoulder, and found Sergeant Andrada and the Chief Pilot waiting for Jaume to unlock the door that gave access to the water. The Sergeant was grumbling that he would gladly exchange this life for a death sentence in a Christian dungeon, where at least he might die with his thirst quenched, his stomach full, and a priest to give him absolution; or even for a bench in a Turkish galley, where he could still cherish hope of rescue or ransom. He interrupted his lament to ask Myn why he had brought so large a pitcher. 'Oh,' said he, 'Myn often comes here to draw water for to wash my Lady's linen; old Jaume he doesn't like it, yet obey he must or Myn will use his axe, like as he chopped off the Ensign's head.'

'So she washes her soiled shifts in our life's blood!' cried Andrada. 'Can such things be?'

No sooner had Jaume appeared than the Chief Pilot snatched the key from him and went straight to the Great Cabin, where the officers were waiting for breakfast to be served.

'Pray pardon me if I disturb you,' he said to Doña Ysabel, 'but you would do well to speak sharply to your maids. They have sent the negro below to draw water for your laundering. Since he threatened the water-steward with his axe, I took away the key to prevent bloodshed.'

'Myn is obeying my orders, not the maids'. Do you think that I intend to rot good clothes by soaking them in brine, or to wear foul linen? The pitcher must be filled at once, and let there be no more argument!'

He checked his rising rage. 'I should have thought that your Excellency would be a deal more sparing of water.'

'Cannot I do as I please with my own property?' she screamed at him.

'You will recall the benediction which Our Saviour conferred upon a cup of cold water given in His name. . . .'

Don Diego measured a cupful from the jug standing on the table and tossed it in his face. 'May His benediction fall upon me,' he jeered.

Wiping the drops from his eyes and leaving God to avenge the blasphemy, Pedro Fernandez continued: 'Already some of the soldiers complain that you wash your clothes in their life's blood.'

'And do you uphold them in this?' she asked, gripping the table-edge and narrowing her eyes.

'Indeed, no! I am still expecting you to display righteous anger.'

'Well, you had better tell them that you have been mistaken. Have you more to say?'

'I could say much, were I not the last man in the world to sit in judgement on your Excellency. But let me warn you that starving men have been known to help themselves.'

'I thank you for that warning, at least. Here, hand me the key! And, Myn, go to the Purser and ask him for the key of the store-room. In future, I'll wear both on my girdle.'

'The men are still waiting for water.'

'They would have received it by now, had you not come here with your maundering insolence. Let them wait until I have breakfasted.'

News of this interview soon spread through the ship. Sergeant Andrada sought out Pedro Fernandez, and asked: 'What shall we do with this Jezebel? My men are all for overpowering the guard and breaking into the aftercastle to seize her hoard of food. I can't control them much longer. Since they finished my pig for me, weeks ago it seems, three children have died of hunger, and the corpses that we throw to the sharks all lack their livers and kidneys—the Colonel's negro, for one, knows how to look after himself.'

Pedro Fernandez, going again to the Great Cabin after dinner, found the Governeress alone. He went up to her without ceremony. 'I am aware, sweetheart,' he said with bitter irony, 'that you intend to goad me into rebellion. You are ashamed of what we did together, and my presence is an odious reminder of your mismating. I am also aware that you lied about that message from my brother-in-law; and that you are in child by me, may God forgive us both!'

She rose from her chair and opened her mouth as if to scream, but he thrust her down by the shoulders, and said: 'Hear me out! Your sister on her death-bed entrusted a sealed letter to one of the ship's company—but whether to a soldier or a sailor, I cannot say. I am told that it contains a circumstantial account of two murders which you inspired, and of other crimes not less discreditable. This letter will be handed to me in your presence a week after we reach Manila, but if I am no longer alive, it will be delivered to the Governor-General, with a request that your brothers be acquainted with the contents.'

She stared up at him inscrutably, as he continued: 'Doña Mariana planned this to ensure our safe arrival in the Philippines. She knew that otherwise your brother Diego's knife, sharpened by you, would soon stick between my shoulder-blades, and that the ship must then be written off as lost. When I receive this letter, I shall make no use of it but pass it to you unread.'

'Cunningly contrived by Mariana,' she replied softly. 'Well, I own that I did not always treat her as a sister should, and this is her revenge. Now I shall have to search the whole vessel for the letter, and when it is found, hang and quarter you for conspiracy.'

'As you please, woman, though were I set in your place, I should neither reveal its existence to your brothers, nor provoke the men by hanging their only pilot. You believe that the forecastle is without arms, but you are mistaken: when you had the arquebuses taken aft, twenty-five were kept back, with ten rounds apiece—more than enough to account for you and your supporters.'

'You have thought it out craftily! A pity that you were born in the gutter. As a nobleman you would have risen high in the service. Very well, I concede you this trick, and to prove that I'm an honest loser, I'll even see what food can be procured to keep your crew on their feet. But soon the flower of the cards will be in my hands, and then you'll repent this day's work. I wonder whether your wife still lives; I sincerely hope that she does not. I should then have adultery on my conscience, a sin I have always been at pains to avoid.'

'It is unlucky for you,' he growled, choking with rage, 'that I am not a nobleman, for chivalry would then restrain me from doing what I do now!' He gripped and shook her savagely until the teeth rattled in her head; then stood glaring down at her.

'I deserved that,' she said in a small, conciliatory voice. 'I have been cruel to you, Pedro Fernandez, but there's a Devil in my bosom. I heartily wish you would beat him clean out of me with a rawhide whip.'

'I can well believe that,' he replied, loosening his hold on her, 'but you must learn to be content with the silent flagellations of your conscience.'

New Year's Day found us in fourteen degrees North, which is almost the latitude of Manila, and the wind being easterly, we ran due west at a good rate, the mast and yards holding staunchly. Pedro Fernandez confided in me that he hoped soon to sight the large island of Guam, about a hundred leagues west of the Philippines, which is separated from another, named Serpana, by a channel ten leagues long. On the 3rd of January, to his great relief, we came upon these very islands and sailed between them, on the Guam side, following in the track of Magellan, who had discovered this channel seventy-five years before. The land was low and well wooded.

A large number of sea-going canoes shot out from a cove to welcome us. Unnerved by eager expectation of food, a sailor who was reefing the foresail lost his hold and fell into the sea, and his comrades could not find a single rope of sufficient length to throw to his rescue. But Myn knew of one: it was stretched across the poop and had the Barretos' washing tied upon it. He had the good sense to fling one end of the rope over the taffrail, just as the unfortunate sailor rose gasping to the surface in our wake. He caught it and was hauled to safety, God be praised! Then because it was Myn, not one of the crew, who had given Doña Ysabel's shifts and Don Diego's shirts a ducking in sea-water, he earned a slight reprimand only.

The canoes came closer. They were double-ended, so that the crews could advance or retreat without having to turn them broadside on to an enemy. Magellan had called this group *Las Islas de las Latinas* ('The Islands of the Lateen Sails'), but his crew *Las Islas de los Ladrones* ('The Islands of the Thieves') and the name sticks. The Ladrones were a lusty-looking race, reasonably fair and well-featured, though with lank, black hair and narrow, retreating brows. Knowing well what to expect from a galleon, they came so eagerly in search of gifts that several canoes collided; the occupants were flung into the water but righted their craft with ease and clambered merrily aboard again. We lay to, but did not drop anchor.

They brought coconuts, bananas, water, baskets of rice and some very large fish, crying *charume*, which means 'Friends' and *herrequepe*, which means 'Give us iron!' Never in my life have I seen vendors so eager to sell, or emptors so eager to buy: these islanders run mad after iron, which they value more than gold, and our poor fellows were so distraught with thirst that they would have bound themselves into a ten years' slavery for a gill or two of water. But Sergeant Andrada and the Boatswain's mate, having consulted together, forbade any man to cheapen the value of iron by accepting too little in return, and made arrangements to buy and sell in bulk. They bargained with the leader of the Ladrones, who came aboard with an escort. It was agreed to set two hundredweight of victuals against every pound of iron, whether it were hammers, chains, spade-heads, keys, bolts, hinges or pieces of broken armour; but Doña Ysabel sent the Purser to see that nothing was sold except the property of the men, and he removed from the heap on deck more than fifteen pounds' weight—the barrel of an arquebus that had exploded, hoops from water-casks long since burned, and parts of the ship's gear.

The Chieftain took this in very bad part, calling Don Gaspar a *ladrón*, and threatening violence. The affair would have ended badly, had not Matia brought out his pack of needles, scissors and razors, and thrown half of them into the common stock. These goods were reckoned at three times the value of their weight; so that our suffering people were given a new hold on life by the abundance of food purchased.

We of the afterguard made our own bargains and revelled in the taste of fresh fruit and pure water; but having another wide gulf to cross before we reached the Philippines, and then a difficult passage to negotiate through the islands before reaching Manila, we would have bought more food at whatever cost, especially rice and oil of coconut, had not an accident interrupted our traffic. The Governeress, leaning over the rails, exclaimed in a fury: 'Look, Diego! Look! Do you see what that thin savage yonder holds in his hand?—a piece of cask-hoop! Tell him to restore it at once, Diego! It is my property and worth a dozen good coconuts.'

Don Diego grabbed an arquebus from a soldier, propped it against the rail, took a long aim, and fired. The ball struck the unsuspecting native in the throat and killed him, as it also killed the man behind him. Instantly the canoes darted off and we did not see them again, or any others like them.

Captain Lopez then asked leave to take the long-boat in search of water, pigs and coconuts. Doña Ysabel gave her consent; but the Chief Pilot said that, much as he desired to comply with the Governeress's wish, he lacked gear for lowering the boat.

'Let us heave it over the side by main force,' said the Captain, and when asked how it was to be got aboard again, answered: 'There is no need, it can be towed behind us.'

The Chief Pilot shook his head. 'Not through the ground swell which we shall encounter at the approaches to the Philippines; it would be swamped and sink. Once we are among the islands, we cannot do without a boat.'

Captain Lopez arguing his case angrily, he stopped his ears, and because the Governeress did not care to lose a boat worth fifty pesos or more, it remained on deck.

We were now running before the wind. The Chief Pilot had never navigated in these waters, but recollecting that the extreme easterly point of the Philippines is Cape Santo Espiritu, which lies in twelve degrees North, or thereabouts, he set a course for it.

Not to prolong the account of our sufferings, at daybreak on

Sunday, the 14th of January, we sighted a mountain peak at a great distance, and Pedro Fernandez announced that yonder lay the Philippines of which we had come in search.

'The Virgin be praised!' whispered a soldier whose skull was dried to a death's head and whose legs were thin as crutches. 'Soon I shall hear mass and seek God.'

Chapter 24

COBOS BAY

We were no longer sailing through uncharted waters and several of the ship's company claimed to know better than the Chief Pilot what course should be shaped. The most insistent was Major Moran, who once, while serving as page to the Governor-General's Lady, had accompanied her on a pleasure jaunt among these islands in a state-barge. That afternoon, when within a league of the coast, which had been hidden from us by dense rain showers, we observed a small opening running north and south. 'Why, what good fortune!' exclaimed the Major. 'That is the Strait of San Bernardino, separating the islands of Samar and Luzon. I know it as well as the sleeve of my doublet: follow the curve of the Luzon coast, and you are brought straight into Manila Bay. Nothing could be easier; there's deep water all the way until you come to the Tuley Reef, south of Fortun Islet.'

The sun had been obscured since the Friday, when the Chief Pilot had last used his cross-staff and reckoned that we were in thirteen degrees, but the wind being north-easterly, and a heavy ground swell coming from the west, he could not be certain whether we were still on our course. His intention was to navigate San Bernardino Strait, which lies in twelve and a half degrees, with the wind astern. At first he paid close attention to the Major, but as we neared the opening he saw that it measured a good deal less than a league across; whereas Juan de la Isla, who knew this coast well, had once told him that the Strait was nearly ten leagues wide, with an island set in the middle. The coastline being still shrouded in mist, he decided not to place overmuch reliance on the Major's childhood memories. If the *San Geronimo* entered the channel and became embayed, there would be no means of getting her out again in the teeth of the wind; besides, it would soon be night. He brought her on a wind, hoping to fix our position by a star, or by the next day's sun, and thus gain some notion of where we were.

The officers, enraged that we had sheered off, went in a body to Doña Ysabel, who summoned Pedro Fernandez to the Great Cabin and demanded an explanation from him. Not in the least out of countenance, he examined the Major in their presence, and trapped him into such absurd contradictions as caused Captain Lopez and Ensign Torres to laugh aloud. But Don Diego still maintained that a chief pilot who failed to make use of local knowledge deserved the strappado.

'God has been pleased to guide us thus far,' Pedro Fernandez answered warmly, 'and I doubt not that he will also bring us into Manila, unless we try His patience by needless folly. Captain Barreto, if you bore the least responsibility for the safety of this ship, you would sing in an altogether different strain.'

Doña Ysabel commanded him to silence. 'We are agreed that this is the Strait of San Bernardino,' she said, 'and you must either conform to public opinion or earn my anger.'

'Hoist me, hang me, or throw me overboard,' he replied obstinately, 'it is all one. But I refuse to steer my ship into that trap. Let the Major play at being chief pilot, if you will, and wreck us all on the nearest reef. You and your family will then take to the long-boat with all the able-bodied men, abandoning the women, children and sick to my charge; and I shall be left to perform a miracle of salvage.'

'When we get to Manila, you will answer for those words, you stinking cod-fish!' Don Diego threatened him.

'We shall none of us get there,' he said, 'unless the master of this vessel is allowed to make his own decisions!' and strode out of the room.

There was no further interference with his seamanship. When the *San Geronimo* had stood off a safe distance, sail was lowered and we passed an anxious night tossing about in the swell, battered by sudden squalls, with neither moon nor stars showing. Day broke, the wind fell light, and the land was not to be seen for mist. Everyone complained that the Chief Pilot should have taken the channel while he had the chance; now it would never be found. But presently a headland loomed dimly to the north-west, and Pedro Fernandez ordered a bonnet to be laced to the foresail. He proposed to round the headland and coast on, keeping the lead going until a clean bottom was found, when he would drop anchor, and wait for the mist to clear.

As soon as the foresail was hoisted, there came a crack and a rush: the additional weight of the bonnet had parted the robbins and the sail collapsed like a tent on the living skeletons who were handling it. Crawling from beneath, they swore that, for all they cared, it might lie and rot for ever where it had fallen. But the Boatswain warned them that we would drift on the reefs unless they made haste; so they groaningly re-bent it, securing it to the yard with new robbins; but these also parted, and down it fell once more. Damian's rope-end and most blasphemous curses were needed to set it a third time.

When I looked aloft, my heart sank. The ship, kept head-on to the wind all night, had laboured heavily: and I saw that nearly all the rigging had carried away, but especially the running rigging of the foremast, and only a single shroud remained to support it on either side. 'Don't eye that mast, Don Andrés,' said Jaume at my elbow, 'for God's sake don't eye it, nod at it, or breathe on it—lest it go by the board!'

Yet it was a good spar and did not give way. In the meantime, an angry and excited babble arose both fore and aft. Some took the reefs for those of Catanduanes Island, to the north of San Bernardino, where many a good vessel had foundered; they said that the islanders line the rocks to shoot at any man who seeks to swim ashore, and will stick him as full of arrows as a porcupine has quills. Others held that we were caught between those reefs and Luzon, and would never get clear again. But the Major, to knit up his tattered reputation as a geographer, swore that we had missed the channel, which lay astern, and that the ship should immediately be put about at all hazards.

Everyone feared that we should soon have to swim for our lives, and Don Diego, running up from below, struck at the mizzen-mast with an axe, intending to assure himself of support while in the water. 'Avast there, your lordship!' cried Damian in horror. Pedro Fernandez wrested the axe from him and bore it off to the Great Cabin in evidence against Don Diego; for it has always been the law at sea that the master of a vessel must strike the first three blows at any mast that is to be jettisoned, and that the punishment for whoever dares anticipate him is death by hanging.

The Governeress had dressed herself hurriedly in mourning clothes and seemed to be making her peace with God before the end came: her eyes turned to Heaven, and a book of devotions in her hand, she was heaving deep sighs, calling piously on all the Saints in turn. Before Pedro Fernandez could begin his denunciation, Don Diego stole up softly from behind; dagger in hand. By great good fortune, Captain Lopez was able to disarm him, saying sternly: 'If the Chief Pilot can save us, it would be folly to murder him. If he cannot, the folly would be greater still: consider, my lord, you would die with blood on your hands and burn for ever!'

'This madman was about to dismast us, your Excellency,' shouted Pedro Fernandez.

Don Diego yelled, cursed, and threatened dire vengeance, but the Captain told him: 'My lord, do not quit this cabin without leave from the Chief Pilot or, by God, you will find this dagger planted where it will cause you inconvenience!'

Doña Ysabel seemed altogether unconcerned with what went on in her presence. She was deep in the *De profundis clamavi*, which she repeated with fervour in a steady voice.

Pedro Fernandez returned on deck, where everyone crowded around him, demanding to know where we were—as though the name of the headland were written on it in enigmatic letters which only he could read. Major Moran was loudest in his enquiries, but Don Luis dealt him a thrust in the groin with his knee, and said that an evil spirit must have possessed him to decoy us to our deaths.

At last Doña Ysabel appeared on the quarter-deck. 'Well, Pilot,' she asked calmly, 'what have you to plead in your defence?'

'Is there a charge preferred against me?'

'Do not answer me back! Where are we?'

'You know well that this is my first voyage in these waters, and since I do not dabble in witchcraft, I cannot tell where we are.'

'Yet you signed on as a skilled pilot! Why not consult your charts and instruments?'

'I own no chart of the East Indies, and you can see for yourself that the coast is befogged and the sky too heavily overcast for me to take the sun. However, if you will restrain your brother from either knifing me or wrecking the ship, God may yet grant us a reprieve.'

He ordered two sailors to secure the foremast with a couple of backstays, but they were not to cut up our anchor-cable for that purpose—the mizzen-stay would serve, if nothing else could be found. Another was to stand by the anchor, ready to let go as soon as soundings were struck. All three turned their backs on him, muttered indecencies and shambled away.

It is not given to sinful man to know at what moment God will grant or withhold His mercy: we rounded the headland, a breeze sprang up, the masts held, and suddenly our bows were turned straight into a snug bay which we entered at speed, though reefs lay to either side!

Three natives in a canoe came out to reconnoitre and, without hailing us, manoeuvred to windward. The crew cheered them feebly, and the noise brought the Major to the taffrail. 'Come, my lord,' cried the Chief Pilot, 'since you know the islands well, address those men in their own language and ask them to show us an anchorage!'

The Major shouted something, the canoe came alongside and two of its occupants scrambled aboard. One exclaimed, with grinning friendliness: '*Duilacapaylat? Juatxir, bulis?**' The other reproved him, and said to us in halting Castilian: 'You are Spaniards. God bless King Philip! I speak good Spanish of Manila; he only three words of English, learned long ago from Captain Don Tomás Candish. He piloted Don Tomás's ship between these islands, by God, and received rich gifts. He hopes to fall in once again with Don Tomás.'

'What land is this?' asked Captain Lopez.

'Yonder is the Cape of Espiritu Santo; and this, by God, is Cobos Bay. Bound for Manila, yes? You are dead on your course, gentlemen.'

'Show us the anchorage,' said the Chief Pilot.

He shouted to the man in the canoe, who thereupon paddled ahead as our guide. We dropped anchor in the middle of the Bay, in fourteen fathoms. This miracle took place at nine o'clock on Monday, the 15th of January, 1596.

'Who holds Manila now?' we anxiously asked our new friend.

'Don Luis Perez de las Marinas is the present Governor, by God. Don Gomez, his father, was lately murdered on an expedition to the Moluccas.'

This answer gave us hearty relief. We had heard rumours in Peru that Taycosama, the Emperor of Japan, who claimed the vassalage of the Philippines, was preparing a great fleet to attack the city; but our friend now told us that amicable relations had been re-established, and that the Emperor had even given permission for four Franciscan friars to preach the gospel in his realm.

The English-speaking pilot then asked for news of Captain Candish, and was grieved to hear that he had died in the Island of Ascension a year or two previously.

The inhabitants of Cobos Bay are dusky-coloured, with long, black hair, not very tall and much tattooed; I saw no sign of a beard even on

**Do ye lack a pilot? What cheer, bullies?*

the elder men. They confess Christ—or, at least, we saw a cross erected on a mound near their village—and also acknowledge the suzerainty of the King of Castile, though I did not think to enquire whether they either pay him tribute or enjoy his protection. Their headman, carrying a white wand of office, came out in a canoe followed by twenty others well laden with food. Like all persons of importance in the neighbourhood, he wore large golden ear-rings, ivory bangles, anklets of gilded bronze (which our soldiers at first mistook for gold) and a long, collarless tunic, of a stiff native cloth called medriñaque, reaching to his calves.

After genuflecting before the Virgin at the mainmast, and bidding us welcome, he let us know that he was a civilized person, who knew the value of money and would not be satisfied with mere promises in payment for his wares. A regular market was soon set up amidships at which he fixed the prices: a pig cost two or three reals, according to its weight, a fowl upwards of six maravedis. Any man who had a knife or dagger to sell might reckon it at a peso, and glass beads were worth twice their weight in silver. Matia came to the rescue of the troops with the remaining half of his venture, which earned him great praise; and I was able to provide for the crew, as well as for myself, by selling a parcel of beads bought at the auction of Miguel Llano's effects. Thereafter both sailors and soldiers ransacked their boxes, and all contributed to the common fund whatever they had left of value.

Besides pigs, fowl and fish, we bought coconuts, bananas, sugar-cane, paw-paws, rice, yams, water in bamboo joints and faggots for the galley-fires, which were not allowed to go out all that day and night; nor for the next two days, either, being the Vigil and Feast of Saint Anthony who had protected us so well. 'Let's all be cooks together' was played in earnest now, and without pause. Men and women who not long since would have strangled one another for the sake of a sour fragment of coconut-meat were courtesy itself again: with 'Pray sample my stew, Gossip!' or 'Comrade, do me the honour of accepting a little of this prime roast!' Nobody troubled to sleep, and had there been thirty hours in the day and night, instead of a mere twenty-four, I well believe that all of them would have been devoted to eating.

Mouths being sweetened and bellies filled, our people were happier than can be described, and a quantity of palm-wine which they had bought inspired in them an almost pentecostal gift of tongues. They toasted themselves, their generous hosts, Our Lady of Solitude and

Saint Anthony, but above all, the Chief Pilot, whom many offered to embrace, swearing that he had saved them from death a hundred times over. Though accepting their caresses, he earnestly bade them thank God, not himself, since he had steered a blind course from the Friday to the Monday.

A starving man is wise to eat only a little at a time, gradually increasing the load in his belly, until it is re-accustomed to labour; but our people would never learn moderation. When cautioned to restrain himself, one man sighed: 'Ah, that would be a glorious end, to die of a surfeit of roast pork!' Before we sailed on, I added three more crosses to my ledger. But this fat time lasted only a day or two longer, our funds being then nearly expended.

The Chief Pilot hoped to have the ship re-victualled and re-rigged within a fortnight, but on the morning of the 22nd of January the wind backed to the north-west, and blew hard, with heavy seas following the gusts. He warned Doña Ysabel that our single cable could not be trusted to keep us from drifting among the rocks and mangrove swamps. It would be prudent, he said, to take off the artillery and munitions, which were His Majesty's property, for storage in the village under the headman's protection; also the women and children had better be disembarked, as well as her own valuables.

'It is hardly worth the trouble,' she answered ingenuously. 'We are staying here for only a few days more, are we not?'

'I cannot warrant our safety for another hour—look how that cable strains!'

'Oh, away with you and your perpetual fears! The rope's strong enough.'

He went into the Chart-room, but was soon back again. 'I have composed a brief statement, and will be obliged if your Excellency signs it,' he said. 'It is a record that, in Cobos Bay, on the 22nd of January, the wind being north-westerly, I asked leave of you to remove Crown property from the *San Geronimo* galleon, which was in peril of running aground, and that you refused my request. I must protect myself against charges that may later be levelled against me. Here is pen and ink.'

She asked, in sudden alarm: 'Are we lost, then? Is there no way of saving the ship?'

'If I take a bold risk, I might be able to berth her safely behind the point a couple of musket-shots to westward. But why not accept my

advice? It would be a pity to lose your wardrobe, jewels and silver, to
say nothing of your life.'

'Put your proposal in writing, and I'll consider it.'

He did so hurriedly, because the gale was rising and the cable was
taut as a fiddle-string. She summoned a council of officers and read
them the document, but he was not invited to attend. Presently Myn
came to him with a brief and absurd order: 'The Chief Pilot is required to resume his voyage before nightfall.'

The wind blew straight down the Bay out of which she expected
him to take the *San Geronimo*, and not only had no water nor victuals
been taken aboard, but our rigging was still in the same dismal condition as when we had arrived.

His curt reply, 'This is impossible,' she countered with a threat that
she would have him hanged unless he obeyed within the hour.

He approached Captain Lopez, the only officer left in whom he
could hope to find even a grain of wit, and 'My lord,' he asked, 'why, or
for whose benefit, have I been told to wreck the ship and drown
us all?'

The other shook his head gloomily. 'They seem one and all bent
on their own destruction. Yet why should we be involved in it? Hark
ye, if you'll defy Doña Ysabel, I engage to protect you against her
brothers. You are the master of this ship, and her writ as Governeress
of the Isles of Solomon does not run in the Philippines.'

'Nevertheless, she commands the expedition.'

Captain Lopez considered for a moment. 'Friend Pedro,' he said,
'leave this to me. You are by far too honest a man to cope with her.'
Then he went to the Boatswain and his mate, and explained how
matters stood. At his suggestion, the entire crew signed a memorial
to the effect that they refused to sail in an unprovisioned ship; and
that since they were now going hungry again for lack of money or
trade-goods, the Governeress must consent to give them either rations,
an advance of pay, or permission to forage ashore.

This document they brought to Pedro Fernandez, and asked him to
present it to Doña Ysabel; which he did.

'How can I give them food?' she screamed. 'I have barely enough
for my own family. Nor can I find them money, until I have pledged
my jewels in Manila; and were I to send them ashore on forage, not
one of them would return.'

'Very well,' said he, 'I trust that you and your brothers are stout
swimmers.'

'Silence, ass! Weigh anchor at once, or hang!'

'At your Excellency's orders.'

I had gone to my cabin to prepare myself for death, when I heard the capstan-chant raised and hoarse orders shouted, followed by a sudden yell of fear. As I knelt in prayer, I was suddenly rapt out of myself, and enchanted by a strange waking vision of my sweet Protectress, the Macarena of Seville. With stars in her hair and a shining lily in her hand, she entered the wide bull-ring, strewn with sand, in which I found myself. Around me rose seats in lofty tiers, thronged by a ghastly company of spectators, the ravaged corpses of men long drowned! A trumpet sounded, the stable door opened, and a white bull ran out with a roar like the noise of waves dashed against a reef. He stood pawing the ground for a while, then made straight for me, and in a moment I should have been transfixed upon his cruel horns and tossed into the air; but, stepping swiftly between, my Protectress drew him off with a twitch of her sky-blue mantle.

'Olé, olé!' cried the spectators, leaping from their seats and dancing grotesquely, as the bull went cantering away in search of other victims.

'The danger is passed, my child!' she said with a pleasant smile. And with that she vanished.

Rising from my knees in confusion, I found that I was not deceived. With great audacity and skill Pedro Fernandez had club-hauled the ship, though in almost no sea-room; that is to say, he tacked by letting go the lee-anchor when head to wind, brought the cable aft as the ship filled on the other tack; then cut the cable and she clawed off shore. At once it became clear even to the Governeress that we could not hope to make the open sea against such a gale. She ordered him to drop anchor again, but being now without one he could not obey; so he steered for the shelter he had in mind. As we luffed close round the point, the foresheet parted, outside the fairhead, and all seemed lost. But the ship carried her way until her forefoot was close to the rock, when the valiant Damian leaped overboard with a line and swam through the raging seas to the shore, where a dozen or more natives ran to his aid. The Chief Pilot bent a hawser to the line, which was hauled ashore; and then they towed us round under the lee of the point, where they made fast the hawser to a convenient palm-tree. The *San Geronimo* was safely moored head to wind.

No sooner had this dangerous manoeuvre been performed, than the crew renewed their demands. Standing below the quarter-deck, they shouted in unison: 'Either feed us, or pay us off!'

The Governeress flew into a hysterical passion. 'Go ashore at once, Major; take horse to Manila and fetch me back a magistrate and a frigate full of troops to suppress this mutiny!' The Major would have been glad enough to depart on this ludicrous mission, if only to escape from her authority, but Don Diego offered to spare him the trouble by spitting a couple of sailors on his sword, which would soon silence the rest.

Doña Ysabel then withdrew the order and, her mood changing, she mildly informed Pedro Fernandez that we might as well take advantage of our enforced stay at Cobos: if he saw to the repair of the rigging, she would consent to defray the expenses of victualling. He gladly agreed, and persuaded the natives to twist him a spare anchor-cable of coconut-fibre, also several smaller ropes with which he secured the foremast and mainmast; but, having no money to pay them, and knowing that Doña Ysabel would not contribute a maravedi, he borrowed the sixty pesos required from Captain Lopez, and gave his astrolabe, cross-staff, backstaff and pocket-dial in pledge. The Governeress, for her part, bespoke three weeks' provisions from the headman, laying down a few pesos as caution-money; the remainder would be added, she said, when he had fulfilled the order.

She then issued a proclamation, with the Royal Standard displayed and a drum beating, that nobody was to quit the ship on pain of death; but it so happened that the Major had already given old Miguel Geronimo permission to go ashore and buy food for a sick child. Later Don Luis saw Miguel returning in a canoe, and ran to tell his sister, who grew so hot that the frightened Major would not admit to having granted any shore-leave without reference to her. He kept silent, even when she sent him on deck to make arrangements for an immediate strappado.

The Boatswain saw him gazing at the mainmast, which had long been lightened of its topsail, and muttering to himself. 'Has your lordship lost anything?' he asked derisively.

'No, not at all, my good fellow. But where is that piece of timber to which the topsail used to be attached?'

'Do you mean the mast, my lord?'

'No, no! The beam that stretched across high up.'

'Ah,' said Don Marcos. 'If you need that yard, you must go to the Chief Pilot: he's hidden it away in the hold for fear of thieves. Why would your lordship be requiring it?'

'. . . You are laughing at me, blockhead, but I won't be trifled with. These are the Governeress's orders.'

'And have you told her who gave Miguel Geronimo shore-leave?' asked Don Marcos with a disconcerting stare.

'I gave him no such thing.'

'Two or three honest men were present.'

'Enough of this, scoundrel! Replace that yard without delay, or I'll run you through!'

'I take my orders from the Chief Pilot, not from any soldier, whatever his rank.'

'But this comes from the Governeress, I tell you!'

'Then pray advise her to think again. There's not a man here with strength to waste on a strappado. Now, if she were to present us with a jar of wine and a jar of oil, and a sackful of flour, and a flitch or two of bacon from her larder . . .'

'Impudence! How do you know what the Governeress keeps under lock and key?'

'One of her maids hawks about a list of provisions; but asks too high a price. . . . Now, if she were to feed us well, we'd willingly hoist every man of the afterguard, your lordship not excepted.'

'Do you refuse to obey me, villain?'

'Hoist here, flog there—it's unreasonable! And the men once again on the knife-edge of starvation!'

Meanwhile the execution party had arrived, headed by Ensign Torres, who was looking uncommonly pale and thin because of a bad attack of the flux. Behind him marched the drummer, dressed in the finery which he had taken from the Colonel. The Colonel had been short and fat, and the drummer was tall and emaciated, so the clothes were not the best of fits, and the drum was fantastically tricked out with ribbons. Then came the prisoner, between two hollow-cheeked halberdiers who, disgusted with their shameful duty, nudged him to leap for liberty into the waves.

'No tragedy without its comic interludes!' sighed I to myself.

The Boatswain sought out the Chief Pilot who, after warning him not to reeve any tackle unless on orders from himself, confronted Doña Ysabel with the facts of the case.

'Your Excellency,' he said. 'I fear for your reputation in Manila. What if the news gets about that you maimed an old man who had already lost all his wealth, and four of his seven children, in your service—an old man, whose one crime was to go ashore, with leave from the Major, in search of a little food for the survivors?'

'From the Major? Is that true, or are you playing another of your tricks?'

'I leave tricks and lies to noblewomen,' he answered bitterly.

'Wait, until we are in Manila, my wharf-rat! I'll set the terriers on you.'

'I am content to wait. Meanwhile, what of this strappado?'

'The man disobeyed my orders and must take his punishment.'

'But what punishment awaits those who disobey the laws of God?'

For some reason, this simple question penetrated her defences. Without warning she burst into tears and he, knowing the profound misery of her heart, was tempted to take her in his arms for comfort; so strong a spell did her beauty still exert upon him. Restraining himself with difficulty, he said in broken tones: 'Doña Ysabel, I pity you with all my soul.'

She replied, sobbing: 'Tell the Major to set the man free. I only wanted to frighten the sailors. Now, get out of my sight, before I do you an injury!'

It is my belief that she was not yet fallen out of love with Pedro Fernandez; otherwise she could never have treated him so barbarously.

Chapter 25

THE LAST HUNDRED LEAGUES

The headman of Cobos delivered little more than a third part of the provisions bespoken and then, shrewdly guessing that Doña Ysabel intended to bilk him, demanded a further advance of money. She was sick these days and kept her bed, but told Elvira that she had never been so disgraced in all her life and that the headman should be sent to the Devil. On Tuesday, therefore, the 29th of January, having recovered our anchor and cable, we set sail at daybreak without having shipped so much as another coconut; what had been brought had been our subsistence during this past week but could not last us out the month.

By five in the afternoon we were already through the Strait of San Bernardino and had left the islet of that name well astern. About midnight, near Capul, we met with a strong cross-sea, which twirled the ship giddily around, like a stick in a mill-stream; yet in the end she answered her helm soberly enough and at dawn a small fleet of baranguays that put out from a port named Nivalon, laden with pigs, fowl, wine and fruit, found us none the worse for our adventure. The crew being penniless, the soldiers in much the same state, and not a knife nor a bead remaining among them all, trade was extremely dull; though the Governeress picked up a few bargains for the Great Cabin. The natives left us in disgust, shouting insults; and Don Diego, since we were now in Spanish waters, was persuaded not to shoot at them.

Pedro Fernandez needed a pilot to guide us through the tortuous channels of this archipelago, much dreaded for their rocks, shoals, and currents; but Doña Ysabel refused to take on more hands at this stage of the journey. Forced to navigate by guess, hazard and the grace of God, he steered the *San Geronimo* through dangers that would have made us gasp, had we been forewarned of them. We kept the

large islands of Ticao, Burias and Marinduque well to port, hugging
the Luzon coast; and on the first day of February reached Galban, a
township only fifteen leagues from Manila by land, if one cuts across
the peninsula, though twice that distance by sea. Here Don Diego and
Don Luis were given leave to go ashore in the long-boat to buy
provisions, not a scrap being now left of what had been bought at
Cobos. The boat was readily hoisted out with the new falls rove by the
Chief Pilot and, at the Governeress's desire, they took with them
Captain Lopez, Ensign Torres, two negroes and three common
soldiers. While the party were descending the Jacob's ladder, Damian
remarked: 'Away they go, and good riddance to them! I'll wager my
life they won't bring back any food. They'll desert the ship and leave
us to starve.'

Don Diego overheard this and, climbing grimly aboard again, drew
his sword and pursued Damian across the deck. He fled up the
mizzen-shrouds and took refuge at the masthead, whereupon Don
Diego returned to the boat, seized an arquebus, primed it and handed
it to Don Luis. 'There's your bird, brother,' he said.

The shot grazed Damian's forearm and cut down the pendant,
which fell into the sea; but he had the wit to cry and groan as though
the wound were mortal. The long-boat then went off, and Damian
slid slowly down, winking at us in reassurance.

He was proved right in his surmise: they did not come back and,
at dusk, Doña Ysabel gave orders to sail without them. That night the
ship seemed so deeply embayed among the islands that we despaired
of finding a way out. Having now no boat left—the skiff had been
swamped and sunk in Cobos Bay—and, standing in desperate need of
a pilot, we hailed several baranguays from which men were fishing
by the light of torches. But at sight of us they all ran for shelter, this
not being the season for galleons to arrive from New Spain; the
Governor-General had issued a warning that they were to take cover
whenever a suspicious sail came in view, lest it might be an English or
Dutch privateer. We proceeded slowly and anxiously by moonlight
through calm water, with little wind in our sails; the shores pressed
upon us more and more closely, until a stone might have been tossed
across the channel. As the first signs of dawn appeared, the fairway
suddenly widened, the breeze freshened, and soon, to our delight, we
were off Cape Azufre in the Gulf of Banbon, having passed between
Luzon and the islet of Maricaba—a course which, it seems, no royal
ship had ever before taken by night, unless to be wrecked for her
temerity.

Since the Governeress had boarded up the door between the Chart-room and the Great Cabin, which she forbade Pedro Fernandez to enter on whatever pretext, he sent me to her as his go-between. I was to announce that if she refused to sell him food against his pledge to pay her in Manila, he would not hold himself responsible for the consequences: the troops, who were now in a worse condition even than when we had sighted the Cape of Santo Espiritu, might mutiny and break into her store-room.

'My good Andrés,' she said, 'ask the Chief Pilot whether he has lost forty thousand pesos on this expedition, as I have!'

'But the men, your Excellency?'

'The soldiers do no work and need not eat; for the sailors I care nothing.' She did not, however, go so far as to reveal what must have been uppermost in her mind: that the smaller the ship's company when we reached port, the less money would she need to expend.

Pancha came nobly to our rescue. She reported to Doña Ysabel that the calf had died during the night, never having recovered from an injury it sustained when the ship was buffeted about off Capul. 'I should not recommend any Christian to try that veal,' she said. 'Its guts were rotted through.'

'My poor brindle!' cried Doña Ysabel. 'And I had hoped to bring you safe to Manila!'

'What am I to do with the carrion, your Excellency?'

'What else but throw it overboard? Ah, if God had only spared me this!'

The calf, which was alive and in the best of health, was then secretly slaughtered, and the carcase thrown into the sea at the end of a line, but presently hauled aboard again. Pancha had bound us on oath not to make a stew, lest the smell might reach the Governeress's nostrils; it was therefore eaten raw. Some found this repugnant, but Jaume reminded them: 'What does not poison, fattens.'

About noon on the 4th of February, we met with two forty-oared galleys coming from Manila. We showed the Royal Standard and hailed them. The officers and crew were Filipinos to a man and the master of the leading galley, as she came alongside, told us in passable Castilian that he was taking a cargo of Chinese trade-goods to the Jesuit mission on Zebu, west of Leyte; a voyage of a hundred leagues between the islands. When Pedro Fernandez, in the King's name, asked for a pilot to steer us past the notorious Tuley Reef, they gave us one at a daily charge of three pesos, which we might pay in Manila.

Observing our famished looks, which contrasted strangely with the sparkling rings which Doña Ysabel was displaying, their purser offered to sell her some rice. She told him that his price was too high and, finding that she could not beat him down by so much as a maravedi, retired in a huff to the Great Cabin. We pleaded with him for a gift, to which he replied that the remedy lay in our hands, and that we deserved nothing if we were not men enough to pull those rings from her fingers. However, Pedro Fernandez found two good pairs of buckled shoes in his sea-chest, for each of which the Filipino paid him with a large basketful of rice. This he divided among the crew, and also gave them leave to chop up the mizzen-yard for fuel.

We then coasted along the islet of Fortun, and on the 7th of February came to the entrance of Manila Bay. Land stretched on either side of us, and we could even make out the distant smoke of the City; but the wind was north-easterly and blew dead against us. For three days and nights we tried to enter, but could not: and though we counted the hours between each flood-tide, hoping that the next would bring us within hail of Corregidor Islet, which commands the mouth of the Bay, we lost distance, rather than gained it. At last Damian said to the Chief Pilot: 'For the love of God, your honour, run the ship aground; our luck is out.'

'But, man, the coast is steep-to and the waves are high.'

'What other chance has this vile woman left us?'

I carried one last appeal to the Governeress, who replied that she had no more than two sacks of flour left and four bottles of wine, all of which she needed to buy masses for Don Alvaro's soul. She was lying, and did not care who knew it; so I refrained from contradicting her.

As I turned to go, she called me back. 'When the Chief Pilot delivers me a certain letter,' she said, 'addressed to him by my sister, the men will be fed, but not until then.'

I took Pedro Fernandez his answer, feigning ignorance of the letter. 'I would gladly give it her,' he assured me, 'to save their lives, if I could be certain that she would keep to her bargain. But I have no notion to whom Doña Mariana entrusted it—unless it were Captain Lopez, who is no longer with us.'

'In that case,' Doña Ysabel told me, when I went to her again, 'I fear I cannot oblige him.'

I miauled at her, like a hungry kitten: 'But what of me? Would you let your own secretary waste away to a ravelling?'

She flung a sheaf of papers at my head. 'Begone with you, little misery! I'm not the fool you take me to be: I know a double-dealer by his way of walking.'

There was no more to be done. Hourly we grew weaker, and I composed myself for death, not having had a bite to eat for a week but a platter of dry rice and a small piece of raw veal, and scarcely a spoonful of drink. Myn, who had been fed well enough, was sent round the ship with a fellow-servant in a brisk search for the letter; he unlocked sea-chests or broke them open with his axe, shook the straw out of palliasses, ripped up the lining of coats, slit open the soles of shoes, chuckling at the feeble protests of the owners. A reward of a jar of oil and half a sack of flour was offered for 'a treasonable letter written to the Chief Pilot, if presented to the Governeress with the seal intact.'

Nothing was found, and Doña Ysabel dared not put Pedro Fernandez to the torture until we were safely past Corregidor.

'One last effort, brave hearts,' said he to his three remaining seamen, 'and Manila is ours! We have made a voyage through uncharted seas which will be famous for many a year, and done our duty nobly by God and the King.'

With dry throats and blackened tongues they croaked back: 'To the Devil with that! The Governeress and her bloody-minded brothers will claim the lion's share of praise. We are only sailors, ragged and dying: what welcome or mercy can we expect?'

They executed his orders sullenly, with reproachful looks, or not at all. The wind blew still from the north-east. I painfully entered my own name in the death-ledger, marking the cross, but leaving a blank for the date, and wondered dully who would complete the entry.

Yet our Blessed Lady always looks pityingly upon her afflicted children and brings succour and solace in time of most distress. At dawn on the 10th of February the wind backed to the north-west, and we were able to tack slowly towards the entrance of Manila Bay, still two leagues distant. Soon after nine o'clock a baranguay was seen approaching from the direction of Corregidor, where a duty-officer is always posted to give the Governor-General early intelligence of the arrival of ships. Four Spaniards were in it, who seemed to us like four thousand angels, and a sturdy crew pulled at the oars. They hailed us and clambered aboard; it was the Duty-officer, by name Don Alonzo de Albarran, with two soldiers and the Governor-General's major-domo. Our people gave them weak hand-clasps and

tearful embraces, and tried to cheer, but could not. Doña Ysabel
came out on the quarter-deck, where the Major-domo handed her a
letter from his illustrious master, full of condolences on her mis-
fortunes, of which Don Diego and Don Luis had informed him in
detail, and high compliments on her single-minded courage and
devotion to the Royal cause.

She showed this to the Chief Pilot, remarking with satisfaction:
'You had best be careful how you behave in Manila, where I am
already famous.'

'We are not there yet,' he answered. 'God may have further troubles
in store for us. Pray excuse me: I have work to do.' He pointed at the
channel between Corregidor and The Friar, a large rock which lies
due south of it.

She invited the Major-domo into the Great Cabin, where she plied
him with wine and wrote a reply to the Governor-General.

Meanwhile, the Duty-officer gazed in horrified wonder at our people
and, seeing them so emaciated, tattered, sickly and covered with
sores, could exclaim only: 'God be praised that you have made port
at last!' Then he ventured below, despite the noisome stink that
assailed him, and saw such a scene of misery and filth as, I suppose,
was never before found in a royal ship. The between-decks might have
been a lazar-house in a city that had been sacked after a two years'
siege. Naked corpses lay putrifying in a row against the bulkhead;
half-naked scarecrows who had once been upright men and comely
women stared at him from sunken, lack-lustre eyes, and whimpered:
'Water! For the love of Christ, a drop of water and a few crumbs of
bread!' A madman raved in the stocks: 'Alas, alas, the black men have
eaten my lovely children, blood, bones and all!'

Don Alonzo retreated, in anguish of mind, murmuring: 'O God!
To think that Christians should have sunk so low!' At the sound of
loud grunts and squeals from the other side of the bulkhead, he
went into the aftercastle to discover what new horror this might be;
and found that the noise proceeded from two well-fed pigs. He called
the Purser, and asked incredulously: 'Man, what are these?'

'Pigs, if it please your honour.'

'Then my eyes do not play me false! But, in the name of mercy,
why are they not slaughtered to feed your starvelings?'

'They are the Governeress's own.'

'What the Devil! Is this a time for courtesy to pigs?' Then, with a
profound sigh, he declaimed dramatically: 'O cruel avarice which,

entering in and taking possesion of so fair a bosom, can turn a living heart to flint!'

He broke unceremoniously into the Great Cabin where Doña Ysabel, radiant with joy, was sealing the letter that she had just written. When he bowed to her, she offered him her best Malaga. 'Wine, too?' he cried aghast. 'I should have a heavy load on my conscience if I even wetted my lips at this goblet.'

'Have you fault to find with my hospitality?' she asked, puckering her brow.

Don Alonzo gazed sternly at her. 'When did your ladyship last call upon your sisters of the between-decks?' he enquired.

With more than her usual haughtiness, she replied: 'I had but one sister, who lived and died here, in the aftercastle, as befitted her quality.'

'Follow me!' he ordered harshly, and she came, with a shrug of her shoulders, not caring to cut a bad figure before the Major-domo. Don Alonzo led her down below where, at sight of her, the women pursed their cracked lips as if to spit, but the men crossed themselves in abhorrence and looked away. She stood there, dressed in jewelled clothes, her skirts lifted high to avoid soiling them. Her cheeks were plump and rosy; her delicate nose twitched in disgust. Don Alonzo snatched a bundle of rags from the arms of a dying woman: it was a child with a face like a shrivelled winter-apple, arms like cabbage stalks, and a portentously swollen stomach. Pressing it on Doña Ysabel, 'Take this, you charitable dame!' he commanded. She let out a shriek and darted off, weeping, pursued by whispered curses and laughter like the crackling of sticks.

At her order Myn slaughtered the two pigs, lighted the galley-fires, and threw the corpses into the sea; and she, with a tearful protest that the Chief Pilot had failed to inform her of her people's plight, engaged herself to dole them out wine, flour and oil forthwith. But at last we reached Corregidor on a long tack, and there our visitors left us, so she did not trouble to keep her promise.

Soon afterwards another baranguay came up, carrying the Provincial Magistrate, the Barreto brothers, and several soldiers. They brought Doña Ysabel wine, fruit, fresh bread and other dainties as a present from the Governor-General. Having learned prudence from her encounter with Don Alonzo, she was now dressed soberly enough, and told the Magistrate with a sad smile: 'Alas, your worship, hungry though I be, I must not touch these good things until the poor sufferers forward have been given their share. Their need is even greater than mine.' She found it easy to deceive him.

The Magistrate took his gifts below, where the wolfish way in which they were snatched from his servants' hands made him exclaim: 'Gentlemen, ladies, remember your manners! You are no longer in the jungle.'

I staggered from my cabin and secured for my share a small loaf and a cup of wine, but the three ship's officers to whom the navigation was now wholly abandoned had been given nothing as yet. In the privacy of the Great Cabin I found Don Diego and Don Luis carousing with their sister and helping her to empty a large hamper of bread and cold chicken. I asked Don Diego whether he would have the kindness to spare a morsel for the Chief Pilot. He would not answer, except to rally me on my appearance, with: 'Why, Fat Cheeks, you'd not cut up very well now, eh? However, I dare say you might still serve for the stock-pot, given plenty of vegetables.'

It was Pancha once again who relieved the distress of Pedro Fernandez and his companions by a timely theft from her mistress. Damian told her with emotion as he ate and drank: 'At one time you caused a deal of trouble in the ship, but I know now that you are on the side of the angels.'

'When a woman loses her looks, she must needs fall back on virtue,' Pancha answered, gazing ruefully at her shrunken body.

That night seemed endless, but with the dawn a capacious barge came alongside, laden with various cooked meats, bread, wine and vegetables, a gift sent at the Governor-General's request by Don Diego Marmolejo, the richest land-owner of the district. This time everyone received as much as he could eat.

The white-washed houses of Cavite, a port two leagues from Manila, hove in sight and we tacked towards them. Don Juan Pinao, boatswain of a royal galleon lying at anchor there, arrived in a skiff rowed by sailors in their best silks and came aboard to guide us into harbour. His men were between tears and laughter at the crazy appearance of the *San Geronimo*, and he told Pedro Fernandez: 'By the body of Bacchus! You must be the most skilful, or the luckiest, pilot the world has ever known.'

'He is both, and more!' said Don Marcos. 'His skill would not have served without extraordinary luck, nor his luck without extraordinary skill, nor either without Our Lady's help.'

The Captain of the Port stood, sword in hand, on the beach, his men drawn up smartly under arms. We made one last tack and ran in. As we dropped anchor, the Royal Standard was broken on the quay, and a resounding salvo of cannon and musketry bade us welcome. The gunner's mate and Myn touched off a couple of falcons in reply, and the veterans discharged their arquebuses.

It was the 11th of February 1596, and on that day I put EXPLICIT to my ledger. Not one of all the marriages contracted in the flagship, but had been dissolved by death. Of one hundred and twenty souls, our original complement, only twenty-five men, nine women and one child still lived; and eight more men, one woman and the child were dead within the month.

Twenty casks of water, twelve sacks of flour, four jars of oil, half a dozen pipes of wine, many sides of bacon and much other food remained in Doña Ysabel's larder: all that Belita had not been able to sell at famine prices (secretly, as though without the Governeress's consent) to the destitute ship's company. But this shameful hoard was carefully concealed from the good people of Manila, who came out in boats, bringing gifts of food and clothing for our relief. With their charitable help the sick and dying were carried to a lazar-house, while those still able to walk went to private homes, where they received much kindness. I stayed on board with the Governeress and the ship's officers.

A stream of sightseers now called to view the marvellous vessel which, as rumour had it, was despatched by the Viceroy of Peru to bring back the Queen of Sheba from the Isles of Solomon. All of them, for good luck, touched the famous cable that still kept us at anchor, and knelt in adoration before Our Lady of Solitude, still smiling tenderly from the sprung mainmast.

Chapter 26

AT MANILA

The Coastal Magistrate arriving on a courtesy visit, Doña Ysabel importuned him with complaints that all the ship's officers were guilty of treason: the Chief Pilot and the Boatswain had disobeyed her orders at Cobos, and the Boatswain's mate had publicly insulted Captain-General Barreto at Galban. Since she laid her accusations on so thick, he agreed to hold a Court in the Great Cabin without further delay, expecting her to appear as the principal witness; then, at the last moment, she retired and he could but examine them informally.

Don Marcos Marin pleaded not guilty, on the ground that the orders in question had been improperly delivered. Damian replied with a counter-charge, that he had been shot at for speaking the truth; he also denied that Don Diego ever held the rank of Captain-General. Pedro Fernandez refused to plead, and asked to be placed under arrest until a regular charge should be lodged against him.

Looking very big and thumping the table with his fists, the Magistrate said in violent tones that he marvelled how any man could hesitate to obey the orders of so pious, beautiful and afflicted a lady as Doña Ysabel.

'Your worship,' boldly answered the Boatswain, 'of her piety let God judge; her afflictions have been for the most part of her own contrivance; and when we few who survive are starved into frightful ugliness her very beauty accuses her of vile avarice and greed.'

He was sternly rebuked and told not to slander the Governeress further, unless he cared to be shut in a madhouse for the rest of his life. 'Look ye, Peruvian rascals,' said the Magistrate in conclusion, 'your countrymen are well-known for their mettlesomeness, but I charge you to remember that you are no longer in the Isles of Solomon where a man can behave as he pleases. You are come to the Philippines and subject to our penal law, with which you will be foolish to trifle.'

Yet Damian had the last word. 'Your worship,' he said, 'even a landsman can see at a glance that we are loyal subjects of King Philip: the patched and cobbled state of our ship is eloquent of duty laboriously performed, and this despite the negligence and cruelty of our betters in the aftercastle.'

For lack of evidence, he and the Boatswain were discharged with a reprimand. Pedro Fernandez, however, was marched off to Cavite gaol, where the Warden on hearing from the Duty-officer, with whom he was acquainted, that his prisoner was the most deserving of men fed him at his own table and freely supplied him with clothes, shoes and all other necessities.

As Doña Ysabel disembarked, walking queenly between two high clerics, another salute of guns greeted her. She was invited to a banquet at the town hall and in the evening conveyed by state-barge to Manila, splendidly illuminated in her honour; there the ailing Governor-General and his Lady entertained her in their mansion as though she were of royal blood.

Her position being now assured, and her reputation further enhanced by the wonderful story which Don Diego had put about, how she had brought the ship safely into port despite a disobedient pilot and a mutinous crew, only one anxiety remained: she feared that Doña Mariana's letter might be conveyed to the Governor-General and prove her undoing. With a pretence of magnanimity, she therefore obtained an order for Pedro Fernandez's release; but the Warden himself escorted him to the Convent of San Domingo in Manila, lest he should meet with an accident by the way, as happened to the luckless Captain Lopez on the Galban road.

I alone knew the whereabouts of the letter and, having recovered a little strength, I walked out from the house of my generous cousin, the Advocate Don Esteban Serrano, with whom I was lodged, and arranged a meeting between Doña Ysabel and Pedro Fernandez in the cloisters of San Domingo. I could count on Myn's attendance: he accompanied her everywhere, axe on shoulder, like a dark shadow and foil to her beauty.

The meeting was agreed for noon, and when I arrived Pedro Fernandez was composedly waiting for me. Fray Diego de Soria, the Prior and an old acquaintance, stood by his side; but Doña Ysabel came above half an hour late, which was her privilege as a noblewoman.

When civilities had been exchanged, I wasted no time and spoke up plainly: 'My lady,' said I, 'Sergeant Dimas, before he died of hunger among the Barbudos, made me promise to do him a service as soon as might be convenient after our safe landing here. Pray, Myn, lend me your axe!'

With my dagger I pried a stopper of wood from the butt, then a good deal of wax, and finally shook out a thin roll of parchment, addressed to the Chief Pilot, which I handed to him.

The negro's eyes rolled in wonder, and he cried: 'By the Virgin of Guadelupe! To think that Myn's own axe could play him such a trick! Have you anything else in your belly, axe?'

Doña Ysabel snatched at the parchment and read it furtively. Then, handing it to the Prior with a sigh of profound relief, she murmured: 'This is a last message from my sister Mariana, who died unconfessed.'

It was short enough: 'God's mercy never fails! Repent before it is too late, and pray for the soul of your loving Mariana.'

The good Prior stared at the letter. 'Those are sweet words; yet why should she have concealed them in the haft of an axe?'

'My poor sister suffered from strange delusions before her death,' said Doña Ysabel. Touched by the unexpected kindness of the message, she drew the Chief Pilot aside, and told him incontinently: 'The Devil was in my heart, friend, but God has punished me. At Cobos I miscarried. How can I win your forgiveness for all the cruelties that I did you?' She offered him her hand, glancing away as though in fear to be spurned, but he took and pressed it to his lips.

'May God forgive us all!' he said. 'My lady, I am still your honest servitor; but our ways should now part, lest we be pained by re-membrance of things best forgotten.'

'Is this venerable Prior in your confidence?' she asked. 'I stand in great need of a confessor.'

The next day I sought out Don Fernando de Castro, whom Doña Mariana had appointed her executor and legatee. I found a handsome young gallant, who five years before had been royal page to his uncle, Don Gomez Perez de las Marinas, the Governor-Elect of the Philippines. When Don Gomez sailed across the Pacific from New Spain to assume office, Ensign de Castro commanded the troops in a galleon of the same convoy, which had the ill-luck to strike a reef off the Island of Marinduque; but he leaped into the waves, her flag wound about his middle and a line in his hand, and swam ashore. Though the ship was lost, all his men were drawn to safety, and he was rewarded with high rank for this heroic deed. Don Fernando had since performed other meritorious services and was now Brevet-General and a Knight of the Order of Saint James, yet not older than five-and-twenty years; he was lately returned from Cochin China, where he had exacted vengeance on his uncle's murderers who sought refuge there.

When I brought the young General the news that he was the sole beneficiary under Doña Mariana's Will, he expressed great astonishment. He convinced himself that, gifted on her death-bed with prophetic insight, she had envisaged him as her brother-in-law, for his bequest of jewels should by rights have gone to her loving sister; and Doña Ysabel did not disabuse him of this fanciful notion. They had already fallen deeply in love with each other; and that same autumn, on the very day that her year of widowhood came to an end, they were married in Manila Cathedral. All her property thereby passed to him, including the rights in the Isles of Solomon, which she had inherited from Don Alvaro. His own possessions were large, his cousin, Governor-General Don Luis Perez, having meanwhile died and left him a respectable sum of money, and the good people of Manila who danced and feasted at their wedding agreed that no handsomer couple had ever before been seen in their City.

Not long after our arrival news came of the galeot. She had reached the Philippines, but there lost her bearings. Passing close to an islet named Camiguin, off the northern coast of Mindanao, the crew had seen a dog on the shore and were reduced to such dire extremity that a sailor sprang overboard, crying that he would kill it and eat it raw, like a loyal subject of King Philip. Some natives came up as he was drinking the blood from its throat and, filled with amazement, took him back to the galeot in a baranguay laden with food; and afterwards guided Captain Corzo to the Jesuit mission at Layavan. The good Fathers, having entertained them well, brought them before the Provincial Magistrate who, at the Captain's request, arrested five sailors and sent them to Manila under escort.

The secretary of Dr. Antonio Morga, our Deputy-Governor, was kind enough to show me the Magistrate's letter which referred to these prisoners. It ran:

Your Excellency:
The *San Felipe* galeot, flying the Royal Standard, has just entered our port, under the command of a certain Captain Corzo, whose

conduct and language are equally reckless, but whom I have received with the respect due to his rank. He alleges that the galeot was separated by a storm from the flotilla of General Alvaro de Mendaña, which left Peru a year ago in search of the mythical Isles of Solomon. If the other ships should have arrived in Manila, your Excellency will know more about the matter than I. The five sailors I now send you are charged by their Captain with mutiny; I have however taken no disciplinary action, since they plead that their sole offence was to protest against his deliberate desertion of the flagship.

Captain Corzo eventually sailed the *San Felipe* to Manila, where she was refitted and fetched a high price.

Strangely enough, the *Santa Catalina* frigate also reached the Philippines in God's good time: she was discovered aground on the coast of Leyte, her sails set, her bulwarks nearly awash, and all her crew dead and rotten. But from that day to this, nothing has ever been heard of the *Santa Ysabel* galleon.

Most of the survivors of our expedition settled in the islands, all the widows marrying again because of the great scarcity of Spanish women there. Doña Luisa became the wife of an ivory-merchant; I am a frequent guest at her house on the banks of the River Pasig, and her daughter by Juan de Buitrago calls me uncle. Damian chose Pancha for his bride, but she whored him sadly and he cast her off. Jaume married Elvira, who has proved a good wife though her tongue is never still. Juarez died in the lazar-house at Cavite, and Matia, much grieved by his death, elected to join a religious Order; as also did Sergeant Andrada, and the gunner's mate, and Federico. They were sent out, after a period of instruction, to one or other of the remote missions in these islands, where the friar is the only Spaniard for many leagues around and acts as a benevolent despot among the untamed natives.

I am now a Provincial Magistrate with a comfortable home and no dearth of silver coin to jingle in my pockets. This country pleases me better than either Peru or New Spain, because its pacification was achieved by priests rather than by soldiers, and its inhabitants are paternally governed. Here we have no silver-mines, tombs of the living dead, and the friars are diligent in their work, though much jealousy exists between the Orders. The danger of invasion from Japan appears to have passed.

In the following year, Pedro Fernandez conveyed Doña Ysabel

and her husband across the Pacific to New Spain. Doubtless, she would have preferred another pilot in the master's cabin, and he another General's Lady in the Great Cabin, and both another ship than the *San Geronimo*, in which they embarked; but necessity compelled them. Because traffic between the Philippines and New Spain had, for reasons of economy, lately been reduced by Royal decree to two vessels a year in each direction, and it was therefore not easy to obtain a passage, even at great expense, and because Doña Ysabel's royal letters patent entitled her to despatch one ship a year to the New World from her Prefecture, Don Fernando had decided to refit the *San Geronimo*, load her with spices and China merchandise, and sail her; and Pedro Fernandez was the only skilled pilot who would make the voyage so late in the season—for they were delayed until August. After almost incredible new hardships and adversities he brought them safe to the port of Acapulco, where he stepped ashore on the 11th of December, 1597, taking leave of Don Fernando and his Lady, who made a profit from their cargo of close on fifty thousand pesos. Don Marcos had sailed with them as Boatswain, but was washed overboard towards the end of the voyage; God rest his honest soul!

On Pedro Fernandez's arrival at Lima in May, 1598, he found his wife and son in good health, and a daughter, born shortly after our departure, already able to walk and talk; but soon he left them again and sailed for Rome on a pilgrimage. I have heard it rumoured that Doña Ana made him wear horns, in revenge for his long absence and hasty departure; discontented alike by her poverty and by the religious excuses he offered.

I never saw him again. Of his subsequent expedition to the South Seas, many contradictory accounts are extant, and here I cannot write with authority. It seems that he sought to avoid the errors of the former voyage; but it was not enough to carry several Franciscan friars and no women on board his two small, well-provisioned ships, nor to install in each an ingenious machine of his own invention for distilling fresh water from salt, nor to obtain a special dispensation from the Holy Father,* by which any member of the expedition, dying without a priest, might confess himself directly to God. He had still to contend with the spirit of bellicose pride, jealousy and cruelty among his troops; moreover, delays at Callao had lost him more than two months of good sailing weather; and he fell sick in

*Clement VIII.

the newly discovered Island of Espiritu Santo, at a time when his authority was most needed to quell disorders. The enterprise miscarried, his efforts to renew it were discouraged by the Indies Council, and he died in Peru two years ago, a broken man. I have often wondered how far it was vainglorious thirst for discovery that animated him, rather than a Catholic desire for saving souls; but when a man slings at two birds on the same bough, his bolt is apt to fly between them.

Let me write lastly of Doña Ysabel. It is marvellous to relate that, once she was married to General Don Fernando, her character wholly altered: she became generous, trustworthy, truly pious and beloved by all her friends and servants. This transformation must be ascribed to God's infinite mercy, and to the affectionate love of a lusty, fortunate husband, who fathered on her the children she had so long desired, opposed manly firmness to childish caprice, and weaned her away from the society of Don Luis, her only surviving brother. Don Diego had long since died in a tavern brawl, at the hands of an angry Indian girl who, armed with a pair of shears, first lopped off one ear and the tip of his nose and then drove the blades deep into his belly.

HISTORICAL EPILOGUE

In 1606, Pedro Fernandez, now usually known as Pedro de Quiros, was forced by foul winds and a mutiny to retire from Espiritu Santo, an island in the New Hebrides which he was colonizing under the impression that it formed part of the northern coast of 'Austrialia.' On his way home to Acapulco in Mexico he again passed within a few hours' sail of the Solomons but, perhaps because General Fernando de Castro and Doña Ysabel had warned him not to infringe their rights, he sheered off. Torres, his second-in-command, whom he had left in the lurch, sailed west to the Philippines by the strait that now bears his name, discovered the eastern end of New Guinea, and sighted the Cape York peninsula of Australia, which he took for an island.

The era of Spanish expansion now ended in national bankruptcy, and though Pedro Fernandez sent memorial after memorial to the new King, imploring him to finance still another missionary expedition, he never realized his hopes.

The Solomons were lost for almost exactly two centuries after their first discovery by Alvaro de Mendaña. In 1767, Captain Carteret of the *Swallow* sighted them on his way across the Pacific, having just rediscovered Santa Cruz, but did not recognize the group because Gallego's hopelessly inaccurate log had placed them more than twelve hundred miles farther to the east; neither did the Frenchmen Bougainville and Surville, who arrived there in 1768 and 1769 respectively. It was left to the geographer Buache to identify them with Mendaña's islands, in a memoir published in 1781.

No attempt was made to convert their inhabitants until 1845, when a Catholic bishop, Mgr. Épalle, landed with eighteen Marist Fathers; but he was murdered and despoiled of his crucifix, ring and vestments on the very first day, and in 1848 the mission was abandoned. The Anglican Bishops of Melanesia have had more success, though some of the villages still remain pagan, and both the Solomons and the South Solomons, which include Santa Cruz, are now under the British flag.

The position of the Marquesas was long kept secret by the Spanish, to prevent their falling into English hands, but Captain Cook rediscovered them in 1774. Since their annexation by the French in 1842, the population has declined by four persons in five; Herman Melville gives an idyllic but trustworthy account of primitive native life on Dominica in his 'Typee,' or, *A Narrative of a four months' residence among the natives of a valley in the Marquesas Islands.*